cream

cream

The Best of the Erotica Readers and Writers Association

Edited by Lisabet Sarai

THUNDER'S MOUTH PRESS
New York

CREAM:
The Best of the Erotica Readers and Writers Association

Published by
Thunder's Mouth Press
An Imprint of Avalon Publishing Group, Inc.
245 West 17th Street, 11th floor
New York, NY 10011

All the stories in this collection originally appeared on Erotica Readers and Writers Association (www.erotica-readers.com), with the exception of "Mad Dogs," by Lisabet Sarai, which is previously unpublished. In addition to appearing on ERWA, the following stories have been published previously: "The Bookseller's Dream," by Seneca Mayfair, was published in the *Scarlet Letters* e-zine, www.scarletletters.com; "Home Ice," by Tulsa Brown, was published in the e-anthology *Blasphemy* (Torquere Press, 2005); "Successor," by Amanda Earl, was published in the *Unlikely* e-zine, www.unlikelystories.org; and "Tears Fall on Me," by Sydney Durham, was published in *Moist* magazine (2004).

First printing December 2006

Library of Congress Cataloging-in-Publication Data is available.

ISBN-10: 1-56025-925-6
ISBN-13: 978-1-56025-925-1

9 8 7 6 5 4 3 2 1

Book design by Maria Fernandez
Printed in the United States of America
Distributed by Publishers Group West

Contents

Note from the Editor

Welcome to the thickest, richest, most delicious, and decadent collection of stories that you will read this year. This is not your typical, ordinary, run-of-the-shelves erotic anthology. In this volume I am serving you the *crème de la crème*: shocking, intense, tender, humorous, and above all, arousing tales of sex in all its guises. A feast for the connoisseur.

Where do these tales come from? The Erotica Readers and Writers Association, or ERWA, (www.erotica-readers.com) is a global virtual community bound together by common interests in sex and the written word. On the ERWA Storytime email list, scores of erotica writers exchange stories and critiques every week. Each month, the ERWA editors select the best offerings from Storytime to be posted in the Galleries of the ERWA Web site. For this anthology, I skimmed the very best from the Galleries to offer to you, my insatiable readers.

One feature of ERWA that I've reproduced here is our theme stories. One weekend each month, Storytime members are invited to submit tales that revolve around a specified theme: Sex Toys, Erotic Noir, Sex in History, Sex for the Holidays, and so on. It's always astonishing to see the incredibly varied ways that different authors tackle a theme.

Another ERWA specialty is the flasher. Flashers are complete, sizzling, sexy stories in a mere one hundred words. I've included a baker's dozen to whet your appetite.

I've been a member of ERWA for nearly six years and the editor of its newsletter for two and a half. The authors that I present in this collection are more than exceptional writers; they are colleagues, friends, almost family. If you regularly read erotica, you'll recognize many familiar names, but I'm proud to introduce other equally talented writers whom you may not have encountered previously.

To get to know all the authors better, go to www.lisabet-sarai.com/Cream.html. You'll find author biographies, links to their Web sites and blogs, and other titillating tidbits of information.

I see you're licking your lips in anticipation. I won't delay you any further with preliminaries.

Enjoy.

Lisabet Sarai
April 14, 2006

Sex Toy Stories

Laying Down the Law

Keziah Hill

I hate some sex toys. Plastic ones that smell funny and have stupid battery compartments. Those irritating slide things always stick, so I end up breaking a nail. And all those cutesy-poo animal shapes in hideous colors. Why on earth would anyone want to be fucked by a rabbit?

Don't get me wrong. There's nothing I like more than cuddling up with my sleek, tasteful vibe on a Saturday night after I've closed the shop. Mine's appropriately low-key. And it's dead easy to change the batteries. No mucking around, just unscrew the end, put them in, and away I go. There's a lot to be said for good technology. But I do miss hands and mouths.

Weekends in the shop are the busiest times. Everyone comes in. Gay boys looking for their porn hit, couples looking for a bit of spice, and weirdos looking for god knows what. I don't care as long as they don't damage the merchandise. Last weekend it was a group of university students doing an assignment on human sexuality. I felt like a dorm mother telling them about the health benefits of a little light bondage. They took notes, gasped at the twelve-inch dildos, giggled over *Tit-fucking Whoredroids from Planet Mammary* and stocked up on flavored condoms.

After they left, I realized one of them had lifted the Ultrasmooth Rainbow Bliss 5000, the *crème de la crème* of vibrators. It was iridescent bright purple. The blurb on the box said it had everything you could possibly want in a sex toy. You could fuck yourself in both holes, get your clit rubbed and snap on an extension cord for the nipple stimulator. When you'd had enough, one press of a button and rose scented massage oil sprayed out the end. A kind of do-it-yourself money shot. I used to look at it with loathing.

But at three hundred bucks, it wasn't cheap. I was more than a little pissed off, particularly after I called the university to explain the problem. A snotty-sounding toad told me her precious students couldn't possibly be responsible. They were from good homes. I couldn't accuse them of shoplifting. I said I didn't think times had changed that much. Shoplifting was the sport of choice in my university days; it was the only way to keep up the stocks of ciggies and chocolate. When she spluttered with outraged denial, I told her she could look forward to a visit from the cops and hung up.

A call to the state's finest didn't fill me with confidence. They said they'd get to it when they could, but other matters had priority. Yeah, sure. I couldn't see them pulling out all stops to recover a vibrator. I guess I could claim it on insurance, but it didn't seem worth it.

I was brooding on the injustice of the world, stocking the shelves with lurid animal toys, when I sensed an unusual presence in the shop. Sure enough, standing at the doorway was a poster boy for tall, dark, and handsome. Central casting couldn't have done better. Sinful dark eyes, a mouth to die for, and a broad, muscled chest. I looked at him suspiciously.

"Can I help you?"

"Ms. Crane?"

I hadn't been called Ms. Crane for a long time. "Yeah, I'm Trixy Crane. What can I do for you?"

His gazed traveled up from my baggy black jeans, to my Weapons of Mass Distraction T-shirt (a vain hope—with my less than ample tits, it was clearly a political statement), and finally to my disheveled dark hair. I could see what he was thinking. Most men had the same thought when they met me. Disappointment I wasn't some kind of silicon sex goddess. Everyone thought a woman who owned an adult sex shop and had a name like Trixy would be blonde, voluptuous, and wear black leather. They were so predictable.

"I'm Detective Andy Pope. You rang to report a theft."

My jaw hit the floor. "You're kidding? They sent a detective over? Wow! My tax dollars are working today!"

He smiled, and my heart kicked up a notch. Not to mention some other parts of my anatomy. I couldn't remember the last time I'd responded to a man with such a welcoming gush.

"Some of the details in your report are similar to some thefts other people have reported in the area. Would you mind if I asked you some questions?"

Would I mind? I don't think so. Not if you keep smiling with that wicked twinkle in your eye.

"Sure. It'll have to be while I look after the shop. I'm the only one here at the moment."

"Isn't that dangerous for a woman on her own?" he asked.

I snorted. "The last time someone messed with me they got a butt plug up their nostril. I can look after myself." In my experience, the more good-looking a guy was, the more of a dope. I tried to reserve my opinion, but I wasn't hopeful. At least he hadn't patted my head and called me "little woman."

I picked up some more vibrator boxes and thrust them higgledy-piggledy on the shelves. Turning, I watched with appreciation the smooth roll of muscles under his leather jacket as he leaned against the counter. That wasn't all. A distinct bulge in his trousers showed me Detective Andy Pope was finding adult sex shop detail just his cup of tea. I wondered if it was the black leather corset on the curvaceous blow-up model behind me, or the rack of gay postcards to his left.

"So tell me what happened."

I shrugged. "Just a bunch of students in here being silly. One of them lifted my most expensive vibrator."

"How do you know it was one of them?"

"There was no one else in here. As soon as they arrived, looking bright-eyed and bushy-tailed, notebooks in hand, everyone else made a hasty retreat. Not many people want to be part of an assignment. Cramps their style."

He laughed, and my heart did a little pitty-pat.

"So you didn't notice anyone take it? Wouldn't it have been fairly bulky?"

I shook my head. "Some of them were wearing those army disposal store overcoats. You could hide an AK-47 under one of them, and no one would know."

He nodded, staring at me intently. It was a little unnerving. He seemed to want to say something but was having trouble. I was getting the impression it didn't have anything to do with stolen vibrators. He kept flashing quick glances at my T-shirt and then, I swear, blushing. On six-foot, broad-shouldered, walking sin, it was kinda cute.

"So," I said cheerily, "any clues? Got a list of vibrator thieves you can look up?"

"We're following some leads. It could be part of a student prank, or it could be something more. Could you describe the vibrator for me?"

"Sure. I've got a pamphlet here somewhere."

I walked over to the counter and rifled through the stack of paper next to the cash register. He stood close to me. Too close. I started breathing in quick little pants as a sharp spike of heat zinged through me. He smelled of coffee, stale cigarettes, and mint gum. Ambrosia. I was in big trouble. Everything about this guy was turning me on. "Here it is," I said, waving it in front of him trying to ignore the sudden tightening of my nipples.

His eyes glazed over, and the bulge in his pants got bigger as I gave him a run through of the functions. He seemed particularly interested in the anal attachment. "A big seller is it?" he asked in a breathless voice.

"Not really. Most people are happy with your basic phallic vibe. Although how they can stand the plastic ones I don't know. I find the sleek metal ones are much more user friendly." I held up a glittering gold vibe.

He gulped and stood there speechless staring at the vibe and then at my T-shirt again. Maybe he had a problem with political slogans.

Shuffling from foot to foot, he looked as though he was trying to pull himself together. Strange man for a cop. Kinda coy and tough at the same time. My cunt shimmied again.

Don't go there, Trix. Not a cop.

Dragging his eyes away from the vibe, he became brisk and professional. "Okay. I'll make some inquires and get back to you."

"Thanks," I said, feeling bewildered. And disappointed. He sure was easy on the eyes. Nothing else that good was likely to walk through my door anytime soon.

The next couple of days went in a whirl. I'd seen it before.

Full moon in Scorpio. It sends everyone into a sexual frenzy. They start rushing into the shop to buy whatever they think will get them through the night. Business-wise, I couldn't complain. But I wished I had someone to share it with in my bed. It had been a long time between drinks for me—months in fact.

Most men thought I'd be a firecracker in bed and were always disappointed when I showed no interest in nipple clamps, handcuffs, or candle wax. The women were worse. I found my main attraction was the range of vibrators I stocked. More than one woman had begged me to break out the Rainbow Bliss. What's wrong with mouths and fingers? I'd cry, tossing them out of bed.

I'd stomp around the place after these less than edifying encounters, furious that everyone seemed to prefer a piece of technology to a living, breathing woman who was willing to make them french toast in the morning. What was wrong with the world? I blamed the Internet.

I was musing on these profound insights when Andy arrived, looking tall, dangerous, and temptation personified. Boy, he packed a punch. Parts of my body I didn't even know I had tingled into life at the sight of him.

It was just at the end of my shift. Being the owner, I hired other people to do the shifts I hated and would disappear up to my apartment with relief. Friday night was usually full of drunk office workers letting it rip before the weekend. I didn't need that.

He saw me and sauntered over smiling broadly, the boxed Rainbow Bliss in his hands. I couldn't believe it! "You got it back!"

"Yeah, it was part of a prank. The kid who took it also lifted a blow-up doll from another shop and was going to leave an artistic arrangement outside the U.S. consulate. Some kind of antiwar protest."

"Subtle."

He shook his head and smiled. "Well, they are kids."

"You didn't charge him, did you?" I had a sudden pang of guilt. If the kid told me what he wanted to do, I would have gladly donated one of the animal vibes. I'd have been chuffed to think one of my sex toys was part of an antiwar installation.

"Nah, just gave him a warning and told him any future liberation of private property would get him into big trouble. He seemed to get the message."

I beamed at him. "Quick work. Are you normally this efficient?"

"I had an incentive," he said stepping toward me.

"Really?" I said, my heart pounding.

"Don't look so terrified. I'm not going to eat you. Well, not right now anyway," he said backing me against the counter.

"What are you going to do with me?" My voice sounded high and panicky as I tried to speak through a suddenly dry throat. This was in direct contrast to another part of my body, which was weeping with anticipation.

"Is there somewhere else we could go where I could show you?" he murmured, lifting his hand to my mouth. He rubbed his thumb against my lower lip, and my tongue slid across his skin. Salt and citrus. Just like a margarita.

I looked up at him as he towered over me. "Are you wanting to trade sexual favors for a good investigative outcome?"

He laughed, and I felt the vibration in his chest against my aching nipples. I pressed closer.

"Investigative outcome? I've never heard it described like

that." He stared down at me with predatory brown eyes and placed his hands on my hips, pulling me tight against him. "What if I was? You got a problem with that?"

He bent and ran his tongue along my jaw. I gasped and realized it was entirely possible to melt from lust.

"None at all," I muttered. "Come with me."

I chucked the keys to the shop to my assistant, Jerry, who'd been watching the whole exchange slack-jawed with amazement. Pulling Detective Andy Pope behind the counter, I led the way to the back of the shop where a doorway hid the stairs to my apartment.

I pounded up with him close behind and threw open the door. We stumbled in and stood staring at each other.

"Do you want coffee?"

"No."

"Wine?"

"No."

"Anything?"

"The bedroom."

"Yes," I said and led the way.

He pulled me to him and kissed me hard. He tasted like onions, coffee, and sin. I couldn't get enough. I wrapped my arms around him and prepared to devour him. When he cupped my buttocks and pushed me against his cock, I wriggled to get my clit against that glorious hardness. My mouth was still on his, pushing, licking, biting his tongue and lips. He tumbled me onto the bed and pushed his hand under my T-shirt, pulling it up and over my head.

Then he stopped and stared at my breasts.

My heart sank. Here we go. He's confronting the reality of no silicon.

"I've been dreaming about this. I bet I can get your whole breast in my mouth," he murmured and proceeded to do just that. He sucked hard, and I nearly came on the spot. I gasped when he took my nipple in his teeth and pulled, a tingle of pain making a direct hit in my cunt.

He raised himself on his knees and ripped off his shirt while I wiggled out of the rest of my clothes. My eyes didn't move from that big, rigid bulge in his pants. When he stood to unzip and step out of his trousers, I almost wept with joy. His cock bobbed up in front of me looking hard and enthusiastic.

I rifled through the drawer in my bedside cabinet, pushed aside my trusty vibe and pulled out some condoms. He grabbed one, ripped it open, covered himself and pushed me back on the bed. I like a man with a sense of purpose. His tall strong body was all over me, and I sighed with bliss. When he made moves to slide down to put his mouth on my cunt, I stopped him.

"Just fuck me, Andy. Just get your cock in me."

He looked dumbfounded. I guess the tired old protocol was get her off first then fuck her. Well, sometimes that just didn't do it for me. Sometimes I only wanted the feel of a hard cock inside me, wanted to be pressed into the mattress with every thrust while I ran my hands down a smooth back. More than that, I wanted to take in the heady smell of sweaty sex and hear the slap of balls against my cunt. There's nothing like the good old missionary position for wrapping myself around a perfectly working male body while he went for it.

And go for it he did. He pushed my leg up around his hip and plunged in. It was heaven. Fast, furious, and frantic. That in-out, in-out, god, how I'd missed it! He went to raise himself on his arms to take his weight off me but I pulled him back.

"Forget it," I growled. "I need your skin against me. Don't be so polite."

He grinned down at me and thrust hard. I gasped, feeling his cock almost to my womb.

"Yes," I muttered through gritted teeth. "Keep going!"

I whimpered with joy as he pummeled my cunt. Sliding my hands down to his buttocks, I pushed him in harder. I wrapped my legs around him and held on as he rocked into my body. He collapsed on me after coming with a hoarse cry, and I smiled with total satisfaction, pinned by him, unable to move. He stirred after a while and to my disappointment, slid out of me. Pulling me against him, he brushed hair out of my eyes and kissed me.

"You didn't come."

"No," I said, smiling. "I didn't."

He looked confused again and lay on his back staring at the ceiling. "You're a strange woman."

"Yes," I said. "I know." I lay on my side and traced lazy circles across his chest with my finger.

"So, was that the most boring fuck you've ever had?" I asked.

He looked at me, horrified. "No! Of course not! Why would you ask that?"

"Because we did it quick and traditional. No mucking about. Some people find that a little boring."

He shrugged and rolled over to face me. "Who am I to argue with tradition? Sometimes the old ways are best. Although, even I think it's a good idea for both people to have an orgasm. Is there something I should know?"

He ran his hand up my thigh and started stroking the sensitive skin on the edge of my bush. I gasped with pleasure when he slid a finger into my cunt and brought it out to smear juice over my clit. He started a good, even stroke, not too direct, with just enough pressure.

"When I sleep with a man for the first time," I said, panting, "I just want to feel and smell him. If I start thinking about orgasms, I don't have as much fun."

"No? What about now? Are you having fun now?"

He quickened his pace and moved down to replace his fingers with his mouth while sliding his fingers deep into my cunt. I nearly shrieked.

"Yes," I said, sounding on the edge of hysteria. "I'm having a lot of fun."

He sucked on my clit, vibrating his tongue against the tip, and I shot to the ceiling. I think I screamed, but I wasn't sure. I wasn't sure of anything except the slow slide of his fingers in and out. As I came back to earth, he pulled them out and licked them slowly, moaning with pleasure.

"You taste great," he said and kissed me. He was right. I did.

I snuggled against him and breathed in his tangy, sweaty smell. As I started to drift off, he stirred.

"Do you ever use any of your stock?" he asked.

"Hmm? What do you mean?

"You know. Have you ever used the Rainbow Bliss?"

I snorted. "God no! I use something much more low key. Why?"

"Just wondering. Seems strange an owner of a sex shop wouldn't use some of the products."

I raised myself on an elbow and glared at him.

"Out with it. What is it you want to use? The nipple clamps? A cockring? Do you want to fuck me with a bunny?" I started to pull away from him, furious yet again that my main attraction had nothing to do with me.

"No, no, no. That's not it. Come back here," he said rolling me under him. I started to struggle as he pinned me and started nibbling on my ear lobe. I kept it up for a while, but the combined effect of his tongue in my ear and his hard cock rubbing against my clit turned my struggles into a desperate attempt to rub as much of myself against him as I could.

As he trailed hot nips down my neck I moaned. "Well, what do you want?"

"I want you to fuck me," he whispered.

"What?"

"I want you to fuck me with your vibrator, the one that's been inside you."

I gulped and stared into his eyes. They were feverish with desire. He rocked against me, pushing his cock against my vulva.

"I want to feel what you feel when I fuck you."

He moved his hand between us and pushed down hard on my clit. I came again with a scream.

Damn, this boy was good. And I had to admit, the idea of sliding my well-used vibe into his tight, round ass was very tempting.

I lay there recovering, while he rummaged in my bedside table and found my vibe and lube. Oiling it up, he presented it to me like a little boy about to get a Christmas present.

"How do you want to do this?" I asked, a flutter of excitement making me nervous.

"Like this. So I can see you," he said, lying on his back and bringing his knees to his chest. His cock was rock hard and sticking up. This could be good, I realized with surprise. Lots to keep me occupied. My cunt started a low, warm pulse as I watched his strong, hard body open for me.

I laid the vibe on the bed while I lubed up my fingers.

Easing one into his sweet little hole, I moved it gently in and out, adding another when I heard his gasps of appreciation. He started moving his hips to meet the rhythm of my fingers.

"Now," he said. "Put it in now."

I put the tip of the vibe against him and pushed slowly. He groaned deep in his throat and closed his eyes. I couldn't believe how gorgeous he looked. Like some kind of wicked fallen angel. Good enough to eat. Keeping up a smooth thrusting rhythm, which he seemed to like a lot, I kneeled between his legs and took his cock into my mouth. He seemed to like that even more.

"Fuck! Trixy! God!" he yelled, as he grabbed the sheets with both hands.

I turned the vibrator on, and he yelped some more, especially when I sucked the tip of his cock hard into my mouth. I started to synchronize the thrust of the vibe with my sucking mouth. Up and down. Down and up. He tasted earthy and musky. This was fun. More so when I felt him on the verge of an explosion.

"Trix, I'm gonna come now!"

"Good," I mumbled incoherently. "Go for it." I don't think he understood me, but I didn't care. I kept up a good stroke with the vibe as he shot off in my mouth. He didn't taste too bad, but the best part of the whole experience was the look on his face when I pulled out the vibe and sat up, wiping my mouth.

Adoration. I had never been adored. He looked at me as if I had given him the most precious gift he'd ever received.

I crawled up his body and kissed him lightly. "You okay?"

He smiled dreamily and bent his head to lick my nipple. "Mmm."

"Hungry?" I asked.
"Sure," he said. "I'm always hungry."
"What do you feel like?"
He frowned, considering.
"French toast?"

A Race to the Finish

J. Z. Sharpe

On this particular Friday, my housemate Connie greeted me in the driveway with a Rolling Rock straight out of the fridge and a cardboard box. "Look, Julie!" she started yelling as soon as I got out of the car. "Guess what came today!"

After nine hours down at the factory, gluing fingerboards onto guitars, I'm hardly in the mood for guessing games. "Give me that thing," I said, pointing at the frosty bottle.

"First you gotta guess."

"I'm not guessing nothing until you give me a drink!" She handed it over with a pout, and I took a long, brain-chilling swig. Several, in fact. With the bottle half drained, I'd be more in the mood for her unique sense of humor. "Okay, Con, now you tell me—what came today?"

"Our toys!" She yanked a plastic bag out of the box. In my weary state, my eyes could have been playing tricks on me (they do that at the end of a long week), but I was pretty sure that the bag contained, among other things, a huge pink plastic penis. She stabbed at it with her finger. "Ain't that the wildest thing you ever saw?"

"Jeez, will you put it back?" I grabbed a quick peek over my shoulder toward Mrs. Pronkowski's house; luckily she didn't appear to be home, the nosy bitch. If she'd been around, she'd have to know what was going on, and then she'd blab to the rest of the neighborhood, of course. As two single girls on a block of all-American families and upstanding, bingo-playing senior citizens like Mrs. P., we were the subject of all kinds of imaginary scandals. Like when we took some vacation time and bought cheap tickets down to Orlando to hang around Disney for a couple days? When we got back, we found out everyone thought we'd gone on some swingers' orgy cruise in the Caribbean. Yeah, I wish!

The only cute guys Connie and I saw, the whole time we were down there, were the pool attendants at the hotel, and they didn't even talk to us (although Connie kept giving them her special look, which always embarrasses the hell out of me). They were too interested in the fashion models who were working at the convention center next door—but that's another story for another time.

"It all came, nothing was backordered. Even the sizzling lube gel! Look at the little red bottle, ain't that cute? Shaped like the devil!"

"You be careful with that. Don't go leaving it around the kitchen, okay? Somebody's likely to think it's hot sauce."

I stumbled inside, Connie bouncing behind me. The closest chair was the shaky one with the duct tape holding on the cushion, but a chair is a chair, so I sat down and started pulling off my shoes. When you're on your feet all day, all you can think about is getting off them. I rubbed that bad spot on my left big toe and thought about pizza for dinner, delivery from the place that hires all those Italian weightlifters to do their deliveries. And the food's not bad, either.

Connie, on the other hand, kept yakking and taking things out of that box, tossing them on the table, which I wasn't too sure about. I mean, we eat on it, for crissakes!

How can I ever sit down to dinner again, knowing that a giant plastic dick had once been placed there as a centerpiece? I lit a cigarette and shook my head. "Jeez, Connie, did we really order all this shit?"

"We sure did. Don't you remember?" She smiled and put another beer in front of me, dropping the empty into the bin with all the other recyclables. "That was the night we made the big pitcher of Blue Hawaiians? And then we ordered all those movies on the pay-per-view? The ones with all the hunky naked guys?"

"All right, all right!" Not one of my prouder moments, to be sure, but we did have fun, I do recall. One of those dateless nights, you know how that goes.

We were hanging out, eating chicken wings and watching TV, and Connie got the idea that we should do a little recreational surfing on the Internet. After wandering around and looking at all these nude photos (some of which were pretty weird and nasty), we found this Web site with all kinds of sex stuff for sale, vibrators and junk like that. Now bear in mind that we'd just seen some of these things in use, and in our less-than-sober state, we began to wonder if maybe this was the missing link in our less-than-perfect love lives. So Connie and I started filling a shopping cart, clicking left and right on everything that looked like fun. Now the results covered our kitchen table, just waiting to be explored.

"It's all here, everything we picked out. Oh my god, my Visa bill is going to be so big this month!"

"Can we send any of it back?"

Connie opened a beer for herself and sat down to study the small print on the packing slip. "Hmm . . . I don't know. But, hey! We don't want to do that anyway!" She jumped up, grabbed some cheese curls out of the kitchen cabinet, and started scooping the sex toys back into the box. "It's Friday! What the fuck! Let's get busy!"

She headed for the living room with the box under one arm, the curls under the other. I picked up her beer and followed, like a good roommate, bringing along the rest of the six-pack, too, just in case. Hell, I couldn't even remember what I'd ordered! But Connie had the list in front of her, and she seemed to know exactly what was mine and what was hers. A little pile grew steadily on my side of the coffee table, including a jar of the sizzling lube and a mystery object, discreetly packaged in a leatherette case, like a small makeup bag.

"What's this?" I asked, peeking inside.

"That's the Magic Bullet Pocket Vibe."

"The what?"

"The Magic Bullet Pocket Vibrator," she repeated, louder and more slowly, the way you have to explain things to Mrs. Pronkowski sometimes.

"How does it work?"

Connie took the case away from me and pulled out the contents, placing them in my hands. About a foot of thin electrical wire connected a small box, shaped like a disposable lighter, to an egg-shaped ball, which fit perfectly in the palm of my hand. "This is the switch, see?" She slid something on the box and the egg began to hum. "You slide it up and down to make it go faster or slower."

I tried it myself. The faster setting really made that baby buzz! I turned the thing off and opened a third beer for courage. "And where do I put it?"

"Here." Connie pointed between her legs.

"There?"

She was too busy tearing the wrapping off the oversized plastic penis to be of any further assistance. "For crissakes, just try it, will ya? I've got stuff of my own over here I gotta figure out."

So I held the egg in my right hand and gave the switch a push with my left. Right off the bat, the thing starts jumping and nearly took off out of my grip and halfway across the room! I turned it off, took a deep breath and another swallow of beer, then tried again, taking it easy this time, sliding the switch ever so slightly until the toy hummed. Then I opened my thighs and pressed the thing up against me.

"Ooooooh!"

I gotta tell you, I ain't felt anything like that since Herbie Scheetz took me behind the pool house at the company picnic five years ago. Man, that Herbie, if you keep the Coors Light coming, that boy will try anything. We snuggled up behind the shed where they stored the towels, and he was kissing me and putting his hands all over me, and while normally I might push away any other guy, Herbie felt so good. He sure did know what he was doing, with his hands under my shorts, doing this little finger dance against my panties. Too bad I found out later he was doing the same thing with half the other girls in my department, huh? But that's another story for another time.

Anyway, I played around with that egg thingy, making it speed up and slow down, while Connie stuck batteries inside the pink plastic penis. Why she had to do that, I couldn't figure out—until I saw her turn a little knob at its base, right behind its "testicles," and it began to buzz just like my toy was already doing so well.

"Woo-hoo!" she shrieked, wiggling out of her cutoffs. "You think Barry Bothwell has a cock like this?"

"Who's Barry Bothwell?"

Connie rolled her eyes. "He's the guy on Channel Five? The one in the morning who does all the local news?"

"Oh, yeah." Leave it to Connie to lust after someone she could never get. At least I see Herbie at work every day, in the flesh, driving the forklift in the shipping department. Even if he's fooling around with half the girls in the factory, there's always the chance that one day he'll get some sense knocked into his head and decide he likes me the best. He does smile at me whenever he sees me, and sometimes he even says hello. A girl's gotta have hope, after all.

Anyway, I was leaning back, sliding the switch up and down, kinda enjoying the way that egg buzzed, when Connie jumped to her feet, swallowed the contents of her bottle in one gulp, and plopped herself right next to me on the couch. She stretched out so her toes were practically in my face, and I could see her pubes and her flabby stomach. The plastic penis whirred away in her hand.

"Okay, Jules, I got an idea." From the way her words slid together, I could tell that she was feeling just fine, maybe a little too fine, and we might need more beer very soon. "I'll race ya, okay?"

"Race me? What do you mean?"

"First one to come wins. On your mark, get set . . ."

"Wait a minute! First one to come? How do we know if we come?"

Connie looked at me, openmouthed. "You don't know what it feels like when you come?"

"Well, gee, I guess—I mean—I'm not sure."

"You get all tingly? All hot? You see stars?" She kicked me. "Come on, Julie. I don't believe you. Not for one minute. You'll know. And I'll be able to tell. Trust me on this one, babe."

"I don't know . . ."

"Come on! A hundred bucks! I'll bet you a hundred bucks I come before you! On your mark, get set . . ."

"Connie! Wait a minute!"

"Go!"

Off she went, throwing her head back so I could see right up her nostrils. "Oh, Barry!" I thought I heard her say. "Tell me more about that traffic jam on the interstate, baby! Oh, yeah!"

I cringed with embarrassment. Thank heaven no one else was around to see her doing this, rubbing that grotesque plastic dick all over her stomach and thighs, moaning for Barry all the while. I closed my eyes so I wouldn't have to look.

Interestingly enough, this shifted my viewpoint so I could concentrate more on the sweet vibration between my own thighs. I found the little egg remarkably easy to maneuver, much easier than Connie's silicone tree-trunk. With a little practice, I could run the whirring sphere up and down my pussy lips, along my thighs, even down to my anus where it actually felt good. But the best place to park it had to be my clit, and I began to circle the happy nub with the toy, making circles that got smaller and smaller, until I had it pressing directly against my magic love spot. Wow! I just might win this competition after all!

Connie, in the meantime, seemed totally oblivious to her surroundings. Hell, the real Barry Bothwell could have jumped out of a cake, right in front of her eyes, and she probably wouldn't even notice! How she could get such pleasure out of someone she'd never meet, I do not know.

My fantasy, on the other hand, was more at my level—

Herbie Scheetz, of course, cornering that forklift by spinning that steering wheel with his stupendous arms, all muscle with a scattering of tattoos. I thought about how he likes to roll his sleeves up when it's hot, and how a little bit of sweat will roll down his temple, and how he runs his hand over his close-cut hair when he stops by my workbench to say hi to me. I could feel an intense tingling all around my clit. Yeah, I was going to come, I couldn't hold back! I'd go insane otherwise!

"Oh, my god, oh, my god—oh! Oh! Oh!" Connie started letting out this little yelps as her hips bounced up and down. "I'm coming!"

"Oh, no you're not, goddamn it!" My own hips began to gyrate, raise up and down off the cushions, and all I could think about was Herbie, Herbie, Herbie—buying me coffee, following me out to the parking lot at the end of the day, kissing me behind the trash containers in back of the factory. Man, did I want him or what? Who cares if he had a whole crowd of women following him around? He was mine—and I was coming, too, panting and shaking my head, Connie barely visible in the corner of my eye.

"I came first!" she crowed.

"No way! No fucking way!" I was gasping for breath, my head thrown back over the arm of the sofa so I was looking at the world upside down. "Oh my god, that was amazing! Where the hell is my beer?"

"I still say that I came first."

I slapped her knee. "Shut up, girl, you ain't getting no hundred bucks from me. It's a draw. We both came at the same time. Hey, let's call for a pizza."

"From Mario's? The place with the weightlifters?"

"That the only place for pizza, as far as I'm concerned."

They sent a new guy over with our order, and although I don't think he spoke a word of English, we admired his biceps and his dark brown eyes. Then, much later, we had them for dessert, digging into our box of toys once again.

In fact, that pretty much describes the whole damn weekend! Hell, I even watched the evening news, because Barry Bothwell was filling in for the usual weekend announcer. And you know something? He's not half bad.

Better yet, on Monday morning, as I was punching in, who should come along but Herbie? He pulled his card out of the rack and gave me this big, toothy smile. "So, babe, how was your weekend?" he asked.

"Just fine," I told him. "Better than you'll ever know."

Erotica Noir

A Little Help

Nan Andrews

They always thought I was just another dame. A pretty face and an hourglass figure. Someone they could hook with a drink and a smile. Well, I had some news for them. I knew what they were up to, what they were capable of, and I didn't trust them a bit.

Harvey's Lounge was only half full that night, just a few poor sods drinking away their weekly dole or avoiding the missus at home. The jukebox sat silently in the corner, no one interested in dropping a dime on dance music. No dames to dance with anyway, until I walked in. A line of faces looked up from their beers and then looked down as I strolled past the bar, coming to the empty stool at the end.

I was dressed for a night on the town: blood red sweater, tight skirt, garter belt and silk stockings, the seams running straight down to the heels of my black pumps. My hair was done up in a french twist, and I was wearing my best perfume. If that didn't get his attention, I didn't know what would.

He was sitting alone, still wearing his overcoat, nursing a scotch and soda. He looked over as I caught the eye of the barkeep and ordered a whiskey, neat. I laid my purse on top of the bar and climbed onto the stool next to his.

"You're not the type we usually get in here. What brings you to Harvey's?" he asked, looking at me sideways as he set his glass down.

"Oh, what sort of type do you usually get?" I asked him.

"Hard luck cases that need a little help, or else sweet young things looking for a new sweetheart." He swirled the ice in his glass before continuing. "You don't look like either of those types."

"No, I don't think I do." I took a sip and set the glass on the bar, turning to him. "My name's Esther. What's yours?"

"George."

"Nice to meet you, George." We shook hands briefly. His was clammy and cold from holding his drink, or perhaps something else. Maybe he had a guilty conscience.

Silence fell, and he went back to his drink. This might be harder than I expected. Crossing my legs and letting my skirt slide up my thigh just a bit, I turned toward him and leaned closer.

"Listen, George. I'm new in town. What's a girl gotta do around here? You know, to get a little attention."

"What sort of attention did you have in mind?" George glanced down at my legs and then slowly back up to my face.

"Oh, a drink, maybe. Dinner?"

George leaned toward me and looked into my eyes. His were bloodshot, probably from the scotch and the smoke in the bar.

"Is that all you're looking for? A drink or a meal?"

He made it sound so sordid, like I had asked him to knock over a bank. "Well, what else did you have in mind?" I smiled up at him, hoping that I was just the type of treat he enjoyed.

"Let's blow this joint, and I'll show you."

He reached for his wallet, pushed a bill across the bar along with his glass and helped me down from my stool. I picked up my coat, and he walked me toward the door, his hand pressed against the small of my back. A few curious stares followed us out, but they may just have been watching me sway along as George's hand slid lower on the curve of my hip.

Once outside, he slipped an arm through mine and drew me away from the front door. The wind almost blew us over. We clutched at each other and made our way past the edge of the building and into the alley. Rain threatened, but it wasn't cold as yet. Too early in the fall for really bad weather.

George drew me along the alley and into a doorway. The lighting was nonexistent this far from the street, and I could barely make out his face in the dark. He leaned down and kissed me hard on the mouth, his hand sliding up my skirt. I slipped my arms around his waist, pulling closer to him. His hands were insistent and none too gentle. One pushed up my sweater and fondled my breasts and the other lifted my skirt. So he liked it fast and rough.

I reached between us and unzipped his fly, pulling his erection free of his boxer shorts. He moaned softly as I stroked it a few times and then he pressed me against the door. Moving my panties to one side, he thrust into me, quick, short strokes, with him grunting at each one. I looked over his shoulder and wondered about his wife.

It was over just as quickly as it had begun. George pulled out his rapidly deflating dick and pushed it back into his shorts. Zipping his pants and tucking in his shirt, he leaned down and kissed my neck while I rearranged my clothes. I guessed that our little encounter was over. His arm went back through mine as he walked me back down the alley. We parted at the sidewalk, and George turned toward the bar, never looking back.

I walked several blocks before stopping to straighten my skirt and smooth my stockings; George's fluids were dripping down the inside of my thigh. Flagging a cab, I gave the driver an address in the toniest part of town. I wasn't headed home, but rather, to see someone.

Wide streets met wider lawns, manicured by hired hands. The streetlights cast a warm glow over the neighborhood, welcoming the residents home but warning outsiders that they could be seen by watchful eyes.

Walking up the brick path, I thought about what I was going to say. The door swung open before I could even ring the bell. The lady of the house, wrapped in a silk robe, invited me in and took me into the parlor.

"Can I get you a drink or a cup of coffee, Esther?" she inquired.

"Coffee would be nice, Betty. Black, please." I liked it dark and strong.

She left to get it, and I took off my overcoat and then slipped off my wet panties and put them in my coat pocket. They were becoming uncomfortable.

"Thank you," I told her as she returned with a single cup and gave it to me. It was almost too hot to hold, so I set it on the table beside the sofa.

"So, what can you tell me?" she asked quietly, looking at me with soulful eyes, eyes full of concern and dread. Her silk robe had fallen open, but she was too distracted to notice. I noticed, though, and saw that she was wearing a silk gown under it, the color of lilacs.

I took a moment to think. This was the hardest part of my job. Telling a spouse about the cheating, lying scumbag that they had married. I always felt bad for them.

"Well, I found George at Harvey's Lounge, just where you said he'd be."

"And what happened?" Her blues eyes sparkled as she waited to hear. "Was there another woman?"

"Well, yes, there was. He left with the other woman and went out to the alley and fucked her."

"Do you have any proof? Anything I can use against him?" Betty leaned closer to me, and I could smell her powder, something delicate and floral. She smelled nice.

I reached into my coat pocket, pulled out the panties and gave them to her. She turned them over in her hands and noticed the wetness in them. I couldn't tell if she found them distasteful or something else. She held them up closer to her face and sniffed them. Putting them aside, she looked at me for a long second and then smiled.

"Was it as bad as I said it would be?" she asked, sliding closer to me and putting her hand on my thigh.

"Yes, just as bad. How could you stay married to him all these years?" I untied the belt of her robe, letting it slide further open. Then I leaned over and kissed her on one bare shoulder.

"Well, now I have all the evidence I need to get a divorce." She laughed and stood up, pulling me up with her. Holding the panties in one hand, she wrapped an arm around my waist as we walked out of the parlor and headed up the stairs.

Because I Could

Daina Blue

He had waited only six days for the supplies he asked for to arrive. He was taken into an empty gray room as stark as the words he would be writing. One table. One chair. His irons scraped against the concrete flooring, the only sound in the room besides the rasping of his breath. Twenty-five years of smoking did that to you.

"One hour."

There was no need to reply to the short statement. It wasn't expected. Permanently nicotine-stained fingertips brushed over the pristine white of the paper stacked neatly in front of him. One ballpoint pen waited for his efforts. He supposed he could jam it through his temple before the guards could reach him, but what would that get him?

Nothing but nothing.

But on these blinding-white pages, he could secure his place in history. He could ensure that whoever read his words would never forget Donald B. Camrooney. He would live forever, perhaps he would even inspire a following. Now wouldn't that be something?

He flexed his hands, enjoying the short respite from the manacles around his wrists. He slowly leaned his head to the right and then to the left, relishing the loud crunching releases of air between joints that followed.

Then, he began to write.

Seems like a lot of people want to know why I killed Loretta Halscott. The police wanted to know why, the reporters wanted to know why. Maybe even you—the you reading these words right now—want to know why. Why?

Because.

Because it was my right. Because she was my property. Because she was my possession. Because. Because. Because, I just wanted to. Because I could.

I met Etta in an online chat room. It was pretty easy to pick out the needy ones. They whimper and whine and spread their legs, hoping that someone is going to rescue them from their boring lives in the real world.

I picked Etta because she had a link to her real picture. Who would think that a looker like that needed to come online to find love? You've all seen her by now. I'm sure there will be pictures in this article when it's published. Would you have turned down legs for miles and an ass shaped like that? Tight as a fucking drum, I can assure you.

Well, it's not hard online to feed people all the lines they need to hear. They are just waiting to hear how you are different. They want a strong man. Maybe their husbands or their boyfriends are slobs who won't work, who won't take them out on the odd Saturday night. See, Etta needed a man who was going to treat her like a lady. Treat her like the female she is. Know what I mean? She wanted me to be who I was. A man's man. Her man.

So, I played the part. I seduced her with all the right words and promises, told her that I was trained to be a Master and that she was the epitome of a natural submissive. She liked that; it made her feel special. Everyone likes to feel special, right? It was easy online to make her fall for me, long before the first phone call, months before she'd come out to meet me. She was my nasty, begging, slut of a thing. My property. She wanted that. I would make sure it would come true for her.

It was eight months after I found her online, that she flew out here to meet me. I told her if she was truly my slave, to come off that plane in a leather jacket with nothing beneath, a short black skirt, heels, and no panties.

She did.

I had my hand up her skirt before we made it to the luggage pick-up. She was as wet as if I'd had her spread with my tongue up her pussy. I fingered her while we waited in line. She squirmed and groaned. I probably could have fucked her right then and there if I had wanted to.

She was as hot as any of her pictures had predicted. All that long blonde hair and those big blue eyes. I'd had her on a special diet for the last five months. Nothing but fruit and vegetables, only water to drink. She was into yoga and pilates and all that other new-age shit that I never cared for. I have to admit, that bitch could bend anyway you wanted her to. And brother, did I make her bend. Of course, I ain't no lightweight. You've seen me on television. You've seen my pictures. I can bench 380 easy.

In the car-ride to my house, I had her suck my dick. So there she is, bare ass up in the air for all to see, my hand between her legs, fingering her pussy, and her mouth sliding up and down my prick like she hadn't tasted dick for years. I took the long way home.

During that first visit, I was her dream come true. You see, you don't reel them in by scaring them off the first time. You have to seal the deal. I treated her to dinners, movies, clubs.

I gave her baths and washed her hair. I whispered all the sweet nothings she could take into her ears while I fucked her every which way you could imagine. She liked it from behind; never heard a bitch wail and moan the way she did when I'd hammer it in.

Nope, I never so much as bruised her on that first visit. You save the good stuff for later.

You have to introduce the good stuff nice and slow to a pet. Train them with diligent patience. You pretty much train all bitches, human or canine, the same way. Before you know it, you could sell her shit on the street corner, and she'd bring all the cash straight back to you and beg you to allow her to kiss you in thanks.

I let Etta come out two more times. The last is when I started introducing her into the hard play. I'd gag her, bind her, blind her, and then beat her for an hour. She wanted those bruises. Brother, let me tell you, she begged for them. I took my time with Etta. She was the best slut I've ever had. Tight little twat, titties that would bounce with each strike. She truly was a submissive. She loved making me dinner, bathing me, sleeping on the floor in a dog collar. Of course, she resisted when I started making her sleep outdoors in the doghouse. I told her if she really loved me and if she was really a slave, she'd do whatever I told her to do and enjoy it. She did it. I rewarded her with a pillow and blanket. God knows, Michigan nights can get cold.

See, there's a small thing called consent. Even a guy like me has his pride. I would have let her go at any time, if she asked.

I never once did anything to Etta she didn't consent to. I made sure of that. I just made sure that Etta loved me enough to consent to anything I ever wanted. So, it wasn't a surprise when she started telling me she would die for me. By this time, she'd moved in with me permanently. Left her job, her home, and come to me. She was mine, in total. I had her branded with my initials. Never had heard a squeal like that before in my life. Got me hard, and I fucked her with her flesh still steaming.

So, we'd been together about two years, and one night, while I was fucking her, I asked her, "Would you die for me, Etta?" She said she would. She swore it in a moan right when she was coming on my dick. I just smiled and said she was a good bitch.

I introduced breath play to her. First, with my hand. I'd choke her until her cheeks flushed, and her eyes looked about ready to pop right out of her skull. I choked her with my prick. I held her face down into the mattress while I fucked her ass. She got off on all that shit. Etta was just as kinky as I was. People are acting like Etta never had a say in anything. But, I made sure she loved everything I did to her. People don't offer to die for you unless they mean it.

So, I decided Etta deserved what she always swore she wanted. To die for me. I made sure it was a special day for her I brought her into the city, and had her hair and nails done, bought her a slinky black dress that did all the right things for that round ass and great tits. I made her dinner, first time since she'd moved in with me. I told her tonight would be a night to never forget.

I enjoyed making love to her that night. I tried to make it like something out of a movie. I took my time. I undressed her slowly. I kissed every inch of that perfect body until she had come three times before I ever slipped my dick into her.

She sang when she came that fourth time. She told me she loved me afterwards. You know, I felt like I loved her, too. You can't own such an obedient pet and not come to have some sort of affection for them. And, well, she was going to die for me. There would never be another like Etta.

I had thought about all the possible ways I could kill Etta. I imagined slitting her from ear to ear, or from her throat down to her pussy. I thought about breaking her neck in a noose. The thought of watching her dangle there for me was kind of hot.

But, in the end, because I did have such a sweet feeling for my Etta, I chose to smother her.

I tied her at both ankles and wrists until she was spread out over the bed like an X. I stared at her body and into those blue eyes for the longest time. I asked her again would she die for me? She whispered yes. She loved me. I owned her. She wanted anything I desired. I told her tonight, she was going to give me everything.

I started with my hand around her throat as I fucked her. I was taking my time, trying to memorize the snug feel of her cunt wrapped around my meat. I came inside her when she was almost unconscious. I let her catch her breath and then had one last throat-fuck, too. I couldn't resist.

Then I straddled her, bunching up a fluffy pillow into my hands. She was worn out from our fucking. She looked content and starry-eyed.

"Etta, will you die for me?" I asked her.

"I will." She had whispered. So sweet.

She must have struggled under that pillow, and under me, for a good ten minutes. I knew it was over when the small twitches in her body were gone. When I slid the pillow off her face, her eyes were wide open and staring straight up at me. Her mouth was gaping.

I don't know why, but I started to cry. I was gonna miss that bitch. I do. Best fucking slut I ever found online. The others had all left me, but Etta, she was true blue. She said she wanted to die for me, and she did.

So, I guess you could say I killed Etta because she wanted it. But, in the back of my mind, I always knew that she didn't really want to die. It was just an expression of how deeply she loved me. It was just proof of how well I had played the game. I guess you could say I killed Loretta Halscott out of ego. I killed her because I wanted to. Because I could.

"Time's up."

"Yeah, all right. I'm done. Make sure that gets over to Rita Durant at the *Times*."

"Sure, Camrooney. I bet you can't wait to be a star."

What Was Lost

Robert Buckley

It was all said and agreed to so matter-of-factly days ago. So why was she feeling the butterflies now? Why was her heart racing as she stared herself down in the mirror? It was a simple request. What harm could come of it? He was eighty-three. That's what he said, but she knew he had to be much older. What else could he do but look, even if he wasn't tethered to an oxygen pack?

It was practically an act of charity. Practically, because he hinted he would pay. But Janet didn't feel like a prostitute. What she had agreed to do was light-years different than prostitution. And she certainly wasn't in the same league as some girls, who were financing their graduate degrees with what they earned working outcalls for escort services.

This was nothing like that. So why was she feeling so queasy? She took a deep breath and slowly slid one hand over her bare buttock and silken hip. Now she draped the treasure in a wrap skirt and gave herself one more appraising look in the mirror.

Stepping out of her apartment, she contemplated the long corridor and slowly ambled toward his door, high heels clicking on the hard wood floor.

She wondered if he would dress for the occasion, but she was almost certain he would wear the plain cotton pajamas and bathrobe he always wore. He lived in those garments.

He had charmed her, she decided. He had bound her in some spell cobbled out of the old magic he wielded when he was king of the city, in the days of flappers and bootlegged hooch. She had counted herself lucky for finding him, just a few doors away from her own, but now she wondered if he had found her, or more accurately, lured her.

It was her landlady who had sent her tapping on his door. Janet had told her about her thesis work regarding the twentieth century's first sexual revolution: the Roaring Twenties.

Mrs. Ponsetti's eyes had lit up like floodlights. "Dear, you must speak with Mr. Havilland. The poor thing can barely get around now with the emphysema, but in his day he was king of the speakeasies. Oh my, yes, you must speak to him. Just knock. He rarely has company these days. I'm sure he'd love to talk."

Janet had thanked her and turned to climb the stairs to her floor, when Mrs. Ponsetti caught her arm and whispered, "You know, they tried to kill him—the Black Hand—but he stood up to them. And the beautiful girls, oh, madre mia, the girls . . ."

It sounded like a warning, if only a halfhearted one. But it was enough to send a shiver up Janet's back, and stoke her curiosity about Mr. Havilland. She had glimpsed him on occasion as he stepped outside his door to retrieve his daily newspapers, but neither had acknowledged the other.

He was a gaunt ruin of a man; in a body made so worn and decrepit by years of abuse it barely contained his soul. His skin was pasty and off-yellow, marked liberally with large liver spots. He wore thick, dark glasses over a face drawn skull-tight. Thin, dull, white hair fell in random wisps over his temples and ears. Still, he seemed to carry himself with dignity, or perhaps a residue of arrogance.

She researched his notorious career at the morgue of the *Herald-Standard*. He was indeed king of the speaks back in the twenties, running five different clubs throughout the city and its outskirts. But the crown jewel was the Sans Merci on Pelletier Street.

It was understood then that Prohibition was an annoyance, and law enforcement was just as likely to look the other way, especially when it was being paid to do so. But there were other incidents that brought the club into conflict with the moral watchdogs of the day.

Janet could read between the luridly purple lines of newspaper reports. The Sans Merci wasn't just a place to drink and party, it was a sex club. It served not only the well-off "swells," but the working man in his rough and tumble desires, so long as he knew his place. And it was a magnet for young girls determined to shed their innocence.

The local Temperance Society demanded action to close down Sans Merci after a father, who had gone there to retrieve his daughter from the den of debauchery, was severely beaten and left bleeding in the gutter. Charges of "white slavery" were made, but no criminal proceedings ever were brought against Havilland, or anyone else.

A simple farm family, sponsored by the local Baptist church, testified that their only daughter had been "sold" to a wealthy couple during an auction at the club, and was indentured to perform "lewd and vile services."

The couple countered that they had hired the girl as a servant mainly to rescue her from abuse she suffered at the hands of her family. They implied the girl was an incest victim. And so it went. Havilland, and his patrons for that matter, wore Teflon long before Teflon was invented.

Then there was the shooting. Thugs working for a local Mafia chief traded shots with Havilland in an alley next to the club. It was understood the Mob wanted to take over the Sans Merci. Havilland took three slugs in the chest and lived. All three of the trigger men died on the spot. A week after the incident, the Mafia chief died choking on a multi-pronged fishhook that somehow was never extracted from the eel he consumed.

Janet could hardly contain her excitement. He was perhaps the last true buccaneer of the Jazz Age, and she had to talk with him.

Early one evening she knocked tentatively on his door. Her heart was racing, and her stomach was doing somersaults. At first there was silence, then a shuffling. Finally the doorknob turned. Some nameless angst caused Janet to step back from the door, as if she expected to see a specter. And as the door opened a stale, dry smell invaded her nostrils. It was the smell of an aged man's abode.

Anthony Havilland stood before her without as much as a nod. He had done his part by opening his door to her. It was up to her to make the introductions. As she explained her interest in early twentieth-century history she felt as though he was scanning her, evaluating her somehow. She became acutely aware that her nipples had hardened.

He asked her inside.

That first evening they talked well into the early morning hours, but she had no sense of time passing. He enchanted her with anecdotes about rum-running and the "Naked Follies," a contest during which the couples danced in the nude, the men wearing a mock vest and tie, and the ladies only feathered boas. He told her of Clara Bow spreading "it" around liberally, and of Valentino, anonymous in drag, seducing drunken young men.

His voice, dry and papery, kept her in thrall for six-and-a-half hours. It seemed like thirty minutes. They agreed to meet again two nights later.

She was bolder then, asking him more questions and challenging his answers or his memory. She had made tea and handed him his cup before settling into an overstuffed chair. He lifted the cup to his lips slowly and deliberately, but without a tremor. It surprised her that his hand could be so steady. She chalked it up to age misconception. She just expected elderly persons' hands to shake.

She took a breath and steadied herself, uncertain how he would react to her next question. "Mr. Havilland, the Sans Merci—it was more than a nightclub where liquor could be had, or where you could participate in a naughty dance contest, was it not?"

"It was," he replied in his soft rasp.

"In fact, it was primarily a sex club, wasn't it? Of course, the liquor . . ."

"The liquor was just another taboo, my dear. It was, of course, a social lubricant, but then it was also a legislated taboo."

"Taboo? That's why people came to the Sans Merci."

"The light shines, and her eyes are opened," he chuckled. "Yes, of course. Prohibition was a sham. If you wanted a drink, you could get it at the corner drug store legally with a fabricated prescription. The Sans Merci offered a venue to shed one's inhibitions, to shake off one's fetters. A place to turn and laugh at all the 'thou shalt nots' imposed by government, religion, morality, whatever the definition of it was at the time."

"I read the press coverage of the day," she said, carefully

placing her teacup on the dull coffee table. "It was strongly suggested that you were involved in 'white slavery.' "

"White, brown, yellow," he tittered. "Yes, we auctioned slaves at the Sans Merci."

His admission startled Janet momentarily, or perhaps it was his thin smile. "We didn't kidnap young girls, or young men for that matter," he continued. "They came willingly and they were grateful to be placed on the block. For them, it was the ultimate freedom from all that had repressed them their whole lives."

"You can't mean—I mean . . ." Janet searched for words. "Human beings don't willingly surrender themselves, surrender their ego . . ."

"You're missing the point, my dear. In slavery there is freedom. Yes, a paradox, but there it is. We sold young women, young men. Occasionally a man would wish to sell his wife, or a wife sell the services of her husband."

"Wait a minute. Married couples?"

"Oh, I see, what God has joined together and so on and so on?"

"What happened to these people, these slaves?"

"They were taken away by their owners. My concern in the transaction ended there."

"They can't have just disappeared," Janet insisted. "No one keeps a slave for real. How long did they remain in their relationships?"

"Relationships?" he laughed. "I have no idea what became of them. Occasionally a couple would return to the club with a girl or a young man they had purchased. Usually it was to show off how well they had trained them. Or they would be required to perform social favors."

"Social favors?"

"I've always liked the phrase, 'a gift that keeps on giving.' What a marvelous gesture to give a friend the use of a lovely young body for a night, or a few days." Janet could feel her blood simmer in her cheeks. Havilland studied her closely. "Do you wish to continue, my dear?"

"Huh? Oh, yes. It's just, I know mores changed at this time, but what you're describing is more than a couple of college kids getting drunk and diving naked into a public fountain, or dancing the Charleston without a stitch."

"My dear, we had just experienced the Great War. A war that was to end all wars. A war so horrible it was, even then, nearly impossible to comprehend. That war pulled the rug out from under all the churches and all the golden rules. If there was a god, he had a sick, twisted sense of humor. And, if you had a brain, any intellect at all, you understood that the Great War would not be the last, and the ones that followed would be that much more horrible." He stopped to suck up oxygen, wheezing painfully.

Janet weighed his words, then responded softly, "You make it sound hopeless. No good, no evil. Just carnality."

"Freedom. It was freedom, my dear. When you stare into the abyss, you step back, and all the illusions, all the fogged glass that has distorted your vision shatters and falls away. You realize all you have is your body, and it is yours to do with as you please. Even if it means giving control of it to another, it is yours to give. Not the churches' with all their shamans, nor the government's and its politicians, it is yours alone."

"But it would seem class distinctions didn't change," Janet countered. "I deduced that Sans Merci was not democratic. The wealthy were treated differently. The working classes were welcome, but they were kept at arm's length, drank at a separate bar."

He chuckled again. "That was as they wanted it. They were free to mingle, and mingle they did—with a purpose."

"I don't understand."

"Then imagine a society woman who spends her week ordering about the help. The gardeners, the cook, the mechanic. They are all her inferiors. Now imagine that perhaps she harbors a fantasy of being taken by her social inferiors. Brutalized by the unwashed, as it were." He paused.

"Now, conversely, you are a working man, or a shop girl, and your fantasy is to subordinate your employer carnally. There are so many variations and permutations of this inkling to immerse oneself in another strata of society." He watched Janet closely for a moment, and then continued.

"There were other concerns, of course. The continuation of many fortunes in those days depended on an heir."

"You don't mean . . ." Janet gasped.

"I do. Stud services. More than a few seemingly virile captains of industry brought their wives to the Sans Merci for that purpose. The ladies weren't unwilling. It makes me laugh today to know that some stodgy director of a family foundation likely has some Dago, Polack, Mick, or Jew genes that were deposited into his mother by an anonymous laborer."

They sat silently for a moment. Janet noticed a wetness between her legs, and her cheeks and ears smoldered. Finally, she said, "It's late. I hadn't realized . . ."

"Will you come back, my dear?"

"Huh? Ah, yes, sure. I would like to speak some more."

"Good. But, I wonder if you would do something for me? The next time."

"Of course, if I can."

"Not if you can, my dear. If you want. You must want to do this thing I ask."

"What could you want?"

"Would you expose yourself for me?"

"I—I'm not sure I understand. Expose?"

"Would you let me look at your ass?"

"My—my ass?"

"Yes. Just your ass. I would not put a hand on you. It's just that, I think you must have a beautiful derrière. May I see it? Next time?"

Janet couldn't fathom a single reason why she shouldn't grant his request. It seemed perfectly reasonable at the time, as did his offer of an "honorarium." She agreed.

Now she was in front of his door. The butterflies were again taking flight in her stomach. She knocked softly and heard the familiar shuffle from inside.

He opened the door slowly and greeted her, "Good evening, my dear. I've been anticipating your arrival."

Janet nodded and stepped inside. The butterflies vanished.

"If you don't mind, my dear, I should like to forgo further discussions for another night and just enjoy your physical gifts."

"Uh, well, yes, of course . . ."

"Show me your ass," he ordered. "Now, please. Turn and face the wall."

Janet turned, vaguely feeling she had no choice. But then, she had no intention of denying his request now. She unwrapped her skirt and let it fall. Behind her she heard a long, labored breath.

"Lovely, lovely," he whispered. Janet smiled, realizing a quiet excitement was building and spreading throughout her body.

"Please, my dear, tilt your hips. Yes, like that. Marvelous."

It continued that way for most of the night. Janet would change poses, angle her hips, and stretch her leg as if she were being choreographed. She had no idea how much time had passed, but again felt wetness that now coated the tops of her thighs. She wondered if Havilland noticed.

"Would you like me to turn around?" she asked.

"No," he said firmly. Janet felt she had been scolded.

After some moments of silence, he said, "I've always regarded a woman's body as a temple, to be worshipped or spoiled, depending on one's predilection. Her breasts are the lavish columns and façade that lure the worshipper. Of course, her cunt is the holy of holies. But her ass, her ass is the altar, and that is where I preferred to perform my rituals."

And so the evening went on. He never touched her. When it was time to leave he placed an envelope in her hands. "Something for your education, my dear."

On the way back to her apartment she opened it. It contained a crisp hundred-dollar bill.

That night Janet dreamt she stood outside herself, watching Havilland as his eyes made love to her ass. She dreamt she could reach out and touch herself. She awoke as an orgasm rippled through her.

Over the next few weeks their meetings alternated between discussions and ass-baring sessions. The discussions maintained an ambiance of the time. Havilland's voice easily transported Janet to the heyday of the Sans Merci, champagne-fueled orgies, slave auctions, live sex shows, and virgin deflowerings.

On the nights she was called just to bare her ass, his instructions became curt. One night he told her to kneel and place her forehead on the floor so she could raise her ass as high as she could.

"Have you ever allowed yourself to be taken this way?" he asked.

She surprised herself by answering without hesitation, "Yes."

"He took you from behind—cunt or ass?"

She swallowed. "Both."

"Excellent, my dear. Who was he?

"A professor. Undergraduate school," she answered, even as she wondered how she was so easily confessing intimate details of her life.

"Have you been intimate with a woman?"

"Yes. After high school, just before college. My best girlfriend and I spent the night together before I went away. We hadn't planned anything. We were just fooling around."

"You enjoyed it."

"Yes."

"Tell me your most lurid fantasy, my dear."

"I—I took a taxi one night. The driver was a large man. Very rough and hairy-looking. He was very rude. Later, I fantasized about him fucking me in his cab, then leaving me naked by the side of the road . . ."

"So you could be ravished again, by anyone who happened by."

"Yes."

"Thank you, my dear. You may go now." He handed her another envelope as she dressed.

Later, Janet marveled at herself. How could she have told him such deep, intimate secrets?

A week passed during which Janet was occupied with work at school. She had set a date to see Havilland on a Sunday evening. He greeted her in his usual fashion, but he stopped her before she could sit down.

"My dear, I think I have told you all I can about bygone days. I would like you, for one more time, to bare yourself to me. This time, however, I wish to touch you. Would that be agreeable to you?"

Janet sensed a climax of some kind was pending. She nodded her head, kicked off her shoes and slipped her jeans down and off. Turning, she pulled her white bikini down her long legs and kicked it off her foot.

For a moment she stood still, then, without instruction, followed the moves he had choreographed so many times for her.

Then he spoke. "Please, be still."

She heard his raspy breathing become louder and more rapid. Then she felt his hand, like cold, hard plastic, flatten itself against her right cheek and move up and over her hip. A chill ran up her spine and gooseflesh emerged on her back and thighs.

His hard finger probed between her cheeks, feigning entrance to her anus, then it withdrew. His other hand, just as hard and cold cupped her other cheek.

Then his hands were gone. She heard him sigh. "Alas, my dear, the desiccation of age has not permitted me to feel your lovely body as well as even a man in his sixties. These hands have lost their ability to touch. Thank you. That will be all."

She dressed as he sat looking out the apartment window. She began to speak, but he cut her off. "Goodbye, my dear."

It was over. Whatever had happened over the past few weeks ended there. She turned to leave. Stepping into the hallway she heard him say, "All lost . . . all lost."

Monday evening Janet came home to find an ambulance outside her building. Attendants brought a sheet-covered form down the front steps toward the waiting vehicle. She noticed Mrs. Ponsetti, wiping her eyes with a handkerchief.

"What happened?" she asked the weeping landlady.

"Poor thing. It's Mr. Havilland. I went to bring him his newspapers, and I found his door open. I went in and found him."

Janet ran after the attendants who had just loaded the body into the ambulance. She tapped one on the shoulder. "What happened?"

"Not sure, Miss. Looks like the old guy just turned off his oxygen. Happens sometimes. They just say 'enough is enough.'"

Janet watched the ambulance pull away until it was out of sight, then turned and climbed the stairs past Mrs. Ponsetti. Climbing the flight of stairs to her floor she walked past Havilland's apartment and along the long corridor to her own.

Once inside, she turned on her computer and reached for the notes she had made from her conversations with Havilland. Calling up her thesis draft she poised her fingers to type.

Her nipples pushed against the fabric of her sweater, and blood simmered in her cheeks. It was hot in the apartment. Slowly and deliberately she shed her clothing. Naked, she again positioned her fingers on the keyboard. No words came.

She touched her labia, which were moist and slick, as were her groin and upper thighs. She stopped to rub a bit of the viscous fluid between her thumb and finger before wiping it across one breast. A warm tingle rose up her back, as if a finger were tracing lightly along her spine.

She breathed deeply, then she began to write.

Holiday Sex

Newborn

Ann Regentin

In her right hand, Martina held the ankle of a teenaged girl, running her fingers over the contours as she examined it closely. How old had she been? Seventeen? Maybe eighteen? No older than nineteen, that was for sure. Certain bones had not yet fused.

Guatemala's thirty-six-year civil war reached a high—or perhaps low—point in the early 1980s, when General Efraín Ríos Montt decided that the Maya were sheltering the Guatemalan National Revolutionary Unity. In retaliation, or perhaps as a preventive measure, he destroyed the indigenous villages, killing everyone in his path. Now it was Martina's job to sort out the remains.

A young girl's ankle. An old man's skull. The legs of a toddler. The ribcage of a teenaged boy.

Martina spent her days putting the pieces together, figuring out which bones made up which skeletons. DNA, of course, was the deciding factor, but that took time and money that she preferred not to squander. Old-fashioned forensic anthropology was her best bet, and that was what she relied on most of the time. In some cases, it was easy. This arm and shoulder belonged to this torso, and then all she had to find was the missing left leg. Sometimes the body was nearly intact. Most commonly, she had a lot of heads that had no bodies, all showing the marks of machetes on the vertebrae.

The bones told their stories more clearly than words. A bullet hole through a ribcage showed her a woman running for her life, trying to out race death at five thousand feet per second. Repeating death; the cowards had used automatic weapons. An infant's smashed-in face brought a vivid picture of a screaming baby held by its ankles, swung high into the air, and brought down hard on the concrete wall of a house. Martina wiped sweat from her face and eased the ankle against the tibia and fibula of a skeleton of about the right age and build, then smiled as the bones snuggled into place. A near-perfect fit, which after twenty years, was the best she could hope for.

The girl was small, like most of the indigenous peoples, maybe about five foot one. Her bones were delicate as crocheted lace, a slight framework to give shape to the muscle and fat that would have filled out her cocoa-brown skin. Black hair, brown eyes, definitely a Mayan face, but a unique face, her own face, a face that was lost to the world forever.

Martina had the bones put together, but identifying the girl would be another matter. In the deep jungle, there were no birth certificates and in the wake of General Montt's scorched-earth policy, odds were good that there might not be any living relatives to claim her. Her father, mother and siblings were probably among the bones still awaiting Martina's expert care. Still, there might be someone who remembered her. The girl had broken her left front incisor. That would be a big help because it would have made her smile quite distinctive. What else? Lots of fractures, but the girl had been tossed carelessly into a mass grave and buried equally carelessly. One break, though, was old and well healed, probably a childhood accident. Right front metatarsal. Probably she caught her foot on something when she was running.

Her pubic bone was broken. Martina bit her lip, took a deep breath, made herself look at it. Hard, blunt force from below.

What the hell had they used? And why? Wasn't rape enough?

" 'Ey, boss!"

She started, and looked up. "Jaime!"

Her lab assistant smiled, his flat Mayan face lighting up in an array of wrinkles.

"It's time for dinner, boss," he said.

"Right," Martina said, shaking herself. She was, she found, suddenly hungry, or perhaps she had been all along. She had a tendency to lose herself in the work and without Jaime's nagging, would go all day without eating any more than breakfast and a quick snack before bedtime. "Give me just a minute."

"Five," he said, still grinning. "No more."

Martina shut her workstation down and looked up, surprised at how tired she was. Still, it was a good kind of tired. She'd put a body together, someone who might possibly be identified before she was given back to the earth with more dignity. Sometimes she wondered why she bothered because that's what was going to happen to all of those bones. They'd be sent right back to the ground. Hers was not the kind of job that created happy reunions. The best she could hope for was closure for the families, if they could be found. It didn't matter, though. Every body reconstructed, every new grave, felt like a victory over tyranny itself. Martina lived for those victories.

When she and Jaime reached the home of their hosts, Martina stared open-mouthed at the table. It was loaded with food: beans, rice, chicken, cheese, two kinds of soup, and a mountain of steaming tortillas. "What is this?" she asked wildly.

"It's Christmas Eve, boss," Jaime said, holding a chair for her and laughing at her confusion. "How did you forget?"

"Christmas Eve," Martina repeated stupidly. She had forgotten. Without snow and lights and pine trees, it just hadn't felt like December at all.

The village hadn't forgotten, though. Martina's Spanish was still weak, but she was able to join in the celebration anyway, with Jaime translating in her ear when she lost the thread of conversation. And it was a celebration. Even the morbid work of disinterring the old bodies could not stop the village from wearing its best clothes, bringing out its best food.

"Who did you find today?" an old woman asked slowly. She had, by a miracle, escaped the death squads, and she was, for all intents and purposes, the village memory.

"A girl in her teens," Martina said, equally slowly. "She had broken a bone in her foot and one of her teeth."

"Where?" the old woman asked.

Martina pointed. She had never heard the Spanish word for "incisor."

The old woman closed her eyes, then spoke in rapid-fire Spanish to her nearest neighbors. The buzz spread down the table, then swarmed back up. "Could she have been nineteen?" the old woman asked.

"Yes," Martina said. "If she grew up slowly." The words for "late bloomer" were lost in the same ether as "incisor."

"Then I think she is Porfiria Estrella de la Cruz. She was nineteen but young for her age. She broke her foot trying to play soccer with the boys, and she broke a tooth in an accident."

Porfiria Estrella de la Cruz. The girl in the lab had a name now, and a personality. In her mind, Martina saw a carefree tomboy. "Does she have a family?" she asked.

The buzz traveled down again, then up among a wave of shaken heads. "No. The village will see to her, though. The priest will pick up the body." Martina smiled, thanked the table at large, and discovered that her dinner actually tasted good.

Afterward, she went out for a walk, wandering aimlessly down the mix of two-tracks and footpaths that connected the various parts of the village. People smiled at her, and she smiled back, but she was in no mood for conversation, and they knew her well now, knew that she wasn't rude, just a crazy foreigner with crazy ideas, and they let her be.

She still wasn't used to the stars. The constellations were strange, unidentifiable. She was too close to the Equator for comfort. It really didn't feel like Christmas Eve. For that matter, it didn't feel like planet Earth. She was trapped in a place where everything normal and good had gone, and there was no hope of it ever coming back. The villagers lived in fear, and so did she. She could be killed for what she did. In this place, memory was a crime.

She walked past the village church, and was startled to see a figure standing in the doorway. It wasn't anywhere near time for Mass yet. Then the figure moved, and she realized that it was Jaime.

"Hey!" she called softly.

" 'Ey, boss!" he called back, his voice glad. "Come look."

For Martina, a lapsed Protestant, the village church bordered on assault. In Guatemala, the Crucifixion wasn't cleaned up before being put on display, and painted blood ran so freely from the body on the cross that Martina fully expected it to drip on the floor. There were Christmas lights, but instead of illuminating trees, they illuminated the sculptured tragedy on the wall and the glass coffin that contained yet another version of the tortured Christ. Martina balked.

Jaime grabbed her arm. "Come on, boss," he said. "You've seen worse."

"I'm not so sure," Martina said without thinking.

"What do you mean?" he asked.

"Nothing," she lied. Perhaps if they had a gentler religion, would these people be gentler? "Do you like it?"

"Yes," Jaime said.

"Why?" she asked. Jaime had not let go of her arm, and she found his touch comforting and oddly familiar.

He was silent for a while, looking up at the body on the wall. "I like the idea of rebirth," he said. "I like knowing that death is not the end. Look at this village. In the bodies we find, you see the village on the cross, bleeding to death, buried wherever a place could be found, but then we go home to see it come back to life again. There are people here, and they are afraid, but they have come back to their homes, to their lives, and to those they lost. The tyrants cannot win as long as people are willing to come back from the dead."

Martina blinked, startled. She hadn't even considered it that way. "Have you ever held a gun, Jaime?"

"Yes," he said, "when I was a boy. I was told that the more people I killed, the more chance there was for peace. Luckily, I lived long enough to learn better."

"How old were you?"

"Fifteen."

Martina stared at him. "How did you survive?"

"I grew up," he said. "I got old enough to know when I was being lied to. They told me that killing would make me a man, but I knew I was a man when I was brave enough to stop."

Martina looked up again at the bloodied wreck on the cross, and fragments of an Appalachian carol drifted through her head. ". . . why Jesus our Savior was born for to die." It was the innocent, she realized, who made up the machine of war; only an innocent could fire a gun at another human being and believe it would do any good. Innocence wasn't such a precious thing at all. In it, the seeds of destruction had their best chance of germinating. "Which side were you on?" she asked.

Jaime smiled, but not his usual, broad smile, just an upward quirk of his lip, nothing more. "I was one of the guerillas," he said. "I was fighting for my country's freedom, at least that was what I thought at the time."

"And now?"

"I am still fighting, except now, I fight against both sides."

Martina would someday go home to Wisconsin, to the snow and the pine trees and the illuminated reindeer, where death was something that happened in private and every grave had only one occupant. This was Jaime's world; he had no other home to go to. She had thought herself brave and noble, walking away from safer work at home and coming down to lend her superior skills to his battle, but that bravery was ashes compared to Jaime's. Reborn as a man of peace, he would die here, probably at the hands of those he bore witness against. He had no embassy to protect him, no superpower government to intervene, only the faith that he could somehow outrun death long enough to make a difference. He had that faith. She could see it in his eyes as he looked up at the cross.

"Come on, boss," he said, finally letting to of her arm. "Let's go home. You need sleep."

The house was quiet when they got back. The children were tucked into bed, and their hosts were napping in anticipation of midnight Mass. Jaime sat her down at the kitchen table and got a bottle of water out of the refrigerator for her. It was lukewarm; the electricity had gone out again. She took a sip, felt Jaime's hands on her shoulders, and stiffened.

"Relax," he said. "I know it's not easy for you."

"How do you know?" she asked as his fingers dug expertly into the knotted muscles.

"I've been working with you for three months. You push too hard."

She was suddenly ashamed to realize that she had worked with him for three months, too, and could barely remember his last name. "Are you married?" she asked.

"No."

She heard the reason in his voice, that he would not put anyone else at risk, and the pain it caused. "I'm sorry."

He said nothing, only moved his hands down to her deltoids, still massaging.

"Jaime, I can't," she said, feeling desire and panic arise in her together. "I'm sorry."

He didn't stop. "Because of Porfiria?"

"How did you know?" she asked.

"I examined the bones, too," he reminded her.

"But you're not . . ."

"An expert like you?" he finished. "I don't have a degree, but I know the difference between a postmortem break and a broken, living bone."

"Why did they do that?" she asked.

It was a rhetorical question, but Jaime's hands stilled for a moment. "Fear," he said finally, as his hands resumed their motion.

"Fear?" she asked, twisting up to look at him.

His face was almost unfamiliar in its distance, the lines of it hardened to basalt. "She was alive, and they were dead. They thought they had to kill her, too."

A slow welling of horror rose in her gut. "You were dead once." It was the closest she could get to asking, "Did you do it, too?"

"Yes." And there was her answer.

The horror crashed in on her, and she let her head fall into her hands, tears welling in the corners of her eyes. Nothing here was ever what it seemed. Not even Jaime.

His hands tightened on her shoulders. "Come here," he said.

With nowhere else to go, she stood, hating herself for it, and he wrapped his arms around her. Jaime was barely her height. She had to drop her head to his shoulder, but that shoulder was hard and warm. So were his arms, and she let the tears soak into his shirt as she inhaled the slightly stale smell of his body. Nobody bathed daily here, including her, so it was familiar, even comforting. So was Jaime. For three months, he had been her bedrock, always there, always solid no matter how stressful things got. If they had a good day, Jaime was calm. If they had a bad day, Jaime was also calm. He had the peace of a Buddha in him, and only then did she realize how much she relied on it.

How could she find comfort in the arms of a rapist? She tried to pull away, but his grip tightened. "Jaime, I really can't."

"Do you think she won't forgive you?"

"No, but . . ."

"You don't have to die for anyone's sins," he said, "especially not mine."

It was obscene to her, in light of the abused body on the table in her lab, that she should have any pleasure at all. Her whole, pampered life seemed suddenly disgusting, and the fact that she was even contemplating sex with this man was grotesque. "No," she tried to say, but it didn't come out that way at all. What she thought was right was losing to something else that she didn't understand and feared far more than the bones lying in her makeshift lab.

"Martina!"

It was the first time she could ever remember hearing him say her name. Usually, he just called her "boss."

"Why?" she asked.

"Because you're a good woman, a caring woman. I want you to live."

Martina was surprised at how close his lips were. All she had to do was move her head just a little to meet them.

Jaime's kisses were surprisingly gentle. Even when they became open-mouthed and passionate, they were still gentle. His hands, too, were gentle, and under her hands, his body was strong and warm.

"Martina." This time it was a whisper as he disengaged, took her hand, and let her to his bed.

He undressed her slowly, patiently, breaking off his kisses only when he needed to, just long enough to remove her shirt, then his. He let her deal with her bra. He unbuttoned her jeans and tugged on them as she wriggled free of both them and her panties. The heat of his hands soaked through her skin all the way down to her bones, turning her insides to water. She had to bite her lip to keep silent, to keep from waking the rest of the house, and even still, tiny sounds escaped from her throat, a rhythmic counterpoint to his breathing.

Jaime's body was solid, not the ripped body of a weight lifter but the powerful one of a man who spent much of his time in motion. His legs and ass were hard as packed earth. His chest was smooth and almost too broad, his pectorals curving to meet deltoids that were just as strong and firm. His belly was soft, not a young man's, and below it, his cock rose hard from its thick nest of hair. She ran her fingers up the length of it and smiled to herself when he had to smother a groan.

He rolled up, wrapped both arms around her, let her get her left arm around him, and wrapped her legs around him for good measure. His body settled easily on hers, his cock sliding over the swollen folds of her cunt, but he simply kissed her, thrust against her, nothing more. She felt the anxious welling of the very earliest hints of orgasm, whimpered before she could stop herself, and he kissed a trail down the side of her neck to her breast.

He sucked, and she arched up hard against him, the near-pain of it sending her anxiety into the stratosphere. The head of his cock left a slippery trail on the inside of her thigh and she reached for it, felt it fall thick and heavy into her hand. Her touch coaxed the ghost of a groan from him, and he thrust forward, the head brushing her groin. Still, he did not push for penetration, only moved his mouth to her other breast as her fingers played with his balls.

He rolled off of her, back to his side, his hand sliding down over her belly to her cunt. He went straight for her clit, a broad caress that couldn't miss, and although it wasn't the precise touch she was used to, nothing like her own, the sheer thrill of being touched by another pushed her anxiety to a fever pitch. She felt that hesitation, as if her nervous system was holding its breath, then she came, burying her face in his chest and shuddering in his arms.

Only then did he nudge her gently onto her side, and she felt his fingers on her cunt, then the blunt head of his cock. It felt too big just before it went in, then just right as it filled her, and his hand caressed her hip as he buried himself to the hilt. It felt unbelievably good, even better when his fingers coaxed one of her nipples back to hardness. He thrust very slowly, as if savoring it, and she relaxed, warmed to the core by it, as his lips brushed the back of her neck.

She was in bed with a rapist. This bothered her less now than she thought it should, and she wondered what his victims would think of her.

She was no longer an innocent.

In the soft glow of Jaime's fucking, she realized that she came to Guatemala believing that she brought moral superiority, as an American and a noncombatant, as well as her skills. She was all but gloating over the battered bones, so certain she was that such things could not happen in her world, that Guatemala and Wisconsin really were different places inhabited by different people. She was not a better person, she realized suddenly, only someone who had not been so tested and who had, in her blind innocence, avoided such tests. They were there, in Wisconsin, just as they were in Guatemala. She had simply chosen not to see them, had clung to her innocence, mistaking it for virtue. She could no longer condemn Jaime. Whatever he had been, whatever price he'd paid, he was now as he was now and she was no better.

Through all of this, Jaime kept up that slow, steady rhythm, off in his own world as she was in hers, but what jolted her out of it was the change in his pace that let her know that he was about to come. She came back to the moment and found that she welcomed it, that her hand was already resting on his hip, her fingertips following the flex of his ass. Then he thrust hard, froze, and she felt him pulse inside her as he sighed into the nape of her neck.

No pillow talk; he simply pulled her close, not bothering to pull out, and they drifted, perfectly content, into sleep.

Martina woke later to the sounds of the household making hushed preparations for the midnight Mass. She had to use the bathroom, but she stayed in bed waiting, not wishing to be invited to go along. Jaime was no longer inside her, but his body was still pressed firmly against her back and she relaxed into him, savoring it.

She didn't feel any different. That was strange because she expected to, she thought that such epiphanies were supposed to leave a mark. All she felt was the glow of a woman with a new lover, that rich peace that filled both body and soul like homemade hot cocoa.

Tomorrow was Christmas, and she changed her mind; she would not work. She would celebrate. Then she would go back to the lab and finish her tenure there, if not the job itself, before going back home, and she wondered idly what she would do when she got there, if her newborn self would survive the inevitable hero's welcome. It was not easy, being born for to die, when one lived in a world where lights sparkled in store windows and Crucifixions were scrubbed all tidy and clean before being put on display.

She heard the front door close, waited a moment, then

got up, pulled her clothes on, and went to the outhouse. There was a faint chill in the air, but only a faint one, drowned out by the humidity that gave her the most persistent acne she'd had since she was sixteen. Jaime, bless him, had made her forget all about it.

She shed her clothes and crept back into bed. Jaime, still sleeping or perhaps half-asleep, held the light blanket open for her and drew her back into the curve of his body.

"Merry Christmas, boss," he murmured.

Martina laughed

On a table in the lab, Porfiria Estrella de la Cruz slept.

Debra's Donuts

Julius

The walk around the lake was a daily event for me. Well, nearly daily. Well, usually three or four times a week. Enough exercise for me to think I was looking after myself. It wasn't a big lake mind you, a forty-minute walk, maybe two miles. Halfway around was Debra's Donuts, in a small shopping mall across the highway. It had loons and a beaver and ducks—the lake, not the doughnut shop.

I'd been doing the walk for maybe eighteen months. Eighteen months! A year and a half since Monica had traded me for a lawyer. Makes you wonder.

Debby had been there since I'd become a regular. Was Debby Debra? I had no idea. But the badge on her left breast said Debby. She was fortyish, which meant thirtyish some days and forty-plus on others. She was an ash-blond, almost skinny, but she always drew my eyes, and I seemed to draw her smile. I always had an Earl Grey and a maple-dip doughnut and sat to get warm in the winter or air conditioned in the summer. The day in question was the eve of Christmas Eve and cold as a penguin's thingy. I tossed hat and gloves onto my usual table and took my cold-freaked bladder Gents-wards.

I unzipped my parka and my pants and advanced towards the urinal. I was fishing for my poor shrunken, chilled whatsit when the door banged open. Enter one of those wheeled-bucket things and a mop, followed by Debby.

"Hey!" I cried, in mildly outraged modesty.

Debby locked the door behind her, smiled her sweet smile and said, "Maple-dip right?" and held one out.

As always at Christmas, the staff had dressed in Christmassy, fancy costumes. Debby wore a little, red, flopped-over Santa hat with white fur edging and a white pom-pom. That and a very short skirt and fishnet stockings or maybe pantyhose. She looked very fetching I thought.

"I'm one of Santa's little helpers," she told me.

"Well, I don't really need any help, not right now!" I said. I'd been on the point of release, and I groaned one of those in-throat, semi-silent groans that you groan when some vital moment has to be put on hold.

Debby gestured at me and at the urinal and said, "Don't let me stop you."

"A guy can't take a leak with a woman watching him!" Anybody knows that.

"I heard a guy can't pee with a hard-on," Debby told me.

"I haven't got a hard-on," I told her and told myself if I didn't take a leak soon I might die.

"I could give you one," said Debby and actually started to move towards me.

"Dear God, woman, I gotta pee!"

"Not with a hard-on."

"I don't have . . ."

She was close by then, and her free hand moved towards my open pants, "You will."

And I did.

She had it free, and in a flash it responded in fine fashion. The little guy wasn't cold anymore, the little guy wasn't little anymore. I gave a groan and Debby said an appreciative, "Quite impressive!"

She still held the doughnut and she slid it down over my cock. It was tight, but it was soft, and my cock wasn't. So there I stood with my very erect erection poking out through a doughnut and one of Santa's elves giggling little, girlishly.

"Go on, try and pee," she said. I didn't pee, and I didn't try, "See, you can't, can you?" She seemed pleased that she was right.

Debby dropped to her knees right in front of me. It was a day for surprises. She held the doughnut and took a small bite out of it and looked up. "We do make good doughnuts don't we?" she asked, a crumb at the corner of her mouth. Slowly, delicately she worked her way around the doughnut while my cock-head hovered an inch from her left ear. I stayed hard.

Debby's next move was to reach over to the basin and squirt a shot of hand soap into her palm. This she applied to my cock and, with no more ado, proceeded to jerk me off. It took maybe half a minute before my body quaked and my cock spurted. My offering came in curving installments onto the floor between us.

A swirl of her mop and my come was gone and, in a flash of fishnetted legs, so was Debby. Through the closing door she called "Merry Christmas! Ho! Ho! Ho!"

I walked around the lake on Christmas Eve, but I didn't cross to Debra's Donuts. The entire staff likely knew. Somehow I couldn't face walking in there. But I did wonder about Debby and our encounter. I did want to see her again. . . . Well, can you blame me?

Maybe after Christmas. Maybe.

On Christmas morning I stayed in bed. Why get up? Too early to get drunk, and a Christmas alone isn't the best reason to crawl out into the morning chill. So I dozed off again.

The bell woke me, and someone was pounding on the door. I crawled out of bed and pulled a bathrobe over my nakedness.

Debby! She stood on the small deck, and told me I looked awful. She wore a long winter coat and her little Santa hat. She held a paper cup with a plastic lid, a wisp of steam rose from its little vent hole. In her other hand was a small brown-paper bag. "Merry Christmas to my favorite customer, and it's cold out here."

I moved aside and let her into the kitchen. She put her gifts on the table and unbuttoned her coat. Underneath? The Christmas outfit, fishnets and all! She shooed me from the kitchen. "You need a shower and a shave and breakfast. Off you go, I'll get us some food."

Half an hour or so later, I felt brand new. Clean and shaved and awake with eggs, bacon, toast, and marmalade, and coffee inside me. "I could get to like this," I told her and added a very sincere thank you.

I watched her wash up and thought how magic she was. The fishnets and the short skirt did lovely things for her and lovely things for me. She wore a white blouse through which I could see a white bra. The little hat made her look Christmassy and so utterly, utterly sweet.

"Merry Christmas," she said from her seat on the sofa. She held up the little bag, and I crossed the room and took it. Inside, a maple-dip doughnut. I took it out and looked down at her.

"I've another treat for you," she said softly. With one hand she pulled up the little skirt. No panties! She put out her hand for the doughnut, and I handed it to her. She placed it carefully on her shaved mound.

She gestured me closer and carefully unsnapped and unzipped me. My pants fell.

"Oh my!" she said. I'd not put on any underwear after the shower, and now my cock was half-erect and rising and, in full view. "He seems to like doughnuts," she said and looked up at me. I think I fell for her at that moment, which sounds a funny thing to say. She looked so happy as she gazed up at me from under her lashes.

I knelt.

"I was wondering about this moment all night," she said. "Would I get up enough nerve to come here?"

She was suddenly shy and murmured, "I wondered if you'd eat the doughnut or maybe fuck me through it."

She picked it up and said in a husky whisper, "Forget the silly doughnut!"

She squirmed her ass forward on the cushion towards me. I leaned forward and kissed her very gently at the top of her cleft. She smelled of soap and of Debby. My mind swam in the scent of her, and suddenly shyness was gone. We might have been lovers for years. I peeled her open with my thumbs and kissed her inside, exploring with my tongue tip.

Two people hungry, very hungry, for each other. She came quickly, wetly, and noisily. She still held the doughnut.

I rested my cheek on the softness of her stockinged thigh and gently played my fingertips over her mound. It was my first close-up of a shaved pussy, and very cute it looked. "What now?" I whispered, happily knowing what was now.

"You know what to do, Santa!" she told me and wriggled her ass half off the cushion.

Santa did indeed and it was beautiful. The slide-in was the most perfect of moments. Her heat, her tightness. A few thrusts, and I came like a boy. She came with me and cried. Near bursting with happiness, I damn near cried, too.

We stayed quiet for a long time. She'd not moved. I sat on the floor between her feet, kind of uncomfortable, but the moment was too perfect to spoil.

Her thighs, her warmth, and most of all, the scents of our lovemaking got to me. My cock began swelling again. Almost embarrassed and afraid she'd say no, I asked, "Would you like to play some more?"

Back came a dreamy, "Yes, I'd like that."

I slid one hand up her thigh and reached for the bottom button of her blouse. Her small hand clamped on my wrist, almost painfully. "No!" The sharp one word response had me looking at her in surprise.

Her words came in a rush. "I lost them two years ago and got my white hair as a bonus. A white-haired old lady of forty-eight."

Her eyes were flooding with tears, "I think I'd better go, the turkey's in the oven and I, well, I was going to ask you over for Christmas dinner, but maybe that's not a good idea."

She tried to get to her feet.

I talked her out of leaving and listened in aching silence. She cried her long-saved tears. I held her, we held each other. I told her that her breasts didn't matter, while we both knew they mattered a lot.

It was a wonderful Christmas dinner.

I sold my house and moved into Debby's.

Now I kiss her scars and thank God I've got the rest of her. And we walk together around the lake every day. Well, maybe four, five times a week. Most days we go for Earl Greys and maybe share a maple dip. Sometimes I go for a leak and think about the girl with a mop and a doughnut one long-ago Christmas Eve's eve.

Ghosts of Christmas Past

Richard V. Raiment

It is six o'clock on Christmas morning, and I wake up like I always do. That way I am awake enough to roll out of the way just before Jake bounces on the spot where my gut would have been, knocking all the breath out of my body being his chosen way of celebrating the excitement of Santa's deliveries, together with his ecstatically whispered mantra; "Santa's been! Daddy! Daddy! Santa's been!"

The same routine every year. Weary from a night too late, too many compensatory nips or glasses of something to while away the tedium of wrapping so many presents, I crawl out of bed, still blitzed, to a household full of the raucous joy of young children, bodies blurred beneath a fake autumnal fall of torn wrapping-paper leaves as they leap from excitement to excitement, laughing and awestruck by turns.

The dross—the rummage-sale stuff—is opened first, the stuff they know will disappoint: the inevitable socks from granny, Auntie May's movie merchandise that is always from last year's forgotten hit, the perfumed soap and candles. Because when that's all over and duty's done, they can focus on the best.

And then it's shrieks and screams and hugs and kisses, for Jodie and for me, though it's Jodie who deserves it most. She makes all the consequential choices, always gets it absolutely right.

But then again, she chose me, didn't she?

Holiday Sex

Jake won't arrive in the big bedroom till seven. Even Christmas doesn't get our heavy sleepers out of bed that early, so there is always time enough for us and for our Christmas Morning ritual. Not that our Christmas Morning ritual is really any different to our every-other-holiday and day-off ritual, except that it happens to be Christmas Morning.

At forty, Jodie's as beautiful as the day I met her. Her legs are long and firm, the gateway to her heaven still an open arch, that lovely crotch-gap unclosed yet by swelling flesh. The slithers of silvery testimony to the three kids she has had are almost too fine and slender to detect. Her belly's a gentle swell of silk, still, easily sinking into an inviting soft concave when she is in repose, and the breasts which fill my own large hands so neatly remain pert and firm—firm as her nature.

And Jodie can be very firm.

Looking at the body warm in bed beside me, I remember all I have known with my lovely Jodie, and I stir, blood flooding warmly where it matters, soft-inflating. I've always woken Jodie the same way, since the first delightful morning of discovery when I found her asleep on her back, one leg diagonally outstretched, one knee drawn up, the lovely sweetness of her sex smiling pinkly open, inviting and sleepy warm.

Not this time, though. This morning is different. The body beside me, in a bed warm and musky with the scents of our sleep and Christmas Eve fucking, lies with its legs still softly together, and the difference is poignant, bitterly emblematic of the change between us. Only she drank as much, perhaps, as I did last night, and I can coax her gently apart without her even knowing.

She sighs and mumbles sleepily as I move her, and it is not the same, not the lethargy of a good, sound, innocent sleep this morning, and I miss that. God, I miss that. I wish I could change it all back again.

My tongue on her full pink lips, softly questing the small pink trigger within, snaps her eyes open, her thigh muscles tautening as her knees draw upward and apart, opening to me, and I sink deeper, both because I know she wants it and because it builds in me, turning me to iron still, the delayed gratification making all hotter and harder when it comes, when "he" comes, I come.

Not yet. Delay. Scent her, scent that animal musk that blends acrid with joy, probe her wet and hard and taste her, taste the salt of cunny juice and morning sweat, nuzzle in the softness of shaven mons, the electric coolness of inner thigh. Slip my hands beneath the lovely gift of ass, finding in the full, firm mounds an intimacy, which, in their nature, in their ever-secret, ever-private function, is somehow even more poignant than intimacy with her sex. I feel their soft, slick weight, caress their infinite smoothness as I lift her to my tongue, then slide away, stroke the inside of her thighs with teasing fingertips.

Long fingers, now, deep inside her, rolling, softly thrusting, tongue flicking and slipping and circling the little, questing periscope arisen in search of fulfillment, then back inside her again, tongue rolling and thrusting, tremors in my ass as my cock seeks to find the same rhythm, hungry for his own completion.

In a sleep-warm bed, I slide up a body warm and slick with perspiration, hers and mine, fill my mouth briefly first with one breast, then the other, licking the hardness of woken, hungry, teat, and she is pulling me upward, urgently, and a hand takes hold of me, urgently, knuckles softly bruising my groin in the clumsy desperation of her want of me, fingers round my shaft guiding him to her lips, and he is sliding, hard, so softly, smooth and wetly.

My mouth tasting of her other, carrying its scent, presses firmly on hers, her tongue sudden and hungry in mine, grappling as if in a dance of serpents seeking to entwine, and I am pushing, thrusting, feel her rhythm matching, the upward shift of buttock and groin as her vulva seeks to grasp me in her, snatching pressures of grabbing muscle seeking to hold me, to milk me. And I am thrusting hard, now, a violence in me scarce-suppressed, groin and balls slapping and punching into that wet-warm, slippery firmness, almost as if I am punishing her. But she is accustomed to it. Perhaps it makes her writhe a little more, perhaps there are small, silent squeals of pain passing unheard from her mouth to mine, but she does not fight me, and I think she likes it.

Mouths part suddenly in hurried, end-of-race exhalations, in cursing and in prayer, the glorious blasphemies of coming, of twin surging, melding wetness spurting white and gushing clear, the hard dry ache of craving balls replaced with the softer ache of release, iron hardness suddenly softening, always reluctant at parting, drawn to curl up and sleep, drawn to remain in warm, wet comfort.

"Boy, that was something!" Her breathless words sound trite in my present state of mind. I fight the desire to be angry with her, to hurt her with my guilt and pain.

It is almost seven. The presents sit wrapped beneath the tree in the parlor, awaiting onslaught, and Jake, no doubt, is stirring in his bed. I look at the woman beside me and try to keep the hate and hurt from my eyes. It is not her fault, after all.

I think her name is Ellie, though in the warm suffusion of

alcohol that made this Christmas Eve so barely bearable I may have misheard her, and she is just another one-night stand, just another pick-up from yet another bar.

And she and the others, my cock-driven follies, are the reason Jake won't be trying to jump onto my belly this morning. She is why my place in that bed, that house, is empty. It is Jodie, after all, who makes all the consequential choices, always gets it absolutely right, whilst it was I who made my own consequential choices and got it absolutely wrong.

And I can't fix it. Jodie can be very firm.

Cross-cultural Erotica

Butoh-Ka

remittance girl

He was lying on the floor, in a rumpled black suit, curled around a large white flowerpot and accompanied musically by the high-pitched, electronic whine of a tone generator.

Having spent most of my life viewing my own body as an inconvenient piece of baggage I had to drag around to make my brain work, the prospect of spending any significant amount of time watching someone else dealing with their body has never appealed to me. What I was doing on a Sunday afternoon, in a small Japanese café, in Saigon at the height of the rainy season watching a *Butoh* dance performance is easily explained. It was all Mitsue's fault.

Mitsue is my best friend and the only Japanese girl I know who talks really dirty. She's thirty-two, single, permanently on the prowl, and gorgeous: bum-length black hair that looks like liquid latex; smooth, clear skin the color and texture of a peeled lychee; tall and willowy. She has a face that, in repose, is straight out of an antique woodblock print from the Floating World. When in motion, it's wicked as hell.

There I was, sitting in this ultra-neat little café with about thirty other expatriates, all assuming we were about to witness something terribly subversive. This is easy in Saigon because, at the moment, almost anything's subversive. And yes, it was Mitsue who had persuaded me to come along by informing me that *Butoh* was nothing like dance as I knew it, I had turned into a terminally antisocial cow, and that I was a loser who had nothing else to do on a Sunday afternoon. Beyond all that, she insisted there was someone I just had to meet. Sitting next to me on one of those nasty plastic chairs that make your ass ache after five minutes, she finally divulged who it was.

"Him. The one on the floor," she whispered, pointing at the immobile black lump with the burning tip of her pink Sobranie cigarette.

"Mitsue, sweetheart, why do I need to meet . . ." I gestured at the paralyzed form on the carpet of the performance space, ". . . this . . . that?"

"Because he's giving a Butoh workshop; I signed you up for it. Six weeks, three hours a week," she said, patting my hand as if she'd bought me a Mercedes-Benz and wasn't it sweet. "Don't worry, I paid. I sent you an e-mail with all the details."

"You what? What the hell were you thinking, Mitsue? I fucking hate exercise!" Behind us, someone shushed me.

"I've been reading Mishima again. You need to be more in your body, Sarah." She lounged back as much as anyone can in one of those bendy plastic chairs. "Lucky I didn't sign you up for yoga class, hey?" she sniggered. "Okay, and he's handsome, too. Wait and you'll see."

She communicated all this despite the high, piercing tone that had slowly turned into hissing white noise. I wasn't going to be able to beat her up verbally to my satisfaction without pissing someone off, so I shut up, fumed, and pretended to be interested in the arty performance crap.

The body on the floor was moving—not much I'll grant you—but he'd subtly changed his position. His hands inched forward and slowly took his body weight as he dragged himself along the ground, some distance from the plant pot. Gradually his upper half rose to reveal his face under a battered black fedora. It was painted as white as snow. The lips, the eyes, the brows—everything was covered in a thick layer of some chalk-like substance, erasing every trace of humanity from his face.

Steadily, he pulled back his head and the slits of his epicanthic eyes opened to reveal nothing but whites and, as his jaw lowered with measured deliberation, I could see that the inside of his mouth was stained black.

It was then I realized his arms were spread wide in midair, hands skewed and contracted, and he'd been supporting his entire upper body with only the muscles of his stomach and back for quite some time. This was more disturbing than the face paint by far; I could manage the makeup but there was no way in a million years of workshops I was ever going to be able to do that.

The performance was bizarre, but about halfway through it I got sucked in. All the movements, all the gestures, were achingly slow. His expression alternated between a strained grimace and a vacant mask, and not once did I see the pupils of his eyes. On his rising from the floor, I noticed he was wearing latex surgical gloves. He brought them to his mouth, finger by finger and tugged lethargically at the tips with his teeth, stretching the digits out into strange bladed shapes until either the latex tore or his teeth lost their grip and it snapped back hard against his skin. The first time it happened, I winced in sympathetic agony. The second time, I watched his face as the rubber snapped back. He didn't flinch—not one iota.

The second half of the performance contained faster

movement, but culminated in the weirdest thing I've every seen. As he moved towards the spotlight at the side of the makeshift stage, he began to shake. It didn't have the same quality as a seizure but the vibration of his body became steadily more violent the closer he got to the light until he stood underneath it and, standing in the pool of it, rippled like a body of water. It went on for what seemed like forever, but was probably not more than a few minutes. Then, suddenly, it was over.

The dance lasted forty-five minutes. At the end of it he grinned and bowed.

"Thank you for coming to see me today. Workshop people please stay. I will get changed, and we can talk." Then, he made a very dignified exit.

"So, what do you think?" asked Mitsue.

I turned in my chair to face her. "I think I'm going to kill you, you bitch. No way can I do that. I'm not flexible, I have no balance, and I'm not remotely interested in learning how to dance anything."

"Never mind that. Did you like the performance?"

"Yeah, actually I did, once I got into it. The bit at the end was amazing."

"Good. So, you stay and meet your new teacher. I have to go."

"Wait a minute! You aren't doing the workshop?"

"Oh, no! All that sweating? Not for me at all. You know that." She put on a nonchalant face and became engrossed in the keys of her mobile phone while making for the exit. Mitsue: mistress of confrontation avoidance.

I hardly recognized the dancer when he came back into the room. His skin color was back to normal, his head was shaved and he wore a sleeveless T-shirt and jeans. His feet were still bare, as they had been for the performance, and the size of them struck me. He wasn't all that tall, perhaps five foot seven or eight, but his feet were about the same size as mine, size five or six.

There were ten other people left in the café, workshop people presumably. I approached him to make my apologies and leave before he got down to business with the rest of them.

"Hello . . . um, damn, I don't know your name." I held out my hand. There's really no point in doing all that bowing crap when you don't even know who you're talking to.

"Kaoru." He took my hand and shook it with bone-crushing vehemence, offering me a smile that bordered on the comedic. At least in one thing Mitsue had been right; he was absolutely beautiful: golden skin stretched impossibly taut over his cheek and jaw bones, eyes set very wide apart, and fine, dark brows. My immediate reaction was to hate him. When I was younger, I used to fall in love with beautiful men on the spot. Later they just made me sweaty and nervous. These days, on the whole, I disliked them outright unless I suspected they were gay. Being unsure of Kaoru's wiring, I wasn't going to give him the benefit of the doubt.

"Great. Look, Kaoru, my friend Mitsue signed me up for your workshop, but I really don't think I can do it. I'm not at all fit, don't do any exercise, and I don't like dance. It was very kind of her, but she's made a mistake."

"Ah. You are the friend of Mitsue. Sa-ra. Good, good, good! Excellent. Welcome." The smile was still stretched across his lean face, and he gave me a little bow.

Christ, I thought, he doesn't speak English properly. I tried again. "Yes, Mitsue's friend. But I can't do this workshop thing. Sorry."

"Certainly you can! Butoh is not about physical strength; it's about the mind." He took a step back and looked me up and down. "You have a most suitable body for Butoh. Excellent."

As excellent as it might have been, after what I'd seen him do with his, I couldn't really take that as a compliment. I persevered. "Well, that's nice. But I'm not at all a physical person. I hate exercise."

He reached out his hand and curled his fingers around my upper arm, giving it a little squeeze. It didn't feel like a friendly thing; I suspected he was doing some measuring. "Me too. I hate exercise. Don't worry, Sa-ra. But, I will be honest with you, after the first workshop, you will be in some pain. But it goes."

He was standing close. I noticed the sheen of sweat on his shoulder, on the blade of his cheekbone, and smelled the acrid taint of it, like burning leaves.

"Pain? Yes, well, I'm not all that fond of pain, really." I tried to take a step back, but the fingers around my upper arm closed a little tighter; it didn't quite hurt but it was definitely a firm grip. The sustained contact surprised me. The Japanese are usually very considerate of personal space unless they're smashed.

"No, Sa-ra. Never say that," he murmured. "Pain is our friend. Pain is an excellent teacher. Pain cleanses the body."

What a load of crap. I'd heard similar words come skulking from the mouth of a fitness instructor at a gym I once joined in a moment of madness. They'd been delivered with a manic, steroid-induced glee. Kaoru's delivery was altogether different; I was being chided like a child for insulting a favorite maiden aunt.

He let my arm go. I felt a sharp twinge of rebound pain

as the blood rushed back into the space where his fingers had been. He had increased his grip so slowly that it was only then I realized how tightly he'd held my arm.

"I will see you on Tuesday. Yes? Five-thirty." He smiled; teeth were still black from whatever it was he'd used to stain the inside of his mouth with. "You have the address?"

"Yes. I do."

That evening I procrastinated, caught between believing that perhaps I could do this and wondering what six weeks of torture would feel like. Monday I was very busy until the early evening, but around six o'clock I thought about phoning the number I had and begging off the workshop. Honestly, I don't know why I didn't do it. I found the e-mail Mitsue had sent me and printed it out. I left it on the coffee table and then never got around to calling.

On Tuesday afternoon, it struck me that I either had to attend or let them know right away. The notice about the workshop had said that there were only twelve spaces available, and I didn't want to do anyone else out of a place. It was then that I decided I never did anything new and interesting, and, if it really turned out to be torture, I could always drop out after the first few sessions.

It took me ages to find the address. It was raining like a bitch, and I took the wrong alleyway twice. Finally I found the street number on the wooden gate to an old villa. I rang the bell and waited in the downpour. Moments later the wet slap of footsteps in the rain gave me hope that someone was crossing the courtyard to open the door. Poor housekeeper, I thought, she's going to be as soaked as me.

It wasn't a woman who opened the door. It was Kaoru. He pulled the gates wide and stood there bare-chested with the rain sluicing down over his body. The baggy cotton trousers he wore stuck to the skin of his thighs. I had a sudden flash of Kurosawa's film, *Rashomon*.

"You are late, Sa-ra,"

His arms were stretched wide, holding the doors of the gate apart, his tiny feet placed neatly together. In my imagination, he'd morphed into Christ crucified, and I felt a little guilty. He didn't move an inch, and the ember of guilt sputtered out as little rivers of rainwater slid down my spine.

"I'm sorry. I had a hard time finding the place. Is everyone else already here?"

"No. You are the first. Everyone is late. Is this common in Vietnam?"

"It is, especially during the rainy season." I smirked and wiped the water out of my eyes, trying to induce a little pity. "Are you going to let me in?"

He didn't move. Obviously, he'd forgotten he was standing in the middle of a monsoon.

"Maybe. Maybe not."

He smiled; it was a tease and perhaps, I thought, a test—a thoroughly Japanese thing to do. Cool. I knew how to play this game.

I crossed my arms over my sodden T-shirt. "Well, I'm soaked now, so please, feel free to take your time making up your mind." I had another shirt in my satchel and was planning to excuse myself and change once he let me in. If he let me in. "No hurry. No hurry at all," I drawled.

A rumble of thunder broke over our heads, and the volume of the downpour increased. Still immobile, he scrutinized my face. It was clearly designed to make me feel uncomfortable. I was so fucking fed up with this bullshit cultural game. I licked angrily at the rivulet that had formed beside the crook of my nose and was snaking over my upper lip. It was getting hard to keep the water out of my eyes, and the light was dying.

Abruptly he let go of the doors and stepped back into the courtyard. "Come in," he said, turning on the balls of his feet and walking into the old house. He left me to close the gates and follow him.

Sonofabitch.

Fascist little prick. I had a sneaking suspicion that, between Mitsue and Kaoru, I'd stumbled onto a Japanese cult of Mishima worshipers who were busy trying to revive prewar imperialist militarism or some kind of Bushido code crap. No wonder none of them were actually living in Japan.

Poseur.

The room I followed him into was bare. Here and there chunks of plaster had fallen from the old walls and left lighter patches against the dark yellow of the paint. The floor was a mosaic of dirty, cracked tiles. On the ceiling, a single bare light bulb of no discernible wattage gave off a weak glow, and, further on, a ceiling fan pushed the moist air around the room.

"Do you have a washroom? And a towel, maybe? I'd like to change out of my wet stuff."

He'd taken up a squatting position, his back flat against the far wall. "Yes . . . and no."

"Sorry?"

"Yes I have a washroom and a towel. But you cannot use it."

I dropped my satchel on the floor with a wet plop. "Why?"

"I say no."

On the verge of my losing my own version of Asian reserve and yelling, the doorbell rang. He rose in one fluid motion and left the room. "Stay!" he called behind him.

The rest of the group arrived in a clump, and I was relieved not to be alone with him anymore. They were all wet, and he gave them the same answer when they asked if they could change or dry off.

"No. Wet cloth is good against the body. It makes you aware of every muscle you move. Like a guide. You will need it." A couple of people protested, but he was adamant.

He made us each find a place to get down and stretch out on the floor, telling us to lie on our stomachs. Then he walked among us, bending down here and there to push someone flatter to the floor.

"Lie as if you were dead. There is nothing between you and the ground. Like you were the ground itself. And relax. Dead people are very relaxed."

Someone giggled. I thought about how dead people don't feel wet clothes.

It wasn't the flattening I had a problem with; it was the nasty feeling of my wet shirt and pants getting cold against my back and legs. Rivers found new avenues of egress beneath my clothes. I could smell the wet dust on the floor beneath my cheek.

After pretending to be dead, we did some stretching exercises. Sitting in a Japanese kneeling position with our feet beneath our butts, then a "grandma" position with the feet out on either side of our hips. Arching backwards with our bodies until we were lying like neat little legless packages. It was all very interesting, although some of it hurt like the devil. Finally we ended up on our stomachs again.

"Now, please. I want you to take five minutes to reach a standing position," he ordered. I felt his foot on my tailbone, pushing it down. "Listen to your bodies. Choose a pace.

Once you begin to move, don't vary the pace. Just slow and even. Go!"

"How will we know when five minutes is up?" I asked. A guy somewhere on the other side of the room seconded my question. I felt his foot lift away and heard him walk towards someone else.

"Don't worry. You will know."

Suddenly the magnitude of what he was asking us to do hit home: to move with agonizing slowness from a position of prostration and, micron by micron, end up standing.

"Don't think about standing. Think only about the next muscle you will need to move to get there, how you will place your body weight, where your center of gravity is."

I closed my eyes and thought: *Okay. In order to get my weight up off the ground, I'm going to need to put it on my hands and my knees. Or perhaps I could roll slowly onto my hip and shoulder. No. Definitely hands and knees.* I began to inch my arm outward, feeling like a lizard.

I had no sense of how long it took to get into a standing position. Somehow, along the way, the time didn't really seem to matter. All I remember is that the muscles in my arms screamed as I made the initial push off the floor with my hands. My back arched, and my inner thigh screamed in sympathy as I pushed my hip off the ground in minute increments. The hardest part was where I least expected it: when I was off the ground and almost erect. By the time I was standing, my limbs were shaky and weak.

I clocked in at four minutes and seventeen seconds. There were people who finished way earlier. We had to stand there, feeling like failures, until the five minutes were up.

Kaoru made us repeat the exercise six times. By the third,

some woman I couldn't see was crying. He led her out of the room and came back alone. On the final exercise, I couldn't feel the wet clothes anymore; I'd broken out into a hot sweat. My lips tasted like salt and dust, and my throat itched with dryness. I looked down at the front of my shirt. It was smeared with dirt. My palms felt horrible, filthy and tacky. I would have done almost anything to be back out in the rain.

"Good. Very good. Now sit please, around me."

I watched him lower himself into a cross-legged position on the floor. One seamless, fluid act, not slow, not fast; he never let his weight take over his movement. We all gathered around him, most of us still out of breath. It felt odd to be panting after what seemed like hours of moving at a snail's pace.

As I lowered myself back onto the floor, my left thigh cramped up. I yelped and tried to stretch the leg out in front of me. Kaoru glanced at me and smiled. Somehow that made me really angry, and I focused on the wall ahead of me, clenching my teeth, holding my breath and waiting for the pain to subside.

Like lightning, his hand was on my jaw, pulling my head sideways until I was looking at him, his face an inch from mine.

"Look at me. Look at me only. Yes." Tiny droplets of his spit hit my face.

"Breathe!" The loudness shocked me, and I didn't listen; I gulped air instead.

"BREATHE!" he bellowed. I pulled in a deep lungful of air and expelled it like a violent response to his aggression.

"Hmm? Now the pain goes away—after it has given you very important information. See?" The tone of his voice was quiet again, as if he hadn't hollered at me at all. "The pain cannot go if you hold it inside. Push it out with your breath."

He let go of my jaw gently and retreated, crablike, back to his place in the middle of the circle on the floor.

"So, now I will tell you about Butoh: how it began, what it is." Kaoru looked around the circle of faces in the room. "Butoh is called the Dance of Darkness because it is not about the normal human body. It is about the soul, and the human soul is dark.

"In 1959 the fathers of Butoh, Tatsumi Hijikata and Katsuo Ono decided to reject the West's definition of modern dance and its idealization of the human body. They felt that, most of the time, the body was not beautiful; it was somewhere in the process of decaying and dying. The first performance was a short piece, without music. It was a story of a young boy enacting sex with a chicken and strangling it to death between his thighs; then an older man comes to him in the darkness to give him a direction for his sexual energy.

"Butoh is not really a dance at all. It is the metamorphosis of the dancer's body. He stops being himself and becomes something else, connecting the conscious to the unconscious. Butoh rarely has choreography as we know it. The dance emerges from the dancer's body like sweat. The story leaks outwards through the skin."

Kaoru looked around at us and smiled. "You cannot come to this place with all your social rules. It is a visceral place. It requires you to be unashamed and then finally unaware of what you are made of—both body and soul—and to use this viscera and spirit to make imaginary architecture or geography."

At the end of the lecture, seven people left the room. Clearly they felt that this was a far cry from the jazz dance classes they'd been used to. The thought of leaving hadn't even crossed my mind, and, considering what a flake I am, that was surprising. It didn't seem to bother Kaoru at all that there were only five of us left. He was very polite to the people who left, and then he sat back down on the floor. The circle had simply gotten smaller.

"Now I want to teach you some 'dialogues.' These are exercises you must undertake to do once a day during the course of the workshop. One thing, though: if you don't do them, do not lie and say you have. It's insulting to me. I will know."

He looked around the group at each of us, making eye contact and waiting for at least a nod of agreement. When he came to me, I said, "I can't promise if I don't understand what I'm promising. Show us the 'dialogues,' and then I'll tell you."

I expected a bad reaction from him. I thought he'd be pissed off or insulted or something. Instead he nodded. "Sara has found no reason to trust me. She's challenging me. I accept this challenge." The statement was so samurai-kitsch, I had to fight to stop myself from laughing out loud.

The exercises he showed us weren't really exercises per se. They involved holding an idea in your mind and trying to express it physically. Some of them were very easy, like reaching: straining from the inside and making your body show it. Others were harder; imagining you were walking through air suspended with shards of glass.

The rain had stopped, and the crickets were shrilling. The din echoed in the bare room as we worked. I could only hear Kaoru's instructions and people breathing, sometimes little sounds of effort or pain. Suddenly the crickets seemed much louder, filling my head until I thought I would scream.

Then it was over, and we were all standing up, shaking hands, introducing ourselves. The five of us all looked like we'd been living on the street—dirt-streaked and exhausted. I picked up my satchel and turned to Kaoru.

"Can I use your washroom now?"

"Yes, of course." He smiled wide. White, even teeth glinted in the harsh light of the bare bulb. I felt him surround my upper arm with his fingers, exactly as he had done at the performance. "Will you do the dialogues?"

"Sure," I answered lightly. "Where is your washroom?"

"Upstairs."

I climbed a dark, damp-smelling staircase that creaked as I ascended. At the landing, I cursed myself for not asking better directions. The only light was coming from a window at the end of the hall, and all the doors leading off the hallway were shut. I tried the first one, but it wouldn't give.

The door on the opposite side was unlocked and swung open. It was a room almost as bare as the one downstairs except for a futon in the middle. I stepped in and poked my head around the door because, hell, I'm a nosy bitch. Further exploration revealed only a metal clothes rack hung with a couple of suits, shirts, T-shirts folded over hangers.

Past the clothes rack was another door, which I opened. Feeling around blindly for a light switch on the wall, I was relieved to see that it was the bathroom, and not a moment too soon. The feeling that I was sneaking around had made me nervous, and my bladder was bursting.

I sat on the toilet and looked around as I peed. Same as the rest of the house, it was in terrible need of renovation. There were bits of tile missing from the floor and walls. What had once probably been a lovely black and white mosaic pattern was marred by gaps and moldy grout. When I got up and took a look at myself in the mirror above the sink, I squealed; I had muddy dirt smeared down one cheek, my hair was matted with sweat. I looked like someone who'd only barely survived a natural disaster, and I smelled worse.

"Is there a mouse?"

His voice scared me witless. I turned around to look out into the bedroom, but it was too dark to see him properly, just a slim form outlined in the wan light from the window. Once the shock had passed, I looked down and noticed an empty mousetrap nestled behind the sink pedestal. I giggled inanely. "No—no mouse. I just saw myself in your mirror. I look like I've been in an accident. Your floor is filthy. Don't you have a housekeeper?"

"You look like a Butoh-Ka." He came and leaned against the wooden doorjamb, smiling past me at my reflection in the mirror. "A Butoh dancer."

I couldn't help myself; I smiled back. He really was so beautiful, and it was hard to keep hating him for it. My hands fumbled blindly for the taps. I turned them on and bent over the sink to wash my face. With my eyes closed against the water, I had a quiet little talk with myself about the perils of getting crushes on beautiful men. It felt good to wash; it was cool and refreshing and brought me down to earth. I swiveled, water dripping from my face, and reached blindly for where I thought I'd seen a towel, but collided with something decidedly more human instead.

Okay, I'll admit it. I can be extremely slow on the uptake when it comes to men. I'm careful not to assume they are interested in me. On occasion, I've been so unaware I had to be told outright. However, this wasn't one of those times. People who dislike me don't keep making physical contact.

"Do you have a towel?"

"Yes."

"Can I borrow it?"

"No."

I opened my eyes to a beautiful expanse of bare chest and followed it up to a face, which was utterly passive. It had a bad effect on me—I wanted to laugh hysterically—until he bent forward, opened his mouth, and slid the flat of his tongue all the way up one side of my face. Then he did exactly the same thing with the other side.

It was the oddest come-on I'd ever experienced, and it wasn't that I didn't appreciate the originality of it, but I had no idea of how to disengage from it gracefully. This begs the question of why I wanted to disengage at all, and I can't really answer that. Perhaps I just wasn't ready to hear the terms of the exchange yet.

I took a step back and laughed inanely. "Thank you, really. A towel would have been as good, but I appreciate the very personal service." I could smell his spit on my skin; it smelled too good. It was definitely time to make a quick exit.

"Okay. I'm going to go now." I picked my satchel up off the floor and backed through the door into his bedroom. Then I turned and ran. His laughter echoed down the stairs after me.

The next day, as promised, I was in pain. Moreover, I was ashamed of how I'd mishandled the previous night's situation. I was attracted to Kaoru, so what was the problem? In truth, I was a little scared of him in particular and wary, in general, of anyone who walks through the world like they belong in it, like they don't have any doubts, like they don't hesitate or waste their time weighing up options.

The state of adolescent fugue lasted through the morning

but, by midday, I'd matured enough—become jaded enough—to decide that I'd probably blown it and that was probably for the best. It was by far the most sensible attitude. But it was inconvenient that, halfway through delivering an afternoon lecture on semiotics, I had vividly erotic daydreams of writhing around on a filthy floor with Kaoru. Worse still, I was hallucinating the smell of his saliva every time I turned my head quickly. It made my cheeks burn and I lost my place in the PowerPoint slides.

That evening, I sat at a noodle stall and had a little heart to heart with myself. I'd been successfully single for more than six years. When I wanted sex, I could and did pick it up where I could find it. I wasn't remotely interested in anything more complicated than that. All I required was someone whose eyes rolled up in the back of their heads when they orgasmed. I didn't need someone who did it for a living.

Absolutely.

Too true.

My phone rang as I let myself in to the house.

"Sa-ra. This is Kaoru speaking."

"Hello, Kaoru."

"Did you do the dialogues?"

It's not often that one feels a twinge of excitement about being nagged. "No, not yet. I just got home from work."

"Ah. Okay. Don't forget."

"Can I ask you something?"

"Please."

"Are you phoning up all the workshop members and reminding them?"

There was a long pause on the other end. My mobile hissed static at him.

"Sa-ra? Why are you asking me this?"

Sonofabitch! Bugger it! I could play that game, too. "Because I'm interested to know."

"No."

"No what?" I wondered whether this wasn't turning into one of those dumb "who's on first" conversations.

"No, I am not phoning all the workshop people and reminding them."

Gotcha, you sly bastard. "So, am I the only one you think has a brain like a sieve?"

There was another long pause followed by a sound I would swear was him clicking his tongue. "Don't forget to do the dialogues."

"I won't."

"Excellent. Goodnight."

He'd hung up before I could return the politeness.

The rest of the week flew by in a flurry of overwork. I met Mitsue for dinner on Saturday night, but, when I tried to get more information about Kaoru from her, she was not her usual gossipy self at all. She'd heard he'd practiced Butoh for eighteen years and had been living at an arts center in Hamburg before coming to Saigon. She said she didn't know much more about him or why he'd moved here. I found this hard to believe. Mitsue made a fine art of knowing everything about everyone.

"Oh, come now, Mitsue. I don't buy it. You are the nosiest woman I know. You've got to know more about him than that!"

She fished around, finally selecting a turquoise cigarette from the multicolored box. I noticed it went well with the off-white dress she was wearing. "Not really."

"Bullshit. You know people at the consulate. And I can't believe the arrival of a Butoh dancer wouldn't have caused a stir there. I've done my research. It's still a really controversial art form in Japan. What gives?"

"Nothing. They don't care about him. He's Korean-Japanese."

"So?"

Mitsue shook her head and shrugged in irritation. "Yours isn't the only racist culture, Sarah. Japanese of Korean descent are really looked down upon."

I saw her with new eyes. I could hardly believe it. That's why she hadn't wanted him for herself, despite all his beauty. He would have spoiled her standing in the inward-looking, xenophobic Japanese expat community.

She had the good grace to lower her eyes. Then she shook it off and asked, "So? What's he like?"

It was hard to keep the anger out of my answer. "I'm not fucking him for you, as a proxy, Mitsue. If that's what you're after, you can forget it."

She sighed and lit her cigarette.

When Tuesday rolled around, I left work early and rushed home to get ready for the workshop. I had been doing my dialogues faithfully all week and, regardless of how Kaoru factored into things, I was pretty proud of my progress. Truthfully, it was having an effect on how I moved. I noticed my body more as I walked around. Disconcerting to have it present after so long an absence.

I did ponder over what to wear. This was laughable, considering how sweaty and filthy I was going to get, but it said volumes about how much I had begun to think about him.

It had rained earlier in the day and cleared up nicely, so I arrived at Kaoru's place dry and on time. The remaining five of us were all waiting at the gate when he opened the door and greeted us as he had greeted me before, holding the doors of the gate wide.

"Come in. But you must come in as one."

"What the fuck does that mean?" whispered the guy next to me. Gary was Welsh and a yoga addict.

"Maybe he wants us all to walk in step or something," said Elizabeth—Australian and way too fit to live. "Like soldiers."

"No. I don't think so." I pressed myself into the group. "He wants us to 'come in as one,' like we're all parts of one body."

Gary nodded in agreement and, being the tallest among us, maneuvered himself into the middle, stretched out his arms and began pulling us tight against him. Akira, who was rather sweet, definitely gay and the smallest of us, wriggled to the front. "Like a jellyfish," he said.

"I don't think that's what he wants," complained Michael, an American and the only dancer among us. "I don't think he wants anything that concrete."

"You're probably right," I said, wriggling in at the side. I linked my right arm into Gary's and encircled Akira's neck with the other. "But let's just go with it, or we'll never get out of the street."

We waddled in, a many-legged thing, arms lashing the components of the strange thing we had become together. The front steps were hard to negotiate but we made it.

"Was that what you wanted?" asked Gary, once we'd reached the workshop space.

Kaoru was laughing. "I didn't want anything. I wanted you to decide, and you did. Excellent!"

I felt Akira bristle beneath my arm and gave him a little

pat. "Let him laugh, Akira. He's laughing because we looked funny. And I'm sure we did." I whispered in his ear.

The first thing we did were the dialogues. Kaoru was checking to make sure we'd kept our end of the bargain. He walked between us, prodding and poking bits of our anatomies. The rest of the class was focused on changing, morphing from one image to another in our minds and then translating it outward to the body. The focus wasn't on the final form but the process of change. I went from mist to a brick wall with infinitely long fingers and thought I did pretty well, actually.

By the time eight-thirty rolled around, every one of us looked dazed and exhausted. Not so much from the physical strain as the mental one. We were dust-covered and, when I looked over at Elizabeth, she stared back with eyes that seemed not to focus, as if she'd been somewhere, seen something, horrible. Oddly enough, Michael seemed the worst affected, he had the hardest time concentrating, and it showed. Kaoru had seen it too, and spent a lot of time with him. Suddenly it struck me that this was much more like baby-sitting people on an acid trip than it was about teaching them to dance.

As we all got up and gathered our things, I was half-expecting Kaoru to say something to me; when he didn't, I was disappointed. Still, I'd given the man some very mixed messages, and I could hardly blame him for not throwing himself in my direction. It was my move, and I knew it.

"Can I use your washroom before I go?" I figured that would buy me some time until the others left.

Kaoru's face showed nothing. "Of course. You know where it is."

His bedroom was exactly as I'd seen it before, nothing had

changed, but the bathroom was a bit of a shock. Someone had cleaned it. It was still shabby and in need of retiling, but at least the floor was clean, and the rust stains on the sink were gone. Funnier yet, there were two towels hanging on the rail, obviously fresh and folded very neatly. I took it as a compliment. Pulling off my grimy T-shirt, I washed my face, hands, and arms. There was a suspect and worn bar of soap; I used it anyway.

In the middle of my ablutions an idea occurred to me. Maybe the towel wasn't there for me? What a fucking little egotist I was! He'd hooked up with someone else. And, of course, it explained his casual yet distant behavior. I sniffed the towel before I patted myself dry. It smelled like, well, like . . . Downy. I wasn't happy to be right. Fabric softener's a sure sign of female incursion.

I pulled a clean T-shirt out of my satchel and put it on, feeling suddenly and uselessly depressed. It was my own fault, after all. What had I been expecting—a courtship? I smiled wanly at my clean face in the mirror, ran my fingers through my cropped dark hair, switched off the light, and headed downstairs. Not really paying attention to anything but my own self-pity, I barreled into him on the dark, narrow stairs. I backed up to give him some room.

"Oh! Sorry. Thanks for letting me use your bathroom," I mumbled.

"No problem. Where are you going now?"

"I'm off home. See you next Tuesday!"

He took the next step up, crowding me against the wall. "No."

I couldn't see his face properly, but I looked in its general direction. "No class next week?" I could smell his sweat again and feel the heat of him in the darkness of the stairwell. For someone who used their body for a living, he was very careless with where he put it.

"Is my English so bad?"

"What? Oh, no—not at all. Your English is fine. Very good, in fact." I was babbling out of nervousness and an acute desire to get the fuck out of there. He was standing too close and smelled too good. "But sometimes you need to be a little clearer with your answers."

"Don't go yet. Okay?"

This was becoming really painful. Between his scent and his proximity, I was getting turned on, and angry at the same time. Mostly I was just confused.

"Look, Kaoru, I don't mean to be rude or anything, but I'm not exactly sure what you want. I'm getting a whole lot of conflicting messages from you, and it's difficult to interpret."

I felt him step into me then, pressing his body into mine, wedging it against the wall. His breath was even and moist against my forehead, and then I felt him press his mouth to it. "Everything must be so black and white for Westerners; hot or cold, dark or light, right or wrong . . . It seems you hate everything . . ."

I could hear him searching for the word. "Ambiguous?" I offered.

He traced the palms of his hands over my shoulders, down my arms and laced his fingers into mine. Then slowly, with great deliberation, he ground his hips against me, just once, but so hard it pushed the air from my lungs. He held them there. I felt his cock get progressively harder against my pelvic bone. It slowly took over room that hadn't been there, making space from nothing. I wondered if he could feel the nipples beneath my shirt harden in response.

"It is clear enough?"

"You want to fuck?" I squeaked with what little air I had.

He stepped back and exhaled. It was a sound filled with meaning, disappointment, I thought, or dismay. He grabbed my hand and took the stairs upwards, dragging me behind him, pulling me back into his room. He was speaking as he went, but it was all in Japanese.

Throwing himself down onto his futon, he pulled me with him. It wasn't graceful or gentle at all; I fell on top of him and smacked my cheek against his collarbone. It hurt like hell but I didn't get to dwell on it before he reached behind me and started tugging my shirt off. I tried to get my balance and sit up so I could take it off easily, but he clicked his tongue and pulled me back down against him.

"Don't make it so easy, Sa-ra. There is no need to make it easy," he said, rolling on top of me. "Everything is better with effort."

It's very hard to explain what happened after that. We did end up getting all our clothes off, but without separating our bodies. It was a lot less like disrobing and more like writhing out of one's skin. By the time I got to feel my bare skin against his, my cunt was throbbing and sopping, my nipples were stinging, and I could hardly catch my breath. The entire surface of my skin was burning from the friction.

I wriggled my arm in between us and closed my fingers around the shaft of his cock. It was wet with fluid, either mine, or his. I wasn't sure which. For a moment, I felt his whole body shudder and then he pulled away.

"No hands," he panted, rolling again and pulling me on top of him.

"Why?" I whispered, frustrated.

"Too, too easy." He maneuvered me until our legs were intertwined, and I could feel the sharpness of his hipbone pressed against my pussy, splaying the wet lips apart.

"Move," he said softly. That's when I got the idea.

I don't remember kissing at all, but that's not to say it wasn't achingly intimate. It felt more so for the stark lack of all the standard moves that come with foreplay. Slowly, we slid and ground and molded our bodies into the gaps and hollows of each other's flesh and, each time we moved, new areas of ingress appeared that needed to be filled. I came, without noticing the wave of it build up, against his hip and, as I did, he pressed my face into his, so that I stuttered pleasure into his skin. My wetness oozed out over him, slicking the skin between us, and everything was suddenly slippery. Moments later, he shuddered and came against my thigh, spraying cum over my stomach. As we moved, it got everywhere.

Rolling me over, he pressed his thigh between my legs, spreading them wide and smearing my ass and back with stickiness. His arms wrapped around my chest, he slid against me, over and over. I could feel him dragging his face through the wetness on my back, the angles of his cheekbones riding over the ridges of my spine, the heat of his breath pooling out over my skin. There were so many sensations, from so many parts of my body, that it crowded my brain. I couldn't think about what any single sensation felt like, I could only writhe in response. His hands were on the back of my neck, pressing my body to the futon in the oddest way; every time I moved, my nipples raked against the rough sheets beneath me. The disparate messages merged into a haze of pleasure, and, for the second time, I came, against his thigh with his body curled over me and under me, not realizing the orgasm was coming until it shook me like a doll.

I wanted him inside so badly I could have screamed, but he wouldn't cooperate.

He stroked himself against the curve of my side, smearing his face into my hair and the side of my neck. The whole room stank of sex. I could taste it at the back of my throat with every breath. We were like blind worms burrowing towards some place of pleasure, some crook or cranny where it felt good to be, wriggle a while, and then move on.

Somewhere, in that subterranean cave where things brush against the earth and liquid seeps through the layers of rock and skin, I begged him to fuck me. And he did, from behind, and when he pushed himself through the layers of me, he put his mouth to the back of my neck, and bit me like a cat. And like a cat, I arched my back and the greed to be filled made me mew and push back harder.

This time I felt the orgasm coming, from the moment his cock slid into me. I came within seconds of being entered, the walls of my cunt almost pushing him out with their contractions. He didn't move, but I felt each of my spasms echoed back to me through his body. And still he didn't fuck; he didn't thrust.

He whispered, "Hold me."

It sounded so hideously romantic that, at first, it confused me, but then I understood. I contracted my muscles, tightening my grip around his cock. And then his body did something quite extraordinary. It started to shake, just like it had done in the performance. Not like the shudders that happen before an orgasm, but like a body in deep cold. An even, steady tremor with no unevenness, absolutely controlled; it was like being on the inside of a vibrator. At first it scared me. I tensed to stop the reverberations of it sinking through me.

"No, Sa-ra. Don't resist it," he whispered, his body shattering each word into odd syllables. "Relax."

I took a deep breath and let my body go limp and, when it did, I almost fainted at the sensation. The reverberations of his body slid into mine and drove it. Nerve endings began to fire chaotically, all over my skin, inside, in my bones, around his cock.

He came in utter silence. Between the sounds of his choppy breath, I thought I heard ripping as he flooded wet heat into me.

Later that night, after we'd slept for a while, I tried to crawl out of bed to get up and wash, but he wouldn't let me. He didn't say no, he just refused to let me get out of bed. Trapped inside the cage of his arms and legs, he smelled me, licked me, ate me, until the scent of sex fluids was masked beneath the smell of his saliva.

We don't talk much. I've had people ask if we get along, if we are fighting or distanced from each other. We think a lot, though, and the thoughts get communicated in other ways. I don't wash as often as I used to, or worry much about how I look or what clothes I wear. I don't have as many moments of doubt and I move through the world very differently; I think I belong in it.

I dance, now.

Mad Dogs

Lisabet Sarai

I'll write about this someday. The cracked, grimy ceiling that's there whenever I open my eyes. The raspy hiccuping of the fan. The momentary relief when it swings in my direction, air hot against my naked, eternally sweaty skin, but moving at least. The scents of frying garlic and rotting fish and stagnant water, the singsong voices of the vendors under my window, the quavering pop music and the honking of the taxis on New Road.

Exotic Thailand. I'll capture it all, the mysterious complexity and the gritty foreignness. A brilliant cross between E.M. Forster and Jack Kerouac. Young man adrift, living on the fringe, self-abandoned in a strange land, victim of bad judgment and bad luck. A suitable subject for a talented writer like myself, full of irony and pathos.

Right now, though, my head aches. Even indoors, with the stained cotton drapes half-closed, the heat is a hammer, mashing my fine mind to incoherent pulp. I lie here paralyzed, arms and legs spread wide on the hard mattress to increase the surface area exposed to the limping fan. I lie here, as I do every day, waiting for the sun to sink low enough to make walking on the baked sidewalks tolerable.

Usually about five o'clock I manage to rouse myself, throw on a T-shirt and shorts, and do my daily business. My pilgrimage to the main post office, only a block away, my daily penance at the poste restante counter, the pitying smile from the plump clerk as she shakes her head yet again.

No, sir, no mail for Michaelson today. Sorry.

It's already mid-April. When I spoke to her last month, Marcia told me she expected a response by the end of March. But publishers are unpredictable, and agents are notoriously busy. I can't afford to call her often, but I guess I'll have to try again Monday night (Monday morning in New York), try to catch her before her week is completely booked and shame her into badgering New American Library yet again. I'm no longer Marcia's top priority. Out of sight, out of mind.

Thailand. It had seemed like such an inspired notion when René proposed it to me over our beers last January. René was buying. I had just been laid off holiday duty from Barnes and Noble.

The gutters overflowed with gray slush. The pitiless wind whistled through the city's artificial canyons.

"I can't afford to live in the city," I complained. "But where can I go? Back to Illinois? That would be career suicide. No serious author ever came from Peoria!"

"Why don't you take a sabbatical?"

"Sabbatical! I can't pay my rent!"

"Sublet your place, take whatever money you can scrape up, and go to Thailand. Beautiful girls. Glittering temples. Fabulous, spicy food. No snow! It's incredibly cheap, if you know the right places. Phone and Internet are just as good as here. You can relax, have a good time, maybe do some writing, while you wait for the news about your novel."

Beautiful girls. Now that sounded appealing. Since Lisa had dumped me, just before Thanksgiving, my romantic landscape had been as bleak as the city streets. I didn't miss Lisa, not exactly. But jacking off is a supremely lonely activity.

So the picture René painted of high-spirited, hedonistic Bangkok sounded like the ideal answer. Especially when he volunteered to join me for a week or two. I cashed the savings bond that was my parents' graduation gift. I found a fairly reliable acquaintance whose boyfriend had just thrown him out to take over my apartment. I had a fifteen-minute meeting with Marcia in which she promised to keep the pressure on NAL. I sent a letter to my mom and dad, vaguely suggesting that I had a writing assignment overseas. Once I made the decision, everything seemed to flow smoothly.

Now, two months later, I'm stuck here, mired in the gooey underbelly of Bankgok like a dinosaur in a tar pit. Money almost gone. Nothing left but my return ticket, my laptop, and my dubious genius. Sure, I could limp back home, a whipped dog with my tail between my legs. Back to what, though? Working with Dad in the hardware store?

I accept the inevitable. Dragging myself out of bed, I put on the minimum acceptable amount of clothing. The loose cotton shirt clings to my damp back. The zipper of my fly grates uncomfortably against my flaccid cock, but the notion of underwear is simply unbearable.

I pull my laptop out of its hiding place behind the scarred bureau. Tools of my trade. I've hardly opened it since I got here. I stuff the computer in a shopping bag and head for the street.

It's well past three. I weave my way along the fractured pavement, trying to stay in the shade. Whenever I fail, the fierce sun pummels me, pounding my skull despite my hat. A couple of bare-headed, red-faced tourists stroll past me, wearing cheap batik and gold jewelry. What's that saying about mad dogs and Englishmen?

I spend three-quarters of an hour breathing exhaust on the open bus before I get to Pantip Plaza. The used-computer places are on the third floor. I ride up the escalators, rock music and video game sound effects blaring from every shop. I catch the scents of Chinese incense and fried chilies.

When I find the stall I'm looking for, the transaction takes no more than ten minutes. I do my best to haggle, but the shopkeeper recognizes my aura of desperation. I stuff the wad of thousand-baht notes in my pocket, sending one last regretful look back at my friendly Toshiba. The skinny young man already has it disassembled on his table.

Feeling flush, I splurge on a taxi back. Rush hour makes it a long, slow ride, but in the sterile chill of the air conditioning, I hardly mind. I close my eyes and lean back. The throbbing in my temples gradually dies away.

It won't be in vain, I resolve. Who needs a computer? Did Hemingway have a computer? I'll pick up a notebook tomorrow, and from now on, I'll spend at least three hours a day working. What else have I got to do, after all?

The irrational pattern of one-way streets means that the taxi has to let me off a couple of blocks from the guesthouse. That's okay, though. The sun has sunk below the horizon by now. There's even a hint of breeze coming from the river, stirring the muggy air.

I'm revived by the air conditioning and my fresh resolution. I stride down the sidewalk, maneuvering around the other pedestrians, avoiding the cracked bricks and crumbling curbs almost by instinct. Maybe coming to Bangkok was a good idea after all. After all, there's that old wisdom about having to hit bottom before you start to recover.

His body slams into me without warning. As I stumble and fall to my knees, I have a confused impression of tight jeans, flashy jewelry, silky black hair. Sandalwood cologne.

"Oh, I'm sorry, sir! Are you okay?" He helps me up, brushing the dust off my pants. "Please forgive me! I'm so clumsy." His voice is soft and musical, with the pleasing cadence of Thai-accented English.

"It's all right. Never mind," I tell him. His arched eyebrows are drawn together in a concerned frown, but a smile hovers on his full lips. "*Mai pen rai.*"

"Are you sure? Can I help you to your hotel?" I'm suddenly aware of his manicured hand resting on my shoulder, light as a butterfly. His exotic scent makes me slightly dizzy. I look him over. His designer shirt, in muted stripes, fits his slender torso and broader shoulders like a second skin. His stretch denim trousers look painted on. He has gold rings on every finger, and one in his left earlobe.

He's a creature of beauty. I'm suddenly ashamed of myself, sweaty and unkempt, with two days' beard. I don't want him to see the dingy hole where I live.

"No, thanks, that's not necessary. It's not your fault. The sidewalks here are treacherous. It's easy to lose your balance."

"Okay, then. See you."

He saunters away, graceful despite the hazards of the broken pavement. I watch him for a moment. There's an odd tightness in my chest, and I still feel a bit woozy. Too much sun, I think, turning back toward my destination. I should know better than to come out during the day. At least I accomplished my goal, though. I pat my pocket, seeking reassurance in the fat mass of folded bills stashed there.

And feel nothing.

My pocket is empty. It's several seconds before I understand. Then I let out a howl that sends both tourists and natives scattering in alarm.

"NO!! No, damn it! You bastard!" I turn back in the direction I came from, trying to run, stumbling and cursing my own stupidity. The slick young thief has disappeared, of course. Before long, I'm gasping from the heat and pollution. Pain lances through my forehead. Black spots dance in front of my eyes.

I sink down onto the step of a shuttered shop, barely able to breathe. Despair washes over me. It's all over. No money, no computer, no future. I might as well be dead. Tears of frustration and self-pity spill down onto my shirt, already muddy with dust and sweat. I squeeze my eyes shut, willing the darkness inside my soul to take over my consciousness.

I smell him before I see him. "Hey, you." The voice is gentle, almost sad. "Don't cry. Never mind. Here." A folded wad of paper is pushed into my hand. "Take it."

Incredulous, I open my eyes. He's crouched beside me, thighs spread wide for balance. His hand is on my shoulder once again. He pulls a silk handkerchief from the pocket of his jeans. It's still warm from his body.

I look down at the beige bank notes in my palm. "It's all there," he says. "You can count it if you want."

"Why . . . ?"

He shrugs. "I like you," he says, his half-smile widening to a grin.

I notice a tourist police kiosk across the street, its occupant watching us curiously. I stuff the money deep into my pocket. I don't care whether or not he's telling the truth.

"Hey, you want a beer? My friends have a place down the next *soi*." He rises from his haunches with a dancer's grace and holds out his hand to help me up. "My name is Bom. And you?"

"Gary." I'm still suspicious, not sure I should trust him.

"Come on, Gary." He throws his arm around my shoulders and leads me away. In the brooding heat of dusk, I expect to find his touch unpleasant, but it's strangely comforting. I guess I'm not over the shock of my near-disaster.

His silk shirt slithers against the bare skin on my arms. I worry about the dirt on my own clothes, but Bom doesn't seem to care.

He leads me down a lane that dead-ends at the river. A dilapidated wooden shack on stilts perches precariously over the muddy water. The door's wide open; inside I see several young men gathered round a table, and an inviting-looking plastic tub filled with ice and bottles of Singha.

Bom introduces his friends. Their monosyllabic names go in one ear and out the other. They're all dressed like Bom, skin-tight jeans and tailored silk shirts, accented by gold amulets and fancy watches.

Bom hands me an open beer. The chilled amber liquid slides down my throat, a sensual delight. He tips his head back to take a swig from his own bottle. My eyes are drawn to the elegant curve of his neck. He wears his hair long, in a ponytail down his back. A lock has come loose and hangs in his eyes, giving him a waifish look.

His friends are laughing and chattering in Thai. The polite host, Bom tries to make conversation. "Are you here on holiday?"

"I'm a writer." This doesn't really answer the question, but he nods as if satisfied. "I'm working on a novel."

"About Thailand?"

"Partly."

"Ooh! Maybe you'll put me in it!" He grins with almost childish delight.

I take refuge in silence, taking another swallow of my beer. I'm surprised to find the bottle is already empty. Before I can even ask, Bom hands me a full one. I drink deeply, gazing out the open window at the twilight river traffic.

The barges make their stately way downstream, ponderous and silent. Swarms of longtail powerboats zip around them, buzzing like insects. A tourist dinner cruise sweeps by, a floating Christmas tree outlined in tiny flashing lights. I'm feeling quite drunk, and oddly peaceful. I let everything flow by me.

The place reeks of fish and rusted iron. Under these raw smells, I catch a whiff of Bom's sandalwood cologne. He has lapsed into Thai with his cohorts, abandoning any attempts to communicate with me. Still, he makes sure that the bottle in front of me is always full.

Overwhelmed by the beer and the day's events, I must have slept. I wake, disoriented, in near-darkness. A halogen lamp mounted on the next pier sends uneven shafts of light into the shack, but until my eyes adjust, I can barely see anything.

The chairs clustered around the formica-topped table are all empty. The table itself is littered with dozens of empty bottles. The room is quiet enough that I can hear the river lapping against the piles that support the building.

Then I recognize the sound of breathing. As this is sinking in, somebody moans.

"Bom?" There's a creaking sound off in the corner.

"Here, Gary." His voice is muffled. Someone bursts into laughter, which breaks off suddenly to become a groan of pleasure.

I'm beginning to be able to make out my surroundings. There's some kind of platform at the far end of the room. The platform is covered with pale, writhing, naked bodies.

"Come on, Gary," Bom coaxes. He is on his knees, poised above the prone body of one of his friends. Even in the dimness, I can see the gleam of his perfect skin, the smile on his ripe lips, the saliva dripping down his chin. He bends once more to the cock jutting up in front of him.

Another of his mates is positioned behind Bom's hips. He grabs Bom's buttocks, pulls them open, and begins lapping at his friend's anus.

I think that I should be disgusted, but I'm not. I'm fascinated. My cock hardens rapidly. If I were sober, I'd probably find this alarming, but at the moment, it seems completely normal. I unsnap, unzip, and wrestle my cock into the open air. It swells further, grateful to be set free. I stroke it slowly, root to tip, my attention fixed on the scene in front of me.

For a while the action is languid, dreamy, slow motion caresses punctuated every now and then by a sharp intake of breath or a sudden groan. My cock surges in my hand in reaction. I can hear the slurp of tongues against wet flesh, but it's a bit difficult to see the details.

Hardly realizing what I'm doing, I move closer, still stroking myself. The guy with his face buried in Bom's ass sits back on his haunches. He looks over at me and grins as he rolls a condom over his impressive prick. He says something in Thai. Bom hikes his rear up higher. He wiggles his butt in invitation.

The other man positions the tip of his rod between

Bom's ass cheeks. He jerks his hips, and his cock disappears from view. Bom wails as though in pain. His partner pulls back, then rams his cock back into Bom's guts, raising another yell from my Thai friend.

I can't really see what's going on, but I can guess. My own asshole twitches in sympathy. My cock jumps with every thrust. I remember vividly the one time I had anal sex with Lisa, the way her hole gripped my cock when I plunged into her, the way her flesh gaped and shuddered whenever I pulled out. I remember her roaring orgasm, and her tears afterward. She wouldn't let me do it again, and she flatly refused to stick even one finger up my ass.

I can't imagine what it would feel like, to have that huge, rigid prick boring into my butt. Just thinking about it, though, brings me close to the edge.

The action's rougher now, and louder, too. Another couple is fucking, between Bom and the shed wall. The one who's taking it is on his back, bent double, his legs practically by his ears. His partner straddles him, drilling into him from above. My eyes are better adjusted to the dimness now. I can see the corded muscles of the fucker's thighs and the sweat dripping down his back as he pistons in and out of the other man's hole.

There's a fifth guy, the one that Bom had been sucking. He's still on back underneath Bom, jerking off energetically in time to the cock pounding Bom's bowels. Just as I notice him, he screams and lets go. His come geysers out, showering Bom's face with thick white droplets.

I'm almost there myself. The ache in my balls is unbearable. I jerk and pull on myself, faster, harder, close but somehow unable to get over the edge.

"Gary," Bom says hoarsely, rising up onto his knees. "Closer.

Please." His partner has paused, cock still buried in Bom's hole. I move to the side of the platform, squeezing my aching prick.

Bom puts his arm around my neck and pulls my face to his. He tastes of stale beer and bitter semen. He smells of sweat. His tongue coils inside my mouth, exploring the possibilities. It's muscular and playful and not at all like kissing Lisa.

I kiss him back, rubbing my swollen prick against his naked, come-smeared belly. Nothing has ever felt so good.

Bom smiles when he feels my cock poking at him. He grabs it, pushing my own hands away, and laughs softly, then pulls my pants down around my knees. "Very nice. Oh yes, I like it. Can I have it?"

He doesn't wait for permission. Bending back down, he sucks my cock into his eager mouth. Sensation overwhelms me. Sultry jungle heat swallows me up. His tongue sweeps up and down, massaging, teasing. I want more and so I take it, ramming my cock down his throat. The bulb mashes against his pallet. He gags, then opens wider, taking my whole length. The next moment, he's using his teeth, nipping at the ridge under the head. I roar and slam my prick back where it belongs, as deep into him as I can go. All at once, his body shakes with a new rhythm. He's being fucked again, I realize.

He moans around my cock. I fuck his mouth while his friend fucks his ass, thrust for thrust. I'm ready to explode. The dark smell of shit rises around us. All at once, the guy reaming Bom yells and shudders. He pounds his hips convulsively against Bom's butt cheeks. I know he's pouring his spunk into Bom's hole. The image brings me right to the edge.

Bom writhes against his violator, but doesn't let up on the suction. I feel hot jets of viscous stuff landing on my bare thighs. Bom is coming all over me.

I can't take anymore. I swell and explode, spurting my come into Bom's mouth, rivers of it, a flood that goes on and on. He swallows, sucks, swallows again. The pleasure is outrageous. I'm totally lost in the sensations. My cock is starting to deflate, yet still I shudder and jerk like a puppet, each convulsion sending new jets of semen onto Bom's eager tongue and a new thrill up my spine.

Finally, my cock slips limply from between the Thai man's lips. He's smiling. Remnants of my come dribble from the corners of his mouth. A Buddha image hangs on his hairless chest, between tender-looking nipples.

I'll be damned if I don't start to get hard again.

Without saying a word, Bom turns his back to me and presents his ass. Dripping down the cleft between those two pale moons, I see a trail of wetness.

I can't help myself. My forefinger reaches out, tracing the path of the other man's come downward until I brush my fingertip over the velvety skin of Bom's scrotum. He sighs with delight. Fascinated, I slide my finger back up through the crevice, and sink it into that slick, dark orifice that beckons irresistibly.

He tightens around the invading digit; I slip in a second finger next to the first.

Somebody hands me a condom.

I'll write about this some day, this crazy night outside of time. The boats chugging past in the distance, the scent of rust and garbage, the mournful folk song filtering in on the tropical breeze. The alcohol-induced haze that makes everything beautiful and unreal.

Right now, though, all I want is to fuck this gorgeous, seductive, treacherous creature until we're both senseless.

Sex on the Edge

Kiki

Jolie du Pré

"Close your eyes."

The tall grass tickles my face as she lowers my head to the pond. One hand rubs my hair, while the other showers it with the water.

"All right, baby. You're done." We stand. She lifts up her T-shirt and pats my eyes with it.

Now my blond locks are black. My parents never let me do it when I was at home, but that's not why I bailed. That's not the half of it.

I grab a strand, letting it slide between my fingers. Its dark color triggers an ache in my pussy, which gets even stronger when I look over at Kiki's face. She's smiling in that way that says she wants to fuck me, the new me with my slick black locks.

"You look hot!"

"I want a mirror."

"Yeah, when we're at the store we'll get one."

What she really means is we'll steal one.

Kiki's bald, but she still has tiny little hairs on her head that feel good under my fingers, fuzzy like a caterpillar's. I move closer to her, kiss her lips, roll my tongue over her stud. She's got another piercing on her nose, five on her eyebrow, and a bunch on her ears. She hooked me up with one through my belly button.

The clouds are forming above us. It looks like rain. We head back to our place under the bridge, just before it starts to pour. Don is there. He sits on a tattered blanket, playing his guitar and singing to the sky. His voice is gravely, and sometimes he'll hit a note, and nothing will come out. The skin on his face is tough like leather, and he's missing three of his front teeth. Kiki says he's about fifty and that he's been drinking since he was ten. The kindest man I know. Last week, when I was crying, he sang me a song, and I pretended that I enjoyed the sound of it, because I love him. He's my family.

Not my real family, who told me I was going to hell for being a dyke. Who beat me. Who sent me off to a Christian boarding school. I'm twenty now. Haven't been home in about two years. I don't miss them, never have.

Kiki walks over to the spot on the grass where she hid the box, and then she digs it up. Crack, the only thing she loves as much as me.

She lights some. Her face looks like she's close to coming after she blows it out. The smoke burns my eyes and smells like burnt alcohol. I turn my head. I don't want it. But if I look at her, at it, I might change.

Later, we sit in a restaurant and look at the menus, acting like we're going to order. Then when some customers are finished, we take the money they leave on the tables. About ten dollars today, enough for lunch. We didn't eat yesterday.

When we're done with our meals, we take a walk. It's Saturday. Lots of people are out and about, shopping at all the expensive stores. Kiki decides she wants to scare some "rich brats" again. She makes faces, which I tell her she doesn't need to do since she looks pretty scary anyway, at least to them.

She runs up to some kid. He's dressed perfectly in matching designer duds. Standing there, eyes bugging out of his head, frozen like a statue, he starts to cry. That's when his mother notices and runs over to grab him. She clutches her purse as they hurry out of sight. I try not to laugh.

Kiki grabs my hand, and we find an alley. She's brought one of the rocks with her and her pipe. She takes a hit, and then she's ready to fuck. We go to the train station, into one of the bathrooms, and lock the door.

Pressing me against the wall, she puts her mouth on mine. Her lips are chapped, and her breath is stale, but her kiss is firm. She takes my shirt and pulls it up. Then she leans down and puts one of my tits in her mouth. Since I'm small, she can suck it all in. While she's doing that, her fingers play with my other nipple. I feel a tingle in my pussy, and she knows it. She knows what gets me hot. She puts her mouth on mine again. I push my tongue inside and find the stud. I like the way it feels. I like to play with it.

We pull down our pants and panties and let them fall to our feet. Then we push our bodies against each other, rubbing our pussies together, starting a fire. I slide three fingers into Kiki's cunt and nibble her ear.

"Fuck that pussy," she says.

And that's what I do, hard and fast my fingers go in and out of her hole, juice all over. I lick her neck and reach under her shirt to feel her breasts. I want to make her come. I push even harder into her. Soon she's hunched over, holding on to me for support, until I hear her moan and feel her pussy close around my fingers. I pull them out and put them in my mouth. She's glassy-eyed and smiling as I taste her.

Now we're back under the bridge. Kiki doesn't rest much. The crack has turned her into a zombie. But for once, she's sleeping. I lean my back against the concrete wall and hold her head on my lap. Don is next to us, stretched out with his mouth open, snoring. Even though the city lights are bright, I can still see some stars. I make a wish for us, and then I close my eyes and go to sleep.

Drillers

Dominic Santi

Elizabeth was going to be mine again. That bitch was going to put her head down and point her ass at the ceiling and beg for my love juice. And when my sperm flooded through her cunt, she was going to keep her ass high and clench her pussy muscles together as hard as she could, so she didn't lose a single fucking drop. My sweet bitch baby would stay that way until my cum had all run deep into her womb and every one of those nasty little drillers was racing up to screw his way into her quivering, defenseless, succulent egg. They were going to stab at her ovum's walls until the meanest, strongest one shoved his way in past the virginal cell barrier. Then my chromosomes were going to take hers, one gene at a time, until our genetic code was bonded in a way she could never rip apart.

And her worthless whoreson husband was going to pay me to do it. Again. God, that was rich. And so fucking easy. I'd intercepted her medical records on their way back from being transcribed in India. Piece of cake. The fertility clinic's records were always turned around within twenty-four hours. I sent out spiders the day after her doctor's appointments, and *voilà!* I knew exactly when fancy Miss High Society Reformed Criminal Piece of Ass Who's Fertile as a Fresh-Plowed Field and her blank-shooting district attorney husband wanted to conceive again.

They wanted to use the same "anonymous" donor who had already given them their two darling daughters, of course. I assumed the brats' dark brown hair was the same shade as mine. Beyond that, I didn't know what they looked like, and I didn't care. They were so different from my beautiful blond-haired, green-eyed love, with her wonderful voluptuous breasts. I had a shelf full of videos of her nursing her babies, shielded only by the lace of the nursery curtains. Day after day, I sat at my desk chair, staring at my monitor, zooming the viewfinder in, and jacking off while she bared her deliciously full breasts and offered them, one at a time, to the anonymous hungry mouth I could see only from behind.

When Dear Don was there, she kept herself demurely covered while she nursed. But when he was gone, she opened her expensive designer negligees and let the milk squirt out of one nipple and onto a towel while the small dark head in her arms moved slowly against the other side. I remembered how soft her nipples had been under my tongue, how they'd hardened to nubs when I sucked them to bruises and she begged me to fuck her. When I closed my eyes, I could see my tongue snaking towards her nipple, lapping at the drips, tasting her milk and washing her satiny skin. Dear Don had never so much as cupped her breast while she'd nursed. I wondered if he'd suck her tits dry if she bore him a son, the way I would have.

This time, they were going to test twice each day, trying to catch the pre-ovulation endocrine spike right away to have a better chance at getting a boy. And the chances would be good. After all, "their" artificial insemination donor already had two healthy sons. The fact sheet showed that. Actually, it had originally shown only the two healthy children and blemish-free medical history required by the clinic's A.I. policy. But, well, Don wanted a son, to carry on the family name and business. And his lovely wife, as always, deferred to his wishes. So, when they'd pressed for more information, donor 369 had reluctantly obliged. He'd provided details about his two healthy sons, young leaders-in-the-making who excelled in sports, football and baseball, of course, and had just enough academic prowess to make the grades without being too bookish. "All boy" boys, if you know what I mean. They loved to hunt and fish with Dad. Oh, and they'd had no problems with the law, of course, other than a couple of "harmless pranks" that Dad had straightened out with a stern talking-to.

I'd had to be careful not to overdo my illustrious little cyber-darlings. "Father is a world class hacker who wouldn't be caught dead playing ball and fucks men as indiscriminately as he does women" probably would have given our wunderkind state attorney general hopeful pause in selecting said donor to impregnate his charming wife. Especially since Dear Don had gone to such lengths to protect society from the likes of me—and from me specifically.

So that night, in between sweeping floors and emptying trash in the dimly lit, empty medical building, my little specimen cup and I made a quick trip to the john. I dropped my pants and took my dick in my hand, working my dick-head under its hood until I was slimy with pre-cum. Then I closed my eyes, stroking and squeezing, until once again, my beautiful Elizabeth was kneeling on the bed in front of me.

She was naked, her creamy skin glowing in the candle-light, her long blond hair flowing in shimmering waves over the pillow. Her lovely bottom was arched up high at me, her legs spread wide and her shaved pussy lips glistening with her juices and my spit. She was whimpering. She knew I'd make her come, knew I'd make her scream before I fucked her. But pussy licking embarrassed her. So I leaned forward and ate her long and slowly, whispering her name, over and over, while I told her how sweet her cunt was and how I loved tonguing her hole. And how I was going to fuck her, after she came.

She'd told her therapist she was "nonorgasmic" with Don. Not that she'd ever complained, per se. After all, dickhead was footing the bill. And even though those records were harder to access, I knew she'd waited quite a while to make her shamefaced little confession. But after a great deal of therapeutic questioning, she'd finally admitted that lying on her back while he grunted over her "failed to arouse her."

She didn't add anything about how the scent of his money got her sufficiently hot to at least take his dick. She just mentioned, one time, about how "a previous lover" (yeah, right, bitch, the only other one, the one who took every cherry you ever had and now you can't remember his name) had liked to do it doggie style, that she'd been orgasmic then, and it might be nice to try that position for a change. But when she'd suggested a change in position to her husband, he'd icily ordered her to sleep in a guest room for a week and cut off her allowance. So she'd apologized to him for being frigid and never mentioned it again.

She hadn't said one word to the counselor about how that "previous lover" had leaned forward and inhaled her scent, smearing her juices on his face while he licked and sucked her smooth, sensitive labia, then tongued her clit until she was slick and begging. How he kept whispering, "Not yet, pretty pussy girl," and "Open your bottom for me, sweetheart." He shoved his fingers up her holes and chewed on her clit, and she'd screamed and screamed and screamed as she came. Then he fucked her cunt and her ass, filling rubber after rubber with his cum until she was just one big raw hole pointing up in the air for him to use until his dick was tired.

And the next day, she was rolling naked in front of me again like a cat in heat, rubbing her face in my crotch. She wiggled her tongue under my foreskin, teased me with her bruised nipples and swollen cunt, until I threw her on her face and jerked her ass up and growled, "Spread for me, bitch." And she did. She always did. And I paid homage to her pussy like she was manna from heaven. Which she was. I treated her body with the reverence it deserved.

And now the fucker who sent me up couldn't get her off. She "wasn't responding" to his cold, dry, ex-cop's dick, only to the plea-bargain he'd arranged and the money she'd married into while I was doing time for the money I stole for her. And his balls shot blanks.

"Suck me, bitch," I whispered, working my foreskin furiously over my dick. My pre-cum was as slick as her saliva had been. "Tug on my balls while you choke me into your throat, so I get up a really good load for you."

My balls crawled up my dick, remembering. I wrapped my hand around my shaft, stroking faster, the way I had when I'd fucked her cunt and her ass and her face, the way I'd fucked her face until her tears ran down and sperm-thick cum shot from my balls. As the heat surged through my dick, I pressed the lip of the cup under my dickhead. It was hard, not soft like her lips had been when I'd pulled back and spewed my cream all over her face, as the long white ropes had spurted out onto her beautiful red lips and her flushed hot cheeks, and her eyelids and the bridge of her nose, and she'd lowered her head in shame and delicately, oh so delicately, licked a single strand off her quivering lips.

I pressed up my dick, draining the last drop out of my tube. Then I sealed the cup, stuffed my cock back in my pants, and tucked the specimen job in my overalls pocket. As always, there was no one else in the building when I grabbed my broom and pushed the mop pail back out into the main office. An hour later, the floors were shining, the sample was properly labeled and frozen, and the computer files had been altered to show that donor 369 vial had just passed the six-months waiting period and his recertified negative serostatus report was inserted in the files.

I was still horny when I got back home, to the guesthouse in back of Elizabeth's next door neighbor's. I turned on my computer and checked the digital "security" camera trained on her bedroom suite. Dipshit was already asleep, snoring on his back in his designer pajamas. But Elizabeth was in the bathroom, sitting on her vanity chair, in her long white satin nightgown, whispering into the phone. I knew my honeypot's cycle, and the glass vials on the counter confirmed what I'd already figured. I flipped on the eavesdropping equipment.

"This message is for Dr. Smythe. This is Elizabeth Dalton. Um, my levels are starting to rise, so I'll need an appointment tomorrow morning. Um, at ten o'clock if it would be possible, for the A.I."

Her voice was the nervous kind of breathless she got when she was getting horny. She ran her hand unconsciously over the soft white satin folds over her breasts. Her nipples hardened, and as she hung up the phone, she glanced at the closed bedroom door, and lifted the hem of her nightgown. She closed her eyes and slid her hand between her legs. My cock started to swell, but I didn't touch it. Instead, I pulled up the appointment desk's password and confirmed Mrs. Dalton's desired appointment time.

Tomorrow morning, at ten o'clock, while her fuck-face husband was screwing people over in his sterile little office and his investment counselor was frantically trying to straighten out the latest "unexpected" glitch I was going to make in asshole's financial records, I'd lie in my bed, and I'd replay tonight's tapes. I'd watch Elizabeth finger herself to orgasm, remembering my tongue. And in my head, I'd see her in the doctor's office, her legs spread wide and her beautiful ass trembling high in the air. I'd see his sterile, gloved hands inserted the long, thin tube up her cunt and push the plunger, and my sperm once more shoot high up into her cunt. And I'd know that while she waited there alone on her padded table with her ass in the air and my expensive, designer, command-performance sperm squirming through her cervix and into her womb, chasing her virginal egg, she was remembering me and wishing she once more had a real fucking man inside her.

Junkie

Jaelyn

I can't remember when I started to crave the sound of the old GTO pulling into the driveway. My stomach turns in anticipation while I listen for Terry to climb my steps. When his keys turn my lock, I am paralyzed.

Last night was intense. I had every intention on ending our relations, but my entire body begged for his touch.

Terry slammed the door open and tossed his keys onto my coffee table. Trying to show my displeasure, I peered over my glasses. He never bothered looking at me.

Terry pulled his shirt over his head. He wiped his armpits with it before tossing it to the floor. He unbuttoned his jeans and kicked them off. His swollen cock bobbed as he rushed towards me. I hardly had enough time to remove my glasses before he was undressing me.

He yanked my shirt over my head, then tore off my panties. I love it when he behaves that way.

Climbing the couch, he pressed his beautiful cock against my mouth. His pre-cum smeared over my lips. The smell of him was intoxicating. I closed my eyes, opened my mouth and sucked.

Terry rocked on his knees with his pelvis thrusting in and out. He reached down between my legs rubbing his knuckles over my famished pussy. I moaned over his dick to show my want. He slipped his thick fingers inside me, swirling them, loosening me. I swayed on his hand while he glided in and out my mouth. It was almost like we were making love.

He bit his lip and looked down in my eyes watching me please him. I thought I saw tenderness glimmer in his eyes. Any moment, I expected him to confess his love. Then my body tensed, my legs shook and Terry pushed himself away from me.

Why couldn't he just pretend we were close? Though I knew I didn't love him, I wanted the illusion.

His fingers dug into my arms as he pulled me off the couch. I let him spin me around and push me over the side. Grabbing a handful of my ass, Terry slipped his penis between my legs. The tip of his head passed my entrance and teased my clitoris. I held my breath until he drove himself deep inside me.

I loved the way he fucked me. He thrashed against me. I held on to the arm of the couch and met his body with the same rage he forced in me. The sweat from his head dripped on my back and rolled down my sides. His hands moved away from my hips and slid up my sides before reaching around to hold my breasts. Only Terry could make me hurt, cry, and beg until waves of orgasm crashed through me in a sensual violence.

My inner walls trembled around him. He withdrew himself, pulling me back from the arm I clutched. I lost my grip on the couch and tumbled backwards to the floor.

Lying on the floor, I smiled at him, loving the force he used. He took his cue and dove right in, fucking me harder. I met his rhythm while I watched our pelvises crush against each other. His cock glistened while it pumped in and out of me. We seemed like a machine.

Terry panted. His body became rigid. His gaze captured mine. Between moans he held his breath until his seed flushed in me with a final exhale.

The last thing I remember is lying on the floor beneath his limp body. My mind swam in the afterglow, pretending that something more could come of this.

Early this morning, I awoke curled up on the carpet. I was cold and sore. Terry had gone. I cramped up. Tears welled up behind my eyes, and I started to shake.

It always ends this way. Never again, I promise myself, waiting for the roar of his GTO.

Speculative Erotica

Absences

Chris Skilbeck

"James, I've got to come again, soon—it's been two years now—I can't hold on much longer."

My heart sank at Petra's words, although I'd known for weeks that she was going to need an orgasm soon.

"Darling—are you certain? Isn't it worth waiting for Donna's research results? Can't you hold on a little longer?

"NO!" Her vehemence made me jump. "I've held on and held on; I'm going mad. I need it soon—tonight, tomorrow, soon.

"Please, James, you'll be able to look after me, and Donna will be here next week. She'll help you until I recover."

She took a big gulp of her mint tea and held my gaze, facing me across the remains of breakfast. I couldn't sustain the eye contact long; my feelings were too mixed up. I had an erection; I was already imagining the rare pleasures that we would enjoy, and I was already pushing away thoughts of the cost that only Petra had to pay.

I looked at her again, could not help imagining her naked body. Two years had passed since I'd last seen any part of her skin other than her face and hands. I remembered the perfect slight upward tilt of her nipples, the breathtaking smooth slide of my hand across ribcage, belly, hip, and buttock.

As I recalled the sight and feel of her, my desire started to outweigh my worry about the consequences. I yearned to suck and kiss, to stroke and squeeze. I ached to smell her arousal and slide into her, to hear her cry of abandon as she reached the dangerous height of pleasure.

"You know I want you, Petra, but it frightens me; I never know how close I might be to losing you."

Petra was not satisfied with my reply; she stood up and turned her back to me. She let her heavy gown fall to the floor as she walked out of the room. The sight of her body galvanized my erection, set my heart racing, and reduced my conscience to an ineffectual whimper.

She called over her shoulder, "If you don't want to join in, James, I'll just have to do it myself. But, I'd much rather die in your arms than all alone!"

I winced at her words: she was exaggerating, but only just, and the risk was always there. She came back to the doorway, leant in just enough to give me a fleeting glimpse of a breast, and said, "Tonight, James, make it tonight. Make sure the generator is okay."

During the morning I went into the lean-to behind the house and serviced the generator. When we moved to the Scots Fringe we soon learned that a reliable power supply made the difference between simplicity and barbarism. Some of our acquaintances lived without power, their homes becoming dirty, dingy throwbacks to an age of ignorance. We keep the generator in good condition, using power to connect to a carefully selected portion of the Civic media and to listen occasionally to some of our music recordings.

Some people around the Fringe regard us as halfhearted. They berate us for refusing to sever all ties with Civic, but they don't know the reason we're here. Most of the New

Primitives, Prims, as they call themselves, are seeking spiritual redemption through self-denial and simplicity.

Petra and I moved here in order to avoid sex.

In Civic it is impossible to walk along a street without being bombarded with sexual images. Adverts are nearly all predicated on sexuality; entertainment is all sexualized.

Clothing in Civic is now an art form, not a means to modesty or comfort. Strippers, tantric "artists," naked contortionists, and any number of other performers can be found at any street corner.

In Civic the air is full of the smells and sounds of mating; people are either doing it or, more commonly, watching others do it. There is an endless cavalcade of attractive young "actors" and "models," conducting their frantic and varied sex lives in the full glare of publicity, urging their prurient and adoring audiences to purchase increasingly bizarre clothing, sex toys, films, magazines.

For a couple who want to be faithful, but who can rarely have sex, Civic is a place to avoid.

For me, it was no fun to be constantly aroused by the eroticism flaunted from all sides, knowing that my only release would be solitary.

For Petra, life in Civic was hell. We could not have a normal sex life, so the relentless promotion of sexuality drove her to despair. She was permanently aroused, and yet unable to seek the pleasure that others take for granted.

Here in Scots Fringe we can live quietly. No advertisements bombard our senses. The few people we see are fully clothed for warmth or for protection while working. We listen to the formal Civic Media Newscasts, but avoid watching the images; the last time I watched, the news reader was toying with her nipple-ring while describing injuries inflicted during the latest Police Action in the riot-torn Berlin suburb of East Civic.

We keep our life as un-erotic as possible. Petra is very considerate. She wears shapeless garments that hide her figure. We do not kiss or cuddle very often. We sleep in separate bedrooms.

Once or twice a month Petra will use her hands or occasionally her mouth to relieve my need. She will come to me while I bathe, or while I'm dressing. When I have come, she rushes away to avoid thinking of her own arousal.

We keep busy. In daytime we exhaust ourselves cultivating our patch of land, and we work long into the evening, preserving and processing the fruits and herbs, delivering them around the area. Throughout the New Celtic Fringe there is no money. Our neighbors keep hens and give us eggs; the next valley is home to potters and woodworkers; we all get what we need and give what we can. It works, after a fashion. There is always something lacking.

Four miles away there is a small community of silent monks who make wine and mead. Petra and I trade with them often. It is good to get quietly drunk sometimes.

But just once in a blue moon, Petra cannot bear her predicament any longer, and I service the generator in readiness, and allow myself to anticipate making love.

I checked that the seals in the fuel pump were properly seated. The thought of fuel leaking, soaking away into the earth, made me think about my seed, so often let loose upon the ground, or into the sink.

I did a complete oil change, renewing the filter. An erection came upon me again as I allowed thoughts of Petra's body to linger. I could not stop myself. I released my semen with a few quick strokes. One glistening drop clung to the casing of the generator, oozed down over the printed metal plate that bore the maker's name.

"Stalwart" I read, with a hollow laugh, "Output Frequency—50kHz." I rearranged my clothing, muttering to myself, "Stalwart. Output Frequency—once in a blue moon."

Sometimes, in the routine of work, in the studied adoption of simplicity, I forget to think about my sexual frustration. But usually, despite my tiredness, I crave sex. I yearn for regular physical contact. My balls ache with a fullness that seems only to increase with infrequent releases. I am tormented by memories of former lovers, of kisses and caresses, of calculatedly seductive clothing, of welcoming embraces.

I constantly long to allow my body to react unchecked to the powerful attraction that Petra exerts. Instead, I accept constant denial, holding myself silent and undemanding.

Tonight! I thought, allowing excitement to override my sadness, tonight we will make love! I will make it as slow and sensual as I can, I will draw out the experience, fill it with memories and loving details. I will arouse Petra slowly, caress and kiss every part of her, gradually overcome her fear and lift her gently towards that overwhelming experience that she can enjoy so rarely!

My reverie was interrupted by Petra, calling me for lunch, which we shared out in the growing-tunnels. It was pleasant to sit in there at this time of year. We were able to leave the ends of the tunnels open now, even at night, and the scent of apple blossom wafted in.

We discussed the priorities of our work, which herbs should be cut early to replenish dwindling stocks, which fruit most needed feeding with our meager supply of fertilizer. I became acutely aware that after that night I was going to have to shoulder a lot of work until Petra came back. I finished eating and got up to start tying in the new raspberry canes, Petra drifted off towards the house, calling back to me, "I'll do dinner a bit early, James. Try to finish that new irrigation pipe, though; the other tunnel is getting very dry."

The work occupied my mind. Once or twice I thought about the coming night, but Petra was right, the irrigation pipe was urgently needed, and I was glad to have something to concentrate on. I got the job finished just as the evening breeze shifted and started to bring the scent of wild thyme down from the hills. I walked into the house as Petra was serving our food.

"I'd better go and have a shower, love; it was hot work lugging those lengths of pipe into place! Can dinner wait a few minutes?"

"I'd rather you didn't. Why don't you just sit and relax? There's nothing wrong with a bit of honest sweat. Sit down."

I was surprised, but sat down to my meal without arguing. In all our years together I had always been careful with my grooming, I would never want to spoil any of our infrequent special times by being dirty or unkempt. But now I sat to eat opposite Petra with bits of vegetation stuck in my uncombed hair and the smell of my sweat, laced with a hint of diesel oil, gradually permeated the room.

As I ate, I looked up to find her staring at me hungrily, her nostrils flaring and her eyes wide with anticipation. She did not eat much, and once I'd had a chance to fill my stomach she cleared the table quickly and said, "James, you've been so understanding over the years, so gentle. I know that our life has been a trial to you as much as to me, and I know that you've always tried to give me as much pleasure as possible on the few occasions we've made love. But . . ."

Petra's words tailed off, and she looked away. I was surprised to see that she was blushing.

"Come on, love, what is it?"

She took a deep breath and looked me directly in the eyes, "Tonight, don't be gentle; don't spend ages arousing me. Just burst into my bedroom, after I've bathed, and fuck me. Throw me around the bed into whatever position you like. Use me. Make me feel helpless."

My cock hardened, and my mouth became dry as I sought for something to say. Petra continued, "I often fantasize, while I'm bathing, that a dirty, savage brute is spying on me, watching me get all clean and tidy, waiting for the moment when he rushes in and ravishes me!

"He doesn't kiss me or caress me; he mauls and bites and pins me down; he thrusts and grunts and takes his pleasure without regard to my feelings. I get so aroused when I have that fantasy! It's dangerous for me because I'm always so tempted to let go and have an orgasm!

"I realized today that we may have only two or three more times that we can make love—eventually I'll be unable to take the risk again—so I thought it was time I let you know exactly what I'd like!"

Petra then did something that she hardly ever does. She reached for me, and as I stood she embraced me, letting our bodies contact fully, pressing her breasts to my chest. We locked our arms around each other, our hips and thighs contacting, my erection pushing against her stomach.

We stood like that for a long time. Gradually our shuddering calmed, and we were able simply to enjoy the intimate contact. We kissed, our tongues joining. Petra loosed her grip of my body and reached for my cock, squeezing it tightly through my rough work-pants. I slid one hand up her body, gasping as I felt the weight of her breast.

Petra broke our embrace and walked off towards the bathroom. I thought about what it would be like, to just burst in and fuck her however I liked. A surge of lust rippled through me.

I went outside and relieved myself against the garden hedge, and on a sudden impulse I took all my clothes off and wandered round the garden in the fading twilight.

I walked carefully around the untidy pile of rubble that leans against the side wall of the house. This rubble was once another house, burnt out and collapsed, pushed up against ours by the bulldozers that tried to clear up the mess following the initial earthquake of '34. The cleanup attempts stopped when the aftershocks came, and the area was completely abandoned when the Big Slip happened. A lot of houses, and virtually all the taller buildings, simply fell over during the Big Slip. A few, like ours, remained standing, but were never quite straight again.

We are the proud owners, signed and sealed—and completely unenforceable since the Fringe Areas declared independence from Civic in '39—of an entire abandoned village, comprising eighty-seven collapsed cottages; three standing houses in fairly safe condition; eighteen that we avoid in case they collapse at any moment; a main road two kilometers long, with three side turnings of half a kilometer each, complete with potholes, broken drains, fallen lampposts, and crevices big enough to push all the rubble into—should anyone ever have a working bulldozer again.

The area immediately beyond our holding belongs, legally, to an almost defunct body called the Abandoned Territories Property Reallocation Authority. If we were able to occupy and use it, no one would notice or care. The area is gradually returning to nature. The road is hard to recognize in places. The Big Slip left huge gaps in the land. It has never been mapped properly, and we could not say for certain where our boundaries lie.

We have built rickety bridges over some of the deeper chasms, cleared rough pathways in and out of the shallower ones. Everywhere the willow and elder and blackthorn are encroaching; the asphalt is crumbling, the "village" is becoming less recognizable as such with every passing year.

When we moved here, we hired a group of Prims with donkeys to carry all our belongings over the rough terrain. The generator was the hardest thing. It could be dismantled into manageable parts, but several of the men would not help with it, saying it was contrary to the spirit of the New Celtic Fringe. They still make comments about it if I happen to meet them while traveling the area. They ask if it has broken yet, if we have yet learned to live with nature instead of with the leavings of the corrupt and decadent Civic.

As I mused on these memories, part of my mind was, as always, forming vague plans about what we should rebuild next, how much of the rubble we should try to clear, whether it would make our house less safe if we removed it. I clambered up onto the pile, picking my way carefully to avoid the splintery beams of wood that still poked up through the heaped stones and bricks. I slipped a couple of times, grazed my shin quite badly, and became conscious how stupid I was being to do this sort of thing naked.

As I got to the top of the rubble I could see over the bathroom window ledge and could just see Petra, through the muslin sheeting that we use instead of glass in the out-of-shape frames. Her bare skin glowed in the warm light of an oil lamp. She was drying herself, one foot resting on the edge of the bath as she stroked the towel carefully between her legs.

I clung to the window ledge. My shin hurt, and I could feel blood trickling down my leg, but as I watched Petra I lost any concern for my discomfort. Soon the only part of my body that I thought about was my stiff cock. Petra dried under her breasts, lifting them, the nipples stiff and wrinkling.

I watched as she shaved her legs, plucked her eyebrows, brushed her hair. I noticed that she'd left the door slightly ajar, and that she kept glancing towards it, as though she thought I would be watching from the gloomy corridor outside the bathroom. She was performing for me, but unaware of where I was.

When she seemed about to leave the bathroom, I picked up a rough-edged stone and used it to pierce and slit the muslin, then heaved myself up over the window-ledge.

Petra turned quickly at the sudden noise. She screamed in genuine shock, and dropped her hairbrush. I grabbed her round the waist, pinning her arms to her sides. My senses reeled at the sudden tactile pleasure as I felt her naked body writhing against mine; I became desperate to thrust my cock into her as soon as possible.

I had not expected her to fight; she beat at me with her fists and flailed her legs, forcing me to play the barbarian a bit more seriously. I pushed her to the floor and held her wrists behind her with one hand. I grabbed a handful of her long dark hair and pulled her upright again. As I frog-marched her to the bedroom, just a few meters along the corridor, she still struggled, bracing her feet against the doorframe and pushing backwards, trying to knock me over. I stepped back, turned quickly and pulled her through the doorway.

Once in the bedroom I pushed her, face down, onto the bed, keeping a firm grip of her wrists and her hair. She kicked out ineffectually as I parted her legs with my own. She screeched as my cock slid, full length and powerful, into her slippery depths. As I began thrusting, her cries turned to a rhythmic gasping, joyful, powerful, and savage.

I let go of her wrists and pulled upward on her hair, forcing her to use her arms to support herself. I mauled her breasts, finding the hard point of one of her nipples, her entire body shuddering as I pulled at it harder than I'd ever done before, making her squeal with a mixture of anger, pain, and satisfaction.

I wanted her on her back. I let go of her hair and pushed her down to the bed again, then pulled out of her and knelt up. I grabbed one shoulder and one hip, hurled her roughly over, pushing her legs apart again with my hips as I quickly guided my prick back to her slippery opening.

She pulled me close, her long, slender legs wrapped tightly round my buttocks as my hard length sank firmly into her.

She gripped me so tightly I could make only the smallest of thrusts, the root of my cock pressed close into the upper folds of her vulva. I could feel both her nipples pushing into my chest and could smell her, wild and musky, as a flood of her moisture suddenly washed my balls. I could feel the firm bud of her clitoris rubbing in the slippery tight space between us.

I felt her shudder, recognized the onset of her orgasm. I thrust my tongue into her mouth, muffling her ecstatic scream. My body continued thrusting, urging her into that last release.

Petra slumped unconscious, her entire body suddenly loose and flaccid. For a few seconds I was tempted to continue fucking her. I was close to coming, but my lust was quickly displaced by fearful concern for Petra. I pulled out of her, rushing to check that her tongue had not collapsed into her throat.

I turned her gently onto her side, arranging her limbs carefully into the recovery position, turning her head upward, opening her airway. I pressed my ear to her ribcage, listening intently. After a few agonizing seconds I heard the slight pattering of her heart, faltering and irregular. I stayed like that for many minutes, ready to roll her on her back and start the resuscitation procedure if her heart should stop entirely.

My cock shriveled, tight with fear and anxiety, a dribble of pre-ejaculate fluid hung in a sticky string, connecting my now very unbarbaric and impotent organ to Petra's thigh as I knelt attentively over her. This time, again, we were lucky; Petra's heart did not stop entirely. After about a quarter of an hour her heart was beating regularly, albeit slowly.

I convinced myself that she was not about to die at any second, and I gently lifted her onto the single bed at the side of the room, carefully arranging her on her back, head supported slightly. I checked her breathing and heartbeat, and found myself whispering to her, "Petra, I love you. Don't die my love, come back soon, I love you." Over and over, as though it might help.

I pressed the three little sensor pads to her chest, in the positions her sister Donna had taught me years ago, and turned on the monitoring machine. I panicked again for a moment, when the screen showed nothing, but then realized I hadn't connected the power supply. I plugged the last connection, and breathed a sigh of relief as the screen fired up and began to display the tiny blips that represented Petra's strange near-death.

I had no way of knowing how long she would remain in this state. Last time, two years ago, it had been relatively brief, only three weeks, but the time before, about four-and-a-half years ago, she'd been gone for eight weeks.

I covered Petra with a blanket then ran through in my mind all the things I had to do. The fluid drip was the first priority, then the catheter. Tomorrow I'd fix up the fluid feeding system.

For three days I ran about trying to get all the routine jobs done and look at Petra every few minutes. Her heartbeat remained steady, gradually strengthening, and I'd got the monitor rigged so that if she faltered it would sound a loud alarm. I could be at her side in a minute, administering the tiny dose of adrenalin, ready to go into the resuscitation routine if necessary.

On the fourth day, while I was dozing fitfully at Petra's side, exhausted, grubby, hungry, and feeling very lonely, Donna arrived.

Donna, Petra's sister, younger by six years, was very similar in appearance and exactly opposite in temperament. While Petra was stoic, uncomplaining, a rock of dependability, Donna was mercurial, militant, a whirlwind of busy involvement.

Donna had trained as a doctor just after the Big Slip, when medics of all kinds were in big demand. She'd worked in some of the most distressing areas of her profession, and served her Civic Duty as a senior military medic in some of the most dangerous trouble spots. She'd been highly paid and had managed to invest most of her income. Her own relative wealth, coupled with an inheritance from a deceased Civic army general she'd had a brief affair with, left her able, at the age of thirty-four, to give up her normal work and concentrate on researching the affliction that had dogged the women of her family for generations.

"Bloody hell, James! What the fuck's going on? Surely she wasn't so stupid as to come with only you around to look after her?"

Donna strode into the room, ignoring any attempt at normal greetings or politeness.

"At least you've got a monitor set up. Is your generator reliable? Has her pulse been steady like this all the time? When did she go? It must have been recent; I had a letter from her dated the eighth. Fuck me! That ferry crossing was horrible! I heaved up my breakfast just before we landed, and I've ridden a fucking donkey all the way here. Honestly, a luxury jet-car to Peebles and then a decrepit old steamer across New Gulf and then a fucking donkey if you please, I'm knackered. I'm just glad you live here at the south end; I couldn't stand a long trek in one of those donkey caravans!

"James, you look as bad as I feel! Get us a cuppa and something to eat will you? Then I'll sit with Pet while you get a bit of sleep. Christ! I thought I was coming to visit my sister, not baby-sit a fucking sex-crazed coma victim! What's up? Couldn't you keep your hands off each other a moment longer?"

I'd learned years ago that when Donna was in full flow it was pointless even attempting to interject. The best thing was to let her run on. I knew she'd calm down after a little while, then we could talk sensibly. I left her sitting at Petra's side, holding her hand gently, while I prepared some mint tea and a light meal of bread and fruit.

After a while, Donna joined me in the kitchen, and we sat to eat. I was lightheaded, letting myself relax now that someone was here to share the burden. For the first time I looked at Donna properly. The years had been good to her. She did not look any younger than her age, but like Petra she was a woman who'd taken a while to "grow into herself" as my mother used to say. Donna, tall and lithe like Petra, was more attractive as a maturing woman than she had been as a rather gangly and awkward nineteen-year-old.

Sensibly, she'd dressed in an all-covering baggy jumpsuit. She knew that the illegal ferry operators and the "donkey men" at Dunkeld would not have taken kindly to anyone appearing among them in the flamboyant dress more usual in Civic. Even dressed as she was, she'd have raised a few eyebrows with her fashionably shaven head and the lingering musky perfume that clung to her. I imagined she'd recently had a scent implant. It would fade in another few days. I caught a slightly stronger whiff as she leaned forward for another apple, and I felt my cock stirring and growing.

I became aware of the smell of her sweat, underlying the scent, and couldn't stop my erection growing harder as we sat chatting amiably about current events in Civic, life here in Scots Fringe, Petra's condition.

After we'd eaten, Donna said, "Look James, give me half an hour to shower and change, then I'll sit with Pet for a couple of hours while you get yourself cleaned up and have a nap—you're smelly, mate! And you look like you need a rest. Where's the bathroom? Have you got any hot water?"

Conscious that my lust had been building up, unrelieved, since I'd made love to Petra a few days ago ("fucked Petra," I corrected myself, "without coming"), I was still hard as I showed Donna to the bathroom. As I explained the use of the rather primitive shower system, I tried to keep my thoughts on Petra, wriggling in my grasp as I hauled her off to the bedroom, I thought about the moment my cock had slid so easily into her.

Donna said, "Oh shit! I've left my bags out by your front door—be a love and fetch the big blue one for me, will you James?"

When I came back with the bag, Donna was in the shower, successfully managing the occasional few strokes on the hand pump that were needed to get some pressure from the little overhead tank of warm water. She'd pulled the shower door closed, but I could still see her bare shoulders; she smiled at me, "Thanks James, just dump it anywhere, I'll see you shortly."

Then she resumed washing herself, and I managed to get to the bedroom before pulling my cock from my trousers and coming in a few seconds. I glanced guiltily at Petra, lying serenely in her mysterious netherworld, and I had a sudden panicky feeling that she could see and hear everything.

When Donna emerged from the bathroom, smelling fresh, dressed in a lightweight but modest blue dress, I gratefully left her alone with Petra while I, too, recovered my personal hygiene. As I showered, the water now barely tepid, I couldn't take my mind off the recent presence of Donna, naked, right there in the shower. My erection returned; I forced myself to think about fucking Petra as I masturbated again, a smaller spurt of my seed mingled with the soapy foam that gurgled away down the drain.

I slept a little on the couch downstairs, then went out to attend to the growing tunnels. I managed to forget myself in the habitual work: weeding, watering, checking for insect pests, thinning the new fruit on the espaliered pears and apples and apricots.

"So, this is where it all happens then, eh?"

I almost jumped out of my skin; Donna put a steadying hand on my forearm and said, "Oh, sorry James, I didn't mean to make you jump. I guess you've been a bit tense for a few days?"

Few years, more like, I thought, as I smiled at her and shook my head, "No, I'm fine, Donna, just lost in thought." The casual touch of her hand left a tingling in my skin. My pulse increased; I felt a stirring in my cock. "How's Petra then? Does she seem okay to you?"

"James, for a woman in a coma, she's as good as she can be. Are you nearly done for the day? I've got a lot to tell you."

We walked together back to the house; Donna's hip brushed mine as we exited the growing-tunnel, and my cock became firmer. Had I been alone, I'd have adjusted my clothing to accommodate it; as it was, I had to let it strain, getting insistently harder as I tried not to glance sideways at Donna. By Civic standards she was dressed modestly, but to me her dress was tantalizing, showing a hint of cleavage and allowing the shape of her nipples to be discerned.

Donna went to check on Petra, and I began preparing an evening meal. A few minutes later Donna rejoined me, "She's fine. There's really no point checking on her every few minutes, you know; it's just a matter of waiting now. I'll leave the monitor on for a few days yet, but her heart is steady. I'd guess she's well beyond the danger stage."

Donna helped me, laying the table, drying and putting away the dishes from lunch. And then, as we ate, she started to tell me about the research she'd been doing.

"I've found out a whole bunch of family history, as well as a few medical things that don't really help. Petra is pretty unique you know—even among our strange family—she seems to have the longest absences, although I can't be sure about some of the earlier relatives. Some of them may have been taken for dead when they weren't.

"Petra's problem seems to be the worst ever from another point of view, too: nobody else seems to have had orgasms so readily. Most of us have just avoided coming too often. Not difficult the way most men behave when they're fucking. Me and all the cousins I've spoken to have had a pretty normal sex life, just rationing out the actual orgasms.

"Cousin Janie over in Bristol has the next worst case that I know of; she comes quite easily, and her absences are usually about two or three days. Her heart goes into a more irregular state than Petra's though, so in that sense she's got the bigger problem.

"I eventually got Mum and Gran to talk about it. Mum's first-ever come nearly killed her —Gran had left it too long without warning her. She nearly drowned in the bath when she was twelve. Gran herself suffered only very short absences, like me, and she didn't take it as seriously as she should have done. If she hadn't needed to use the loo herself at the time, Mum would have been dead.

"I've talked to the few specialists that are left, and the general agreement is that the pleasure center in the brain must have some abnormal connection to the brainstem, triggering disruptions to basic body functions. This aberrant link is obviously inherited, so some little strand of DNA, peculiar to our family, must be identifiable somewhere.

"The trouble is we don't have the means to look for it. All that wonderful research that was going on back in the twenties has been abandoned. They had the whole genome mapped, and were gradually working through it, finding the function of each little bit, then Yellowstone decided to blow its top. The medical world has only recently started to think about getting back to any serious research; we've been busy dealing with more pressing problems."

"Talking of Yellowstone," I asked, "has anything been heard from the U.S. yet? They can't all be dead, surely?"

"Oh, yeah! The Civic exploration team finally reported back just a few days ago. They'd had all their communication gear impounded by the interim government over there, and they'd all been held as suspected terrorists. Apparently a lot of people in the U.S. thought that they'd been subjected to a massive coordinated nuclear attack. Of course, when the lava-flow hit Idaho it released a lot of radiation from the stored nuclear waste, and that helped convince people of the attack theory.

"Everywhere was like us, tremors and quakes of every size and type; confusion and panic and no harvests for several years. They've got a communication network running again now, and have just reestablished contact with some other countries. There are about five million survivors on the eastern seaboard, a few thousand in California—which is now a long thin island about forty miles off the west coast.

"And there's a couple of million up in the northwest. They've decided to forget the old U.S./Canada border; no one was sure where it was anyway. Vancouver and Seattle are gone. They've just declared the existence of the Nation of Columbia, capital city Spokane. The Canadian government in Ottawa, and the USA itself, still based in Washington, D.C., have accepted the secession. Nothing much else they could do really, with a couple of thousand miles of ash, lava, and new oceans between them and the new state!

"The global death toll was probably about five billion altogether, but we can't be sure yet. We still haven't heard from a lot of places, and it'll be decades yet before anyone launches a communication satellite again."

Donna fell silent, a faraway look in her eyes. I knew, from some of the letters she'd exchanged with Petra, that she'd seen some terrible sights during her military service, and had helped deal with major epidemics. It was an open secret, a shameful but accepted fact, that "dealing with" epidemics had often involved the mercy killing of many thousands of people who, injured and ill, were beyond real help. The Civic Military Medical Corps, in which Donna had been a colonel, was said to have helped more people to a quick death than it had saved.

I could not concentrate on these thoughts without feeling panicky, I was always acutely aware of how little medical help was available in our new world. I found myself distracted by the physical closeness of Donna, as we lingered over glasses of wine, the kitchen door standing open to the mild evening air, the scent of apple blossom wafting on a light breeze. I could still smell Donna's alluring perfume, and was finding it impossible not to imagine reaching across the table, kissing her, touching her. My cock had grown stiff again, and it was an effort not to touch myself under the edge of the table.

Donna suddenly shook herself and sat up straight,

"So, come on, James, let's get this washing-up cleared away. I need to get some sleep; it's been a long day. Do you want me to look at Petra again before I turn in?

"Not unless you think there's any point; as you say, she's perfectly stable now. Don't worry about the washing-up, Donna, I'll finish it. You get to bed. I've put a few things ready for you in the room next to the bathroom. Everything is a bit primitive by Civic standards, I'm afraid, but there's plenty of spare bedclothes in the chest in there, so you won't be cold."

"Hell, don't worry about me, James, I've been used to worse than this, you know! During the Hungarian plague-riots I never actually got out of my clothes for nine weeks! We all had lice by the time we got back to the R and R base in Geneva! Your home may be simple, dear, but believe me, if you're clean you're a cut above a lot of people these days. Most of East Civic is still short of clean water.

"Look," she rooted about in her big backpack, "I want you to take one of these. It's just a mild sedative, but it'll give you the best night's sleep you've had for ages, and I think you need it, James. You're looking really tired and tense. I'll hear Pet's alarm if there's any problem."

I took the pill from her hand gratefully, swallowed it down straight away with the last sip of my wine. The thought of a relaxed sleep was truly tempting.

"Don't stay up too long then," Donna added, "that'll work within half an hour! Goodnight."

Donna leaned close to me and kissed my cheek lightly, I felt a shudder of guilty arousal. She was so much like Petra; I felt that same rush of sexual chemistry and couldn't help but think of what people often said—if it's that strong it goes both ways.

I decided that the washing-up could wait till morning, and I went off to bed, gazing at Petra's serene face as I got undressed. I kissed her cheek gently as I always did, then got into my lonely bed and fell quickly into a deep sleep.

I guess it was the effect of the sedative; I had the most intense and vivid dreams. I seemed to wake, and thought Petra stood over me, in one of her drab neck-to-ankle dresses. Her hair, which usually hung free, was scraped back, out of sight. She stroked my face gently then trailed her fingertips firmly down my chest, caressing my nipples. I struggled to sit up and take her in my arms, but I couldn't move a muscle, nor make a sound. It was then I realized that I was dreaming.

I relaxed, drifting in and out of the dream, enjoying the unfamiliar feel of Petra's hand, then her mouth, on my swollen cock. Several times I felt about to come, then would drift away again into the depths of sleep.

At another point in my dreaming, I seemed to hover above my own body, looking down as Petra's head moved at my groin. My dream-self watched then as she walked back toward the bed at the side of the room, and I saw her gaze down at her own inert body.

As I drifted in and out of deep sleep, still hazily aware of my arousal but unable to move, my dreaming shifted into a more tense phase: I seemed to hear a sibilant whispering, and it seemed that I was lying on Petra's single bed. I had breasts, and someone was kneading them, pulling hard at the nipples. A jolt of arousal shot through me, moistening the vulva I could now feel as my own. I was still unable to move or speak as the harsh voice hissed a stream of vitriol into my ear and the unkind hands pulled my legs apart and began mauling my groin.

I strained in my unfamiliar dream-body to make out the words:

"You're st . . . a bitch, Pet . . . big sister . . . never forgotten . . . you muscled in . . . my first boyfrie . . . when I was sixt . . . you didn't want him . . . You just didn . . . me to have him . . . remember . . . you showed me . . . to wank when I was twelve . . . could have killed me, you c . . . Lucky . . . my absences are so short . . . really pissed you off . . . came round after half an hour! . . . were you thinking about?

"And I knew . . . you were doing, Pet, th . . . when I came back . . . found you play . . . ith my clit! You thought if I came aga . . . ile I was absent . . . kill me! . . . it might have done, Pe . . . second disrupti . . . signal to the brai . . . before recovery from the first o . . . might well kill any . . . Not that life is so precious any more, Pet, not that I couldn't stand one more death in the world!

". . . jealous of me, . . . after I'd grown up . . . cause I wa . . . taller and had bigger . . . It . . . ly chews me up sti . . . And you turn . . . um and Dad against me . . . decided to go into the military . . . wrote . . . loads of times . . . ey never repli . . . I was crawling thro . . . charnel heaps, closing my min . . . horror I saw ever . . . day . . . ave been quite . . . ood to have my parents' suppor . . . you took it all away. . . . your fanciful drea . . . new age of peace and love—Christ! Who do you think was trying to clear all the shit out of the way so the world could start again?"

The dream-voice became stronger, and the insistent rubbing in my vulva became so intense that despite my fear I could feel the first hints of an orgasm, deep in my belly.

"The military, Pet, that's who. We were the ones who had to drive through the tilted, smoldering ruins of Hamburg out to the new East Cliffs of Jutland, past the lopsided towns and villages full of corpses. We were the ones who had to look out over that vast new ocean and watch the waves bringing in the drowned debris of Copenhagen.

"We were the ones who had to sail out over that new ocean, Pet—while you fannied around dreaming how nice the New World could be—out across what should have been Stockholm, Helsinki, Tallinn, Saint Petersburg, hearing over the shortwave from the teams who were failing to find Riga and Vilnius and Minsk.

"So, Pet, while you were busy with the lucky citizens of London, Paris, Brussels, and Amsterdam, sweeping up the debris of the 'Big' Slip, and finding out how to grow vegetables again in your pretty little slightly difficult world, I was in Hell, and you and Mum and Dad were busy disapproving of me because I wore a gun at my hip.

"I'll tell you this Pet: Civic, and your little fledgling New Celtic Fringe, only exist because the military had to grit its teeth and eradicate the vast hordes of plague-ridden refugees heading up from the drowned shores of the Mediterranean.

"My gun did more to create the new world than your fucking fruit and vegetables did, Pet, and I wouldn't have minded if only you didn't keep wanting to take it all away from me all the time! You're a selfish bitch, Petra, you always were, and you've made James's life hell. Just because you can't come you expect him to live like a monk, too! He loves you, Pet, though I can't see why, and you don't even give him a regular blow job or anything! You don't deserve him, Pet, you truly don't."

In my dream I seemed once more to wake up, this time as Petra, but still unable to move or speak. I continued to lie helpless, my arousal now focused intensely in my engorged clitoris. I could feel the bitterly gentle touch of a fingertip circling, tickling, caressing—then pinching, cleverly and knowingly turning the last moment of pleasure into intense pain.

My orgasm was inescapable, as the tremors started to shake my body and the sparks started to fly in my brain, I was jolted back into my own male body, sobbing in grief and fear and relief as I arched uncontrollably, all tension flung out in a few seconds of racking convulsions. My semen spurted from me, sliding onto my belly.

I slumped back into flaccid helplessness; a deep and relaxed sleep overwhelmed me, pulling me down into blissful slumber.

I woke in a panic. My bladder was near to bursting, and I had swung my legs out of bed before I realized that Petra's heart-monitor alarm was wailing and that Donna was standing over Petra pummeling her in the rhythmic pattern of the resuscitation routine.

Donna stopped, delivered the two deep breaths of air into Petra's mouth, then resumed, gasping, "James, wake up! I don't know what the hell's happened! I heard the alarm and came straight away, but it looks like she's gone! Pet! Oh Pet! Come on!"

I was standing beside Donna by this time, and said "Let me take over the compression, you do the breathing." Donna complied immediately, and I waited while she delivered two more breaths, then I started the fifteen pushes, hard, desperate, willing the impact to jolt Petra's heart back into motion.

I don't know how long we continued.

Eventually we looked at each other, not needing to say a

word. Donna drew the blanket up over Petra, concealing the reddened skin where I'd been pounding her unresponsive chest, the wet stretched lips where Donna had been forcing breath into her unwilling lungs.

I wept as I staggered to the bathroom. As I relieved myself I became aware through my grief that I was still naked from bed, and a crust of dried semen pulled at the hairs on my belly. I wrapped a towel around myself and went back to the bedroom. Donna was gone, but reappeared a moment later, dressed in her baggy jumpsuit again. Had she been naked before? I couldn't remember. The scent of arousal lingered in the air around Petra's bed.

Two days later Donna and I stood beside Petra's grave. We had performed as good a funeral as we could manage between us, and I felt empty. Petra had been the focus of my life, its bedrock. I thought to myself that I wasn't the sort of person who'd be very good at living alone; I thought about all the ways that she'd enriched my life, and then I thought, guiltily, of the ways that my relationship with her had impoverished me, too.

Donna was quiet, had said almost nothing since Petra's death. We'd eaten together; she'd worked alongside me to do the essential daily tasks in the garden; together we'd prepared and buried Petra's body. I hadn't mentioned my deranged dream of the night of Petra's death.

For a few more days I drifted through routine jobs and periods of grief-stricken inaction. I sometimes noticed that Donna was beside me, helping, observing, quietly crying on a few occasions. Once, in an intense moment, we caught each other's eye and a second later were holding each other, weeping, consoling. Only after a few minutes, when we had calmed down, did I realize how tightly Donna held me, and how my cock, impervious to grief, rose hard and desperate, pushing against her stomach. When I tried to move away, she held me tight a moment longer and seemed to move her belly against me as we parted.

She said, "James, I've written a letter to Mum and Dad. How do we send it?"

"Um, what day is it? Is it Thursday?"

"Yeah, I think so. Yes, it is."

"Okay, well, sometime tomorrow Dougal will call by, probably about lunchtime. He's our Brehon, the nearest thing we've got to any sort of official. He tours the area, calling in on all the holdings, hearing about problems, arbitrating disputes, collecting and delivering post, telling us where and when to turn up to help with harvests or building projects. He'll take the letter to Dunkeld; the ferrymen will post it in Peebles."

"Fine. So did this Dougal guy know Petra then? Will he pass the news around here?"

"Oh, Dougal knows pretty well everyone. Petra never liked him; she thought he wasn't sharp enough for the job. Being a Brehon is very demanding; he ends up being general advisor and counselor to everyone, too. There's one for every county of Scots Fringe, from Moray to Bute, and I think the other parts of the Fringe have the same system. All the Brehons are kept in touch with each other by a few specialist ones, who travel about all over the Fringe."

"Does he have any actual authority?"

"Yeah, in theory he can enforce his own decisions in arbitrated cases, and deal with anyone who's violent, but I don't think he's had to do much of that sort of thing. We're all too busy to make trouble for each other!"

"So," mused Donna, "he's like a sheriff and a vicar and a postman and a gossip all in one?"

"Yeah, I guess. He's just our Brehon—and he's the one that the donkey men would tell if any strangers came on the ferry. I bet he knows about your visit already."

"Hmm! Well, I'm going to have a shower. Then I'll start getting some supper ready. You'd better get this bit of weeding finished if you want these beans to stand a chance. See you in an hour or so."

When I went in to eat, Donna had changed out of the baggy jumpsuit she'd been in for the last few days, and was wearing a tight black T-shirt over black leggings. Her hair, now a short stubble, was wet, and I noticed that the T-shirt clung to her breasts, showing the shape of her nipples, as though she hadn't dried herself thoroughly.

I said, "Dougal, the Brehon, is quite a dedicated Prim. It would be easier all round if you wore something more modest tomorrow."

Donna's eyes flashed in anger for a moment, but she only said, "Hah! This is a bit too sexy for your local sheriff, huh?"

"Well, you know, he'll be wanting to know how Petra died, and he'll want to know all about you. There's no point making everything more difficult by antagonizing him."

"Well, I've got my medic ID with me. I presume he's not going to argue with me about Pet's death? He's not a doctor as well as everything else?"

Donna's voice carried a note of worry that I hadn't heard before.

"Of course not," I said, "and I've no intention of trying to explain to him about her absences! She died of heart failure didn't she?"

"Yes, of course."

We ate our supper, chatting a little more easily than on the last few evenings, and as Donna carried our used plates to the sink I found myself captivated for a few moments by the sight of her thighs and buttocks, tightly emphasized in the close-fitting leggings. When she stretched up to put the salt back on its shelf, the leggings pulled tight into her groin, and I felt such a surge of lust that it was all I could do to remain seated.

When Donna kissed me goodnight later, she held me close for a moment, and let her lips linger on my cheek, she seemed about to say something but then didn't.

Dougal arrived shortly before lunch. I was working in the growing-tunnels when I heard the sound of his horse's hooves on the crumbling tarmac of the yard. I went out to meet him just as Donna emerged from the house, and I started to speak.

"Good morning, Dougal. This is Petra's sister, Medical Colonel Donna Rensworth; Donna, this is Dougal McFadden, Brehon of Tay and Athol. I'm sorry to have to tell you, Dougal, that Petra is d . . ."

Dougal cut me off short with an impatient gesture, he had not moved from beside his horse since catching sight of Donna. He stared at her appraisingly; his hand hovered near the rifle that protruded from its saddle-holster.

Donna, too, stood unmoving; she stared back at Dougal, her right hand hidden inside the pocket of one of Petra's big gowns. For a moment I could hardly recognize either of them; I did not understand what was happening, but suddenly felt very nervous.

After what seemed like hours, Dougal relaxed, stepped

away from his horse and spoke very loudly and firmly, offering neither Donna nor me a chance to interrupt.

"Good morning, Petra, I'm pleased to see you looking so well. I'm sorry to have to tell you that I've received a request from the Civic authorities, asking for information about your sister Donna, and asking for permission to send an investigator here. It seems she's been charged with various breaches of the Civic Human Rights Code. Some nonsense drummed up by the silly media, no doubt, calling her names like "Donna Death" and "Colonel Corpse." Too stupid for words, in my opinion. The military did what it had to do for the good of the healthy communities.

"I heard yesterday that one of the passing donkey men saw you digging a grave, James. No doubt that was for Donna Rensworth, who unfortunately had a fatal fall while crossing that rickety bridge of yours.

"Now, Petra, I have a proposition for you. Times are changing again; the population of the Fringe is growing. We need to recruit more Brehons and increase the law-enforcement side of our work. We thought that with your knowledge of your sister's experience and her connections in the military, you'd make a good traveling Brehon, maybe give us all a bit of weapons training, maybe put us in touch with arms suppliers. It's the sort of life that would keep you out of sight of those who want to pester you because of what your sister is supposed to have done.

"You could stay here with James until the apple harvest, while your hair grows back. By then I'll have had a chance to explain the situation to my colleagues. What do you say?"

Donna stood silent for a few seconds then spoke briskly.

"Assuming that I don't have to answer to idiots, Dougal,

and assuming that I end up having some reasonable comfort in between the active service, you've got a deal. Perhaps you'll stay to lunch? And perhaps I should write to my parents telling them of Donna's death; I believe you can carry post to Dunkeld for us?"

"Lunch would be very welcome, thank you, and yes, I'll carry your letter. The Civic Authorities will no doubt intercept it, mind."

Donna gave Dougal a withering look, as if to say, 'Do you think I don't know that?'

Over lunch, Dougal said, "Well, James, you'll be needing some help around here if Petra takes up the Brehon duties. She'll be traveling from Norway to Brittany and all points between; she'll not be picking many herbs for you.

"There's a couple of young widows, living in Dunkeld at the moment, who are looking for a new start. They're sisters, about thirty and thirty-three. Their men both went down with that ferry that was lost. They were at Kirkmichael for the last rye harvest; perhaps you'd remember them, Anne and Bridget O'Connell, quite tall, dark-haired. Anne has a boy of twelve, a sharp-witted lad, good with animals. Bridget has twin girls, only eight at present, but already able to help in the house."

I vaguely remembered the women; I'd helped with the rye harvest at Kirkmichael last autumn while Petra had looked after our holding for a few days.

"What are you saying, Dougal? Are you trying to find a new wife for me?"

"James, Anne, and Bridget need a new home, away from the sea, and you're obviously going to need help here. If either or both of them look on you favorably, so be it. They have a small herd of goats too, and two horses. Shall I ask them to come and help with your apple harvest so you can get to know each other?"

"Yes, okay, Dougal, I'll meet them. To be honest I believe I could make this place quite a productive holding, with enough help. I'd better get a shed and paddock finished if I'm to have goats!"

When Dougal had left, carrying the letter that I'd had no chance to see, there was an awkward silence. I started the washing up; Donna went out.

When I went out later to do some work, I found her sitting at Petra's graveside. Her face was streaked by tears but held no expression that I could make sense of. When I spoke to her she jumped up, startled, and wiped her face. She turned away. "I'll see you in the tunnels in a while, James. I'm just going to wash my face."

She joined me ten minutes later, dressed in her tight black leggings and T-shirt, and apparently cheerful. We weeded and watered together, and she helped me move a rusty, leaky old water-butt that I'd been meaning to get rid of for ages. By the time we'd maneuvered it out into the yard, we were both sweaty and streaked with rust. Outside, we were able to push the butt onto its side and roll it. Without discussion, we both seemed to have the same idea. We pushed the thing across the yard, onto a rough grassy area, towards the nearest open chasm, and watched delightedly as it rolled on its own the last few meters. When it fell, producing a loud crunching boom, we cheered and hugged each other.

We couldn't seem to stop hugging each other; Donna's lips found my earlobe and I was lost in a hot mist of lust and need. I kissed her mouth, and she opened to me, sucking on my tongue as she slid a hand down my body to find my erection, pressing and squirming against me.

With one hand I squeezed Donna's buttocks, pulling her close, with the other I got inside her T-shirt. The feel of her breast in my hand almost made me swoon. I gasped with delight at the large size of her hardened nipple and could not decide whether I wanted to continue kissing her mouth or to suck on this treasure.

Impatiently, she pushed me away, making space between us, and began pulling at my clothes.

"Quick!" she gasped, "Oh, James, quick! I want you!"

In our clumsiness it seemed to take ages to get our clothes off, but then we were lying naked on the grass, panting and moaning as we tried to grope and kiss every part of each other at once.

It was vertiginous, a fall into the inevitable. Within seconds Donna's hand had gripped my straining shaft and pulled it towards her vulva. She wrapped her legs around me as I pushed past the hot, slippery folds and felt her body rise to meet mine.

We thrust at each other madly. She tilted her pelvis up to grind her clitoris against me, gasping and trembling as we found the right movement. It lasted only a few more seconds before we were both crying out in ecstasy, locked together, rocking in that timeless, all-too-brief glimpse of eternity.

I lay breathless, still inside her, my cock still gripped by the fading spasms of her orgasm. I saw her eyes turn up, heard her breathing falter, and felt the slump of her body as she fainted away.

Panic gripped me, though I told myself not to be stupid. I listened for her heartbeat and found it easily. Quick, but firm and regular, it reassured me. I lifted Donna up and carried her into the house, laying her gently on the floor in the kitchen. I sat on the floor beside her, gazing at her breasts; at her toned, muscular legs and arms; her flat stomach; her vacant inscrutable expression as she drifted by the nearer shores of the vast ocean that Petra once sailed.

By the time I'd fetched our clothes, and dressed myself, Donna's breathing was strong and deep. By the time I'd brewed a pot of mint tea she was snoring quietly. She woke after about ten more minutes and sat up, momentarily confused.

"Shit! I wish that didn't happen. Oh, James, tea! Thank you. Pass my T-shirt; it's a bit nippy in here!"

Throughout the summer Donna and I slept together, though we never recaptured the urgency and need of that first time. Her hair is long now, and the apples are ripening.

In a few days a crowd of people with their tents and donkeys and children and noise will arrive. The place will be a whirl of activity as we pick apples, wrapping the good ones for storage, pressing the poorer ones for juice, which will go to the brewers at the monastery near Kirkmichael.

In a few days, I will meet Mary and Bridget and their children, and we will make the decisions that will shape our lives.

In a few days, Donna will be gone; traveling Brehon Petra will set off to meet Dougal's colleagues at a meeting near Ballater, where they use the old Royal House at Balmoral as their headquarters. She'll take with her a string of eight donkeys, carrying the trunks and cases that have been arriving here mysteriously over the last three months.

When she has gone, I will erect the little gravestone we've made, inscribed with the name "Donna Rensworth." Petra's grave must remain unmarked.

So much is gone; absences shape my world.

Secondhand

Chris Bridges

A parking space up front! A good omen, Martha thought. She got out of her Jetta, locked it carefully—she'd been wearing gloves for so long now that handling car keys was nothing—and headed into the thrift shop to see what her sex life was about to be like.

Not very crowded today. Good. She grabbed a shopping basket and made some perfunctory browsing motions through the skirt aisle, but her attention was on the rack at the far end of the store, where the lingerie was. There was a large woman over there now, sifting through the hosiery and underwear bin. Martha shuddered. How could anyone buy secondhand panties? I mean, doesn't she know where they've been? Martha did, better than most people.

After a few moments of sideways observation it became obvious that the woman was living in a dream world anyway. She consistently passed over clothing that might actually fit her to grab for undies that would have to stretch to fit Kate Moss. Martha smiled to herself. Any minute now she'll get fed up and . . .

The woman left, but not before storming over to the counter and complaining loudly that all the clothing was sized wrong and how dare they treat their customers that way. The door slammed loudly after her passing, and Martha fancied she could feel a collective sigh of relief from the other shoppers. After glancing around to see where everybody was, she meandered, in a purely accidental, totally coincidental path that led her directly to the lingerie rack.

It was full. Martha took a deep breath at all the possibilities. Too many weekends she had come in to see the same threadbare rags hanging in the same place. This looked more like someone had turned in a collection of quality things, and she knew without looking that the prices would reflect it. But that was okay. Martha got a lot more out of these garments than anyone would think. She looked around a final time—no one was paying attention—and she carefully pulled off her right glove, and brushed her hand against the first nightie.

. . . red driving thrust and purple-black fuck and biting to taste his rich blood as he attacked, pounding and splitting her with his cock . . .

Martha yanked her hand away. Bit too rough for me, she thought. I always have stomach trouble after one of those. She began lightly touching the next few dainties, just enough to get the barest hint of each one.

She had looked it up once. It was called psychometry, the ability to touch an item and "read" its history. Thank God it only happened when she touched something with her bare hands, or she'd have gone insane the first year. While she'd always been very sensitive to her surroundings, it wasn't unmanageable until the night in high school when she started to get into a friend's new (used) car and suddenly found herself in the midst of someone else's flaming maelstrom of heat and death. She had screamed and clutched at her face with both hands, and the vision had stopped cold, even if the memory of it didn't.

Thus followed years of therapy, during which she was very careful not to reveal any more psychic ability than she had to. She'd seen the *X Files*, she knew what would happen. After that were many more years of loneliness. A few abortive relationships and traumatic experiences taught her quickly that it's not good to know everything about your loved one. How could she live with anyone when every time she picked up something of theirs she became them, thought their thoughts, knew their secrets? She wore gloves every second she was out of her apartment, and was careful never to touch anything she had owned for less than a year in case it carried memories of its manufacture, or some horrible disaster that happened in the store while it was on the shelf.

One night, depressed and lonely, she was doing her laundry in the basement of her apartment building (with her own detergent, and without ever touching any of the dirty, memory-laden quarters) when the young blond girl from the apartment above hers came in with her own basket. Lucy was her name, Martha knew, and she was a college girl with a cat and a boyfriend and a red Miata. They nodded pleasantly to each other and went about their business. Martha kept her eyes downward, slightly embarrassed; many a night she had heard the thumping and gasping coming from the room above, and she considered her own bitter envy to be inappropriate. Lucy dumped her clothes out on the wooden counter and started separating them, only to realize she'd forgotten her change. Martha agreed to watch her pile, and she dashed upstairs, all bounces and golden shining hair.

On the top of her clothing was a crumpled nightgown.

Martha listened for movement outside, and then lifted the nightie. It was a sheer thing, pink and lace-trimmed and entirely useless for modesty or comfortable sleep. Martha, flannel to her very core, had never worn anything remotely like it in her life. In her mind she heard the sighs and the moans and the gasps.

Quickly, before she could change her mind, she slipped off her glove and grasped the nightie tightly in her fist.

When Lucy came back down with a Pringles can half-full of quarters, Martha was just finishing up her load and heading out. She waved to Martha, that nice lady, before turning back to her washing. She never noticed the missing nightie, or the way Martha's face glowed with sweat, or how Martha trembled as she hurried back upstairs with a basket of wet laundry.

Martha was trembling again at the cash register. She always did; it seemed impossible that the cashier couldn't tell why she was buying five pieces of lingerie, no two even remotely the same size. As always, there was no outcry of screams of "Pervert!" and she clutched the bag to her chest as she hurried out to her car. She rushed inside her apartment, locked the door, and tossed the bag through her bedroom door so she could begin her weekend ritual, crystallized over the last few years.

One glass of red wine, to accompany her into the bathtub. One capful of "Amethyst Dreams" in the steaming water. Exactly one-half hour in the tub, to relax and soothe her and to make her skin soft and smooth. Dry off with a thick, fluffy towel, and then walk naked-but-for-gloves where her fantasies were waiting in a white plastic bag.

She stretched luxuriously across her covers with a delighted, anticipatory smile, and then sat up with her legs straight out in front of her. Her gloved hands shook the lingerie out of the bag into a small silky heap. Martha brought her hands in front of her face and began to slowly tug at the fingertips of her right glove. The heat began to build, a purely Pavlovian reaction built up over the last two years, and she felt her nipples tighten into knurled buttons. With naked hands, she grabbed the first nightie, bunched it up against her breasts, and she was.

. . . she was Michelle and she was slipping her new teddy on over smooth shoulders, feeling it drift down to caress her curves. Hank was due home any time now, and she was ready to show him that the honeymoon wasn't over yet, not by a long shot. She slipped on some panties so he could tear them off, applied perfume in the five main areas, and scooted under the covers to wait for him. She wasn't waiting long; she heard his car almost immediately and the front door right after.

"Honey?" he called. "You left me already?"

"I'm in here," Michelle/Martha called in a husky voice. "Did you bring dinner?"

Hank appeared in the doorway, a burly bear of a man with a big grin and a large bulge leading the way. "Happens I did, ma'am," he said. "Hot and ready, if it's not still tired from last night!" He all but leaped out of his clothes and jumped onto the bed, capturing Michelle in a rough embrace and kissing her throat and breasts. She arched up to meet him and her fingernails dragged lines across his broad back. His hands pushed her teddy aside to pinch at her nipples. His cock was a hard, red-hot presence below, pushing stubbornly at the sheets to get to her. Michelle swept the bedclothes aside to reveal herself in all her glory—tanned, tight, and aching with need—and she slowly rolled ov[illegible] her hands and knees, planting her face solidly [illegible] and pushing her rounded ass into Hank's cro[illegible]

"You know what I want, lover," she said. Michelle shook with desire as she felt the first touch of Hank's cock pushing against her asshole . . . .

"Whoops!" Shivering, Martha pitched the nightie away and took a deep, cleansing breath as she fought to ignore the pulsing signals coming from her groin. It wasn't that she was against anal play, exactly. She certainly had no problem with anybody else enjoying it, she just didn't particularly want to enjoy it herself. And enjoy it she would have, she knew from experience. If the person she became enjoyed what happened, then Martha would enjoy what happened just as much, at least until she let go. It was the feeling of revulsion afterwards that she wanted to avoid.

Anal sex was just so undignified, thought Martha, virgin and untouched at thirty-seven. That was one advantage, she supposed. She could try all the sexual kinks she wanted without fear of discovery, disease, or social acceptance, and so eventually, hesitantly, she had. Martha had, at times, been a lesbian, an exhibitionist, a swinger, a submissive (dominants didn't wear nighties, apparently, or else didn't give them to Goodwill afterwards), old, young, white, black, brown, yellow, red, handicapped, athletic, thin, fat, and every possible combination of those and more. Intact though she may be, she had figured that after two years she had fucked almost a thousand men, sort of. She would have had an impressive roster of women as well, but while lesbian memories invariably caused massive orgasms, she always felt uncomfortable about how much she enjoyed them.

Her disappointment was easy to quell. She usually counted herself lucky if even a third of her purchases were keepers. She firmly put away the insistent memory of how badly she had wanted her ass filled and she picked up the second nightie.

. . . one last bow and it was tied in place and look at you, aren't you the pretty, pretty girl! The diaphanous white cloth clung to rounded curves and the full-length mirror faithfully reflected every one. Balding head, bright eyes, straggly mustache over unshaven face, skinny pale shoulders, whorls of chest hair disappearing into the delicate neckline, middle-aged pot belly pushing the cloth out over Bill/Martha's dick which was rising, rising . . .

This time Martha threw the nightie all the way out into the hall where it snagged on a picture frame. The gift had its drawbacks, that was for sure. It had taken quite a bit of trial and error before Martha settled on her routine. At first she thought, despite her first encounter, that panties would provide the strongest charge. Unfortunately she quickly discovered that while they were often filled with incredibly powerful memories of toe-curling foreplay, they would usually go cold right when the owner (or owner's lover) yanked them off, leaving Martha shuddering with interrupted passion. Two or three traumatic menstrual memories after that and she decided to avoid other people's underwear forever.

When she heard about porn stars and amateur Web girls selling used panties, she did wonder for a moment whether or not there were others like her out there, buying them for the memories inside, but it wasn't enough for her to consider buying any herself. Besides, secondhand lingerie was cheaper.

The third one was a long nightgown with little lace roses at the neck. It looked like something Martha might have chosen for herself, should she ever wear anything to bed that wasn't chosen for warmth, and she had been intending to save it for last but after the first two she badly needed one to work. Casting caution to the winds she rapidly pulled it over her head and wrapped her hands around her breasts, crushing the thin cloth between them.

. . . and she was Anne and she was holding the nightgown up to look at it, while a handsome man sat next to her on the bed. He was in his forties, with a salt and pepper beard and some streaks of gray and silver in his hair that made Anne/Martha want to run her fingers through it, again and again. Right now he looked absurdly pleased with himself at having chosen correctly. Anne held the nightgown to her chest and leaned over to kiss him soundly on the mouth before shooing him out the door. She stood up and let her robe fall to the ground, then applied powder and lipstick before putting the nightgown on. It felt incredible, exciting her nerve endings and tugging her nipples erect so they formed points in the cloth. She could hear John brushing his teeth in the next room, and she smiled to herself at his thoughtfulness.

John came back to a darkened room. He made his way to the bed to find a double-armful of scented delight. His hands roamed over the familiar wonders made new again by a satiny wrap that slid like oil over blood-hot skin. Never once did he fail to find a sensitive spot or a fiery nerve ending, and within seconds Anne was panting and nearly mindless with want. She gasped aloud as he ran his hand along her side, over her hip, to squeeze at a ripe buttock before slipping between her legs. His knowing fingers pushed the slick cloth against and around her, tugging at her skin and setting her folds aflame. The sensations threatened to overwhelm her and push her too close, too fast, so she grabbed the hem of the gown and wrapped it around his cock, drawing it back and forth and causing him to cry out in surprise and desire.

A race began, the fever building and cascading, until both combatants surrendered and merged into one. The nightgown slipped up over her thighs as he entered her, and it slid between their bodies as they moved, adding an intoxicating sensation that drove them harder and harder until they roared into each other's mouth and . . .

Martha bucked and came and came, feeling John deep inside her, tasting his mouth, bearing his weight, her heels drumming on his back. She let herself drop flat to the mattress, her arms and legs straight out, and rode out the afterglow. It was always an odd experience—the rapture of the climax, the joy of togetherness, the feeling of loss as the memory faded, and the relief at being Martha again. This one had been more exciting and more painful than usual. A happy, loving relationship was Martha's own secret fantasy, and this pale version was the closest she could get.

She wrapped her hand in the sheet to move that nightgown over to the side. Painful though it was, that one would get saved for later. Psychometric memories never lasted long; her own experiences quickly overrode the lingering traces of former owners. But they were usually good for two or three times before they became too faint to read, and she already had a crush on John. Not surprising, she often got crushes on some of the men she experienced. It never lasted. The sensation of abruptly knowing everything about a strange new man was a heady one, but there was always another one to replace him in the next touch.

It was a source of private amusement to Martha that she

had become a psychic slut. One more sip of wine, and she touched the next pile.

. . . tug it down over fat hips, hippo hips, and a butt that could feed China. Dunno why I wear stuff like this, no one else will ever see it, and God knows it's not as comfortable as a T-shirt. But, oh, it feels so nice on my skin, and with the lights off I can pretend I'm a beautiful model, and these hands aren't mine, they're the photographer's because I'm so beautiful and he's seen a thousand women but he can't resist me . . .

Off came the gown, and Martha resisted the impulse to throw this one even farther. She hated, hated hearing thoughts of single, unloved women. They were too close to her own, and they just depressed her even more. Fantasies were supposed to be better than your life, that was the point. What was more depressing still was that in the few seconds while she was Jill and hated herself, she remembered having a perfectly good body that was probably more attractive than Martha's own. She felt a moment of pity and sadness for Jill. At least Martha had a reason to avoid people.

Last one. She looked back longingly at the one John bought for Anne, but steeled herself to try the last one. Not a good idea to obsess on a perfect lover who's never met you, she thought, and reached for the new one. It was peach and white, and it eased over her head like smoke.

. . . and John, her John, was over her again, thrusting and grunting, the old fool. Anne/Martha tilted her hips forward to push against him and speed things up so he'd pop and she could go to sleep. Faking arousal was easy, but it did begin to wear on you after awhile. John was a good man, a decent husband, but oh Lord, Rick was incredible and young and the things he did to her drove her wild. Anne let herself remember what Rick did to her with his tongue earlier that week in the motel, and for the first time tonight she felt her juices flow.

There we go, she thought and closed her eyes. That isn't John on me, it's Rick, and he's sucking my cunt till I see spots, and he's jumping up to ram it into me and it hurts and it feels so good and I'll be damned I think I'm going to come. The phone rang. John lunged forward to pick up with a movement that nearly sent Anne over the edge, but the next words out of his mouth sent a torrent of ice water down her spine.

"Hello? Hey Jimmy. Look, I'm kind of busy right now, can I. what? They were where? The Motel 6?" Unexpected terror captured Anne's mind as John looked down at her, anguish blossoming across his face. "No, no, thank you for telling me, Jim. I have to go now." He hung up, looked at her for a long, questioning moment, then got up and left without a word. Anne shook quietly for a long time before the wracking sobs broke free and consumed her. . . .

. . . and Martha tore the gown in half, ripping it off her body with a strength that surprised her. How could Anne have done that? How could she have hurt such a good man? For she knew John, knew him and Anne intimately and completely, and as the intensity of the memory faded she realized that the first nightie she had touched in the store had been Anne's as well, the one she wore to the motel. John was the most handsome, responsible, loving man she had ever encountered, and she could hardly conceive of why any woman would stray from him, even though she had just been inside the mind of one who did. What fool would throw that away? John was perfect, and the memory of his tortured face looking down on her tore at her heart.

Riding Anne's mind she had learned all there was to know about him, his tastes, his loves, his life, their wedding day, his favorite Chinese restaurant, everything that Anne knew. She had felt the thundering passion, and she had cut out his heart, and living through both events in a matter of moments was enough to tear her own soul in two.

With a shock, she also realized something else. This had happened recently. The feelings were too fresh, too intense. That night, the night John found out about Anne's infidelity, somehow led to Anne's lingerie ending up in a thrift shop, and the possible reasons why were all Martha could think about for the rest of the night.

Sunday morning at the thrift shop, the cashier opened the front door and jumped aside as Martha rushed in, yanked the glove off her right hand, and began grabbing at every article of clothing in the store. Weirdest thing the cashier had ever seen, in a business guaranteed to attract weird customers. The lady would grab a nightgown, her eyes would pop, and she'd sag a little, then she'd shake it off and grab the next one. It was like each one gave her a migraine or something, and she was desperate to get 'em all. She went from rack to rack, shuddering with spasms, and almost went to her knees in the underwear bins, but that lady never once slowed down. Weirdest damn thing she ever saw.

Martha drove herself on, memory after memory, life after life. She dashed through the thoughts and lives of thousands of people, searching for clues to John's life, his present situation, and where she might find him. She had to know if he was all right, if he was recovering.

Her own life completely forgotten. All she could think about right now was a man she had never met, a man she had loved and lost in the space of ten minutes, a stranger with whom she was deeply in love. Waves of thoughts washed over her mind, threatening to overwhelm her in the flood, but she kept on doggedly grabbing everything within reach, looking for traces of her fantasy lover.

If I don't find him here, she thought raggedly, there are an awful lot of thrift shops out there. It's amazing the perfectly good things that people throw out. And she reached for the next memory.

My Dark and Empty Sky

Teresa Wymore

In the lulling hours of late afternoon, when my sons are with their tutor and my husband is at his office, I usually take tea and sit with my daughter watching the birds along the lake shore, but not today. Today, my daughter is dancing with other well-groomed girls at the Haverton Society, and a woman lies naked in my bed.

She kisses me with deliberation, her lips rubbing across mine, as if trying to pleasure every nerve. After she accustoms my mouth to her caresses, she moves down my neck, and her lawless touches speed my heart. I live for these secret afternoons, when an infidelity to reality becomes my only freedom, for I can imagine a better world than this perfect one.

The satin comforter slides from the bed into a burgundy pile. We snuggle under a sheet, and my adoring hands knead her powder-white flesh as it pulses warmly. Damp skin offers up its feminine musk, and when I reach lower, moisture allows an easy glide. As my fingers plunge into her, she moans and rolls onto her back. Her face slackens and strains as I stroke her wet walls.

I can imagine her wading through the foamy Mediterranean, her lithe limbs beading with water, as we love each other among the waves. I can imagine our intimate talk as we huddle close in a roof garden at sunset, seduced by the sea's moody hues and sipping wine at a café table. I can imagine many pleasures that we'll never know because our only choice is an afternoon in a country villa, drapes drawn against discovery as we love each other on sheets that smell of a man.

We roll among gold and white pillows until the annulling beauty of her eyes startles me, but I remain vigilant, appraising her like a sailor evaluating a perilous current. Men aren't the only dangerous things. Her husband manages her well, so she questions herself far more than she questions him. I worry that she may one day assume a settled indifference, as so many have, or that she may confess and be sent away. Love like ours doesn't exist, at least not on its own terms, because a century ago, science showed that desire lies beyond choice, and when gene therapies found the means to make us all desire alike, no one wanted it any other way.

When her kiss again breathes heat into my mouth, a new hunger takes hold of me. Sliding down, I brush my nose through the pillow of hair and nuzzle her tender flesh. Salt and sweat stir my blood with a scent I crave but can never truly remember. Content to lick and tease her clitoris, I lay between her legs for almost an hour before she comes in my mouth, slowly, like honey spreading. Her back arches, and she cries my name. Her legs and hips tense with each convulsive wave. Later, as I watch sweat trickle down her cheek, I wonder just how science could claim what was so obviously untrue.

Fresh from their success at demystifying desire, men of the twenty-first century began to praise unbelief as a virtue, as if science had liberated their minds, when it had merely unburdened their consciences. Science made other classes of outsiders vanish, too, like the darker races and the poor. Their utopian moment was brief, however, because the world that remained after the last ghettos disappeared disintegrated rapidly into chaos. After men had no outcasts left to unite against, no victims to certify their victory, everyone became a potential enemy, and competition became deadly. Violence erupted everywhere.

Decades of war followed, and savagery nearly eclipsed civilization altogether before men found a way to bond again. They resurrected a common enemy, an ancient group whose exclusion could transfigure their radical violence into righteousness and give them back their religion. They took away our economic freedom and our reproductive freedom and our physical freedom because they needed their vitality to build personal futures with our bodies. Lawless violence was a less appealing prospect than organized violence.

The afternoon ends too quickly. Our love must make way again for husbands and children. Feeling torn open, I shut my eyes against the sting of tears. She holds me against her chest, comforting me with her steady heartbeat. My heart aches because my faith is a woman's faith, one that doesn't translate the words of men but scenes of grace lived out by those tossed from heaven into a dark and empty sky. I know God doesn't require a victim. Only men do, because they don't realize the one sacrifice that counts is their own.

She chastises my attempt at romantic penitence and calls me decadent, and she's right, but I tell her that those who refuse healing remain blind. Her psychomachy seems like an artifact from another age, when people could legitimize their desire only by denying it was a choice. I have no such conflict, for my body and soul blissfully embrace each other, if only in her presence, for she is blessed among women. She is benediction.

Gender Bending

Boy Toy

J. T. Benjamin

I'm in a gay bar called Lester's. The strongest smell of the place isn't that of the gin or the beer or the cigarettes; it's the testosterone. All those homosexual men walking around are putting off a sexual scent so powerful it's making me dizzy. It's also making me horny.

I've spent the whole evening talking with Gary, a young man I just met tonight. He's barely twenty-one, and he's beautiful. Wavy, sandy blond hair, broad shoulders, blue eyes, and absolutely perfect teeth. He's talking about college, but I'm not paying as much attention to what he says as I am watching his mouth move and wanting to nibble on those full, red lips.

We're sitting in a booth in the back of the bar, leaning forward so we can be heard above the din of the music and the people talking. I can smell Gary's cologne. I can also smell his sex.

I find myself stroking the hairs of my goatee again. I always tend to do it when I'm thinking of sex. The gesture both smoothes the hairs and scratches the itch. I used to think it made me look distinguished, but now I fear it just makes me look pretentious. Unfortunately, it's been a much easier habit to acquire than to break.

My self-awareness is making me even more uncomfortable than I already am. I can't sit still much longer. I want to loosen my necktie and rip off my shirt and walk around naked to the waist for the rest of the night. The rigid bulge between my legs actually hurts. I'm aching for Gary to touch me and when he places his hand on my thigh, I almost jump in relief. I put my hand on top of his. I whisper, "Want to go into the ladies' room?"

Gary blushes. Since Lester's caters exclusively to men, the ladies' room doesn't get much use. Somebody had the bright idea to put a lock on the door, so that a person could have someplace to spend a little quiet time with a new friend. Gary says, "Sure. Let's go."

I lock the ladies' room door behind me. Gary's waiting in the nearest stall. His pants are down around his ankles. His huge, erect cock is staring at me. I get down on my knees in front of him and caress the big, beautiful thing for a moment. He lets out a quiet little moan and then, when I take him into my mouth, his moan becomes a groan.

My nostrils are full of the musk that his cock is giving off. I can taste his salty pre-cum almost instantly. I slide my tongue up and down his shaft and then relax my throat muscles, letting his cock go all the way into my mouth.

Gary doesn't say anything for a while, and I'm happy to simply hear him breathe and grunt while I blow him. When I sense he's getting closer, when his cock throbs and swells even larger, I pick up my pace. I also pause long enough to wet the middle finger of my right hand, and when I resume sucking on him, my finger works its way between Gary's firm, tight ass cheeks, and it finds his anus. I massage it with my finger for a moment, and then the finger slips inside.

Gary gasps, involuntarily tightens his sphincter muscle and then forces himself to relax. My finger goes inside up to the second knuckle and I begin thrusting into his anus and continuing my blowjob.

It doesn't take Gary long to orgasm after that. If he didn't convulse just before he cums, I might have been taken by surprise. I'm not, though. I gulp down his hot semen as fast as he shoots it into my mouth. When he's done, Gary's knees buckle, and I'm pleased at my performance.

Gary stares at me, trembling. My finger's still up his asshole, and he shudders when I wiggle it. "Do you like that?" I hoarsely whisper.

Gary gulps, nodding his head.

"Want more?"

He nods again. I don't have to tell him to turn his back to me; he obeys my unsaid command and spreads his legs.

Gary's buttocks look incredible. They're smooth and so firm. I want to claw at them, scratching the skin, tearing at them. Instead, I gently massage them for a moment. I slide my suspenders off my shoulders and unbutton my pants.

Gary says in a trembling voice, "Don't forget the condom."

"Of course." I barely say the words, but they seem to resonate in the deserted bathroom.

The lubricant is warm from having been in my jacket pocket. The gel oozes between my fingers. A little of it goes into Gary's anus, and a lot of it goes onto my organ. I even reach around Gary's waist and put a little of it on to his cock, which is still hard. It stiffens a little bit at my touch.

I move forward. The anus always resists the initial intrusion, and when I move past that resistance, going deep into the man I'm fucking, I always think of a penis breaking a virgin's hymen. I wonder if they feel the same degree of pain.

Gary's cry echoes around the bathroom as I slide deeply

into him. He widens his stance and forces himself to relax. I thrust slowly, but more easily every time. I clutch at Gary's hips, and I can hear his breathing becoming labored. I stare at his large, strong hands, which are braced against the wall. They form into fists and then spread out again, pressing flat against the wall and then back into fists.

Gary's trembling again, and I fuck him faster and faster, letting the burning sensation between my own legs grow and grow. With my final thrust I cum, and I drive deeply into Gary's ass, making him cry out. Pressed up against him, I reach around and grab Gary's cock. I have to stroke it only two or three times before he cums again, spurting and dribbling semen all over his cock and my hand.

I quickly withdraw. By the time Gary's recovered and he turns around to face me, I've already pulled my pants back up.

Gary smiles, sheepishly. "Hang around here often?" he asks. It's one of those awkward post-fuck moments when there's not much to say besides meaningless small talk.

I return the smile. I whisper, "I plan to, if there's a chance to see you again."

Gary says, "Great." Having run out of things to say, he bows his head and says, "I've gotta run. See you around." We share one single, tender kiss, and then he's gone.

I lock the bathroom door behind him, clean up the mess, thoroughly wash my hands, adjust my appearance, and then leave the bar as quickly as possible.

One side effect of these encounters is an empty, hollow feeling I have. I've never been completely satisfied afterward. I always crave more, and the knowledge that I'll never get more makes me want to cry. I force myself not to feel hollow as I drive home. Instead, I focus on the smell of Gary in my nostrils and on my lips.

My roommate, Angie, is awake when I get home. She sees me, and a disgusted look overcomes her face. "You went out again, didn't you?"

"Don't start with me," I say. "I'm going to take a shower." I remove my suit jacket and drape it over the closet doorknob. I slip the suspenders off my shoulders and loosen my necktie as I walk toward my bedroom.

Angie follows me. She asks, "Who'd you meet tonight?"

I talk while I undress. "His name is Gary. He's on his lacrosse team in college. He's still in the closet and scared to death of getting caught."

Angie says, "You should be, too. Your ass is grass if you fuck up."

"Don't worry about me," I say. Slowly, I peel the false goatee and mustache off my face, rubbing the spirit gum off with my finger. I can still smell traces of him, mingled with the odor of the soap from Lester's ladies' room. I try to deflect Angie's criticisms by getting back on the subject of Gary. "Every time Gary has sex with his girlfriend, he feels entitled to go to a gay bar and really enjoy himself. Isn't that pathetic?"

I unstrap my latex dildo and toss it onto the bed. Not only does it look and feel like a real live cock, but it's got a special feature; tiny little latex knobs that press against my clitoris while I've got it strapped on, enabling me to enjoy myself while I'm using it.

Angie says, "You know what's really pathetic? A straight woman so horny for gay men the only way she can get off is to dress up like one." I sigh and begin unwrapping my breasts. The hollow feeling is back. "You're right. That's really pathetic."

A Man in a Kilt

Helen E. H. Madden

The first time we met, Jimmy called me a "wee lassie." I swear it's the only time in my life anybody ever called me "wee," but that's what Jimmy kept calling me even after I stood up and towered over him by about seven inches. We were at the Velvet Dark, a local hot spot for the fetish community. I'd been going there every Saturday night for over six years, but that evening was Jimmy's first time. He showed up on leather night wearing a pair of faded jeans and his favorite Saint Andrew's rugby shirt. I think the only leather he owned back then was his belt.

We didn't talk much that evening. The Glenlivet Jimmy drank made his brogue so thick I could barely comprehend a word he said. But I understood the way he looked at me. His stormy gray eyes wandered from my breasts to my face and back again. When the music turned slow, Jimmy asked me to dance. The top of his head only came up to my chin, but he didn't seem to mind. I was wearing a kidskin corset, the kind that shoves the breasts up high and close together. Mine were up so high my nipples kept popping out to play peek-a-boo. Like a naughty little boy, Jimmy laughed and played right along with them as he rubbed up against me on the dance floor.

When we left the club, Jimmy slipped an arm around my waist and buried his face in my cleavage.

"Take me home, lass," he murmured. His wavy red hair

tickled my chin as he nuzzled my breasts. "Ah'll spread yir legs and fuck ye till ye scream! Ye know ye want me to. . . ."

How could I say no to a proposition like that?

An hour later, Jimmy was moaning and swearing, straining against the leather straps I used to tie him to my bed. The remains of his clothes lay on the floor next to the scissors I had used to remove them. I sat between Jimmy's legs, playing with my clit while he watched.

"Dammit, untie me! Ah want to fuck!"

"I know what you want," I said. "But I'm not giving it to you."

I slipped my fingers between my legs, enjoying the feel of my own slick pussy. I spread my knees wider to give Jimmy a better view. His cock sprang up hard as a rock, and he struggled again to get free.

"Ah'm not playing any fucking games here!" he shouted. "Untie me!"

"If that's what you want." I leaned over and pulled the quick-release on one of the wrist cuffs. As soon as his arm was free, Jimmy grabbed at me.

"No!" I slapped his hand hard enough to make it sting.

"Ow! What the hell do ye mean 'no'?"

"I mean I'll untie you, but then you walk out the door, and that's it."

"Jesus Christ! Why can't Ah just have a simple fuck?"

"Because, lover. If I give you what you want, you'll disappear as soon as we're done, and I'll never see you again," I explained. "But if I give you what you need, you'll be mine forever."

Jimmy's face flushed bright red. "What the hell makes ye think Ah need to be tied to the fucking bed and tormented like some bitch?"

I looked at his cock, swaying like a flagpole in a high wind. The tip was already leaking. "Trust me, you need this."

He stared at me, completely speechless. I doubt a woman had ever said such things to him before. While he lay there dumbfounded, I sat back between his legs and teased open the folds of my cunt. When my fingers were good and sticky, I brought them to my mouth and licked them clean. Jimmy's eyes got real big.

"It's your choice. Do you want to stay, or go?"

He stayed. Jimmy spent the rest of that night strapped to my bed. He came three times, and I never even had to touch him. By morning he was mine.

Jimmy had never dated a Dom before. I'm sure they have Doms back in Scotland. He just never knew he needed one before he met me. I spent six months showing him the ropes, the chains, the handcuffs . . . well, you get the picture. I took things slow at first. Short though he was, Jimmy prided himself on being a big man, and guys like that can be skittish. They don't always realize they're still big men even when they're down on their hands and knees with a butt plug tucked securely between their nether cheeks.

So I wasn't surprised when Jimmy balked at the idea of introducing me to his family and friends. He wanted to keep his extracurricular activities separate from his normal life, like they were two different worlds. But as he soon found out, worlds have a habit of colliding.

We were at Jimmy's place one night when the phone rang. Jimmy was kneeling on the floor with a spreader bar between his ankles. I sat behind him, binding his wrists behind his back. We were busy, so after the fourth ring, the machine answered for us.

"Hey Jimmy! It's yir brother! Pick up the phone!" Jimmy started as a Highland brogue rang loud and clear over the answering machine.

"Sorry," I told the machine as I stood up to survey my handiwork. "Jimmy's a little tied up right now!"

"Nan!" Jimmy strained against the cotton ropes, trying to free his hands.

"Don't worry, love," I cooed as I guided his head to the floor. His ass came up as his head went down, presenting me with a picture-perfect view of his anus, scrotum, and cock. "He can't hear me."

"Where the hell are ye?" the voice continued. "Nobody's seen ye in months, and Ah'm starting to worry. Come down to the pub tomorrow night so Ah know yir not dead."

The phone clicked, and the answering machine fell silent. The only sounds in the room now came from Jimmy as he continued to struggle.

"You're never going to get free," I said as I knelt behind him and fastened a leather strap around his balls. "Why don't you just relax?"

Two pieces of lightweight chain dangled from the strap. Jimmy gave a little moan as I hung a small weight between them. With a push of the finger, I sent the weight swinging just a bit. It tugged his balls back and forth as it swayed.

"Oh God, Nan!" Jimmy gasped. "What are ye doing to me?"

"Something you'll like. Trust me."

I waited while Jimmy bitched and moaned. The weight gradually came to a stop, and he calmed down a bit. Then I slipped my fingers between his legs and started rubbing the sweet spot just behind his balls. Jimmy moaned and rocked his hips, which sent the weight swinging again.

"Ah! Me baws, Nan! Please!"

"Now, now. This doesn't hurt, and I promise your family jewels won't fall off. Oh, speaking of family, you never told me you had a brother!"

I continued to massage his perineum with one hand as I slid the other around his hips to stroke his cock. Jimmy couldn't help himself. He stiffened right up and pushed forward into my grasp. The weight swung in a wider arc and Jimmy swore.

"Language, dear!" I chided him. "So what's your brother like? Is he nice?"

"He's just . . . oh god . . . he's okay . . ." Jimmy gasped. I quit stroking his shaft and began toying with the Prince Albert dangling from the tip of his cock. He shuddered as I twirled the shiny steel ring in and out of his urethra. The piercing was my gift to Jimmy on our one-month anniversary, my way of saying how special he was to me, and I played with it every chance I got.

"He's okay, huh? Maybe you should take me to this pub tomorrow night so I can meet him."

"Ah, I don't know, Nan . . . oh god!" He jerked as I left off massaging his perineum and pressed a finger against his anus.

"Oh quit fussing! It's not like I'm exploring virgin territory here. Besides, I've got plenty of lube." I let up on Jimmy's trap door long enough to grab the nearby tube of gel and flip the top open. I squeezed out a dollop and slowly spread it between his cheeks. "So why won't you take me to see your brother? You too embarrassed to introduce me to your family?"

"No!" Jimmy's hips came up high as I teased the rim of his little brown hole. The weight arced between his legs like a fortune teller's pendulum.

"So why not take me to the pub?"

"Oh god Nan! Ah'll do whatever ye want!"

"I want to meet your brother tomorrow. Think we can do that?"

This time I pinched the head of his cock. Jimmy bucked uncontrollably, and the weight swung wild.

"Yes! Yes! Please Nan! God please!"

"Good boy. That's exactly what I wanted to hear," I said as I slipped a finger inside him.

Jimmy's older brother Hamish moved to the good ol' United States a few years back when a friend invited him to come work at his pub one summer. The friend had a sister, a pretty redhead named Maureen that Hamish fell in love with and soon married. A year after they married, Maureen's brother sold the pub to Hamish. A few months after that, Hamish bought Jimmy a one-way ticket to the States in hopes so that his younger brother might find a nice American girl of his own and settle down.

It took me all night and most of the next day to coax these few details out of Jimmy. He didn't want to talk about himself or his family. Instead, he chose to bitch about other things.

"Ah thought ye were going to wear a skirt tonight."

Jimmy sat next to me in the car, drumming his fingers on the door handle. He scowled at the frayed knees of my jeans as we waited at a stoplight.

"I hate wearing skirts," I told him. "Besides, you're wearing one already."

"It's a kilt, not a skirt!" Jimmy snapped. "And why the hell couldn't ye let me drive?"

"Because the last time I let you drive my car, you nearly

killed us both by trying to drive on the wrong side of the road."

"It would have been the right side of the road if we'd been in Scotland!"

"Of course it would, dear."

I didn't know which side of the road was the right side in Scotland. The fact was, beyond Sean Connery and single-malt whiskey, I didn't know jack about Scotland. I had no idea what a wellie was and no desire to find out. A haggis was the nasty bitch that lived next door to me, and as far as I was concerned, a macintosh was just a computer. And when it came to the more exotic aspects of life in the UK, well let's just say I wouldn't have known a spotted dick if it jumped up and bit me in the ass. At least not the kind you eat.

You know what I mean.

Anyway, I didn't know Scotland, but I did know Jimmy. Even when he wouldn't talk, I had a pretty good idea what was going on inside him.

"So who are we going to see at this bar?" I asked as the light turned green.

"It's a pub, not a bar. Just me brother and some old friends."

"Would any of those old friends happen to be old girlfriends?"

Jimmy grunted and stared out the window.

"Ah ha! So that's why your shorts are all in a knot," I said.

"Ah'm not wearing shorts."

"Oh really? Too bad you're not wearing patent leather shoes either. I bet the view would be spectacular!" I reached over and tugged at the hem of Jimmy's kilt. He glared at me and crossed his legs.

We spent the rest of the ride in silence. Jimmy sat

hunched in the passenger's seat, fidgeting like an eight-year-old boy. By the time we reached the White Horse Pub, he had switched from drumming his fingers to cracking his knuckles. It was after nine o'clock when I drove my SUV into the parking garage across the street from the pub. The bottom levels of the garage already overflowed with the cars of people who liked to get an early start on their revels. I drove up the ramp, through three levels of compacts and sedans, ignoring every empty parking space Jimmy pointed out until I reached the top floor of the garage.

"Jesus Christ, Nan! Ye've parked us all the way out in fucking Egypt!" Jimmy complained as I pulled into an empty spot.

"I don't want anyone to scratch my ride," I said.

"Well, no fucking chance of that happening! The nearest car has to be two levels below us. We've got the whole damn place to ourselves!"

"I know. It's kind of nice and private, isn't it?" My hand sneaked toward the hem of Jimmy's kilt again. He jumped as I touched his knee.

"Dammit, Nan, lay off!"

"Oh come on," I teased. "Just let me slip my hand under there so I can tug on your Prince Albert!"

"Forget it. Ah took it out!"

"You what?" I stared at him. "Jimmy, the hole will close up if you leave the hardware out too long."

"Ah don't care. Ah'm not wearing that thing to go see me brother!" Jimmy said, and then he bolted out of the car.

"Fine," I muttered as I grabbed my leather jacket. "Be a bitch then."

I followed behind Jimmy at a leisurely pace, giving myself

some time to cool off. Jimmy was just anxious, I told myself. He was taking his Dom to see his brother, and even though we both knew he wasn't going to introduce me as such, that still had to make him nervous. In fact, a lesser man probably would have chickened out long before now.

I inhaled deeply and blew out all my frustration in a single breath. Things would be all right. I just had to be patient. To boost my mood, I decided to focus on something pleasant, like Jimmy's kilt. I'd never seen him wear it before. The red and blue tartan hung from his hips like a schoolgirl's uniform. A thick black leather belt secured it at the waist, the hem just grazing his knees. Above the kilt, Jimmy wore a plain black T-shirt stretched tight over his chest. Below, a set of matching wool hose molded themselves to Jimmy's calves. I could see every muscle, every detail of his tight, lean body except for what the kilt covered. It swayed with each step, as though inviting me to come explore what was underneath. I grinned and picked up the pace.

"What's this?" I asked as I caught up. I brushed my fingers against what looked like a small leather purse hanging from Jimmy's belt. It rested right above his cock.

Jimmy pushed my hand away. "It's a sporran. Leave it the fuck alone!"

I wanted to grab him by the short hairs at that point and tell him to be nice, but we had reached the entrance of the pub. Jimmy strode through the double glass doors, not bothering to hold them open for me. I gritted my teeth and followed.

Walking into the White Horse Pub felt like stepping into Scotland itself. It was all low ceilings, wood beams, and stone walls hung with photographs of a small town that I'm sure Jimmy called home once. Celtic rock music blared out of the jukebox, competing with the din of customers laughing and shouting as they enjoyed their drinks. I heard more Scottish accents than I did American in that crowd. Most of the patrons rallied around the rugby game being played out on a large screen television that dominated the front of the pub. A few gathered around a billiards table for a friendly game. The remaining customers focused their attention on a group of guys throwing darts in the back area. The players all wore kilts, but it was the tallest fellow who caught my eye. He sported the same wavy red hair and square jaw as Jimmy. But while Jimmy stood only five foot six inches, this brawny fellow was nearly six feet tall.

"Hamish!" Jimmy shouted as he plowed his way through the crowd to reach his brother.

"Jimmy! Hey everybody, Jimmy's back!" Hamish grinned from ear to ear as we approached. He caught Jimmy in a big bear hug and pounded him on the back. The other players whooped when they saw Jimmy, and everybody piled on top of him.

"Get off me, you bawbags!" he shouted from beneath the crush of bodies.

The other guys backed off grinning, but Hamish continued to pound his back. "Dammit, Jimmy! Where ye been the last few months? Ah was starting to think ye'd been killed."

Jimmy shrugged. "Ah've been around."

I came up behind Jimmy and slid my arm around his waist. I smiled as Hamish's eyes rose to meet mine. I was probably the first woman he had ever looked up to.

"Damn, yir a tall one!"

"Six foot two with eyes of blue," I quipped. I held out my hand. "I'm Nan."

"Nan, huh?" Hamish cocked an eyebrow at Jimmy as we shook hands. "So yir the reason why me little brother hasn't been around lately."

"Sorry about that. I've been keeping him locked in my dungeon," I joked, wincing as Jimmy elbowed me in the ribs.

"Oh, that's okay. I knew he'd come back."

A petite blond stepped out of the crowd of onlookers and sidled up to Jimmy. Even in heels she was shorter than he was. Just a tiny bundle of tits and ass, all packaged up in a low-cut, venomous green dress. But there was an air of conceit about her that made up for her minuscule stature. When she touched Jimmy's hand, he started as though he'd been stung.

"I missed you, Jimmy."

The blond caught Jimmy's gaze and held him transfixed. He stood very still, caught between us, not saying a word. After several long moments, Hamish broke the silence.

"Ah, Nan, this is Fiona," he said with a grimace. "Fiona, this is Nan."

"Nice to meet you, Ann."

"Nice to meet you, too," I lied. "And the name is Nan."

"Oh." Fiona slithered a little closer to Jimmy. "So, you're Jimmy's current girlfriend."

"And you're his ex."

She smiled, showing all her teeth. I swear I saw poison dripping from her fangs.

"Nan, do ye like darts?" Hamish jumped in.

"Never played before," I said, not taking my eyes off Fiona.

"Well, Jimmy's a real pro at darts! Maybe he should teach ye to play. Right, Jimmy? Jimmy?"

Jimmy couldn't hear his brother. He was too busy staring at Fiona, taking in all those sinuous curves. I'm sure in his mind he was remembering what it felt like to fuck her. I imagined she was quite a screamer in bed.

"Jimmy!"

Hamish poked his brother in the ribs. Jimmy looked up at him, startled. Then he noticed me and blushed.

"Yeah, Ham, we should play darts."

"You guys go play," Fiona said. "Nan and I are going to have a little chat."

Jimmy hesitated. He looked from Fiona to me and then to her again.

"Go on!" Fiona said, pulling him out of my arms. She rubbed up against him in a not-so-subtle move before shooing him toward the dartboard.

Jimmy stumbled away like a drunk. Hamish shook his head as he walked after his brother.

"Nice meeting ye, Nan." He said it as though he never expected to see me again.

Fiona grabbed my arm and dragged me toward a table. "Let's talk, shall we?"

"Oh yes, let's," I agreed.

We flagged down a waitress and ordered a couple of beers. While we waited for our drinks, Fiona looked me over, taking note of my leather jacket, faded jeans, and jet-black hair.

"Well, you're something of an Amazon, aren't you?" she said. "Tell me, do guys really like that?"

"Some do," I replied, propping my feet up on the chair next to hers.

The waitress came back with our drinks just as a loud cheer rose up near the dartboard. I looked over and saw Jimmy standing in front of the target, picking darts out of its checkerboard face. Judging from the noise of the crowd, he must have made a good score. Jimmy glanced over at our table as he headed back to a white line marked on the floor. He nearly walked into the bar when Fiona smiled at him and leaned forward to show off her tits.

"Looks like ol' Jimbo still knows how to toss his dart," Fiona said, returning her attention to me. "So, Nan, how long have you two been going out?"

"About six months."

"Really? Jimmy and I broke up about six months ago." She took a sip of her beer. "I guess you caught him on the rebound."

"However I caught him, he's mine now."

Fiona sniffed. "For the moment."

We watched Jimmy prepare to throw again. He held up a dart and aimed for the board. As he did so, one of the other players snuck up beside him with a billiards cue and slipped the tip of it under Jimmy's kilt. Just before Jimmy made his throw, the cue popped up. Jimmy's kilt flew up above his waist to expose his naked cock.

"You bloody-arse bandit!"

Jimmy yanked the kilt back down, but not before I spied the gleam of a stainless steel ring dangling from the tip of his gorgeous rod.

"Oh, you sweet bastard!" I whispered. My heart leapt. Why the hell had Jimmy lied about wearing the Prince Albert?

I knew the answer when I glanced over at Fiona. Her cheeks flushed bright pink and her mouth made a little "oh" of surprise. She had seen it, too.

"Well! He didn't have that when we were going out!"

"I'll bet he didn't have a lot of things when you two were together," I said with a sudden understanding.

Fiona's eyes narrowed to flinty slits. "Let me tell you something, Ann!" She jabbed a finger at me.

"The name's Nan."

"Whatever! Jimmy and I have been together a long time. Every now and then he gets a wild hair up his ass and decides to chase after some whore, but it never lasts. He always comes back to me. Always! And do you know why? It's because I give that man whatever he wants. If he asks, 'How about a blowjob,' I suck him dry. If he says, 'Let's fuck,' I spread my legs and let him have at it. So there's nothing you've got that I haven't already given him!"

"If that's true," I said, "then why does he keep leaving you?"

That took the wind out of her sails. Fiona sat there, gaping at me.

"You know," she said after a long moment. "I was going to be nice about this, but now I'm not. Jimmy's mine, you bitch, and I'm taking him back from you tonight!"

"You're welcome to try," I said, getting up from the table. "But I think Jimmy's made other plans."

"Oh, like he gets a choice here!" she snapped.

"Fiona, he's always got a choice."

I left her spluttering at the table and headed for the ladies' room. How many of Jimmy's other girlfriends had she bull-dozed over? Probably a lot, I realized. In fact, she'd probably scared off so many that she didn't think she could ever lose Jimmy to another woman.

Well, it was time she learned otherwise. I stepped into the ladies' room, entered the first empty stall, and unzipped my fly. Jimmy wasn't the only one going without underwear that night. Unless of course, the strap-on harness I wore counted as an undergarment. I ran my fingers over the black leather straps, double-checking the fit. From the inner pocket of my jacket, I produced a silicone dildo. It slid into the O ring at the front of the harness smooth as silk. A few quick adjustments settled the base of the dildo over my clit. I rolled on a condom before zipping up and stepped out of the stall. With my jacket partially closed, no one would notice the bulge in my jeans.

I left the ladies' room and headed back to the table. Fiona was already gone, as was Jimmy.

"Bitch moves fast," I said to myself. Before I could look for them, Hamish turned up at my side.

"Uh, Nan, there's something ye should know—"

"Fiona's going after Jimmy," I said matter-of-factly.

He blinked. "Yeah. Yir not upset?"

"Not at all," I said, scanning the room. A flash of blond hair and a bilious green dress caught my eye. I turned and spied Fiona lurking near the men's room, waiting for Jimmy. She snared him as he came out, wrapping both arms around his waist to keep him from escaping.

"Fiona doesn't fight fair, Nan," Hamish said in a low voice. As if on cue, the bitch turned and looked right at me. She winked as she took Jimmy's hands and placed them on her full breasts. Jimmy hesitated, but he didn't pull away.

"Nan?" Hamish gave me a questioning look.

"Come on, Ham. Let's play darts."

I strode over to the board and grabbed three darts. Hamish scrambled after me.

"What about Jimmy? Aren't ye going to do something?"

"Like what?" I asked as I stepped back to the white line. I picked up my first dart and studied the board. The numbers around the rim probably had something to do with scoring, but they didn't mean a damn thing to me so I decided to go with the obvious shot.

"Bulls eye!" I called as I threw the dart. A few cheers went up as it landed smack in the center of the board.

"Nan, ye've got to protect what's yirs!" Hamish exclaimed. I glanced back at Jimmy. His hands had shifted from Fiona's breasts to her buttocks. He kneaded her full ass like it was bread dough, all the while pulling her closer to him.

"Hamish, I know what I'm doing." I focused on the dartboard again. There was just barely enough room in the center for my next shot.

"Bull's-eye!" I called again.

Thunk! The second dart landed impossibly close to the first. More cheers went up from the onlookers. I smiled and bowed. As I reached for the third dart, Hamish grabbed my arm.

"Don't ye get it? Once Fiona sinks her claws into him—"

I brushed him off. "Fiona is about to be declawed."

As I picked up the last dart, I saw Fiona press Jimmy up against the men's room door. Her hand caressed his face, and then slid down the length of his body, heading for the hem of his kilt. Jimmy leaned back slack-jawed, and closed his eyes. I aimed the dart and threw.

"Bull's-eye!"

The dart flew across the room and landed with a *thunk* in the men's room door, nailing Jimmy's kilt in the process. Fiona let out a shriek and yanked back her hand. The rest of the pub fell dead silent. Jimmy's eyes flew open, his face bone white as he stared at the dart sticking out between his legs. Then he looked up at me and roared.

fast, but my legs were long. I had already reached the top level of the parking garage when Jimmy caught up.

"Ye put a hole in me kilt!" he shouted, his face boiling red. "What the hell did ye do that for?"

"To remind you, lover, that there are things you don't want to do," I replied.

"Oh, so Ah canna spend time with an old friend?"

"You can walk down memory lane all you like, Jimmy, but I better not catch you fucking there."

"Ah wasn't fucking her!"

"Oh really?" I said as we reached the car. "It sure looked like you wanted to."

"Well maybe Ah did. Maybe just once Ah'd rather be with a real woman than some dyke bitch who thinks she's a man!"

I grabbed Jimmy and shoved him up against the car. He grunted in surprise as I spun him around and pressed his face against the hood.

"Oh I'm a man all right, lover! I'm Nan the fucking man, and tonight I'm going to teach you some respect!"

I kept one hand on his neck, pinning him in place. With the other hand, I pulled up his kilt to expose his naked backside. His pale white buttocks dimpled in the cold air of the parking garage.

"Jimmy, you've just been begging for what I'm about to do to you," I said. I slapped his ass hard enough to leave a bright red handprintburning on one cheek.

"Let go of me, ye fucking bitch!"

I reached around his waist and grabbed the sporran. Jimmy struggled against me as I opened it, but he couldn't

his feet wide apart to throw him off balance. Jimmy had to grab the fender to keep from falling.

"Ye fucking bitch! Don't ye dare do this to me here!"

"Sweetheart, if you didn't want to play, why did you pack this?"

I held up the tube of lubricant I found in his sporran. Jimmy squeezed his eyes shut the moment he saw it, as if that would make it go away.

"Ye damn bitch! Why here? Why in the fucking garage?"

"Oh come on, Jimmy. You know why! You snipe at me all damn evening, and then you start screwing around with your ex in the pub. Did you really think I was going to let you get away with that kind of behavior?"

When he didn't answer, I gave him a shake.

"I asked you a question, Jimmy! Did you really think you'd get away with it?"

He screwed his face up tight. "No!" he said, almost choking on the word.

"Well then, you know you have to accept the consequences of your actions."

I had to take my hand off Jimmy's neck to spread his ass cheeks apart, but he wasn't struggling anymore. He clung to the hood of the SUV for dear life, gasping and moaning as I spread the lube between his buttocks and then into his little brown hole. I started with one finger, sliding it in and out until Jimmy was rocking his hips back and forth. Then I gave him two fingers to pry him open just a little wider. Jimmy bit his lower lip to keep from crying out. I just grinned and slipped in another finger. I'd been waiting for

whispered as I fingered him. He shook his head. "I'm going to make you cry like a baby!"

I yanked open my jacket and unzipped my jeans. The dildo sprang out, just like a real dick. I let Jimmy turn his head just far enough to see what I was doing.

"Oh shite, Nan! Don't do this, please! Ah'm sorry!"

"It's too late for apologies, Jimmy!"

By now, I was fingering him hard, forcing his backdoor to open up wide. When he was ready, I pulled out my fingers and pressed the tip of the dildo up against that little puckered mouth. The dildo slid home, its full length gliding into Jimmy's ass. He squealed and bucked, but it was too late. I was inside of him, and there was no way he could get me out.

"You like how that feels?" I whispered. I found the answer to that question under the front of his kilt. His cock felt stiff as a tree trunk, and it stood straight out from his hips. I wrapped a hand around it and started stroking.

"Oh God, Nan! What are ye doing to me?" He arched his back as I pushed into him. On impulse, I slapped his ass again. The sound reverberated in the empty garage.

"Nan, don't!"

"What's wrong? Afraid somebody will hear us?"

"Yes!" he hissed.

I cackled, stirring up even more echoes. "You know what? I'll bet somebody does hear us. In fact, I'll bet somebody sees us! I'll bet sweet little Fiona followed us here, still hoping to get lucky with you. I'll bet she's hiding in the shadows, watching everything we're doing!"

Jimmy really did start to cry when I said that, and that was

inside it roared to life, sending sweet shivers through us both. My clit swelled up, hungry and aching. Jimmy sobbed and gasped, bucking his hips back and forth so hard I could barely hold onto his cock. The tartan cloth of his kilt flapped around his legs as I pumped into his ass, and my jeans slid off my hips and fell to the oil-stained pavement.

"Louder!" I ordered. "I want Fiona to hear you! I want her to know how much you're enjoying this!"

Jimmy obeyed, throwing his head back as I thrust into him and shouting at the top of his lungs.

"Oh god! Don't stop!"

"Beg for it!" I told him.

"Please Nan! Please fuck me hard! Ah want it! Ah need it!"

The garage rang with his cries. Jimmy clawed at the hood of the car, scratching up the wax job as he shouted, then shrieked, and finally bellowed his way to an orgasm.

"Oh god, Nan!"

He came all over my hand and the inside of his kilt before slumping over the hood. I held onto him and kept grinding into his ass until the vibrator overwhelmed my clit and I came, too. When I finished, I draped myself over him. We stayed there for long moments, both of us gasping for air. Then I stood up, and slowly pulled out. Jimmy staggered around and dropped to his knees.

"Oh god, Nan," he whispered. "How did ye know? How do ye always know?"

I stripped the condom off and tossed it into a nearby trash can. Jimmy leaned forward and kissed the tip of the dildo.

"I know because I love you," I said as I stroked his soft

We didn't need to say anything else. Jimmy pulled up my jeans, tucking the dildo neatly inside before zipping me up. When he stood, his kilt fell back into place, with the sporran conveniently hiding the come stains. Jimmy slipped an arm around my waist and pressed his face to my breasts, nuzzling them beneath my T-shirt.

"Do ye want to go back to the pub?" he asked.

"Sure. Let's get a drink."

Back inside, we found a quiet table and sat down. Hamish brought over a couple of drinks and set them in front of us.

"That was some pretty fancy throwing, Nan." He regarded me with a cautious look, probably wondering if I'd throw a dart at him next. He turned to Jimmy. "Are ye okay?"

Jimmy nodded. "Nan took me out to the parking garage and gave me a proper spank. Ah'll be a good boy now."

Hamish threw back his head and laughed. "So that's yir secret! Too bad for Fiona she never figured that out!"

"Too bad indeed," I replied.

Hamish headed back to the bar, chuckling all the way. Jimmy and I sipped our drinks in a comfortable silence. I nudged Jimmy and pointed to Fiona sulking near the entrance of the pub. We lifted our glasses to her and smiled. Fiona favored us with a scathing look and stalked out.

"I think your ex is disappointed," I said.

"Well Ah'm not," Jimmy replied. He slipped a hand under the table to caress the bulge in my jeans. "Ah've got exactly what Ah want right here."

"No, you don't," I told him as I leaned in for a kiss.

"But you do have what you need."

cream

A Picture Paints a Thousand Words

Successor

Amanda Earl

Inspired by Eugène Delacroix's "The Death of Sardanapalus"

Today another tragedy
of Sardanapalus
this is where the blood stains
the ground
I can't let you go
my lips are the shield
that armors your body
my arms surround you
like a womb
sirens paint crimson
on our walls
this is where my legs
tangle with your own
I clench to hold you
in the cinnabar light
that binds us at last
while others feast on the empires
of dying stars
I devour your body
and you swallow mine

cream

The wail of sirens grows louder. Sarabella holds the needle steady as she pierces her inner thigh, watching in fascination as the blood runs down and pools, dripping against her cock. The high-pitched wail of sirens and the sharp, tight heat of the puncture force her to take a deep breath and smell the thin oxygen air mixed with absinthe and opium.

Albumar takes his finger, dips it in Sarabella's artistry and delicately licks the ruby nectar off the white moon of his thumbnail.

We are back to powdered wigs and secret, shameful sex acts. We hide from the soldiers patrolling the streets as we hunt for the starved, sex-crazed sinners looking for shelter.

No one would recognize our skeletons covered not in the crimson crinoline of high society, but in rags and the old sackcloth of friars, except those who need us. Need us to find them. Need us to fuck them and fuck them hard.

This is how Sarabella and Albumar discovered me. I was scavenging for anything to eat, but really I just wanted sex. The soldiers keep the citizens starved so that they weaken and die. Only those who are prepared to fight may have food. Then they save the women with childbearing hips for the fighters to impregnate. And this is how the world is supposed to work, but there are those of us who resist. We cannot fight, and our women refuse to bear the children of fighters, who will themselves be raised to take on the mission of death.

It had been one month since a soldier fucked me. He bent me over a garbage can in an alley. I wanted him to. I met him in a bar. One that he shouldn't even know about. That kind of thing had been outlawed years ago by Christian funda-

took me. And I enjoyed it, knowing I was taking the seed away from some poor woman for even just a little while, so she wouldn't get pregnant with the child of this killer. So I allowed him his little death. Yes, I could kill him easily with one finger pressed on his throat, but I wanted him to live with himself and his own disgust afterwards. He left me in the alley for dead. But I was very much alive.

Sarabella and Albumar took me back, bathed me and introduced me to the others. We share a bed. Every night we fuck till dawn. No one goes to a separate room. If they are going to try to kill us, they'll have to battle every one of us at the same time. They have no more bombs, they have no more galaxy destroyers. There's no more money to develop these weapons. Now they have their guns, knives, and bare hands. The cunning genius behind this war is the son of the same inbred bunch of bastards that have been ruling us since the beginning of the new millennium. Since they taught people how to fear. Since people listened to their lies. But there are those of us who didn't listen, and we are finding one another. Slowly.

Tonight I am lying on the bed beside Marcu and Joachim. I watch Marcu spread Joachim's ass and lick it with his long pointed tongue. He asks me if I want in on the action, and I might as well agree. I've been eyeing the small round butt-hole all night and my cock is full of blood and sperm. I need to relieve myself inside Joachim's deep asshole. I need to shove my cock inside his ass and have him clamp down on me so tight that I am finally warm again.

Marcu pushes Joachim's head down on the bed.

another cock in that hole. And yours is big enough to roger him right. I'll hold his hips steady, and you fuck him hard."

Marcu takes out his cock, and I see that his is short and thin. I walk over to the edge of the bed.

"Crawl over here, Joachim boy," I say. "Let me see you wiggle that tight ass, and make it quick. I don't have all night.

Joachim moves quickly, and as he crawls, I can see that his own cock is rigid and ready to be used.

"Marcu, go get the CBT. I want to see how hard this boy can get for me."

"You're a wild man, Mikael. I have never seen Joachim's cock so hard. Maybe I'll let him suck me off once you're done with him."

I inch my thick cock slowly into Joachim's tight brown hole. I slap his ass hard a few times and pinch his thigh.

"Get that ass up in the air, you little bastard," I say.

By now Sarabella and Albumar have abandoned their own games and are standing around, watching us. Sarabella is still mildly buzzed from her earlier adventures; she strokes her hard cock. Albumar gets down on his knees to worship it for her. There are many TGs and TVs in our shelter. The soldiers want nothing to do with them and have been known to shoot them on sight or maim them.

Sarabella looks lovely in a red velvet blazer, open to show her tits and the black pants firmly fitting her tight, boyish ass. Albumar is her little puppy dog, and she keeps him well fed with cock.

Other members of our little group are attentive on the big wide bed that covers the room. Maliendo is striking

not homes for women waiting to give birth to the soldiers' children. Once these women are due, the midwives arrive and open the doors of the car, scooping the babies into baskets and leaving the women for dead. The stench is strong until some kind soul rolls the car into the nearest dump and lights a fire. The most popular vehicle for sheltering in is the SUV, formerly super-useless vehicle of the early millennium, now having an important role.

"Tighten that little hole of yours, Joachim, or I'll get that whip from Maliende and take a few stripes off your back, boy," I say as I'm about to come.

Joachim's cock is still blood hard and ready for the torture he adores. I hear him squeal with delight as I use the words he's told us all to use on him to get him going. He can't fuck without this. He needs to be humiliated, degraded, pissed on, and fucked like a hole to get off.

Marcu arrives back with the Jaws of Strife, a leather cockring with nickel studs all along the inside and a ball spreader attached. I wrap the ring around Joachim's cock. "Do you want to do the honors, Marcu?" I say.

"Abso-fucking-lutely," he says and takes the magnets, adding them one by one to the chains dangling from the cockring. Soon Joachim is groaning in a mixture of pleasure and pain, and rocking his hips back and forth. I am still inside him and ready to shoot another load.

"You can't come yet, fuckface. Keep that load inside you until Marcu tells you. Marcu, would you like to get in position?" I say.

Marcu goes to the edge of the bed and sits down, turning

animal he likes to be. My cock rams hard into him, and he moans as his come shoots into Marcu's face, dripping down his chin.

I shoot my load, too, and we are all sated once more. For one brief moment we have escaped from the knowledge that hell is just outside the door.

"Good boy, Joachim. Now lick up Marcu, sweetie. Clean him up all nice, and he'll find you a nice plate of goodies to eat." I stroke Joachim's head, and he purrs like a little kitten and rubs his face against my thigh.

We all curl up; Joachim falls into a deep sleep beside Marcu and me.

"Marcu," I whisper," are you still awake?"

"Yes Mikael, I can never sleep after sex; I'm too wired."

"I need to ask you something. If something should happen to me . . ."

"Don't think of it, Mikael," Marcu says, putting his strong hand on my naked shoulder.

"I have to, Marcu." I say as I return his caress feeling his heart beating strongly against my cold hands on his chest. "If something should happen to me, I choose you to succeed me, to keep everyone safe, to seek sanctuary."

Marcu leans over Joachim's slumbering body, takes my face in his hands. I see his deep brown eyes glittering in the firelight.

"Mikael, for you I will do anything." He pulls me in close for a kiss. Joachim slides further down on the bed, still asleep.

"Not for me, Marcu, but for our family. Help them." I return his kiss, and we remain like that for a few mi

tonight. Chances are we'll have to pick up and move our stuff again. We're pretty good at hiding out, but lately the soldiers have been finding us. If only they didn't keep hanging out in the gay bars, looking for a screw.

I close my eyes and feel sick when I think of the last time they infiltrated our sanctuary. They thought they could destroy us by killing Sardanapalus, our leader, descendant of Assyrian kings. He fought them to the end, and was forced to watch a soldier cut the throat of his favorite slave, Myrrha, her blood running onto the white satin sheets and merging with his own as he bled from their swords. As he lay dying, Sardanapalus whispered to me to take over his reign. Now I am responsible for the well-being of our enclave of sexual deviants.

I gathered as many of our family together as I could. We ran, leaving him and the other massacred bodies unburied, but mourned, deeply mourned. In the middle of a quiet night, when all is still, I hear Sarabella weeping for her lost lover, her king. He understood her needs, allowed her to shove her cock roughly in his ass over and over like a man and then would gently caress her womanly breasts.

Once Sarabella was caught by the soldiers, who thought they'd found another womb to fill. When two of them stripped off her long skirt and revealed her thick penis, they were brutal. One took out a machete and would have cut off her cock, but she kneed him in the nuts and brought her sharp stiletto heel down on the other soldier's cock before either of them had time to act, and then she ran. Albumar found her in the gutter outside our sanctuary.

He nursed her back to health. The soldiers had scarred

he is her slave, licking her boots clean. Every night he washes her uncut cock, pulling down the foreskin and tenderly soaping it and rinsing it for her. Sarabella treats him well, chaining him to the foot of her bed where he remains all night as her pet.

I hear a sound as I shower off the night's debauchery. Perhaps it is Sarabella filling Albumar's water dish, or Marcu and Jochim fucking again. Footsteps are coming toward me. I turn off the shower and take up my position, nude behind the door. My body is no longer the weak skeleton of brittle bones that Sarabella and Albumar discovered in the alley. I am hard muscle, strong hands, powerful legs. I know how to kill with one small movement of my hand to the back of a soldier's neck. I hold my hand upright as the door cracks open.

Four sets of shiny black boots march in to the room.

I feel the sharp tip of a rapier sword puncturing my lungs as I kick and punch and pummel, but I am overpowered.

You don't expect to survive long in this world. I am not surprised.

As I die, images flash before my eyes: Joachim's tight round ass filled with my come, the ring pulling tightly around his cock, Albumar lapping at Sarabella's erect nipples, and Sardanapalus, the smile of death in his eyes as his children find another home. I know that at this moment, they run and will find another sanctuary. At least for a short time.

I smell fire. The soldiers are burning our house down. With my last breath, I throw myself into the flames:

Rather let them be borne abroad upon

A Picture Paints a Thousand Words

Of slaves and traitors.
In this blazing palace,
And its enormous walls of reeking ruin,
We leave a nobler monument than Egypt
Hath piled in her brick mountains, o'er dead kings . . .
So much for monuments that have forgotten
Their very record!
—*Sardanapalus, A Tragedy,* Lord Byron, 1821

Color Less Ordinary

Sydney Beier

Inspired by Robert Mapplethorpe's "Ken Moody Eating a Blue Shoe"

Gray. From the sky, to the cool waters of the Sound, the entire city was a thousand shades of gray. The Emerald City in January. I plodded through it on my way home from work one random Tuesday evening.

The shortest distance between A and B is normally a straight line. I knew this and normally followed the formula, but not that night. I wanted food. Something decadent. Crème brûlée! I had been good and lost five pounds. I deserved it. I wanted company, too, even if it was a crowd of strangers. I refused to be lonely.

Hunger and aching pulled me splashing through puddles into Brasserie Margaux, a place I had passed at least a thousand times.

A bored-looking host placed me in the shadows near the noisy kitchen. My chair was too low, and I had to pull my breasts back to keep them from resting crudely on the tabletop.

Underneath the tablecloth, I fiddled in my purse with a new lipstick I had bought at the drugstore. I popped the cap on and off as I watched the grouchy host return the extra silverware to a cabinet at the front

me. Feeling defiant, I unbuttoned the top of my blouse for them and wondered what they would do with the ice cubes from my water glass. Run them up and down my neck and into my cleavage? Around my nipples? Stick them in my cunt and drink the water as it melted? Whisper naughtily as they did these things?

I was having nasty thoughts, and I loved it.

The lipstick, perfect and new, was silky across my lips. I left prints on the edge of the glass and the filter of my cigarette. It adhered to the starched white napkins as I dabbed water from the corners of my mouth. Someone would know I was there, even if it was after I had left.

I waited fifteen minutes, and no waiter came to take my order. Gazing at my parted lips in a tiny compact mirror, I applied another layer of color. I tilted the mirror down slightly to sneak a peek at how much cleavage I had revealed. Pulling my arms in at my sides, I accented it even more. I continued to play until, finally, someone approached. I looked up when nothing was said and, in that instant it was as if my entire world shifted to technicolor.

Before me stood perhaps the most striking man I had ever seen. I had to squint at his beauty, it was so fine. His features appeared etched in hematite; the dark, nearly black landscape shone in the flickering candlelight from votives throughout the café. He was completely bald and wore a simple white shirt, a dazzling contrast to his ebony skin.

I could not look away. He was staring back at me, and it didn't appear to be in disgust, shock, offense, or irritation. Interest? I was more confused than I had ever been. I

cream

The burn in my stomach was so sweet, I had to stifle a gasp at its intensity. My bones of reason and control were splintering. I tried to gather them as quickly as I could, to hold them together and make sense of everything again. I said the only thing I could think of in that moment.

"Um."

"That color looks fabulous on you," he said, pointing to the lipstick I had dropped on the table in my surprise. His voice ran over and through me, smooth, warm, lovely. My body pulsed with longing to hear it again. My legs spread under the table. Everything trapped between my thighs engorged and became uncomfortably cramped.

"Thanks," I squawked clumsily. "It's Garnet Chrome."

"Sassy." He grinned wide.

"Excuse me?" The idea had never occurred to me.

He cleared his throat, "What would you like for dinner?"

"I'm not here for dinner."

"Dessert?"

"Yes, please."

"Then what would you like for dessert?"

You! I wanted to shout.

"Crème brûlée," I managed, in a mousy voice. I trembled in panic. What could I do? What could I say to keep him at my table? I was losing my mind.

"Sorry. We don't serve crème brûlée," he informed me, his eyes radiant and locked with mine. His voice had an unmistakable teasing quality to it. A dare? A provocation? On the outside, our conversation might have seemed quite banal, but I detected an unmistakable buzz of sexual tension in the air

that shadow into the open and being seen, I felt brave, "What do you have?" I leaned forward and rested my arms on the table. I smiled triumphantly when his eyes darted to my chest. He licked his full lips with a sultry pink tongue and arched an eyebrow.

"Should I wait for your boyfriend to return before I go over the menu?"

"That would be a long wait," I said, glancing at the missing place setting.

My heart was racing. I could hardly wait for the next words out of his mouth. I wanted to lick them from the air.

He leaned in close to deliver them with a deep voice. "You like chocolate?"

The blush brewing just under my skin exploded and rushed so quickly to the surface, I felt dizzy. I realized I was holding my breath as well as the edge of the table. It released in a burst of giddy, nervous laughter. His huge grin only contributed to the explosion.

Conversations throughout the café halted, one after the other, and patrons eyed us curiously. I covered my mouth to suppress the giggles, but it was no use. I laughed until tears ran from my eyes.

When I finally composed myself, I looked at him again. He convulsed with a few more chuckles, his shoulders bouncing heartily. His head shook with a sigh as he grabbed the menu off the table.

"I have the perfect thing for you. You'll love it! Trust me?"

"I'm in your hands," I shrugged with delight.

He clapped once then bounced away into the kitchen.

knew how much I look like a chipmunk when I grin that big. The battle was lost, and I gave up. I suddenly didn't care how silly I looked.

I contemplated how quickly it happened. How, in an instant, it seemed everything was different. So alive at last. I didn't have long to think about it. He was back after hardly any time at all, carrying a plate in one hand and a handsome cognac glass in the other.

The dessert was a cleverly crafted plate of ice cream, half chocolate, half vanilla, and shaped as a yin/yang. The two halves fit perfectly together along a swirling border. I watched him flick a lighter from his pocket and ignite the liqueur. The flame danced a brilliant blue.

"I'm Constance, or Connie."

"My name's Darren, or Darren. And I'm off at ten."

My excitement surged again. The flame before me flashed wildly with my sigh of relief. He moved on to other customers, and I dug into the ice cream as it started to melt, the colors coalescing together.

Darren's apartment lay in the fashionable Capitol Hill district. The old, wooden stairs creaked under our weight. Tipsy and happy from two flaming cognacs at the café, I held Darren's hand as we made our way along the burgundy carpet to his apartment.

He led me in with a warm hand on the small of my back. I stood in the nearly empty studio trying to catch my breath from the short walk, which had seemed a million miles. The exhilaration of his company was uplifting and exhausting at the same time.

A Picture Paints a Thousand Words

"Sure." I walked around the room, happy to explore his space. Aside from the bed rumpled with white sheets, an armoire in the corner and a vanity under the window, there was not much to see. No posters on the walls. No television. He didn't even have a stereo. "You just move in?"

"About five years ago." He joined me next to a cardboard box resting on the floor. The flaps were open, and I could see a variety of things inside.

"What's this?" I pointed to the collection of CDs, novels, and a pair of blue, three-inch-heeled pumps.

Darren laughed his way through a sigh I suspected was quite tired. "My next meal."

I looked at him quizzically, took a shoe out of the box and turned it over and over in my hand. The material was cheap, tacky, probably plastic. A Payless special, circa 1980.

"You're selling this stuff?"

"Yeah. Gotta pay some bills. As nice as the Brasserie is, the customers don't tip for shit."

"Whose shoes are these?"

They had to be at least size eleven. I feared I danced in the wake of a past supermodel girlfriend. Even if she did have bad taste, my gut clenched.

He sighed again and set the tumblers on the floor. His sudden melancholy transformed my apprehension to panic. I gripped the shoe tightly as he cupped my face in his hands and kissed my mouth. The ember of arousal that had been glowing all night and infusing my blood with the most delicious warmth enflamed as his tongue parted my lips and slipped inside. I was on fire then, burning blue, so hot I began to melt.

He nodded, avoiding my gaze, then bent down for his whiskey and knocked it back in one gulp.

"Some—no, many—women can't handle it. I'd rather be up front about things."

Darren sat on the edge of the bed while I stood by the door, blinking in bewilderment. I sensed he thought I'd leave then. I still held the shoe in my hand. It felt right.

"How much you think you'd get for these?" I asked.

"Maybe three bucks at a consignment shop."

I grabbed my purse and fished for my wallet. "I'll buy your next meal."

I found the money, but thought better of it.

"On one condition," I informed him.

Darren's eyes narrowed, "Which is?"

"Model them for me."

"Aren't you shocked?" he asked, and I wondered how many times he had been through this. How many other women were halfway down that creaky stairwell on their way out by now?

"Yes," I answered. "Put them on."

His eyes still wary, he removed his shoes and socks and brushed the lint off his feet. Then he was still, sitting on the bed with his hands in his lap and his legs lolling in front of him. I handed him the shoes, then lowered myself to the floor to watch him put them on.

He stood up in those terrible, tacky pumps and raised his pant legs to display them. In another time, in another life, I might have found it amusing. At that moment, I wasn't sure I had ever seen anything sexier.

"Well?" He asked quietly, caution lingering in his tone

He complied silently, removing each piece of clothing slowly and dropping them to the floor. His physique was chiseled, from those blue pumps to the top of his bald head. All of it wrapped in thick, flawless, black skin.

When he was down to his underwear, I could see the outline of his cock curved up his abdomen, the mushroom tip peaking above the waistband. He caressed it with his hand, stroking through the material, his eyelids narrowing in pleasure and mischief, his lips parted and glistening.

"You're beautiful," I moaned and slid my skirt up my thighs.

"So are you."

He hooked his briefs with both thumbs, slid them down his thighs and let them drop to the floor. His erection sprang free, glorious and proud above a heavy scrotum. A chain reaction of excitement commenced within my body from my nipples to the moistening slit between my thighs.

Darren tossed his briefs aside with a kick of a blue heel then walked to me. That close, I could feel the heat radiating from his body. I leaned forward and rested my cheek against his muscular thigh.

Cocoa butter tainted with a hint of sweat filled my nostrils and made my head swim. I caressed the shiny tips of the shoes with one hand as the other wrapped around the back of his leg and slid to his buttocks. They clenched once, then relaxed. I slid my hand between the cheeks.

With my face still pressed against his quivering thigh, I tilted my head up to look first into his eyes, to see his desire, then back down to his cock just inches from my face. It knocked with each deep inhalation, bouncing heavily. The foreskin pulled back

I pumped slowly at first, my touch light against the velvety smoothness. Like little feathers, I fluttered my fingers up and down the shaft until Darren was bent at the waist and gasping.

"Not yet." He held himself steady with a hand on my shoulder, the other clinging tightly to the base of his cock to avert the orgasm. I rolled to my knees, kissed his outty navel, and he helped me to my feet.

He began with my breasts, kissing them through the fabric of my blouse before liberating them with tender movements. He was so swift and seductive, it only took a moment before I was completely naked. Completely ready. With others, I burned with embarrassment at this juncture, but this time was different. The way he looked at me at that moment, I would have done anything.

Darren reclined on the bed and pulled me on top of him. I tried to position myself so I didn't lay too much weight on him, but he insisted. I slid up his body to take his cock and that was when he refused.

"Turn around," he said and made a twirling motion with his finger. I crawled over him and positioned myself to face his cock. Taking it gently in my hand, I pulled it to point straight in the air.

"Woman, you got a gorgeous ass," he groaned from the pillows and traced my labia with his fingers. He played in the slickness, running his finger from my asshole to my clit and back again. I whimpered.

Mouth gaping and watering, I looked past the magnificent cock in my hand to his feet and those blue heels. It was all the courage I needed. I arched my back as much as I could, thrust

point. Complete abandon. I rode and sucked wildly. We came together, moans muffled by mouthfuls of each other's pleasure.

"No, no, no. The other one!" I sat on Darren's bed, wrapped in the sheets, and watched him at the vanity trying on different wigs.

The doors of the armoire were open. Half his wardrobe consisted of extravagant, brightly colored women's clothing. I favored the straight black bob with the kimono robe. He liked the curly red mane that matched the fabric.

"You're right," he said and tamed the wig with a silver handled brush.

He looked incredible, but there was something missing. I searched through the sea of clothing on the floor until I found it.

"What you got there?" Darren asked as I straddled his lap. He grabbed my ass with both hands and pulled me closer.

"Garnet Chrome." I gasped when he took my nipple between his lips and sucked until it was hard again. "Make an O."

"With pleasure." He slid a hand between my legs.

"No, with your mouth. Like this." I demonstrated by opening my mouth wide and stretching my lips tight. I popped the lid of the lipstick and rolled up the tube. I leaned in to apply the color.

"Darren, stop smiling," I giggled. "I can't do this if you don't stop smiling. Stop it."

"I can't."

I gave up and ran the lipstick over my own mouth. I covered his lips with mine then pulled away to admire my work.

"That color looks fabulous on you."

Cross-cultural Erotica

cream

Kinks

Cross-cultural Erotica

Vegetable Medley

Madelynne Ellis

My job is not glamorous, but it fills the lonely hours between dusk and dawn, if there's nobody at home and you burn up in the sun. If in fact, you're someone like me. My bony white hands stick out from the checked sleeves of my uniform, palms tinted red from work and the heat of my skin. A fringe of white-blond hair tickles the bridge of my nose, obscuring my eyes. It's my shield against the world, my little curtain to hide behind.

"Rachel, you can leave those tins. Could you take these cabbages to aisle four, please?" calls Jeremy, the evening supervisor.

He's trying to be nice. He's also grinning lewdly at me, which emphasizes his ferretlike features. Long face, coarse gold-brown hair and beady eyes. He's almost as bony as I am, and looks just as bad in the store-issue blue-checked top and never-fit trousers. He's also the only person who ever uses my real name. To everyone else, I'm just Ghost.

"Playing favorites again." Maggie is working next to me. She jams her elbow into my ribs. "Better be careful, Ghost, he'll have you in the bakery next, rolling the dough."

"Yeah, yeah," I say, rising quickly before my cheeks start to glow. I leave her stacking tinned tuna and head off towards the vegetable stands with the Savoys.

his cock busting his fly. Is it possible to let someone down gently? I mean, can you imagine us together, all those hard edges, hips grinding like flint and steel. We'd probably ignite the whole bakery. He's all right, just not my type, and he's been trying it on for weeks now. People have started to make remarks. I really hope he doesn't make some cringe-worthy announcement over the Tannoy on Valentine's Day. That'd be too horrible, and I look like some weird kind of dip-dyed tomato when I blush.

Now, if Shawn Munro wanted my personal attention, that would be different. Shawn's a nobody around here, like me. I've overheard him telling people that it pays the bills, but he's really a sculptor. The only thing he seems to have sculpted so far is himself. We're talking a clear six-foot of corded muscles, satinlike ebony skin and eyes that sparkle like buffed obsidian. He's my fantasy pinup made flesh and the image I get off to every morning before I sleep.

His mouth—he tries to hide it, but tiny laughter lines betray his warmth. I long to explore his mouth. I want to trace my white fingertips over his lips and feel the whisper of his breath. I want to taste him, be pinned beneath him. He could probably hold me down with one hand.

To my delight, he's standing by the exotic fruit display when I arrive with the cabbages, carefully balancing mangoes, lychees, and passion fruit—an artist at work. I watch his butt as I push the trolley between the vegetable racks. His trousers pull tight each time he bends to lift a tray, the seam riding up into the channel between his buttocks, emphasizing the hard muscles of his cheeks.

flanks, then dig my fingers in for a good measure, enjoying a nice firm squeeze.

"What the . . ." he snarls, while his body jolts forward in shock, upsetting the display. Fruit bounces squashily on the floor. I hope he hasn't been at it too long.

"Dammit!" He kicks a fallen mango, then turns his outrage upon me. I freeze and try to look innocent, but it's hard when my arm is still extended and there's no one else around. His face is beautiful, even in fury. His eyes blaze, and his anger sharpens all his best features, cheekbones, jawline, eyes.

"Ghost," he hisses, his temper subsiding. I'm surprised he knows who I am. Most people don't. I'm one of those people others look through.

"What the hell was that all about?"

"What? I don't know," I bluff and confess in one breath. I know I should say sorry, but I can't make myself. My heart is racing. Feeling his arse beneath my palm is the biggest thrill I've had since I started working here six months ago. I want to do it again to his other cheek.

He stands very still as he awaits my apology. After a moment, when he realizes it isn't coming, he cocks his head to one side and regards me with a faintly sadistic smile.

"How would you like it?" he asks.

I cock my head too. Nobody has ever spanked me. "That depends," I say as nonchalantly as I can. "From you, I might like it." Lordy, the devil has my tongue today.

"Is that right?" He sounds intrigued. "Then let's do it. Where are you working? Let's see if I can wreck your display." He glances at the trolley full of Savoys. "Cabbages." He takes my hand and tugs me towards the appropriate stand.

"Up." He tips me headfirst into the winter vegetables.

Cabbages and turnips roll and bounce away down the aisles. Potatoes press into my stomach and chest, and I find myself gripping a carrot. He pulls down my store-issue pants to reveal my white cheeks, divided by the whisper of my thong.

"Hey," I complain. "I only smacked you." This is getting a bit heavy. Fantasies don't just come true. Or do they? I wriggle, trying to get down, or comfortable, I'm not sure which. The potatoes shift beneath me, while his hand settles over my rear, firm and warm.

"Ready?"

"No!"

"Too bad." His hand comes down upon my rump with a sharp crack. The impact stings and then disperses as a warming prickle.

"Ouch!"

He rubs away the heat then lays on two more slaps.

"I owe you two now," I say, unable to stop myself wriggling. Despite my indignation, I want more. Not just smacks; I'm enjoying his attention. This is much better than my masturbation fantasies.

"Keen, aren't you?" he remarks.

"You're enjoying this." I look back over my shoulder to find him grinning.

"You blush very nicely," he says, rubbing circles over my now pink cheeks. I'm surprised they're not burning red. They feel that way. Still, I puff the hair away from my eyes, letting him see the excitement in them.

"Are you going to say sorry?"

I shake my head. If this is what I get for misbehaving, I'm not about to reform.

"Then I'll have to try something more persuasive."

"Do your worst," I say, anticipating the sting of his palm. Instead, he unbuckles his belt. The supple leather slithers through his belt loops, and he coils one end around his hand. Suddenly, I'm not feeling nearly so cocky. "Someone might come," I hiss. This kinky stuff could cost us our jobs.

His grin broadens. "Let 'em. I'm sure they'll enjoy the sight of your raw behind."

Jeremy would, I'm sure. For a moment, I picture him joining us, hand rubbing his crotch, while Shawn kisses my warmed behind. Then I banish him to the warehouse, and hope he doesn't turn up for real.

Shawn drapes his belt over my bum, sliding it against my skin and teasing me with its promise. I stare resolutely at the display of curly kale, determined to seem aloof, despite the fact that my insides are churning. One of the potatoes beneath me is pressing into my bladder, and coupled with the pleasant heat in my bottom I have to fight the urge to shake my arse at him. I await the next blow, desperate for an excuse to wriggle and squirm.

Smack.

"One," he counts, after the belt lands against my right cheek. It stings far more than his palm.

Smack.

"Two."

This time it's the left. And the heat is explosive. It streaks down my legs and up my spine, then flows back to concentrate on the point of impact. "How many?" I whisper. I'm not panting yet, though I suspect that's what he's aiming for. It won't take many to achieve. Only five, I suspect. Only five until I'm whimpering, and begging him to give me what I really want—his thick, hard cock inside me.

The next lash is directed across the very tops of my thighs, where it raises a burning welt to match the two already scoring my cheeks.

"Three."

I'm shaking. My nipples are now two hardened points, and my clit is swollen, ready for an insistent touch

"Two more," he says.

Four and five land across my bum. A crimson flush sweeps over my whole body. It rushes into my face, causing tears to prickle my eyes. Then my thong rubs into my cleft. "Oh!" I squeal. Just the brush of the cotton is almost too much.

"Easy," he says, stroking me gently. His thumb traces the path of the most vibrant welt, then follows the line of my thong into the cleft between my cheeks. The fabric is damp. He pulls it aside, and his thumb teases my swollen clit.

"Gently, gently!" I beg, groaning loudly. The sensation is so intense it's like pinpricks all over my skin. My clit is on fire, and I just know that too much pressure will be too much and leave me numb. "Ease off," I whisper.

"How about I ease in?"

"Seriously, here?" We're going to get caught. I know it. Know it and don't give a damn about it.

"Don't move," he says as if he already knows this. I don't question him. He dashes off down the aisle, turning left at the end, to return a moment later with a pack of condoms and a one-kilogram tub of Flora.

Condoms! Whoa, things are happening fast—good fast. I ought to try smacking guys more often, if this is what comes of it. Just watching him rip open a foil packet with his teeth turns the space between my thighs molten.

"What's that for?" I ask, nodding towards the margarine.

"Just a little lube," he replies, peeling off the lid. I can't help wondering why he didn't just pick up a tube of KY. Not that we need it. I'm already wet and warm. Suddenly he lifts a parsnip from a nearby crate, and looks at me.

I look at the parsnip. And the parsnip, well, it looks kind of hard and knobbly, and let's be honest, what I want is his hard black cock, not a white tapered root.

Aghast, I watch him dip it into the margarine. I've a feeling it's headed somewhere not used to being stretched.

Confirming my guess, he scoops margarine onto his thumb and rubs it in around my anus. The slow spiral lights nerves I never knew existed. He circles around with the tapered end of the parsnip next. The tip dabs and teases, until each brush flutters through me to trace phantom caresses on my clit.

When he finally pushes it in, the shock drives me deeper into the potato stack. They roll like vibrator beads beneath me as I arch and lift my hips trying to acclimatize myself to the unusual stretch. It takes a moment or two, and then I realize that he's only pushed it in maybe an inch.

"Relax," he whispers against my shoulder, between kisses. "I've got something else for you."

"Bring it on," I urge, praying it's his cock and not a nice banana or a cucumber.

His clothing tickles my smarting red cheeks. The parsnip presses in deeper, setting my back passage alight once more. Its presence is weirdly invasive. The urge to expel it is great. I'm almost shaking with lust by the time his cock-tip brushes my inner thigh.

The intimate contact steals my breath away. I don't inhale again until he's inside me. I feel as though a missing part of me has been reconnected.

The fit is just right. We rock together. He tries to hold me steady, but I want to race. The dual penetration and the delicate rub of my cotton thong are hurrying me on. My orgasm sparkles ahead of me like a glitter stream. I go stiff as I fall into the rainbow, then shake to the natural rhythm of my body. For perhaps half a minute, time has no meaning.

I stretch. Shawn wiggles the parsnip in my arse, making himself buck. I guess he can feel it, too, and he obviously likes it. His breathing becomes increasing ragged as he strokes in and out. He leans right over me so that I can feel his breath against my hair, and he weaves our fingers together.

A trolley squeaks nearby.

I don't know if he hears it, too, but he clasps hold of me tight and rides me faster, coming almost immediately in three long shudders.

I want to lie together until he's soft and slips out, enjoying the intimacy only fulfilling sex brings, but the squeak and now footsteps are getting closer.

Shawn takes a step back from me, pulling the parsnip free as he does. I slide off the potatoes, and hitch my trousers. There's still a distinct Ghost-shaped impression amongst the winter vegetables when Jeremy reaches us pushing crates of leeks.

"Haven't you done those cabbages yet?" he says. "I've brought these for you."

He positions himself between me and Shawn, who hides the used condom and the parsnip behind his back.

"And what is this doing here?" Jeremy lifts the open tub of Flora. I shrug. Shawn returns to his fruit-stacking endeavor. "Well?"

"It was here when I got here," I lie. "Maybe a customer changed their mind."

He eyes me suspiciously. "What about the rest of this stuff?"

"Kids," I suggest, scooping up a turnip. "This mess is why I haven't begun stacking yet."

He nods. "Better bin this." He puts the lid on the margarine. "Rachel, can I have a word?" His beady blue eyes turn an impressive shade of indigo. "Are you busy later?"

Timing I think, truly awful timing. "I'm afraid I've got something booked."

"Another time?" he asks hopefully.

I glance at Shawn. His trousers are pulled tight across his bum again. I know I already have what I want. I don't have to settle for second best, even if I do feel sorry for him. I brush the back of his palm gently. "Sorry, I'm afraid I can't."

"Oh!" he says, following my former line of sight to Shawn. "You two. I didn't realize." He gapes at Shawn then shakes his head. "Forget what I said. Get back to work and less gossiping."

I wait until he's gone before I retrieve my discarded trolley. There's an added spring to my step.

"Are you free later?" Shawn asks. He presents me with a passion fruit as though he's a magician.

I peep up at him from beneath my fringe as sexily as I can with no makeup and the store uniform. "What did you have in mind?" He produces the parsnip from behind his back. "I'm a bit bored with still life." He laughs, and I smile with him.

Dirty Velvet

William Dean

Well, how does one come to these things? Experience: intense, perhaps excruciating, experience. Some come to theirs early on. A childhood trauma or some arbitrary circumstance in adolescence, just as the urges bloom. Who can say? Everyone is so different, responses unique. The loss of virginity for some becomes obsessional. They want, no, rather, they must duplicate it over and over again. With as many of the same elements as possible. Well. That's how it is with some people.

But then. We're not here to talk about other people, are we? Of course not. Only you and me. That's one of the blessings of privacy, isn't it? Quiet little intimate talks just between two people. Sitting here, just you and I. The fire's not too warm, is it? I'll refill our glasses. Oh, please. Don't worry. I won't make you go first. You see, I'm comfortable with myself.

Beginnings, then. I was starting to say how it began for me. Not too early in my life. Not that I'm a late bloomer, so to speak. The opportunity had simply not arisen before. I won't shock you by using, well, coarse terms, will I? No. I thought not. There's a certain, what shall we call it, frisson? Yes, a frisson in using the more base words. So, then. We'll just say I'd fucked a number of women before it happened. I see you smile that cynical little smile. Well, of course, some could be called making love. Just as some, oh, yes, some resisted. At first. Some women prefer it that way. But, on the whole, you know, I've discovered that once beyond the first few orgasms, those who still want more respond to direct fucking, animalistic, raw, passionate. Yes, we can share a little laugh about that, can't we?

No, I'm not hedging, really. Beginnings always have beginnings before them, don't they? So. It's a truism that the more sophisticated you become, the more you can be jaded by simple fucking. Thirty different women, all ways, all places. A man can find himself drawn to exteriors, details, settings. How many times can your libido be stimulated by baggy sweats or tight satin before you simply glance at it, nod to yourself. The people today, what do they call that? "Been there, done that."

That's me. Done her, done that. Move on.

I like the way you look at me now. It's different. No need to deny it. You see, as I said, I notice details. The curiosity was there before, but now there's something quite different in the look. A glow? A new intensity. I understand it well.

Have you been to one of those out-of-time places? Oh, not as a gaping tourist. Nothing so base. Shirking around in a baseball cap, T-shirt, Nikes on your feet? How could you hope to reinvent yourself in such tawdry clothing? Not at a Renaissance fair, I assure you. Yes, I'm getting to the good part, as you call it. History is its own place, you know. They call it a dimension, but it's more than just that. A place in the world, a place in your mind. So. A Renaissance fair.

In the heat of summer, with the brusque smell in the air of dust and dirt, sweat and incense. The senses begin to reel. Here a dainty dance tune, there a skirl of pipe, a wisp of ballad, a martial drumbeat as the tramping soldiers pass, some unidentifiable drone of strings, the lowing blast of horn. Ale flows into your steps as you drink and wander. You go back, you see? Time drifts away, your time, I mean. The watch on your wrist seems alien. You strip it off. You wonder if you're becoming a child at a circus. That's not it. You're still a man, but now you're rooted in another mind, a mindset.

Did I mention I never knew her name? That helps, really. Anonymity is wonderful. Who was it? That Jong woman I think, who invented the term *zipless fuck*. And Brando in the Paris Tango movie. No names. It's good that way. At least, I thought so afterwards. I still do. She could have had any name. Esmeralda or Juliet or Venus. I can give her any name I choose, you see? Your name, if I knew it.

No, don't tell me. It's better without knowing.

She was as alone as I was. That was obvious even to my spinning mind. Long hair, loosed in tresses that seemed tangled and curling around her small face. Odd, now that I think of it, her face. You know how the faces of some of those people from old paintings seem familiar. Like that. Like some form of déjà vu. Seen you before, but where, but when? No matter. There's a recognition though. Yes, I know. You felt it tonight when we met. I did, too.

May I? There's something I'd like to show you. Just a moment. I had it made for me. Well, not for me, but for: a woman. Here. Yes. It is very lovely. Yes, velvet. No, it's not the one she wore. Hardly. But, you see, I remembered it. Had a costume maker do it up, just like this.

Will you? Just for me, just this once, right now? You can dress in the bathroom. It's quite easy to get into. Just slip it on. You can leave the laces undone, if you like. Yes, yes, she did have them undone. Would you like to wear it that way?

I'd like to see you in it like that. Take your time. Get it comfortable before you come back. I'll refill our glasses, all right?

That was quick. Some women, well. You can put your other things just there on the chair. Hmm. Have you ever felt psychic? No, I just ask because I see that you've taken your underthings off, too. That's how she was. Not a stitch on under the velvet dress. It feels, it feels so good that way, doesn't it? Come, sit down here again. Shall we have a toast? To, what, to old times? Perfect.

You do remind me. Can I be honest, direct? The swell of your breasts, just blush of nipple showing. It takes me back, you see? Very like hers. I have a notion it was that way back then. Women had a seductiveness about them and weren't so afraid of showing it. In their eyes, in their very breath, I think. You smile. You're enjoying this, aren't you? Why else do it?

I saw her coming down a dingy alley. Walking like a tart, like a wench. A swaying roll to her hips beneath the draped folds of velvet as she came. And, as I said, the faint pink blush of nipples peering over the bodice. Did I mention about the psychic? I feel it sometimes. Not that you can read another's mind, but there are things you just suddenly know by looking at them. Here the woman came, dressed in her velvet, and she looked to me as if she'd just been fucked, not a nice, clean featherbed fuck, but a roll in the dirt, whimper-and-laugh fuck, if you know what I mean. Yet looking into her eyes—very like yours right now—looking deeply there I could see—I knew!—that she hadn't fucked. Not yet. But, lord, how she wanted to.

Eyes met and spoke without words. You know how that can be, I'm sure. And she turned, looked over her shoulder at me, and slowly walked back down that little alleyway between some stalls or booths. Back into shadows. I followed her, of course. And when I'd caught up with her, she turned again. Just stood there. My fingers trembled. How strange that was, I thought. A man like I am, trembling to reach out and encircle her waist. I leaned over, without a word, and gently kissed first the pink of one nipple then the other. I felt her shudder in my hands, beneath my lips. God, it was incredible. I was hard as a stone already. Well, as I am now, you can see.

Will it matter to you? When you're whispering, when you're sighing, when you feel my tongue move across your clit, swathed in the velvet? Will it matter whether it's you or the velvet or the dress or the moment? That's so lovely, that you close your eyes right now. You don't have to speak, not a word. I know what you know.

Who cares what it really is? Destiny, fate, serendipity. We might have fucked anyway. True. But that dress, that sweet, sweet, soft velvet around you, touching me, too. It's powerful. You can feel it, I know, as I pull you closer.

No, please. Say nothing. It's not needed. I'm trembling again, feel the vibration from my fingers as they slide up under your dress. Your thighs are warm as a summer day. Your lips tasting of warm, bitter ale. Don't worry, you won't ruin the dress. Sweat in it, stain it, no matter. Make it part of you, make you part of it. Hush now. Hush. Hold your sounds in. Bank up every sigh you want to cry, every muffled scream of pleasure. Hold it. Hold. Until we, until we . . . fuck.

An Evening at Katzenspieler's

Cervo

Her heart thudded inside her chest and then skipped a beat as she lifted the phone. In her free hand Patsy held her very own copy of Empress Theodora's wine goblet over the mirrored surface of the reproduction Venetian table. There in the glass appeared the number of Katzenspieler's. It was etched upside down into the metal of the goblet so that only she could decipher the ten digits of the phone number. These she tapped into the phone. After the first ring, her vision was getting blurry from the need to hear Nera's velvet, cool voice.

The phone rang and rang. Her nipples started to ache. The torment of uncertainty would continue until someone picked her up. Katzenspieler's still refused to have an answering machine or voicemail of any kind. At last she heard Nera's voice murmuring hello. Then she was almost able to exhale.

"Oh, you *are* open?" trying for disingenuous and wanting to be casual. The flutter in her voice gave her away.

"Yes." Then a pause followed by, "Are we ever closed?" Katzenspieler's did not close. Someone was always there ready to serve. Sometimes the whole staff was totally booked, and no one answered the phones. When Nera traveled, she left the place to her staff, who were not averse to letting the phone ring twenty times before they answered. She knew about waiting for an answer from them. Now and then the phone company simply cut you off. Then you had to start ringing again until someone finally picked up the receiver. They were always polite, quick, and distant. Their manner hurt her feelings, but she kept calling even more often.

Recognizing her voice, Nera asked, "Do you want someone, Patsy, in particular?" It sounded too direct, a little gauche. Patsy thought herself clever by turning the question aside. She heard a piano and the sound of light laughter after a pause. Nera played the piano sometimes all by herself in the music room. Then she realized that Nera had answered on a speakerphone.

"Nera, can you send the Packard?" she asked. She thought she would faint. Her thighs were hot, and the little ridge between her puss and her anus had started to itch. She could hear the sound of low, female laughter in the background. Crystal glassware struck metal somewhere. Lately it seemed she could think of nothing but pressing her face into the bodies of others.

Voices chatted quietly. She thought of skirts and trousers wrapping around thighs. Other, more complicated sounds came to her. She felt the warmth between her legs grow and then a spreading, buttery moisture came between her own legs. She would soon be there among them. She would be laughing, close, and again a part of their evening. But first she needed special attention. Her fingers gripped the phone so hard they became cold.

"The Packard?" repeated Nera. "Some of the other girls asked for that. Are you willing to share?"

"No," Patsy snapped. She knew that Nera had three matching limousines from the 1940s all restored to a deep hunter green with brass fittings inside and out. They all had the same long, thick snouts. Their perfect antique engines grumbled when they were made to sit still like restless, petulant lions. All three had been specially fitted in the backseat to accommodate Katzenspieler's clients. But Nera would admit to owning only one so that she could be generous or stingy as the whim came upon her. Tonight she teased.

"No?" sounding a little taken aback. She made herself seem defensive with a dash of mock surprise.

"No, please. I don't want to share. I want the car to myself and I want—I want Cosimo again, please." It was not meant to sound like a plea.

"Cosimo? Really? Well, well. I'll see if he can be had." This meant that Nera would disappear from her end of the conversation for half an hour even if Cosimo were standing nearby her. She waited for Nera's voice, but her other hand could not avoid leaving the goblet and trailing across her thigh in search of the division in her robe.

She started to pant in short waves when the phone came back to life.

"I can send Cosimo. And do you want his special kit?"

"Um, yes. Yes, please. I do." Of course she did, and Nera knew it. Nera broke the connection. Patsy hung up her phone and rolled onto her side to calm her breathing.

Madame Nera cut off the other woman's voice and then dialed Junker, the chauffeur. They spoke briefly after which Junker got out two black alligator leather cases. One was much heavier than the other. He swung them about like toy balloons with his enormous arms and chest. He had spent all his free time lifting weights since the age of ten. It gave him a gnarled look despite his pale skin and bald head.

His long arms and legs added to his powerful stance. The

only truly peculiar thing were his enormous, rippling buttocks. His hips were of average width but the cheeks of his ass were nearly eight inches in depth and stood out like boulders. He had once nearly suffocated a male client who was trapped between their powerful grip during a "sitting."

Junker opened the empty suitcase and hefted the other next to it in the back seat. Then he took a silver canister of warm water and placed it on the floor in front of the backseat. Following this he went to a small apartment at the back of the garage, which faced out onto a tiny lanai. The apartment door stood open, and the room was in near darkness except for the light of a single candle. Through the glass doors to the garden, Junker could see that the plants in the tiny garden were covered with snow.

He tapped twice on the open door, "Cosimo, we have an appointment."

A small gravely voice replied, "I know. She wants me again. Nera called. I'm ready," and the door glided further open to reveal a dwarf of about three feet in height with one arm, wearing a heavy silk kimono, a satin shirt, and tailored slacks all in shades of light gray. Cosimo's one remaining hand had only three tiny fingers, and yet the man was a neat bundle of tightly connected muscle. The front of his small trousers bulged tenaciously.

"Indeed you are," said Junker, who took care of Cosimo's equipment with Germanic zeal, sucking and bending to the smaller man's whims whenever time permitted. Cosimo always had a pronounced hard-on. It was no longer a matter of humor between them. Junker was reverently impressed by the thickness of the dwarf's member. His mouth watered.

"You are always ready," he said.

Cosimo smiled at him. "These people we serve are shopkeepers who got lucky, Junker. They create nothing. They just move money around. I am an artist. So are you."

"You are? What do you create?"

"Dreams, Junker. I create illusions. Most of all I create hope."

"And me, Cosimo? What do I create?"

Cosimo smiled up into Junker's huge face. Then he reached out and stroked the larger man's cock. Finally he patted his enormous bottom and said, "A place for them to dream, a saddle for their thoughts, my dear friend. A coach and four, an ocean liner at sunset, a magic carpet, a Packard on a country road. In short, you give them the clichés they love best and are too lazy to find for themselves. They are cruel but full of fear. They mince along their dark inner roads. You give them their clichés. I am their secret deformity made real."

When they got to the car, Junker waited and then closed Cosimo into the open suitcase. In this way his clients could know he was nestled nearby without causing them embarrassment. Junker lifted the plush-covered panel in the center of the rear seat. He spat into his handkerchief and ran it around the mother of pearl seat of the bidet to brighten the shine. With a light whisking, the spun aluminum bowl and drain beneath the seat reflected his shadowy face to his satisfaction.

He pressed a small button centered in front of the bidet seat and felt warm ionized air blow up into his face from the circle of tiny jets. The ionization made their pubic hair glossy when dried. Then he tested a small electric pump that whirred beneath the seat. A warm fountain of scented water spouted about two feet in the air when the on switch was fully depressed. Finally he tested that the gold inlaid lid of the bidet closed with the firm snap of fine workmanship. He put six small squares of finished ecru silk in a small compartment in the back of the front seat in case the lady wanted to wipe herself.

"Many costly asses and cunts have been washed there, eh, my friend?" chuckled Cosimo. Junker kept his face set in stone as befits a chauffeur. He made sure a small silver box of tampons was in its place concealed within the armrest on the passenger side. Each had an engraved silver applicator. A bottle of Krug was chilling in the ice chest of the drinks console.

After a twenty-minute drive through the snowy darkness, Junker opened the door of the rear seat for his passenger. Light perfume filled the interior cabin of the car as Patsy climbed in and sat down. He could smell the light urine scent of her pussy and the heat of her body through the perfume. Her hand flew to the surface of the cases next to her on the seat, but Junker took her shoulder gently to restrain her.

"Soon" was all he said. He let his fingers crush her skin against bone, but not enough to bruise. She winced and let go of the case. She sat like a lamb with her heart in her throat as they pulled away from her house.

They drove toward the park at the center of the city. As they neared the park, the snow stopped. When they reached the gardens at that center, the Packard's special tires bit through the virgin white without pause until they were alone in an open circular plane of snow. It surrounded a winged statue. The blue moonlight of evening touched every frozen surface. The woman took a small silver egg from under her left breast and thumbed it open. From within she took a large white pill, which, though its taste was bitter, gave her a measure of temporary calm. She took it with champagne. She had eaten nothing but boiled eggs for two days. Her heart slowed a little, and the ache between her legs seemed to ease. Her nipples burned. The moisture increased as she started to relax and drift a little.

She could make out the winged statue of Venus in the center of the circular garden. One stone knee was lifted, and the wings spread as though she was just landing on her pedestal from some joyous flight. Patsy thought Venus might have come to be with her. The goddess was poised with snow resting on her prominent nipples and even the crest of her belly. She wished this divine cunt would take her in her great stone arms and crush their breasts together as they kissed.

Half of the stone face was rendered secret by the snow. In the same way, the woman felt half of herself to have disappeared in the life she lived now. She was a slave to the place between her legs. If only Venus would call, she saw herself making tiny footprints in the snow or perhaps gliding over it to embrace the statue in flight. She could let her hand trail over the goddess's broad, firm, round bottom and reach down between the cheeks for the touch of her pussy. Then she would make those hard stone thighs yield to her touch by applying her fingers and tongue to her divine sex.

The fantasy distressed her. She had never made love to a woman before she met Nera. She had never even tried when it was offered by her friends. She was sure she would do it wrong. Now she longed to lick the goddess or any woman. She shuddered when she realized she wanted to be at the mercy of Venus or Nera, to do their bidding, to defile herself at their command. She wanted to be free to prove her submission to a woman, a man, anyone who would take control of her. She wanted to feel human, but the statue did not move. Venus was impervious to her desires. Patsy's thighs burned as though she had a rash, and yet the goddess showed no mercy.

Instead, Junker opened the rear door letting in a blast of cold air. She shrank back from the shock as his huge shoulders thrust into the rear cabin. Her nipples bit her in protest of the sudden cold. Junker snapped open the near case, withdrew and closed the door. He then walked off toward the line of trees to smoke a short, fat, black cigar.

Cosimo unfolded his small body slowly from inside the suitcase like a magician being his own rabbit. Then he rose to his feet and opened the second case. He stripped off his shirt to reveal his muscled chest and horribly scarred shoulder. His olive skin was otherwise flawless, and so he was handsome despite his stature and the mark where his arm had been.

"I will remind you that my arm was torn off in a tragic golfing accident. Therefore, I must ask your assistance in one thing. Please remove your underpants." This abbreviated tale, though true, was told thus incompletely to all the ladies who "used" Cosimo. They longed for a fuller explanation but were never granted it.

He made a point of referring to their handmade undergarments as though they were army issue. Being demeaned made them feel the experience was personal for him. His caustic style in referring to his cruel fate on the links only added to his mysterious appeal. She had one erotic dream of him threatening her with a wedgie as she lay staked out in a sand trap.

While she removed her stockings and panties, he opened the second case, which contained a finely wrought silver pump with two articulated hoses. One he attached to the silver tank on the floor, noting that the gold and silver rampant eagle at the top had been polished to a rich, dull shine. The other he inserted into an ivory dildo with a series of small holes running up each side. It had been buttered with olive oil for the evening's use.

Cosimo restacked the cases to make room, and invited the lady to shift to the center of the rear seat so that she would now occupy the bidet at its center. He flicked on the warm air so that her ass and pussy would remain cozy while he inserted the douche. He opened the small drain that vented into the snow beneath the car. The water would form an odd block of ice in the frigid snow. He wondered if dogs would find it interesting and lick it.

Then he knelt between her thighs and started to massage her pussy as he made low, happy sounds in his throat. His three-fingered hand found her clit and began to amaze it. Then he applied his tongue, and his fingers located the slick opening of her vagina. He was frigging her with his whole hand. Once confident that she was ready, he inserted the fat ivory dildo into her pussy and flicked on the pump on the button next to the air jet. Soon warm water was flowing into her and dribbling with a pleasant tinkling sound into the bowl beneath her.

He shut off the lights and checked his palm pilot for her musical preferences. The strains of *Tristan and Isolde* began to rise from the eight speakers in the Packard. She lay back against the gray-green plush upholstery of the back seat as pint after pint of warm fluid flowed into and out of her pussy. He licked her clit firmly as his face grew soggy. When she was fully relaxed, Cosimo eased back the cuff of his one sleeve with his teeth, exposing his forearm.

"And now it is time to behave," he said. He reached between the seats where Junker had left a small plastic tub of lube. It was the color of bubble gum and smelled of a heavy sweetness. He plunged in his three tiny fingers up to the middle of his forearm and waited for the goo to soften and penetrate his skin. Then he removed his hand from the bucket and started to invade her anus. She squealed and tried to pull back, but not from his mouth, which was sealed to her cunt again.

She whimpered and wiggled, but at last the hard wrinkles of her anus began to relent and slowly her ass opened to his assault. She felt she should resist but his tongue on her clit would not allow it. When all three of his fingers were inside her, she knew that this time his whole hand and wrist would follow. She eased drew up her legs so as to fully expose and open her ass to his authority. Slowly he screwed his fist into her and continued to twist it within her until it was halfway to his tiny elbow.

Tears rolled down her cheeks as her body gave way again and again. Sighs came from her. She stared at the dark stone goddess leaping in the endless darkness. Her chest felt as though a great anvil of sorrow rested on it. She wanted the love of that cold hard thing. She was powerless against her desires. What had she become? What would she become now?

Her sighs turned to moans and then short barks as she was overtaken by cascading spasms. Pushing and then pulling his fist in her ass, Cosimo watched her melt impaled on his arm. Then he took out his greasy, stained hand and found her nipples through the thin fabric of her dress. He bit her clit as he did so again and again just as her body rose and fell from one precipice to the next.

After forty minutes, Junker stamped his cigar butt into the

snow and headed back to the close heat of the Packard. By then the bidet was closed, the cases were again shut, and Cosimo was nowhere to be seen. He was in fact taking a leak in the snow. In the car the heavy camembert sweetness of cunt hung in the air. Between the heat and the pussy smell, Junker became a little dizzy.

The woman lay curled in the dark as the Wagner neared its end. She was nearly naked except for the rags of her dress in the hot car. He would give her another dress sent along by Nera. She was turned away from him on her side with her face toward the corner of the seat and her legs drawn up to her. The crack in her round, white ass glistened with gobbets of shiny grease. He would have to wipe her to protect the Packard from stains. Was she ill? Sad? Nuts? It seemed odd to Junker that she might be so withdrawn. *Don't they do this for pleasure?* he wondered. It costs them enough. He found a linen towel and wondered how to approach the subject of wiping her ass.

Patsy felt a surge of nausea from the stale cigar smell, which came into the hot cabin of the car with Junker. It was like the steam-heated bathroom at school on days when they had all sauerkraut for lunch. Then she thought again. No. It was like discovering fresh dog shit on one's shoe, and the idea made her queasy. She wanted to roll down a window and wondered if that would be allowed. Then she remembered who was paying here. She sat up and grabbed the towel from Junker. Then she wiped at her behind a little and sat on the towel in the far corner. Junker decided that would have to do. She did not look ready to discuss her ass with him.

There was also a deeper funk around Patsy's nose that lingered under the other smells that made her wonder if perhaps Cosimo had secretly come while frigging her. He had only one hand. Could he do that? Had it been a spontaneous reaction to her? Passion? Was she pleased or horrified at that idea? Why did it matter to her?

She gave a short laugh. She was sure he had no hand free to help himself. She liked that idea. It meant that he was subject to her weaknesses. It made them companions in pleasure. That might be somehow comforting. But she did not like him thinking he was entitled to take the liberty of pleasure in her presence without permission. His pleasure should be a gratuity, not a presumption. She liked this thought. Its construction made her feel safe.

Junker found his sandwich under the driver's seat. It was his snack that he carried when he drove in case he had to wait for some reason. The pecorino cheese in it had gotten quite warm from the heater blasting away in the car. The salty, pungent smell in the front seat was quite pronounced. He supposed the reek of pussy overwhelmed it in the back. He discretely ditched the sandwich in the snow dispelling the odor from the car. He was not hungry at the moment anyway. Cosimo was again next to him in the front seat. He stroked his perpetual hard-on thoughtfully through his trousers. Junker smiled.

Soon the Packard swept under the portico of Katzenspieler's. Patsy's panties were greasy and stained, but it did not seem to matter. She left them on the floor of the car. She put on the dress Nera had provided and the fur coat she had worn that evening. Her cunt was sore, and her ass was on fire. She released one silent, experimental fart. It burned unpleasantly but then what could one expect?

A greasy slickness radiated out from her anus and down her thighs. She felt drippy. It was not nice, and she wanted to wash a little. Once inside she was greeted by Nera, who pressed two tall flutes of champagne on her one right after the other. A small spoonful of white powder cleared her nose and her thoughts. Nera understood completely that Patsy would need to take a shower and a short lie down before joining the party.

Patsy could see into the emerald party room. At once she felt strangely forgiven, like a little girl after a severe punishment who is again allowed to be among her family. She felt at home. She could relent here to those things that made her what she was. She could be as nature intended her—fulfilled, happy, at one with herself. She wondered if Cosimo was again available.

Small indirect lights in the party room beyond revealed three women. They stood relaxed and happy in a small circle of warmth. They were caning a young man with a beautiful slender body using a long, slender leather-clad rod with brass studs. He was tied with brocade ribbon over the end of a chaise lounge, which bent him over sharply. Three peacock feathers emerged from a thick wooden plug jammed between his buttocks. An older woman had snaked her hand beneath him in search of his cock, which she now pinched forcing him to rise up on his toes and tighten his muscles. The cane bit violently into his thighs.

Laughter rose as more stripes were applied to the young man's body. They were already evident from his shoulders to his calves. Nera turned Patsy away and climbed the broad marble stairs. With the last of her strength Patsy tottered down a corridor toward her usual room. It faced the sea to the east. In the darkened gloom of the corridor, she suddenly found herself staring into the naked ass of a young girl. The ass seemed inches away like a cake on a shelf in a bakery. The girl had been tied face down to a steel truss so securely that she was held motionless. Her dress was thrown up to expose her ass and hips. Her panties had been yanked to her knees.

Nera tried to steer her along, but she resisted. She recognized a friend from her garden club with whom she played cards. The friend was standing next to the girl's ass with a heavy rubber strap in her hand. Sweat covered the card player's face, and her eyes were large with rage. Her lips were drawn back from her teeth in a rictus of loathing. Her nose flared above her gritted teeth. Her face was contorted within the frame of her salon-blackened hair. She clearly did not want the spanking interrupted.

"I will teach you not to return hearts to no trump with six points!" The rubber strap slapped fiercely over the girl's bottom. The girl with the beaten ass clenched her strapped, raw buttocks and moaned.

"Do you play cards?" asked Nera. She let her hand brush down Patsy back to her hip and come to rest with authority.

"Yes," she said.

"Perhaps you can take the girl's place next time." Nera giggled, having seen in Patsy what Patsy did not see in herself. Then the strap landed with a hard, loud crack on the girl's ass, and Patsy's cunt twitched.

Wide, dark, purple welts covered the girl's cheeks. Patsy wanted to feel that last terrible spank. The rubber punctuated its point with blood blisters and torn spots in the flesh. She looked at the card player with the strap. The image of their last bridge game flashed across her mind. She remembered how badly the bridge player took the slightest mistake in bidding or play. She looked at the player's hand gripping the rubber strap with white knuckles. The player's tight anger made her body start to flow again.

"Get out!" screeched the card player. Patsy wondered how much of a beating would satisfy the woman. Her cunt reacted as though a tiny jolt of electricity had touched it. She pictured her own pale ass tied to that iron monstrosity. She saw herself with the ropes just above and below her plump ass cheeks. They would be holding her completely still as the girl was, totally vulnerable to the spanking, and without escape. She felt the shrieks that would come from her own mouth during a punishment like that. She felt her cunt go warmly damp and wished Nera would do something about her.

The sharp crack of the rubber hit the girl's bottom again. Nera leaned into her and whispered, "That girl knows what she's doing, you know. She knows how to take a beating. Would you?" Nera's hand moved over Patsy's ass traveling over the crest of each cheek and pausing there. She could feel the heat from Nera's touch build in her skin.

She was taken to her room, lay down on the bed, and worked her fingers between her legs until she got off. She quickly went to sleep hearing the sharp smacking and the pleading squeals of the girl continue. Loud tears began to interrupt the card player's shouts.

When she woke, the room was dark and silent. She looked into the hallway which was now softly lit and looking quite normal. The heavy, iron truss had been removed. She felt a little disappointed. Then she saw that the rubber strap tossed there onto one of the brocade chairs that lined the corridor. Clearly it was meant for her to find.

She used the toilet trying to empty herself completely. She wanted her body ready to receive. Then she sponged herself between her breasts, thighs, and buttocks. Oily residue remained. She did not want to shower. She wanted the scent of the early evening to remain. Then she swiped hard under her arms, which gave off the odor of nervous sweat. She hated that, but she never wore deodorant at Nera's insistence. The hot cunt smell she gave off earlier had settled down a little to a mossy undertone, but it was still there. She slipped into a fresh dress and freshened her makeup.

Finally she slipped a small silver plug from her handbag into her anus. It was dry, heavy, and cold, making it hard to get into herself. She wondered if someone would oil it later. She realized then that she rather hoped it would slip out at some embarrassing moment. She might even be punished for that. Then she wondered if she cared. Finally, she hoped she might be punished quite severely. She moved toward the light at the head of the stairs and the sounds from the gathering below. Then she headed for the door of the party room.

In his apartment, Junker was kneeling before Cosimo slowly and carefully sucking his thick, hard cock. In time, Cosimo came to their mutual satisfaction. Cosimo slipped a tiny cassette from a recorder he kept in his back pocket. This would be encrypted and transferred to a CD. He placed it with the others in Junker's collection of Kenny Rogers albums. Soon it would find its way with two ABBA CDs into a collection that was heading for the northern border. Names and dates were all there for the record. It was not the deeds but the embarrassment that mattered.

"Sometimes, my friend, we must do them a favor."

"Yes?"

"Yes indeed. We must turn their dreams into reality. Their tastes are so gratuitous to our purposes. We must give them a dose of the real shame they so crave and deserve. You are a man who understands bad taste, Junker. Why do you think they need us so, Junker?"

"Because they do awful things."

"Well that's true, but not with us. No, it's because they think they do awful things with us for which they wish to be punished. You love Barry Manilow, Junker, but you can be forgiven for that. It's an honest mistake. They want to be punished for their whims in order to feel important. They want their appalling sensibilities to seem significant, so they are. It's karma you see. The wheel may be an illusion, but it still turns."

Junker and he prepared flank steaks with mushrooms in cognac. Afterwards they had a beer and a cigar apiece. They would leave well before dawn. Cosimo looked in the mirror. He was thinking of growing a beard. He would start it soon when they crossed the northern border for the last time.

The Bookseller's Dream

Seneca Mayfair

I'm a bookseller.

I love books, and I love women, and I love women with books, especially women who know how to love a book. That kind of woman delights in the smell and the feel of a grand old book with a cover made for her pleasure. They made books for women a long time ago, but not anymore. Now, it's a use-them-throw-them-away kind of publishing that's going on. Other bookshops sell those one-night-stand books. I don't, because I know what women like.

Most of the other bookstores on the street have been bought out by the big chains, but not my shop. I have lots of customers. Most of them come back to my shop again and again. It's not because of me. I'm an ordinary middle-aged man, tall and thin; my hair, what's left of it, is graying; and I wear bifocals and tend to squint a lot. You won't find me on the cover of one of those bodice-buster romances. It's my knowledge about women and books that keeps this shop going.

I'd probably be out of business right now if it hadn't been for Alexi, and what she taught me. That girl opened my eyes. She brought my dream to life, and she gave life to a dying shop. Alexi made me see the purpose of my life—to bring happiness to those women who need me. Most of them don't realize they need me, but they do after they visit my shop.

Thirty years ago, I didn't specialize like I do now. I bought what felt good to me. I've always loved the smell of an old book, and the feel of the heavy leaves sewn together. Some of those pages never yellow. They weren't made of newsprint and other waste papers. No, many of them were made of cotton, and they were made to last. There's something solid and sensuous about the feel of those pages between your fingers.

It was a rainy Saturday afternoon when I first saw Alexi. I was in the back of the shop, so I didn't see her as she stepped through the door. I was rearranging, for the hundredth time, some old sets of encyclopedias. My favorites are those published in the late 1800s like *The American Educator.* It's amazing what's in those books. The whole wealth of knowledge at that time was contained in as little as four volumes.

As I was saying, I was in back when I heard the bell above the door ring. I turned, and there she was. She was breathtaking. The rain had curled and frizzed her long red hair. It stood out all around her head, and the light from the shop windows was enough to make it look as if she were on fire. She looked up from the book she was holding. Her eyes were the purest emerald green; the kind you read about but never expect to see in real life, but there they were. I must have been staring with my mouth open, because her lips did this quirky little dance, which I now know is her smug smile.

She held an old library copy of *Ramona* in her hand, and was running her palm over its surface. Those glorious emerald eyes were closed, and she had this look on her face as if she were a million miles away. It wasn't a pretty book, but the binding and cover were hard and smooth, and made to last a thousand years. I learned later this was her favorite kind of book, and with good reason. They're getting harder to find, but I buy a lot of those old library-bound books. They get a lot of traffic in my store.

I moved up to the counter at the front of the store. I knew I'd be able to watch her from there, and I had every intention of watching. She was the first customer I'd had in days, and she was by far the best-looking. I sat down behind the counter and coolly observed her. She was a voluptuous woman with lovely rounded curves. She wasn't wearing a raincoat, just a blue cotton sweater over a white peasant blouse. I couldn't quite tell, but it didn't look as if she had on a bra. I guessed this from the swell and dip of her large breasts. She wore a simple Indian print skirt that gracefully flowed over her full hips and hit her about midcalf. From what I could see of them, her legs looked as delicious as the rest of her.

Did I say I coolly observed her? No, I was at full attention. I felt as if I'd been licked by her red-flamed tresses. I was on fire as I watched her slowly caress her cheek with the book she was holding. She ran the book's cover over her jaw and then lightly over her slightly parted mouth. The pink tip of her tongue grazed the cover. I'd never been so aroused by anything in my life.

She put *Ramona* down and pulled a slightly larger book off the shelf. It was another one with a library binding, and was sickly green in color. Swinging her hips, she walked over to a chair at the end of the shelf range. She propped her left foot up on the chair's seat cushion. Spellbound, I watched as she ran the spine of the book up the inside of her leg and under her skirt where it disappeared. I could imagine what she was doing with it.

Alexi knew I was watching. She enjoyed it. I could tell. When she pulled the book out from under her skirt and turned to me, I could see the moisture glistening on the edge of the book. She smiled and looked at the clock behind me. I'll never forget her first words to me.

"Shouldn't you be closing?" she asked. "I seem to have stayed too late."

As far as I was concerned she could stay forever.

"No," I said. "Keep on looking. I'll just close the store and you can finish." Idiot thing to say, but what else could I say to a woman who had just turned me on by the way she was fiddling herself with one of my books? I've thought about this over the years, and I have yet to come up with the perfect answer.

I locked the door to the shop, turned the CLOSED sign over, and pulled the blinds. When I turned around, Alexi had taken off her sweater and blouse. She was rubbing the open pages of the green book against her hardened nipples. It was then I knew that everything in my life had changed. Those nipples were omens.

"You don't mind, do you?" she said. "I always like to try out my books first. It makes the experience so much better, don't you think?"

Alexi pushed her nose into the spine of the open book and sniffed, then looked up at me with an impossibly sexy smile. I was lost. As far as I was concerned, she could rub her nipples against every book I had in stock.

I stood there staring. My part in this was nothing. It was Alexi who was everything. She dropped the book, untied her skirt, and let it slide down her legs. She wasn't wearing any panties. No wonder the book had been wet. I'd be, too, if I'd been under her skirt with that gorgeous red bush and lovely lips peeking out.

Alexi sat on the chair and lifted one leg up. Divine, is what it was. She spread her legs as wide as she could and, ignoring me, took a red book and plied the edge of it gently through her pussy's lips. She fanned the edges slightly and pushed her swollen lips in between the pages and closed the book. She looked up, but not at me. Her green eyes were partly closed, not seeing anything around them as she moved against the book wrapped around those wet lips. I remember thinking I wouldn't mind having a bookmark like that.

She wasn't making any noises. Alexi never does. She moved against the book with her eyes half-open and a smile on her face. She sure was enjoying herself. I don't think she came, though the pages of that book were wet by the time she stopped. I couldn't tell because she stopped too abruptly. She got up from the chair and moved back by the encyclopedias. She pulled books off the shelves and laid them out in a straight line on the floor. As she pulled each book out, she'd run her palm across it and then touch her cheek with the cover's flat surface.

She pulled out an old college edition of *Webster's* and, holding it, lay down on top of those books she'd arranged on the floor. I'd followed her and stood just below her feet. Looking up at me, she spread her legs and began to rub the spine of *Webster's* against her wet pussy. This time she was really moving. Those beautiful hips were rising up to give full access to that old book. I knew the book was ruined, but I wanted to see it completely soaked by this woman. I'm standing there, looking down at her and rubbing my crotch when the angel on the floor in front of me opened her eyes, and said the most wondrous sentence I'd ever hear in my life.

"Fuck me, bookseller."

She didn't have to say it twice. I fucked Alexi by the encyclopedias, on top of a bunch of library bound books, and with one she'd put on her stomach so that it was flat between us as we moved. The book was cold, but wonderful against the skin. As I said before, I love books, and I love women; and nothing is better than when you can have the two of them together.

Many of the books in my shop look as if they've been dropped into a bathtub. I'm careful about mold, though, and I've never had a problem with it. I always dry out the books my customers use. Sometimes on a hot day you can walk into my shop, and you can just smell drying pussy. It's glorious.

I've kept up the practice Alexi taught me. She showed me the signs to look for in a woman who wants a good book. She's the one who pulls a book off the shelf as if she's caressing her lover. If she thinks I'm not looking, she'll run her palm over the book's cover. Usually she'll smile, and that's about the time I step in and encourage her to touch her cheek with it. From there it's just a matter of time until I close the shop for a while and let the woman have her way with my books, or with me.

Alexi doesn't mind. She says it's my duty to book-loving women everywhere. She thinks someday someone will write a book about me, and she wants to be the first to have her way with that book. I just smile.

Yes, Alexi and I are still together. Today is our twenty-fifth wedding anniversary. I have a special treat for her. In the shopping bag by the counter I've packed away all four volumes of my favorite encyclopedia, *The American Educator.* Since that first day Alexi walked into my shop and changed my life, I've saved it for a special occasion. Tonight I'm going to give the encyclopedia set to Alexi. I think she'll enjoy each volume, one by one. I know I will.

Just Sexy Stories

Avril's Name

Thomas S. Roche

I thought I had her figured out. I thought she'd be an easy fuck, a casual lay to rinse from my mouth the too-fresh taste of a broken love. I thought we'd fuck, I'd go home, I'd forget her. And she'd forget me. No harm, no foul, no long goodbyes.

"Once," she told me, leaning against me in the bar. "I'll sleep with you once."

I'd seen her so often, looked at her body with lust in my eyes. She tended at Markers, the bar I frequented, a hip bar filled with young tattooed punks and staffed entirely by women. She knew what all the other bartenders knew—sexy clothes spelled big tips. But she didn't go the route the other girls did—tight, low-slung jeans showing off their hips and the fact that they wore no underwear; short skirts and knee-high leather boots that made their thighs more tantalizing than a pair of high heels ever could have; belly-baring T-shirts showing off sexy tattoos and pierced navels.

Instead, every inch of Avril's flesh was always covered except her hands, her face, and—just occasionally, when she bent forward within sight of me—the small of her back. Her tattoos were dense, indistinguishable; they adorned the small of her back so tight and finely woven that I couldn't make them out. The tight leather pants she always wore kept them hidden most of the time; her long-sleeved, tight black turtlenecks forbade any real view of her slender arms, her flat belly, or her ample tits. But that didn't make her any less sexy; on the contrary, the clothes she wore were so form-fitting that no contour of Avril's body was unfamiliar to anyone who went to the bar. She was a frequent source of discussion among male patrons, speculation often centering on how the hell she could have gotten into pants so tight they looked sprayed on, how she managed to make her breasts stand so firm like that when it was clear through the tight, stretchy material of her turtlenecks that she wasn't wearing a bra. Nobody knew, but it titillated them to speculate. It titillated me, too; it made me want her more than I already did.

The bar girls at Markers were notoriously slutty, most of them recently out of college and moved to the city to be hip and be seen, to get high and get laid. A joint, a hit of E, or a baggie of Ketamine tablets, it was said, would get you pretty far with one of these girls. But Avril was different—no older than the others, probably, or at least no more than a few years. But her reputation was pristine despite her provocative clothes. Rumor had it she'd never gone home with anyone. Not men, not women. Not anyone.

But she flirted with me. When I dropped in for a drink near closing time, when she was the only bartender on duty, she would kick everyone out, lock the door and chat with me while she cleaned up. She wanted to know about me—my interests, my dreams, my desires. She avoided all the like questions I sent her way. Even after a month of regular flirtation, I knew only a few things about Avril, all of them relevant but none of them terribly illuminating. She was straight. She was single, had been for some time. She was from Nebraska, but had lived in dozens of towns since running away from home at an early age. She was of mixed Italian-Dutch parentage. And she never, ever showed off her skin.

But I knew one more thing, just a rumor, murmured by one of the bar girls I'd taken home one night: Avril's mother had been a tattoo artist, had died young, of a broken heart.

As she finished counting out her drawer one Thursday night, I sat at the end of the bar watching her, smoking cigarettes—another testament to the fact that she liked me, for the health department could have fined them even while the bar was closed. She glanced over to me between stacks of ones and clanking rolls of quarters, her eyes hungry, her lips full and red with lipstick.

"I was thinking I might stay up for a while," I said. "My place isn't far away. Would you like to come over for a drink?"

"I have to work," she said nervously.

"Friday's your day off."

"Oh, yeah," she said, and blushed.

"One drink," I smiled. "I promise I won't try anything."

She turned to me, her face washed with sadness. She ran her hand up the length of her sleeve, as if it itched.

"I want you to try something," she said.

"Then I will," I told her, fixing her dark eyes with my stare.

She came around the end of the bar, put her arms around me. She smelled like a mix of flowers and Johnnie Walker. Black Label; maybe even Gold. We kissed, and I felt the press of her body against mine, the slick rub of a tongue piercing as she explored me. The taste on her tongue was definitely Gold Label, a brand Markers didn't carry.

"Once," she told me. "I'll sleep with you once."

I smiled, shrugged. "Who said anything about sleeping together? I'm talking about a drink."

"Once," she told me. I opened my mouth to protest—if we liked it, couldn't we do it again? She put one finger across my lips, finding them still moist with her spit.

"Once," I told her. "I'll sleep with you only once."

My apartment was a few blocks away, and as we walked she leaned against me, seeming to need support. Perhaps she'd been single for long that the thought of being with me scared her. I wanted her so bad I knew once wouldn't satisfy me; perhaps if I were good enough, she'd be open to a repeat performance.

I slipped my hand down the waistband of her pants, feeling that she, like the other girls at Markers, wasn't wearing anything underneath. She cuddled up next to me as we walked. I took a deep breath of her: scotch and flowers, fear and fire. I fumbled with my keys and let us into my apartment.

We tumbled onto the bed without turning on the light, and her mouth was insatiable. She pushed up into me, her back arching as my swelling cock found her leather-clad cleft. She moaned and pulled me hard against her. She kissed me like a savage, like a cannibal. She slipped her hands under my T-shirt and massaged my back, pushing her hands into my jeans to cup my ass. Her pussy rubbed firmly against my hard cock. She pulled her mouth from mine and my tongue worked eagerly after it, seeking. She grabbed my hair and forced my head back. I stared into darkness, Avril nothing but black, not even a shadow.

"Undress me," she said.

"Let me light a candle," she told me. "I want to see you."

"Not yet," she told me. "Take off my clothes first."

Kissing her tenderly, I unfastened her belt, peeled the moist, painted-on leather pants down her thighs. I could smell her bare cunt the moment I exposed it; her musky tang was thick and hungry. I unzipped her boots and pulled her leathers off. Then she put up her arms, and I pulled off her top.

My mouth found her tits and I felt the smoothness marred by tiny, almost imperceptible lines. They were barely there at all; my tongue could feel them, but my fingers couldn't. Her nipples were pierced, which I'd known ever since I'd first laid eyes on those perfect orbs in their stretchy silk prison. I suckled her tits and teased her metal-cool rings with my tongue. She moaned softly, and as I slipped my hand between her legs I found her wet. One finger slid easily into her; two made her tighten around it and moan louder; three, with a thumb on her clit, made her arch her back and gasp.

"Fuck me," she said, her voice hoarse with desire. "But I need you to see me first."

I got up in the blackness, fumbled for the candles in my night stand drawer. I'd done this often enough with enough women to know the procedure without being able to see. Before I lit a match, I stripped off my T-shirt, kicked off my shoes, dropped my jeans and stepped out of them. My under-shorts joined them on the floor, and I lit the match.

Avril stretched beautiful and pale on the bed, her white skin crisscrossed with black lines from the top of her throat to her wrists, from her shoulders to her hips to the lengths of her slender legs, all the way to her tattooed feet. Only a dead white spot at the top of her left breast remained unadorned, her natural skin color without benefit of ink.

"What the fuck?" I whispered.

"Light the candle," she told me, and I did, snugging it into an old whiskey bottle.

I joined her on the bed, bending close to inspect her

body. My eyes wide, I ran my fingers over the black lines, disbelieving.

They were names: hundreds of them. Written tiny in ornate script, large in dripping-blood horror-letters, medium-sized in faux-typewriter. And a hundred other variations, two hundred, more than I could count. I ran my fingers over her, eyes wide, reading.

Richie. Darius. Mac. Jonah. Jerrold. Roland. Frederic. Quinn. Jeremy. Sean. Stanford. Walker. Mikhail. Tobias. Saul. Lawrence. David.

And on and on, in swirls and slants and grids around her naked body, leaving only her heart untouched. Names repeated, but were they the same names? Or simply echoes of past loves?

She looked into my eyes, her dark orbs flickering in candlelight.

"Men," she told me. "Men I've been with. Every one of them. Even a kiss," she said. "Even the smallest touch. Every one of them."

"You're crazy," I said. "Is it your . . . your mother?"

"You heard," she said.

"I heard," I told her. "Is it true?"

"That part's true."

"Is it why you do this?" I asked.

"I don't really know," she told me. "It just happens. Every time. It's too late now," she said. "We're here. We've kissed. You're mine." Her hand moved to mine, took it, pressed it to the blank spot in her breast.

"I'm running out of space," she said.

I kissed her, hard, and her tongue swelled against mine as her back arched and she pulled me onto her. My tongue traced a path from her mouth to her heart to her nipple, then down her belly to her pussy. I could barely see with the dancing shadows from her body writhing on the bed, but there were names there, too. Even on her lips; even on her pierced clit, so tiny I couldn't read them. But the names above it I read; Anton and Val and Conrad stitched on the shaved, smooth mound of her sex. I closed my eyes and listened to her moan as my tongue worked her clit. When she came, she begged me to enter her, and I did, climbing atop her and sinking into her pussy so smoothly I almost came, myself, right away. But I held back and fucked her, my fingers tangled in her hair, each strand parting to show names written there, too, on flesh that must have once been shaved. I kissed her hard when I came, and she pulled me down onto her so hard I could feel her pubic bone against mine; she bit my tongue, drawing blood in the instant my orgasm peaked. When our lips parted, her lips were glossy with blood. "I love you," she said, shuddering. "I'm sorry. I love you."

Deep into the morning, I rested, Avril clutching herself against me, sighing almost sadly and murmuring in her sleep. The candle burned down to a ruined mass of wax, leaving acrid strains of smoke curling through the apartment, illuminated by the slanted light of the rising sun, segmented into improbable patterns by the jolly roger hung in my window.

I stared into the smoke and asked the question all men ask, or perhaps only most. How many? Hundreds, clearly, but how many more? Were names written in names on Avril's body, the writing so dense that the names of new men had covered those of long-lost ones, the kind of cover-up you get when they throw you out of the street gang?

And what of the blank spot on Avril's left breast—virgin white over her heart? Untouched, unspoiled, unknown?

Avril lolled to one side, dozing fitfully. She rested in a hot band of sunlight shooting molten from the window. I looked down at her and froze.

There it was. Written large, in block letters the color of blood: My name.

I might have thought I'd only missed it before; my name is not uncommon, and Avril could have had one of me before. But there was no mistake. My name was written on her breast, in the spot that had been blank.

My name was written on her heart.

I shook her, softly, whispering her name. She stirred and shivered. She looked up into my eyes, and saw the question there. She looked down at her breast and her mouth dropped open slightly.

She turned her face to mine, sad, and shook her head.

She curled up onto me and whispered into my ear, her breath warm and scotch-scented.

"I'm sorry," she said. "I'm so sorry." When I woke she was gone. She'd left no trace except for her discarded leather pants and turtleneck top, her discarded boots. Perhaps she'd borrowed clothes from my drawer; smaller than me, Avril never could have fit in my jeans or my boots or my turtlenecks. Nonetheless, she was gone, the only trace of her the scent of her cunt on my body, the smell of her scotch and her sweat and her tears on my bed. I went into the bathroom to wash her from me.

I stopped.

Staring into the mirror, I drew my hand to my breast. An inch above my left nipple, it was written in letters the color of blood. In feminine script, but shaky, fragmented, as if rendered by a tattoo artist being forced to do so at gunpoint.

The tattoo was fresh, as if she had rendered it while I slept, without waking me. Blood oozed from the fresh marker, trickling down.

I knew she wouldn't be there when I went back tonight after work. I knew she wouldn't be anywhere that I would find her, ever again. I knew she was gone, vanished into the wind, roaming the planet wearing my name on her heart, touching it sometimes, late at night, whispering into the darkness: "I'm sorry . . . I'm sorry . . . I'm so sorr. . . ."

I stood there in the mirror and ran my fingers over the bloodied script of Avril's name carved across my chest like the notebook scrawlings of a very small girl, lovesick and alone.

I could smell her in my nostrils, taste her on my lips.

See her named on my body, rendered by a lovesick girl in the middle of the night.

Tears Fall on Me

Sydney Durham

Part I: I Won't Care

How many times have I watched her come to me? How many times have I peeked at her breasts and the furry mound of her cunt as she crawls to me over the foot of the bed? How many times have I enjoyed her flickering self-conscious grin as her impudent eyes betray her and stray to my cock?

She stops by my waist, beside my hairy sprawling balls and cock, and settles herself, sitting on tiny feet, manicured hands resting lightly on the arches of thighs that nearly hide her tidy pubic hair. Her breasts are elevated slightly by the curve of her dancer's back, and move slowly as she breathes. Her hair hugs the back of her neck, and I am tempted to grasp her there, to pull her head down to my groin. But it would be offensive even to me to do that.

She redefines usual clichés: style, class, poise—yet none of these words fit her. All are beneath her. There is so much that separates us. I smell of beer and motor oil; she smells of class and money. I am hairy and bearded; she is cultivated and clean. I am plastic; she is porcelain. I am her cock. She is my cunt.

It is hard to imagine sweat pooling between her breasts as I rut over her, but I have seen it. It is hard to imagine the slippery sheen on her body as I hammer into her, but I have seen it. It is hard to imagine the eager way her mouth swallows my cock, the swarming of her tongue as she humps her head over my pelvis, the delight with which she gulps my come as it flushes against the back of her throat. It is hard to imagine her fists knotted into my hair as my tongue probes and laps her cunt. It is hard to imagine the sounds of her sopping cunt receiving my plunging cock. It is hard to imagine seeing her juices mingled with mine, coating her inner thighs as she sprawls, sated, gaping, and oozing, hair wild and sweat-tangled, panting, whispering, "oh fuck, oh fuck . . ."

For a tiny interval in the history of the universe she sits quietly, poised, eyes downcast, looking at her hands. There I can see the matching rings. She has never worn them when we have been together, but this time they are there, foretelling, haunting me with an expectation of unwelcome truth. I wait.

She lifts the hand carrying her rings and traces a fingerpath on my slowly swelling cock. Reaching the foreskin she takes a pinch of flesh and lifts, enclosing me with warm fingers. I stiffen quickly in her gentle embrace, and her nipples harden in empathy. She turns her head to me, and I see tears.

"I'm letting him come back," she says.

"I saw the rings." It's all I can say.

"It's not fair to the children," she says, as if I have not spoken. Her hand begins to move on me, up and down. "We can't do this anymore."

"He won't fuck you properly. He won't make you come. He won't eat your pussy."

"He thinks I'm clean and pure. He wants me to be that way."

I hear a catch in her voice but ignore it. "Make me come," I say, unable to manage my anger. "Suck me. Just make me come."

"Don't," she whispers. A tear oozes along her nose. She

begins moving her hand faster. "Besides, I could ask him to—to try harder." she offers, hesitancy wrapping her throat.

"He wouldn't. He doesn't know how. Make me come."

"You won't fuck me?"

"No," I say, watching her breasts move.

Her hand slows, stops. "Maybe I should go," she says, her voice tiny.

My mind betrays me, flooding me with memories. "Just do it," I mutter, moving my hips, sliding my cock through her slack fist. "Make me come."

She lets go of me, hiding tears with her hands.

I am remembering. I remember her prim reserve the first time we fucked, her slut-lust after that. I remember the first time I came in her mouth, how I surprised her, how readily she was angry at me for it, and how soon she wanted to suck my cock again. I remember when she asked me to fuck her ass.

She gets off the bed and goes to stand in the doorway with her back to me, leaning against the jamb. Her shoulders move with soft sobs she tries to hide. Her perfect wealthy ass is canted, twisted in a way that would get any man's eye, the same way it got mine the first time I saw her.

"Whose cock are you going to suck?" I call out. "Who will fuck you in the ass? Who will eat your pussy and fuck you so hard you scream? Who will come in your mouth? He won't. You know that."

"Stop," she says, her voice muffled by distance and tears. She turns to face me. "I have to do this."

Even her pubic hair is perfectly trimmed, a narrow stripe that can hide behind designer beachwear. "Make me come," I counter, pumping my still-rigid cock.

She returns to the bed, crawling again. Seating herself

astride my thigh she takes my cock in her hand and begins, up and down. In rhythm she moves her hips, sliding her slippery pussy on my leg.

I stack my fists behind my head and watch. Her right hand works my cock this time, and her left hand is behind her, hiding the rings. I twist a little and reach and get my fingers into her wetness, making her gasp. I hook a finger into her, and she rocks her hips harder, jerking at my cock as she does. Tears streak her face.

I am about to come and give in, grabbing her hips and lifting, guiding her over my cock. She brings her ring hand around and parts her cunt lips and lets me inside. Slippery wet and warm, she settles on me slowly, getting that dull, eyes-half-closed look she always gets when she is full of cock, when she is being properly fucked. It's a look that makes her seem animal-mindless, a look he would never tolerate—and the only thing I can give her.

"He doesn't want you to come," I say. "It wouldn't be ladylike."

She pulls me, rolling to her back, taking me with her, and spreads her raised knees wide so that I am buried deep inside her. "Fuck me," she says.

I push hard, and she grinds herself against me, locking her legs behind me, grunting, mouth agape, eyes still lidded, muttering, "Fuck me . . ."

"I can smell your cunt," I say. "Can you smell it? You won't smell it again. You're his princess. He won't want your cunt to make that smell. He won't fuck you. He'll stick his cock in you and he'll come and he'll call it fucking, but he won't fuck you. He won't care if you come, and he won't want to smell your pussy."

I fuck, slamming hard the way she wants me to, and I know when she is ready and pull out and straddle her, grabbing her wrist, forcing her to take my slippery cock in her hand. "Make me come!" I shout.

She opens her eyes and glares at me and starts jerking my cock. Her other hand, the one with the rings, slips under me, working in her cunt.

She throws back her head and lets go a long, breathless, shuddering moan that rises into a hoarse scream. My semen falls, thick gobs on her breasts and stomach.

And it almost works; for a few minutes I don't care.

Part II: Sufferance

I know she's here before she says anything. I know the sound of her car; I know her expensive perfume. I continue to twist the oil filter, pretending to snug it into place. Finally I look away from my work, unable to stall any longer.

"He said it would be okay," she tells me. Her voice takes me back against my will, dragging me into that final Sunday afternoon in my apartment.

She stands beside the hoist, as if afraid to come under the car. Her hands are behind her back, hidden by her bottom the same way her hips and ass are hidden by her proper red shorts, the same way her breasts are hidden by her expensive white silk blouse. Her eyes drop when mine meet them. Her eyelids come down, covering the black of her irises, drooping the same way they do when she's coming.

Or the way they used to. Before she let him move back into the house. Before she stopped coming to my bed.

"What would be okay?" I ask. But I already know. I know there's only one reason she would be here. I know it's because she wants to fuck me, wants me to fuck her. She wants to come, to wail, to clutch, to scratch and sweat under me.

"Okay if we f—" She looks up at me, angry. "Don't make me beg, please."

Her nipples have hardened under the silk, and my lust comes back, slamming into the front of my mind like a hammer blow. All I want in this instant is to see, hear, feel, and smell her as she comes. I know this hunger has never really been gone, but I can usually keep it hidden, keep it from bothering me until I'm in my bed, in the dark, alone.

I don't care. I say it to myself, in my mind, a thousand times in the space of a millisecond. I don't care that she left me. I don't need her. I don't miss her. I don't care.

I don't care. My mind has room for that chant another thousand times, and still has room for more. It has room for an image of her white silk blouse with my oily, dirty finger-marks on it. It has room for an image of the way she used to smile at me sometimes while I was coming. It has room for memories. I do have room for her in my mind, and I do care. I do care.

"I didn't think you'd be back," I say.

Her face drains its blood; her color leaves. "Is there some-body . . . ?"

"No." I'm anxious to tell her that and hate myself for it. "Nobody."

"So we can—you'll take me back?"

I feel my cock swelling under my coveralls. "You never belonged to me," I say.

"You knew my rhythms."

"I made you come." My throat closes a little, choking the words.

She pauses, staring at me. "Oh god . . . you loved me, didn't you?"

It isn't really a question, and I can hear her surprise: she knows the answer. I look away.

"You did," she whispers. "It wasn't just about sex for you, was it? I'm sorry."

"It doesn't matter," I say, pulling a shop towel out of my pocket and wiping my hands on it. "It's over."

She comes toward me timidly. Her throat arches as she looks up, as if she's afraid the hoist will drop the car on her. I want to put my lips there, in that hollow place at the base of her neck.

"I didn't know," she whispers. "Let me make it up to you." She reaches for my cock.

The gesture demeans her. I grab her wrist before her hand gets to me and pull her along as I go to punch the button that lowers the big door.

"I'll make it up to you," she says, hurrying behind me. "He doesn't care if we fuck."

Peachy. We have his blessings.

In my office, beside the big cracked-leather couch, we undress as if we're in panic. When I see her breasts and the wispy hair that coats her cunt I begin remembering the dreams I've been having since she left.

Wearing nothing but her sandals she squats before me and grabs my cock, sliding her mouth over it, sucking and rocking on it. I stand there feeling stupid, wanting to grab her head, wanting to encourage her, but my hands still feel oily and dirty. Instead I put them on my hips and watch her pale lips move along my dusky prickskin.

On her hand I see the rings, the ones she had returned to

her finger that spring Sunday, the rings that had been my signal of the end of us. Her fingers enclose my cock and follow her lips, and her expensive manicured fingernails seem to threaten my balls.

Even squatting, naked, sucking my cock in a dirty garage office, she is proper and cultured and untarnished. My cock will corrupt her mouth and fingers, just as it will corrupt her cunt. She will be soiled by me, and she wants to be soiled by me. I am her source of perversion and her connection to the earthy place in her soul.

Her eyes come up, meet mine, her carefully cultivated eyebrows arching, questioning, seeking acquiescence. I can see her plea there; I can see that she, too, is lonely.

Her willfulness hardens my cock even more, and I can feel myself getting ready to come. I reach and pull her away and lower her to the sticky leather, my oily hands marking her porcelain skin. It's the same dusty, broken couch where we first fucked the day she brought her expensive little red car to me a third time, to fix some imaginary rattle.

We took a test drive that day, with the top down, the wind and sun washing us with an invitation to join nature. We were close in the little car, her face near mine, her hair whipped in the wind, breasts and knees and thighs dragging my eyes away from the road. Back in the garage she bent over the couch, and I flipped up her tiny skirt and pulled her panties aside to fuck her from behind. It was an auto mechanic's dream.

I watch her arrange herself. Her breasts flatten a little, but they still arch up toward me. Her nipples are extended and rigid, but I know they will yield to my teeth, making her gasp sharply.

She opens her legs, an invitation. My cock hovers over her body, making a blurred shadow on her in the fluorescent light, as if threatening her.

The hair that mounts her groin is trimmed carefully, neat and tidy, as always. But the hair deep between her thighs, in the place where she is already open and wet, seems thick and tangled as if I have already been there, pummeling her inside.

I lower myself into her, drawn in easily by her suction, up and well into her as her legs lock behind me. "He isn't fucking you?" I ask, kneading one of her breasts with my oily palm.

"It's the same," she says, grunting as she raises her hips to rub herself against me. "Nothing for me. He comes, and it's done."

I press hard and hammer her a few times. That scent comes up to my nose, her scent, the one she is so quick to make. It seems her scent is our hallmark. She grunts and rubs against me again, coming hard and quickly, rapid beats against my cock, helpless gasps falling like feathers on my ear.

"You were right," she says. "He can't make me do that." She strokes my shoulders. "That smell, he can't make that happen. Only you can do that for me. And only you can make me come."

I move my hips, sliding, and without warning my cock sobs into her as I groan, my face lost in her hair.

"Be sure to clean yourself of him before you come to me," I say, pulling out. My wet cock drags across her thigh, marking her.

Part III: Don't Ask

It comes to mind that I have not been in a public place with her. In the diner the people know me; I eat many of my meals here. But they do not know her, they do not know about her. They are reserved, quieter than usual, as if she has startled them, or perhaps as if they feel an awkwardness, as they might in the presence of royalty.

She has that effect. Across the chipped and stained Formica tabletop she seems small in her chair, yet her presence there realigns the room, centering it on her, adjusting its tempo to meet hers. I am tempted to shout in celebration of my discovery, of my delight in finding that I am not alone in succumbing to her elegance.

I feel an unseemly pride, knowing that I am the only person in the room who has heard the sounds of this woman in passion. I am the only person in the room who has plundered her body. Across the table from me is a woman whose rhythms have aligned with mine as powerfully as the tides with the moon, and I know that no other man has been able to do that for her. As I watch her I can see her nipples, hardened beneath the black T-shirt she is wearing, and I can remember watching her breasts rise as she pulled it over her head that morning.

She studies the menu, sipping water from a scratched green plastic water tumbler. Her lips purse around the straw. The image thrusts me backwards, flooding my mind with another way she used her lips, her hand, not more than an hour before. The fine lines on her knuckles seem to wink at me.

"What's good?" she asks, raising her eyes to meet mine.

"Fucking you." I only mouth the words, but the diner seems to go silent for a heartbeat.

Her face flushes, color rising out of her collar into her cheeks. Her breasts rise and fall as she takes a deep, involuntary breath. "Stop that!" she says, grinning, her white teeth flashing at me. "I'm starving. Besides, if you keep that up I'll come across the table after you."

Blanche appears as if signaled, as if we are in need of being rescued from ourselves. Her thick cylindrical body nudges the table. "Who's your friend, Rafer?" Her pencil is poised over her order pad, but her eyes lock on mine. I think I see mischief in them. Blanche and I have known each other a long time.

"A friend," I say. "Judith, meet Blanche."

A silent greeting passes between the women, and I imagine telepathy happening. Suddenly there are no secrets. "Eggs over easy, bacon, wheat toast, short stack," says Judith, smiling. It's one of those smiles full of secrets, the kind women reserve for each other.

Blanche writes nothing. She glances at me. "Wheaties, hon?" she asks, one eye squinting a slow wink.

I feel the heat of blood in my face. "The same as the lady's having," I say, and Blanche is gone.

"What have you told her?" Judith asks, grinning.

"Blanche sees all, knows all things," I say, "but I've told her nothing."

Our eyes lock. The intimacy of the moment, the revelation of our secret, the realization that somebody now knows comes as a flood of affirmation. We have just spent our first full night together, and unexpectedly, in the crisp morning that follows, our union has gotten sanctity through the unruffled acceptance of a waitress. I smile, delight filling me, and Judith smiles back. "I'm glad you brought me here," she says. I don't answer, unable to speak.

We eat quickly, driven by hunger and an urgency to move further into the day. It is another threshold for us, our first meal together. I am tempted to linger over coffee, to prolong the time, but I am also eager for us to walk together, holding hands, to wander the aimless way lovers do.

We visit a quiet park, one of my favorite places. Dew-fresh grass lingers in shady hideaways, but we find a bench in a spot of sunny warmth and sit side by side, holding hands, watching clouds. It is early; we are alone.

"What are we going to do?" she asks.

I am tempted to snatch her from the bench and swing her in circles, but the door she has finally opened acknowledges that we are not just fuck partners, not just concupiscence, not just cock and cunt. But it does not reveal a way to tranquility. My mind cannot shed its dark awareness of her husband, her children.

I lower my head over hers. Her lips are still sticky with maple syrup, and my tongue savors her sweetness for a moment. Her hands tangle into my hair, pulling me even closer, and her breath touches my cheek. Her hips roll, urging me, pressing against my thigh, and I work my hand into the waistband of her shorts, down into the swampy heat of her cunt. She is thick with want and comes softly, pulsing rapidly on my fingers as I probe.

"I can do that for you," I say. "But I can't give you or your children what he can give. I can't—"

"And I can't ask you to wait," she whispers.

It's a question, not a statement. My silence is like a wall. I am unprepared. I have long since resigned myself to nothing more than a physical relationship with this woman, insulated from the pain I felt before.

I close my eyes, blocking out the peaceful sky.

I feel her move, I feel the press of her breast on my arm. "That was unfair," she whispers. "Forgive me."

The day spins past too quickly. We spend the morning visiting small expensive boutiques where she is regal while I am as inappropriate as a bear. I buy her expensive lingerie, and the saleswomen peek at me. Judith's lips brush my ear: "They're jealous," she says.

We visit haberdasheries, where she dresses me up as if I were her doll. In the end she buys me colorful French briefs while the men in the store peek at her. We both notice and grin over our shared secret.

Lunch is beer and greasy sausage, at a sidewalk table. I am caught in the silence of melancholy, and Judith seems to be the same. Our conversation is composed of brief exchanges about meaningless things: the color of a passing woman's scarf, the frown on a businessman's face.

We attract attention. People passing on the sidewalk glance at us a second time. It is our contrasts that draw this attention. Her look, the delicacy of fine china, the elegance of old lace, is a stark contrast to my bulk and sharp edges. We create the impression that my slightest touch will break her into pieces, a feeling I've had myself. Sometimes I have been afraid to touch her.

There is no fit for us. We are north and south, light and darkness, yin and yang. But in bed we are oxygen and gasoline. Each of us needs the other for this, and out of it has grown an unexpected communion.

A cold rain chases us back to my apartment midafternoon, and there, standing on opposite sides of the bed, we undress in silence. This is not our plan; indeed, we have no plan. But as we come together our bodies blend with a softness and passion that startles me. I lie beneath her, and she writhes in silence, pinioned on me, silky caresses on my cock driving me like a tuning fork: rigid, but in crisp, pure tremors.

Tears fall on me, and I cannot stop them.

Part IV: Sometimes I Can Hear Myself Crying

There's an old blue F-150 in the lot, with the tailgate down and a big crack in the windshield. Joey comes out, wiping his hands on a shop towel. He takes the box of donuts from me and looks inside. "Max is gonna be late," he says. "His kid missed the bus again. And there's some woman in your office."

Some woman, he says. It's his slang, but he nailed the truth with it. I don't recognize her at first. From behind, in my visitor chair, she's just another customer. It isn't until I walk past her to my desk and turn that I know who "some woman" is.

She still has that smile, those lips, those eyes, fragments that are burned into my memory, un-erasable flickers that have lasted almost fifteen years. She might be Joey's "some woman" but she's no longer *that* woman. Her jeans are faded, frayed at the cuffs. Her canvas shoes are green and soiled, and her fingernails are clipped, with no polish. There's no trace of makeup, and straight brown hair, silver-streaked. I can see squint-wrinkles, big smile marks. She is happy. Once "some woman" would have been fashionably dressed, maybe in designer jeans and a crisp, tailored, button-down blouse instead of a faded sweatshirt with a cartoon duck on it. In those days she wasn't happy.

"How have you been?" we say in unison, and laugh, making nervous noises. She stands, her arms come up, and we fold into one another. I go away briefly, and I hear my breath whistle out my nose, as if I have relaxed at last, after an endless wait. The earth inches another fraction in its rotation as I begin to feel calmed in the warmth of her body against mine. She smells clean but mysterious, like a hint of cardamom. The perfume scent I remember, some forgotten brand I bought her, is not there.

I stall, holding on, looking at her face, prolonging contact, watching her eyes search mine. Words seem wrong. Empty, polite, fatuous language—you look great, how did you find me, fill me in, what a nice surprise—seems too empty, too ordinary, an insult to the moment. Our silence carries enough information, maybe too much.

My mind is unwinding its sluggish reels, pushing me back, giving me flickering glimpses of her in those months we had. I see her head thrown back, her breasts lifted, a flush on her chest, as her stomach folds in small convulsions. I see her lips, puffy from my hard kisses. I see her over me, under me, surrounding me.

I see us fucking. It was what we did. It was all we did. Simple fucking. We were only animals. That was it, we thought. Until one day we found out it wasn't just fucking. Until one day, when my guard was down, I revealed just what she was giving to me, what I needed, and then I knew the same thing had happened to her. Suddenly fucking was only part of the glue. Suddenly we wanted to walk in the rain together, or sit on a park bench and watch the sky go by and envy the flowers for their happiness. Suddenly we wanted to give, not take. But give was something we could not do.

"Is that your truck out there?" I ask, still stalling, walking behind my desk to hide a little.

"It needs a new head gasket." She grins again and sits back down. "I hope you're not too expensive."

Price was never important before, when she had that little red car. Her hair was short and tinted then, curled and stylish.

Then her skin was machine-tanned, carefully made up; not weather-tanned and scrubbed. Money didn't matter to her in those days, the days when she would ride my cock and come so hard it would make me jealous.

My mind is filled with questions. What had happened while I was gone? "I'll make a good price for you," I say. "How did you know I was back?"

"You're a famous author. A celebrity like you can't just sneak into town."

I'm also broke and recovering, but I don't say that. She probably knows that part, too. Everybody does. "Famous. A load of crap," I say. "What about you?"

She gives a smile. "I'm on my own now," she says.

Joey appears in the doorway. "Somebody's here for the lady," he says, pointing with his head.

Judith grins at me. "That's my daughter. Sorry, but I have to go now, or I'll make her late for work." She stands. "I'll call you about the truck."

I stand, trying to keep up, trying to be polite, but she's already gone, just that quickly.

Joey watches her go. "You know her?"

"Once," I say, realizing Joey would have been just a kid then. I am still behind my desk, locked in place like a gatepost. I sit again as Joey goes back to the grease rack. I spend a few minutes wondering if I should have apologized.

If you don't bother saying goodbye, the mechanical parts are easy. Pack, get in the car, drive. I did that. I eased out of town in the dark like a skulking thief. I drove past their house that night and stopped at the end of the long driveway. It had just snowed, and the world had that gentle, content quiet that comes after a snow. There were a few lights on in the house, spilling out and making the snow glitter, and even in the crisp cold there was a warm, safe feeling. I wanted to escape the snow, the cold, the industry, and its gray skies, trading it for the soft, warm silence of the south. Another myth I wanted to believe. She would be safe where she was. She and her children would be safe. Her husband would take good care of them. They had security. They had plenty of money.

I had none of that. I had only one thing to give her.

I can still remember, and my mind fills up with it as I sit at my desk, letting the memories in: she would come so hard it was almost frightening. It was always best for her when she was astride me because she could control things, and it was best for me that way because I could see and appreciate what was happening with her, taking my own pleasure in what little I had to give her. Sometimes when it was approaching, she would gasp, taking in air sharply as if afraid of what was about to happen. It was like the sound of fear a person might make when death is approaching, just cresting the hill. Her body would go rigid, and she would lift her hands the way babies do when they've just started walking, and her eyes would close, and the first spasm would slam into her and make her grunt as if she had been punched in the gut. Her mouth would fall open and her face would slacken and her stomach would clench and her shoulders would tremble and her arms would tuck down against her ribs, pressing her breasts together and she would begin to shake. I would feel her convulse on my cock and the tremors would start, transmitting the rhythm of her ecstasy to me so powerfully I could only hope to cling to some fragment of the memory as I was swept into her undertow, swirled and tumbled, jolted; compelled to erupt suddenly, involuntarily, violently into her, air ejecting through my clenching throat in a deathlike groan as my passion, triggered by hers, was amplified by hers.

My memories of these physical things are strong: they are unforgettable. But memories of feelings aren't the same thing as actual feelings. The memories fade faster. And when you turn around to look back, to refresh your memories, you find the feelings are still there, but they've gotten a little different. So every time I looked back I got over her a little more, and every time I looked forward I got fucked up a little more.

And all at once she's back in my life.

I get up and go to start on the truck, thinking about how I almost laughed when she told me I'm famous. I am a joke and everybody knows it.

She crosses her legs. I can see that there's actually a little mud on her shoes, old mud that has dried and anchored itself. They're functional shoes, like the ones I wear for my work: sturdy, comfortable, not fashionable. They're the kind of shoes she wouldn't have even considered when I knew her before.

Suddenly I see how beautiful she really is. She has become the person she wants to be.

She inspects the bill and writes a check, not speaking. She hands me the check and our fingers touch. "You're not going to succeed in this business, Rafer. You don't charge enough."

"I'll get by," I say. "Listen—"

"I was really nervous, coming here," she says, in a hurry, as if she hasn't heard me trying to speak myself, trying to work up my apology. "I didn't know if you would hate me. There was so much anger in your first books; I was afraid it was about me, or that I caused it."

"That's not the way it works," I say. "I write to keep the voices in my head quiet. Sometimes, at night, they would talk to me about you. But a lot of the time, in the dark, I could only hear myself crying. That anger was about me. I was never angry at you."

Joey has the grease gun going. He's a virtuoso with it, and the pop-hiss sounds fill the air. Judith gets up and closes the door. I know Joey and Max will huddle. The last time the door to my office was closed was when I fired Alex for stealing a tire.

"Tell me about your life," she says, sitting back down in the chair. "You're so secretive! I never knew you were a writer. Any woman would want to think she was the cause of your passion. I have wanted to tell people about us, you know." Her smile is tentative, as if she's confessing more than she intended.

"I hate writing," I say, staring at my desk. "But you already know about me if you read the papers. I made money, and then I fucked up."

She doesn't answer, and when I look up I see tears in her eyes. "You didn't do that to me," I say. "I did it to myself. I made all the choices. Most of the time I wasn't writing, I was bleeding, spilling my guts, ripping things out of myself and putting them on paper."

I hear my words floating out into the air, but I see alarm and more tears in her eyes, and my mind is screaming at me: Shut the fuck up! You're trying to hurt her again! So I do.

"It wasn't about you," I mutter. "I was just a mess. But I figured it out, I wrote, I got drunk. Then I got over it and bought this place. Now I fix cars and trucks, and I write a little at night." I am trying to sound cheerful. "So tell me what's up with you. I'm more interested in what happened to you. You're the real mystery here."

She wipes her eyes and grins a little nervously. "Well, I still like to think it was my fault. A girl can always hope she ruined some nice guy's life," she says, looking sly. I laugh, but my throat is tight, and I wonder if she can tell. Even my dense brain can figure out what is happening, that we have reached a détente of sorts, that we have agreed to forget about things we could never have controlled anyway.

"We did our best," I say.

She smiles for a few seconds. "My life hasn't been glamorous at all," she says. "There was a terrible automobile accident, about two years after you left. He was drunk, but thank God no other cars were involved. It was a terrible time, and the worst part was how the children suffered. I used the insurance money to do something crazy: I bought an orchard. I raise apples now; the kids call me Mommy Appleseed."

She's smiling; she seems happy. But my mind has fogged up again with grief, with pain for her, and with guilt. I can only stare at her face, her smile, her large brown fawn-eyes—how could I have forgotten these eyes?—and search for the words that will tell her what I feel. Could I have helped? How will I ever know? The truth is that I hadn't been there, hadn't helped.

Judith sees the emotions washing across my face. With a sudden look of concern she stands, comes to me. I get out of my chair to meet her as her hands come up to cradle my face. Her fingers and palms are rough; her lips are soft. I pull her to me by the waist and hold her head against tight my shoulder. In my imagination I can hear the sounds again, the sounds of the halting, choking way I would cry, if I were crying, if I could ever let myself cry.

She breaks, moves away, turning. She stops at the door. "I'm so sorry, Rafer. About everything. I really am." I see tears again.

"So am I," I say, struggling with my voice. I follow her out into the bay where her truck is.

She sees the stove in the corner. It is one of those stainless steel commercial things, with big burners and a hood. "What's this?" she asks.

"My pride and joy. I got it at a bankruptcy auction. A restaurant went bust."

"What's it doing here in the garage?"

"I cook breakfast Saturday mornings. You know, eggs, french toast, bacon, hashed browns. The employees, some customers, some old friends come by. I'm even teaching them to enjoy grits."

She gets in her truck and looks at the stove for a few seconds and then grins at me. "Are ladies invited?"

Joey leers at me as she pulls out on the highway. All I can do is smile.

Challenger Deep

Kathleen Bradean

Pop rode from Oakland to Guam in my lap. I put my vintage green and yellow A's baseball cap over him so that people wouldn't notice the plain cardboard box with the gold-embossed stamp, Black and Sons Funeral Directors. A dusty cobweb clung to the back corner of the box. It had taken me a while to make good on my promise to him. The first two days on the island, I let Pop sit on the dresser in the hotel room. Afraid that a maid might think he was trash, I decided I had to carry out his final request. Until I closed the past, the rest of my life was suspended.

I removed my hat as I ambled into the hotel lobby. By the time I reached the granite and glass reception desk, the hotel staff beamed expectant smiles.

"Hi. I need to find out how I can hire a boat."

They nodded, as if they understood everything. "Yes, sir."

I grinned at them. It helped that I was so athletic and lanky, barely any hips or breasts. My look was boy-next-door, suntanned, with a white-toothed California smile. The short blonde haircut, the way I moved, the unisex clothes, worked magic. I passed as a man!

Then, recognition set in. "Um, ma'am. Miss Erica." Fear that they'd offended me pulled at the corners of their eyes. They still smiled, but a little less certainly, less brightly.

My smile faded, too. Funny how one little word had

enough power to make me feel right with myself. But they snatched it away from me as quickly as they offered it. I wanted to be sir. I wanted that magical word back.

"I need to hire a boat to take me out over the Challenger Deep." I set my A's cap on their polished counter.

The smiles drooped a bit more. The staff shrugged.

The hotel manager stepped forward to handle me. He wore a lei of waxy cream flowers over his dark green suit. The rest of the staff faded back, but their ears were tuned to the conversation, and I saw their gazes slide away from their tasks to watch me.

"No good fishing over the Marianas Trench," he told me with a tight smile. He folded his hands at his waist as if that closed the matter.

"I'm not fishing. I'm—" Who knew how many local laws I broke carrying around Pop's ashes, much less dumping them into the ocean? "I'm paying my last respects."

"It's all the same ocean. Same water. Why not take an island tour and pay your respects during that?"

He tried to hand me a glossy three-fold brochure of feral blonds on a sailboat, each clutching a tropical drink. I didn't accept it from him.

"I made a promise. My father was on the Trieste survey team that measured the Challenger Deep. He wanted to go back."

The manager's smile grew more fixed. "There's nothing out there. Just ocean." He decided a minor problem with the Japanese tourists at the far end of the desk needed his attention. No one was interested in stories about Pop.

They didn't care that being on the team that measured the deepest place on earth meant something to him, and they couldn't understand how important it was to me to carry out Pop's final wish. I made a promise. Pop raised me to keep my word.

Pissed off, I shoved my A's cap over my cropped hair. My walk as I crossed the lobby had a definite female motion to it. I tried to get back into my male groove but couldn't.

I decided to explore past the fenced hotel grounds. The day before, I saw boats beyond the hotel's private beach. I figured I'd simply go hire one myself.

I reached for the brass handle on the lobby's glass doors.

A chubby, flirty doorman rushed to open the door for me. He was the one who always offered to bring me boys, girls, or smoke. "My brother has a boat," he whispered out of the side of his mouth.

"A big boat?"

The doorman shrugged his rounded shoulders, a common answer on the island, I was learning. No one wanted to say no. "Last week, one of his customers caught a tuna! Big fish." He threw his arms wide, inviting me to imagine it. Across the lobby, the manager cleared his throat.

The doorman scooted behind a potted palm. His dark green uniform blended with the plants.

"It's the distance I'm worried about." I felt silly, talking to a huge terracotta planter, but when I stood closer, the stiff palm fronds poked my face.

"My brother goes out there many times, I think."

And made it back apparently, which was my bigger concern. I shoved my hands into the pockets of my khaki shorts. "Can I meet him? See the boat?"

The doorman peered around the potted jungle. "I'll make the arrangements. Meet me beyond the security gate at five o'clock tomorrow morning."

"That early?" It felt so cloak and dagger for such a sunny, tropical island.

"The trench is very far. Better to start at daybreak so that it isn't dark when you come back." The doorman moved from behind the big planter. "Bring lots of water, three times what you think you need, food, and beer," he told me as he moved across the shiny marble floor. Then he trotted back. "Best prices, just for you, at the market in the blue building. Don't go into the other store. No good there. They rip you off. Charge you tourist prices. Go to the blue market. Ask for Gogui. My cousin. Tell him I sent you. You get a good price." He nudged my elbow then glided away to open the door for the Japanese tourists.

The pure white sands of the hotel's imported beach gave way to Guam's domestic brown sand past the hotel's bamboo gate. It was just after dawn, and the air was already torpid. Bright flags on ships' masts refused to flutter in the light breeze.

The doorman called out to me from behind a scraggly hibiscus bush. I wondered about him. Maybe skulking around playing games of intrigue made days of endless perfection seem more exciting. Pop's box of ashes poked my back through the pack, prodding me on, or warning me, I wasn't sure.

Morning was rising, flat and harsh, over the sullen waves. Guam sat near the International Date Line, so we were among the first people on earth to witness the beginning hours of a new day.

"You went to see Gogui?"

I nodded.

"I told you. Best deal around."

Why we were whispering was beyond me.

The last high tide left a meandering line of tiny pink shells, seaweed, and dried foam along the sand.

"Tano!" The doorman greeted his brother as we trudged through the deep sand. "This is Miss Erica. She needs a boat."

Tano worked fishing line in his brown hands, his long fingers arcing high over his palm. He glanced up at us when the doorman hailed him, but he didn't say anything. When we were a couple feet away, Tano set aside the knot he tried to tease out of the line.

Why was it that men always had the thick, long lashes that women wanted? His eyes were like tropical water over shallow white sand beaches. I could see the line of his hipbones above the low waistband of his shorts. A large hook, carved in bleached bone, hung between nipples like melted chocolate kisses.

I should have negotiated the price before I saw him. There had to be a premium for all that languid sex. He caught me looking, so I pulled the brim of my cap low over my eyes. Tano and his brother chatted in Chamorro, the island idiom. Whenever they laughed, as sparkly as sunlight on water, I felt as if it were about me. I shifted my backpack and dug the toe of my black Vans into the sand.

Tano's boat looked like shit, but all the sport-fishing boats along the beach were as weathered as the men who captained them. The metal fittings were speckled with rust. The dingy red stripe running along the hull was crusted with salt.

I looked past the surf to the ocean. It went on without end, and the boat seemed so small.

"No good fishing in the deep. Fish like warm, shallow water," Tano said to me.

I glanced up at him again. High cheekbones, thick lips: he

was too incredible to look at straight on, like the sun. Sparse hairs on his chin curled wildly, one lighter brown than the others. A flush of heat hit my lips and cheeks, as obvious as a hard-on. I felt the welcome, warm tingle of interest between my legs.

"I'm not fishing. I want to release something."

The doorman tried to infect our halfhearted haggling over the price of the trip by baiting Tano and then me in turns, but we already reached an understanding between flitting glances.

It took most of an hour to get the boat ready to go. The doorman disappeared when the work started. Tano told me what to do, sometimes showing me by covering my hands with his dark brown ones. By the time the boat was on the water, we had a casual flirtation going. It was easy. No forced chuckles, no posturing.

Tano asked, "What's with the hat? You touch it like a talisman every time you mention your father."

I caught myself touching the brim again and gave him an embarrassed grin. "Pop and I were big fans of the A's. He bought this cap for me when I was in seventh grade. We caught a foul ball that day."

"I touch a tree every time I return to shore. Superstitious, both of us," he chuckled.

I gave him a friendly little nudge with my shoulder as we bent to lift the cooler onto the deck. Tano bumped back, grinning and showing a gap in his front teeth.

We set sail as the sun broke above low clouds. Land slipped from sight, and I felt as if the world went away.

"You don't get seasick, do you, Erica?" Tano asked as we hit open ocean.

We slammed up and down waves until he tacked enough to cut through the troughs. The side-to-side rocking was harder, but at least my teeth didn't clack together.

I patted my stomach. "Something I inherited from Pop. Sea legs. Sea stomach, I guess. He was in the navy." The sun was already strong, so I put on my sunglasses and tugged at the brim of my cap when I felt the wind try to lift it. "He was stationed near here for a couple years."

"Good, because it's going to be hours of this," Tano warned. He squinted at the bright light bouncing off the white surfaces of his boat.

There were large padded captain's chairs at the back of his boat for fishers, but I settled onto the worn red cushion under the sun shade and propped my feet on a cooler. I sipped from a cold beer. "Your brother told me that you go out to the Mariana Trench a lot. If there's nothing there to see, as everyone keeps telling me, why do you go?"

Tano stared at the water. Damn, pissed him off, and I wanted to sweet-talk him into a little bump and grind. He was just my type—a jock. It was going to be a very long day if he wasn't going to talk.

Tano did talk, though. His eyes focused past me as if he were remembering a distant, hazy past. "About three years ago, I was unhappy. I was in love. There was a man . . . He consumed my heart and soul. I lived for the sight of him. On the day he married a woman, I sailed to the edge of the trench. I hung over the railing, staring into the deep, wondering if I had the balls to jump. Instead, my tears fell. Maybe, they are still falling."

"The trench is deep," I agreed. "Seven miles from the surface to the bottom of the Challenger Deep, the lowest spot along the trench. Pop told me that you could toss Mount Everest down it and still have a mile of water left." I almost touched the cap, but saw Tano's teasing smile and held onto my beer instead.

"Big enough to hold all the sorrow in the world."

Tano leaned far over the side of the boat. It was body poetry, the arc of his lean brown torso, the grip of his long toes on the railing of the boat, the way his hand slapped against the rising waves.

After he swung back onto the deck, he dragged wet fingers across my lips. I licked the drops away.

"Tastes like tears, doesn't it," he asked softly. Our bodies touched.

We stayed there, pressed together, staring down into the water as if it held answers.

"Pop once told me that the human body is mostly sea water."

Tano smiled slyly. "Does that mean we're mostly sorrow?"

It was my turn to stare off at the intensely blue water. I ran my fingertips over the lumpy white A on the front of my cap. "Some of us."

We played his CDs of local technopop and danced like we were in a club. The unpredictable motion of the water made it hard to keep my footing, but Tano put his hands over his head and moved like curling waves. I wasn't as steady so I bumped against him a lot, but I closed my eyes and imagined I was a hot boy under the flashing lights of a foam pit, and everyone wanted to take me home. When his hands went to steady me, I pretended strangers couldn't stop themselves from reaching out to touch my boy flesh.

When the batteries died in his player, I collapsed onto the cushions, laughing. "I haven't danced like that in a long time.

I expected, you know, a tropical paradise, people to be so much more open about their sexuality. But it's worse here than back home. When they think I'm a man, I can dance with a girl, but the moment they realize I'm," I gestured down to my body with contempt, "this, they get angry and move away."

Tano rested his elbows on the boat's console. He still panted from our dancing. "I have to be careful. That's why I couldn't tell him that I wanted him. I could only suffer, and want, and be silent."

"Sorry."

I wanted to tell him that I understood, but at Pop's funeral, people said, "I know how you feel," and I'd think, *You can't even begin to guess what I lost*. But I'd nod and stare down at the carpet until they moved on to the food laid out on the dining room table.

I had to move under the faded red sun shade to stay in the short shadows. Noon already. He watched me out of the corner of his eye. "It's a strange thing to be doing, burying your father."

I shrugged.

"Usually the son does that, around here."

I peeled the label off my beer bottle with my fingernails, trying, as usual, to take it off in one piece. Another superstition. I wasn't even sure what curse a whole label blocked.

What the hell, he came out to me.

"I'm not a woman. I mean, not inside. Just on the surface." I got the big label off and worked on the smaller one at the neck of the brown bottle. "I was supposed to be a boy. I have two older sisters. They're girls."

I knew that sounded stupid. I set aside my beer.

"I mean, they're girly-girls. Real girls. Inside and out. Not me. See, everyone knows if the two older kids are the same sex, the third child is the last try for the other. Mom even told me that the only name they had picked out was Eric. In the hospital, they slapped the *a* on the end to make me Erica."

I pulled off my hat. I worked my hands around it in an unending circle while I spoke to the inside of the cap. "I would have made a great boy. I hung around Pop and helped him work on the cars. I was the only one who went to baseball games with him. We both liked gingersnaps and root beer." As if that described the bond we shared that excluded my mom and sisters. I was Pop's son in every way but the one that mattered to me.

Tano asked, "Do you like girls?"

I gave him that frank look that I learned in bars, the one that got men to follow me to dark corners. "The individual person matters more than the gender. Men, I understand. Women are like a separate tribe with weird rituals and a different language. I don't get women, but I like making love to them. I like men, too. More."

"You like everyone except you." He sipped from his beer. "I only like men."

The waves whooshed and hissed. It was a vast desert, the surface of the ocean. No birds overhead, no signs of life in the water. I drank more beer than I should have and watched Tano because there was nothing else to see.

Every movement he made was sure, slow. I envied the way his fingertips trailed over the boat's chromed steering wheel. His lips were so rough and cracked from the sea that I thought they'd feel great nibbling on my skin.

Sweat shone on Tano's slender neck. I wanted to lick it away. Sex surged through my blood, in my chest, in my belly, between my legs. I wondered if men felt that, too, or if it was all in the dick for them.

Shit. I was dumping Pop's ashes, a funeral of sorts, and I was cruising the island boy. I was going to burn in hell.

"Did you ever think of changing to a man?"

After hours of silence, his voice startled me.

"Yes." I drew my feet off the cooler and leaned forward with my hands clasped together. "I mean, I looked into the treatments. The stumbling block was that I had to live as a man for a year. Not that I didn't want to, but I didn't know when to begin. On the way home from the doctor's office? I got onto the bus as a man, but three stops later someone called me ma'am and I was back to being female. The next morning I planned to start off fresh, but I couldn't escape my body. Every night I'd go to sleep swearing, 'This is my last day as Erica,' but then I'd get dressed and go to work and still be stuck in the twilight world between who I've been and who I want to be."

Tano smiled out at the waves. "You can't become who you already are. You can only accept it. Maybe you're not male; maybe you aren't female. Maybe you aren't straight; maybe you aren't gay. Maybe you're simply you." He made me see myself in a tilted mirror. "There are vast spaces in the between. There's more ocean than island."

"Maybe I'm the shore."

The bottom dropped out of the world. I clutched the boat railing. I was falling, falling while we were floating. Dizzy, I gulped air.

Wave. Trough. White foam. In the distance, the water was

unrelenting blue, but the crest curling off the bow of the boat was green and gray. Nothing was different, yet primal instinct told me that I was in danger. Intense pressure squeezed my chest as if I dove into the depths.

"What is it?"

He answered in a whisper, "We're over the trench." He cut the engines. Even the waves were hushed, as if we'd stepped inside a great cathedral.

The swells knocked the boat.

"Is it always like this?"

He nodded. His pale eyes were as wide as mine. It didn't seem possible, but we could feel it, the void below us. I stared up at the azure sky, afraid that if I looked down, like a cartoon character, I'd fall.

I didn't think I believed in such things, but I swore I felt the immense presence of God.

I wanted to run. I wanted to hide. I lurched to my backpack and pulled out the box of Pop's ashes.

"Maybe you shouldn't drop your father over the side. Maybe you should throw in your sorrow, like I did. Let it sink."

"It's not that easy."

Tano snatched my A's cap off my head. He tossed it onto the waves like a Frisbee.

"Hey!" I was too afraid to jump in after it even though I was a great swimmer.

That much water could drown you, I thought. The weight of it would drag you under the surface. You'd never see the sun again. My hat bobbed on top of a far wave, disappeared on the rolling surface, reappeared even further away.

"That was the *a* at the end of your name. Now, you are Eric."

My mouth open and shut like a hooked fish.

"Your life as a man has begun."

He was an idiot. He didn't understand. "It isn't that easy. It can't be that easy."

"But what if it is? That hat was a *gris-gris*, a magic charm. Throw it away, and throw away the *a* that made you into a girl."

Anger welled up behind my eyes.

Tano pleaded with me. "Believe just enough to make it real. Go back to shore as a man. You don't know when to begin? Begin now! Right now! Because the now is the only time you ever really have."

My throat was too tight to breathe.

"I let my moment pass. I'm stuck in a now that never ends, the man I want living with someone else. Before that happened, I should have acted," Tano told me, and I saw tears in the corners of his eyes. "Don't waste your now, your chance."

The hat slowly absorbed water, growing darker. The big white A on the front sank lower as it absorbed tears. When it was full of them, it fell below the surface. Feeling as if I were drowning, I gasped in salt air.

"You can only tread water so long before the misery will pull you under. It's not sink or swim. It's sink or fly."

The hat was gone. Could I cast off my outer self as easily as he cast away my hat? I inhaled again and relaxed my fists.

"I only like men," Tano reminded me.

He came to me, wrapping his arms around my waist. I felt his dick against my thigh. He kissed me, and it was like kissing the sea. I tasted the salt on his mouth and felt the tug of his chapped skin over my smooth lips. His skin was hot from the sun.

"Fly."

I was Eric. Kissed, suddenly I was a prince.

I shoved Tano to the floor of the boat. His shorts came off in a quick tug. I was more aggressive than he probably expected, but he didn't seem to mind. We fucked like men, raw energy wildly spent. I spat white foam on his cock and jerked him while we kissed, bodies pressed together. Rough, I grasped his balls the way a man would, sure of the grip, not afraid of hurting him.

My thumb pressed under his cockhead. His eyes widened and I said, "I know. I know," because I did know what felt good. When I was a man, I was pure balls and sass. I fit in my skin.

He drew his knees up. I tightened my strokes over his dick. He thrashed under me until white come spurted across the hollow of his dark brown stomach. Tano scooped the load away from his belly button and flung it into the abyss. Giggling, we kissed.

Pop told me that the day he sailed to the edge of the Marianas Trench was a profoundly spiritual day for him. He didn't use those words exactly. Being a navy man, he said something like, "God grabbed me by the balls and made me take a hard look at the man I was becoming."

Maybe Pop knew I needed to face it. Maybe he wanted it for me. Maybe that was why he made me promise to bring him there. I was sorry that I wasted three years keeping that promise.

The breeze ruffled my short hair like a friendly paternal pat. Tano started the boat's engines and turned the boat around.

Against the Challenger Deep, the hurdles ahead of me suddenly seemed like nothing. A drop in the ocean.

Pop always said that the measure of a man was in how he kept his word. Out of habit, I reached for a cap that wasn't there, and, remembering, smiled a little.I tipped Pop's ashes into the vast blue. The wind picked them up and scattered them further. Pop flew on gusts of wind, and then he fell, soft as tears, and is probably falling still, into the mourning wake. I felt every inch a man.

Up in the Morning

Mike Kimera

I'm fifty years old, and my erection still greets me most mornings like a faithful dog. True, it's not the puppy it used to be, bouncing around and leaking everywhere when it gets excited; these days it stands patiently and waits for me to do something.

If time is pressing or I have somewhere to be, I can distract myself from my erection's passive insistence and get on with my life; but on those still dark winter mornings, when I wake earlier than I need to but am reluctant to leave the welcoming warmth of the duvet, I'm much more vulnerable. Then my erection snags at my attention, stretching itself slowly as it wakes from sleep, letting the foreskin slip back just far enough to release that salt-sweet-sweat smell with which it marks my territory.

Perhaps if I didn't sleep naked, the erection would be easier to ignore, but it is the only thing between me and the duvet cover, which nestles against it like an old friend. Turning on to my belly only lets my erection show off the firmness of its resolve.

If this happens when I'm traveling alone, I give myself up to it at that point. I lie on my back, eyes closed, legs stretched, feet crossed at the ankles—I have no idea why—and let it off the leash.

Of course, by now I've had a lot of practice, and I know

exactly how to please myself. I have a particular hold I like to use, developed unconsciously over the years and now effectively involuntary. It is, as most things to do with my sex life are, complicated, slow acting and very, very effective. My thumb sits behind the head where it can roll the foreskin with ease. The index finger stays free, ready to stroke the sensitive skin of the head. The long second finger curls firmly below the glans, just at the point of lubrication. The third finger folds back against my palm so the back of it pushes the shaft out against the second finger and thumb. The smallest finger runs lightly, or sometimes firmly, over my balls.

Initially the erection swells just with the joy of being touched and knowing what comes next. Very little motion or stimulation is necessary. Then its short attention span asserts itself, and it demands a mental porn show to prick it on to greater things.

These are never elaborate or even pretty. These are fantasies I would never admit to. The ones that I hope no one who knows me would ever attribute to me. In thrall to my erection, there is nothing I won't imagine doing or having done to me, no boundaries, no decency, no love, just the need for one more twitch of the nerve endings, one (or more) holes to push into, women (mostly women, sometimes men, sometimes both) to use and abuse, until finally, back arching, legs stiff, hand moving rapidly and firmly, my erection sprays its hot sticky triumph over my belly, dribbling the remnants over my fist, like melting ice cream, to pool in a sticky mess in the hairs on my balls.

During the actual release it is as if I am not there; there is just a blissfully blank moment of nonconsciousness. Then, after a few seconds of pleasantly warm exhaustion, I am alone again and aware that I stink of sweat and semen, that the sheets are damp, that my hair is matted to my head and that I urgently want to be clean.

This, I think, is what sin feels like; the opposite of grace, it drains the spirit and stains the soul. It occurs to me that poor old Onan, patron saint of masturbation, sinned not because "he spilt his seed upon the ground," but because he did it again and again and again, like an alcoholic soaking himself in booze although he knows he will wake in some gutter, covered in his own vomit.

Like most sinners, I indulge most when I am away from hearth and home, but even in my marriage bed, on mornings like this morning, in those vulnerably truthful moments between sleep and life, my erection sometimes snares me.

I test the extent of my temptation by rolling onto my side, pulling my erection up to the side and then releasing it. The thud it makes against the mattress tells me that it will not be ignored today. I turn and look at my wife, sleeping soundly beside me. I take in the reality of my love for her, the central place she has and will always have in my life, and I get out of bed.

My wife is not a morning person. She'd be accommodating I'm sure, but in a "not for me thanks, but please help yourself" kind of way that I find bleakly discouraging and besides, when we have sex I want it to be about more than scratching an itch, so, needing to take care of things and not wanting to wake her, I head for the bathroom.

My erection wags as I walk, pleased with itself and pumped up by the idea that it's leading me somewhere. I follow behind, with the same muted sense of embarrassment as a man walking a dog that insists on trying to hump every passing leg.

Showers are often advertised with pictures of soap-slick beauties achieving bliss under the spray. In reality, I think it is men, not women, who are most likely to masturbate in the shower. It's private, you don't have to explain why you're taking so long, and the mess is washed away immediately.

When I was young, my erection would point upwards fiercely, as if trying to touch my, then much flatter, belly. Now it manages something just about at right angles and still feels proud of itself. Even when I don't touch it, I can feel the pressure of its presence nudging me. Giving in to it, I brace my legs slightly apart, turn the shower to full force so that the warm water bounces off my chest and reach for the liquid soap that is so much a part of this ritual.

I pretend that my eyes are closed to keep the water out; the reality is that I want to concentrate on the phantoms I bring with me to the shower. Today my subconscious furnishes two women, both redheads. The one in her twenties is slim and pale with taut breasts, hipbones like water-smoothed stone and that small tight gap between the tops of her closed thighs that makes my erection whimper with need. The second woman is a forty-something version of the first, with fuller breasts, a rounder belly and a large, fuckable arse.

I picture them kneeling, of course, each one pressing up against one of my legs, faces up-turned, eyes eager. They ignore each other as they compete to explore me, but they cannot help, in this confined space, but rub up against each other. The enforced nature of this intimate contact adds to my arousal. In my mind's eye the younger one soaps my belly and works my balls with her long slim fingers, while the older one, perhaps more adventurous or perhaps merely more needy, parts my buttocks and pushes soap into that dark ripe crevice. In reality my hands are busy working up a foam front and back while my cock is screaming for attention that I enjoy delaying.

Swirling around me, the two change places with an ease only fantasy could support. The older woman opens her mouth and swallows me until her jaw strains and her eyes bulge. She grips my buttocks firmly and forces me further down her throat all the time looking up at me so that I can see what this effort is costing her. The younger one has retained her hold on my balls and is pulling them backwards, using them to help her balance so she can push her tongue impossibly far up my arse.

Anyone looking into the shower now would see an older man, on the balls of his feet, one hand strangling his cock, the other pushing one long finger up his arse. My erection refuses to acknowledge this reality and drives me onwards.

I'm close now and need a final image to push me over. I imagine the older one with her back to me, hands above her head, stretching to reach the showerhead, legs spread improbably wide. My arms are wrapped around her chest and my fists are closed on the soft meat of her breasts, pressing her back against me. Beneath us, the younger one kneels, also with her back to me. Her arms reach up between the thighs of the older woman and then lock on with a trapeze artist's grip as her hands grab the woman's heavy buttocks and part them. Gleefully and brutally I feed my cock up the woman's arse, relishing the grunts she struggles to suppress. The ballet is complete when the kneeling girl leans back; still clutching the legs of the woman I'm sodomizing and stretches her long neck at an impossible angle to clamp her lips around my balls.

This Circe-de-Porn triptych is so effective that I manage

to ignore the pain in my calf muscles long enough to squirt off-white cum onto the pure white tiles in front of me in three short but tremendously gratifying blasts.

The moment the heels of my feet touch the base of the shower, I start to come back to myself. Mechanically I lift the showerhead from the cradle and rinse the tiles clean. Then I switch off the water, step out of the shower, wrap a towel around my shoulders and recover my breath leaning against the sink.

Why do I do this? I ask. My erection is no longer there to answer me, and in its absence nothing I have just done makes sense anymore.

I try to distract myself by toweling dry my hair, a task that doesn't take as long as it used to, but my mind goes back to the roughly sketched women that I just pressed into service. Who they are, what they did, what I did to them, all these things break taboos or cross barriers that, in my real life I would regard as a violation and yet, what is more real in my life than those seconds of tension just before my balls unload?

The answer, of course, is that the man in the shower really is me but he is not really all of me. Ever since puberty I've lived with being someone who is sometimes driven to places he'd rather not admit visiting, much less enjoying. I've dealt with it by containing it; keeping it between me and my right hand. But it refuses to stay in its box. It seeps out through the cracks and leaves me covered with the snail trails of its slow escape.

Perhaps I misunderstood Onan's sin. Perhaps it was not the repeated self-indulgence that was the sin but the increasing isolation of a diminishing self that this indulgence creates. I wonder if Onan had a wife and if he did, whether he thought of her when he spilt his seed or whether he, too, sought extremes that distanced his act from his reality.

Well, I know where the best of my reality lies under a duvet that's a damn sight warmer than this rapidly cooling bathroom.

I pause long enough to spray myself with the scent my wife likes the most and then head back to the bedroom.

When I slide in behind her, Claire is just surfacing from sleep. I lean into her neck and kiss her, letting myself absorb the richness of her early-morning smell. She stretches like a cat as my hand slides up her warm skin and presses herself back into me when I cup her breast.

Mmm," she says. "That's nice."

She turns over slowly so that her face is against my chest. I wrap my arm around her.

You smell nice, too," she says, running her hand across my chest and down my belly.

Her lips reach my mouth at the same time that her hand cups my penis. I have a stab of concern that I will fail her; that I will stay limp in her hand, useless and insulting. I just couldn't face that. I concentrate hard on the Claire's lips on mine and to my immense relief, my recently used and sometimes unresponsive flesh stiffens slowly against Claire's palm, like a fern unfurling in the sunlight.

"Well, good morning," Claire says in a voice that tells me that it's going to be a very good morning indeed.

"Go slow," she says as she straddles me, "you're not the only one who's stiff in the mornings."

We both laugh. Then she kisses me. I open my mouth to speak but she puts her finger across my lips as if to say "later." She moves slowly down on to my now-respectable erection. When I'm all the way inside her, she closes her eyes and smiles.

Looking up at her, I wonder how many of the mornings when I have made my way towards the shower, could have been spent like this? I put regret aside and offer myself hope instead. For once it seems that I have led my erection rather than letting my erection lead me. This, I think, is what living with it should be about.

Home Ice

Tulsa Brown

"Damn! I used to jimmy this thing all the time. Where's the flashlight?"

I glanced over my shoulder at the road, then back to Guy's shape hunched in front of the door. "I think the battery's dead."

"Don't chicken out now, Maur," Guy said, teeth gritted from cold and frustration. I sighed and turned on the light, then huddled in close in hope of hiding the beam. In my heart I knew it was already too late. I was certain our dark outlines had been recognized against the arena wall, and phones were ringing throughout the little town of Iles des Chênes.

"Maurice is home! And that wicked Guy LePont is with him!"

I imagined my mother and father had just sat upright in their narrow double bed and somewhere in a Montreal graveyard, the almighty Rocket had flipped over on his side, preparing to shoulder-check his way out of the grave.

Guy and I had come home to commit something worse than mortal sin.

Metal clicked. "Got it!"

He pushed the heavy door open. I handed him the light and seized our duffle bags, which had been sitting in the snow. The first breath of the old arena was a staggering dose of memory. Popcorn and angst—the smell of my childhood. Our childhoods.

Guy and I had both grown up in Ile des Chênes, a dot of a town on the French-Canadian landscape. It was three hours' drive from Montreal, and a world away from Satan's Metropolis, the city we lived in now. Neither of us had been back in over a year, and never together. When I'd casually, carefully mentioned that I'd "run into" Guy LePont in Toronto, my mother fell silent.

"Well, once couldn't hurt," she said at last.

He laughed a short gust when I told him, but later I felt the force of his pride. Fists clenched in my hair, he bucked hard into my mouth, the swollen, meaty bell of his cock head striking the back of my throat. I clung to his legs, the driving power of his thrusts nearly gagging me, squeezing water from my eyes.

"Is this it? The once that doesn't hurt?"

He kissed my battered mouth afterward. "Coward," he said gently. "You've got to come out sometime. I'm ready when you are. Hell, I was ready before I was *born*."

I believed him. I'd been in awe of Guy all my life. What did a ten-year-old boy have to do to receive the appellation of "wicked"?

My father's searing look could have melted the ice on the driveway. My mother simply said, "Never mind. Keep your eyes in front of you. Study hard."

"Play hard," my father intoned, the command that eclipsed all others.

There were two forms of worship in Ile des Chênes: the church and hockey, and the former only got one day a week. Growing up, I hadn't known that sports were something people chose to play. I'd been thrust onto the ice at four, maneuvered into the game by the same deft hands that steered me into church and school. The rest of the boys in Ile des Chênes met the same fate, yet the press was a little harder on my shoulders: my very name was an incantation, a prayer. I had been named after Maurice "the Rocket" Richard.

It was no use even suggesting that there had been other greats in the NHL: Hull, Orr, Gretzky. My father would clench his fist over his chest, as if squeezing the blood from his heart.

"Skaters." He spat the word out. "Did any of them start a revolution?"

It wasn't the scoring records Richard had set, or even the five straight Stanley Cup Championships he'd led the Montreal Canadiens to win. In 1955 the Rocket had done something no Francophone had ever dared: he'd publicly criticized the team's arrogant *anglais* owner. Retribution was swift—Richard was suspended for the season. In answer, riots exploded in the streets of Montreal and raged for seven hours. It was the beginning, some said, of French activism. Defiance.

In our house, admiration tipped over into reverence. The winter of 1956 was renowned for its storms, and one howling night in January, my grandfather opened his farmhouse door to a snowman.

"You couldn't even tell his coat was black," my father would say, as if the memory was his own. In truth he'd been only three, and already in bed.

The man had missed his train to Montreal and tried to drive it, hit a snow patch of ice and put his car in the snow-filled ditch. Could he phone a tow truck? When he unwound his scarf and took off his cap, my grandfather realized a god was standing in his kitchen. He didn't own a TV, but there wasn't a soul in the country who wouldn't have recognized the Rocket.

My grandmother was struck dumb; my grandfather had to call for the truck himself, with instructions to come, "but not too quickly." For an hour they entertained the legend with whiskey and laughter, and a plate of stew. When the truck finally arrived and put the miraculous evening to an end, my grandmother recovered her senses and ran out after it, in her slippers. Maurice Richard graciously signed the dinner plate he'd eaten from, a piece of turquoise Fiestaware. The fact that my grandmother didn't even catch cold was a sign, some said, of divine intervention.

By sheer bad luck, no more boys were born to the family until me. I was their first chance to brand someone with the name of the deity, and no one ever let me forget it. "Maurice" was the epitome of bold French-Canadian spirit, of manhood itself.

"The Francophone dink on skates," wicked Guy LePont said—although not too loudly.

Guy had been the saving grace of my teenage years. He was slight and nimble, a quick-thinking forward with a diamond-shaped face and pale skin that flushed pink at the first bite of frost. He had dark, dark hair and hard-knotted muscles; I was entranced by the abrupt point of his Adam's apple.

The chance to see him and hear his laughter, or feel his wiry body jostle my big-shouldered frame during practice, helped me survive a game I loathed. Sometimes, in the middle of donning his uniform, he would look over his shoulder at me, and the shock of it—pads and skin and twisted smirk—sent me sailing on an erotic drunk. Guy LePont's heavy-lidded gaze was thick with both promise and menace, the ultimate mystery.

When we met again in the city, I came to understand that look and quickly discovered I couldn't resist it. I was bigger than Guy, but never his match. Sex in an elevator, or the parking lot outside a busy club—he found my boundaries and goaded me over them.

"We should go home together," he said one night, in the close curl of the sheets.

"Sure. When is hell due to freeze over?"

He brushed my light words aside, slipped his hand between my legs.

"This winter," he said with conviction, "you and I are going to Ile des Chênes."

I sputtered an argument but my erection was hardening, stroked by fear and his touch.

"No one has to know. This is just for the two of us." His voice kinked with a smile. "If you come home with me, I'll suck you off at center ice."

My cock surged, a steel piston against my belly. The threat of it, danger and defiance wound tightly into my most secret teenage dreams. Would he really? Would I?

Guy flipped over deftly on top of me, pinned my wrists above my head, a call to scuffle that I never answered.

"And if you get that, I get a little thrill, too." He told me what he wanted.

Sound vibrated in my chest, laughter or a scream. He couldn't be serious! Guy muffled me with a bruising kiss. My alarm twisted into a moan, then another as we writhed and slid into eager, familiar rhythms. Yet all the while the shock of his blasphemy swirled, molten in my belly, lapped in fiery waves at the base of my balls. Coming was like hitting a wall of sex.

"You're a madman," I said afterward.

Guy's voice was ethereal, as if he was drifting near the ceiling. "It's only a plate, Maurice. It's washable."

Fear smacked me fresh. He wasn't asking permission. He planned to do this, and he knew I would agree. I felt the dizzying sway of realization: it's dangerous to love someone from your hometown. He knows you too well.

The flashlight's beam danced wildly over the walls, lingered on the windows. He was trying to unnerve me.

"Guy, stop!"

"It's after one. They're all in their coffins," he said cheerfully.

I was relieved when we got to the windowless dressing room and turned on the lights. In the stark fluorescence I blinked at familiar things made strange by time and memory: benches, gray lockers, the spongy black-mat floor. The white board was in its usual corner, leftover plays marked in red arrows, blue *X*'s and *O*'s. Manhood's road map, still incomprehensible.

Guy was already hauling equipment out of his duffle. "Get changed, Maur. And remember, no shorts or jock."

The room was chilly enough to see our breath. But I felt safer hidden deep in the building, and when I glanced over at Guy, the sigh of his naked ass against the wooden bench caught me in a long lick of desire. How many fantasies had I spun in this room? Wasn't this where it all began?

I crept in from behind, leaned down and kissed the base of his neck, the enticing hollow of skin above the breastplate of his shoulder pads. He stopped dressing. I dropped to my knees and began to stroke his hair, naked thighs, my cheek nestled in the furrow of his spine. I could hear his heart, the quickening rise of his breath. My hand closed around the base of his cock, a thrilling column of want. I had him. I'd win this time.

He caught my wrist. "No. On the ice."

I pulled back, got to my feet. "Your way! We always do it your way. Maybe I don't want to go out on the fucking ice."

Guy twisted to look at me, and his erection swayed, a ruddy, earthy shock of sex in a mausoleum. I felt a whiplash of desire even through my anger.

"You like it my way," he said.

"Well, not this time. So you've got issues. Welcome to the human race! But yours aren't mine, guy. You want to jerk off on my plate? Go right ahead. I'll stand here and clap." I pulled it out of my duffle and thrust it toward him, a shock of 1950s turquoise wrapped in cellophane.

Guy's face was untouched, as if I raised my voice to him all the time. His gaze touched on the plate. I noticed it was trembling.

"I know you're scared." His voice was quiet, a distant swish of steel on ice. "But if you didn't want this, you wouldn't have come. Get changed, Maur."

I dropped to my bench, outmatched again.

There is no footwear that grabs you like skates. I tightened the laces row by row, and the leather clasped my ankles like hands, a familiar death grip. When I pushed myself up, four years fell away, and my body shifted to accommodate the sudden height, the precarious balance of blades. Some things you never forget.

One sensation was new. Hockey pants fit loosely, and

without shorts or a jock, the nylon fabric caressed me in strange and exciting ways. I felt both liberated and . . . licked. I hesitated before I pulled my old jersey over my head, black and red, Ile des Chênes' proud home-ice colors. It seemed sacrilegious to have a hard-on in uniform.

I followed Guy wordlessly down the unlit hall to the rink. He guided us with the flashlight, and I carried the turquoise plate, making sure my fingers didn't smear the grease pencil signature. Neither of us had helmets or sticks. My heart began to knock in my throat, my body grew light with anxiety. What if we'd made a mistake? What if someone had followed us in? I had a mental flash of a terrible ghost, the fiery-eyed blaze of the Rocket himself.

Then, space. I felt the darkness soar above me, a canyon's worth of air moved listlessly by half-speed fans. I smelled the ice, vast, ionized. Clean. A whole town's crystallized hope.

Guy cut swaths with the beam, illuminated slivers of wooden seats. He laughed, a whoop of joy. "Anybody home?"

"Guy!" I pleaded.

"Meet you at center ice. I'm going for a spin." He pushed open the gate and hopped down. I watched in disbelief as he lit around the perimeter of the rink, a shadow behind a beacon, skates hissing. Flying.

In that instant I both loved and hated him. His bravery taunted me. If I could push him once—just once!—the way he pushed me, that would be enough.

I made it to center ice a half-second before he did. Guy twisted to a halt, sprayed snow over the tops of my skates and caught my arm. I could smell the faint rise of perspiration, feel the new heat beam from his skin. Excitement. Even in the dimness, he seemed to glow.

He set the flashlight on the ice. "Do you know where you are?"

"Stop this . . ."

I'll tell you. You're in the heart of your hometown, dressed up like a gladiator, the good little man. They're all out there, Maurice."

As soon as he said it I felt them, hundreds of reproving faces surrounding me in the expansive darkness. Their collective gaze burned past my uniform to where my desire coiled like a spring. Wicked Maurice. Worse, I'd brought my family's icon, the thing their hero had touched, eaten from. And I was going to let Guy jerk off all over it. Shame prickled like rope burn; my cock thickened, throbbed. This was so wrong.

I tried to turn away. Guy gripped me harder, made me look into his glittering eyes. His other hand fumbled under my jersey, tugged the drawstring of my pants.

"We got such good advice, didn't we? Keep your head up. Skate fast. Shoot hard."

There was a cool draft on my erection, then cradling heat that made me catch my breath. I'd surged out into his hand.

Guy grinned. "I'll help you, Maurice. To shoot hard."

He dropped to his knees and sucked me into his mouth. It wasn't a coy seduction—he swallowed me in a single gallop of wet heat, pulled me into the center of the earth. A low moan rumbled up from my belly. I was transfixed by raw sensation as he rode up and down my shaft with his virtuoso mouth, tugging me soft then hard, teeth grazing the engorged head of my cock. He was devouring me.

Guy burrowed his hand into my pants, and they loosened—fell. Oh, god! The sudden chill and alarm smacked me across the ass; I twitched in his throat. Before I could think of retrieving them, he reached between my legs and gripped the loose skin behind my scrotum. My balls rode up against the base of my cock in a luscious squeeze. New pleasure unfurled down its length.

Again and again he sucked me deep, his hand working my balls in exquisite undulations. I was helplessly pinned by a machine of lush gears moving in unstoppable rotations. Faster. As if from a distance, I heard Guy grunting beneath me, curious animal noises that verged on . . . alarm. I glanced down and saw that I clutched his hair in my fist.

Revelation. I wasn't trapped, I was fucking his mouth, driving into him, shaking his body with my need. And I couldn't have stopped even if the stands were filled, even if the Rocket himself was watching my bare ass pumping at center ice.

White on white. My orgasm kicked open a door and hurtled through, a geyser of bliss flecked with guilt. I shot, eyes squeezed shut, balls pulsing; my toes curled inside my skates. Guy continued to suck, a slower sensuous rhythm now, winding me around until the relief was raw, sweetness at the edge of pain.

I pushed away at last, rubber legs trembling, and reached down to pull up my pants. Guy leaned over and spat the hot mouthful of my come onto the ice. A christening.

"Better now?" he said.

How could I not be? I felt bold, audacious. I'd had sex here, on my home ice. What the hell could scare me now? Yet at the same time I resented him. He'd known how this would be. Damn him anyway. Guy always knew—what frightened me, fueled me, what I'd do and why.

"My turn," he said, reaching for the plate.

The impulse caught me like a comet. I spun around suddenly, arm extended like a discus thrower. I felt the plate wheel out of my grasp, an exhilarating, terrifying emptiness. There was a long second of silence, then the crash shattered the distant dark.

Breath, blood, time all suspended. Had I really done that? Had I meant to? I looked at Guy. His elfin face was flat, cherubic mouth agape. I'd actually shocked him, wicked Guy LePont.

Then he started to laugh. "Cheat me, will you? You sneaky son of a bitch!" He grabbed me by the shoulders, eyes sparkling, his astonishment still beaming from him in waves. "Well, you're not off the hook. You can bet your Bauers I'm going to shoot *somewhere*."

He steered me off the ice, but I reeled, drunk on sex and the unthinkable. Was my family's treasure really in pieces somewhere near the rafters? I could still feel the smooth ceramic edge as it spun out of my hand, pressing each finger as it left. My old life pitched away.

In the locker room, Guy tossed his gear, and let me take off everything but my pads, garters and leggings. It woke me. Now the familiar straps seemed tighter, and stretches of exposed skin were more than bare. On display. I *felt* like a gladiator, large and powerful, stripped down for the delight of a devilish, brown-eyed king.

He slipped one hand under my breastplate, tweaked my nipple so hard I winced. His rising cock nudged my thigh.

"Nice pecs. Must have been all those push-ups they made us do." He tweaked me again. "Now drop and give me twenty."

I seized his forearm. "You first."

We'd never sparred. He was surprised by how strong I was; I surprised myself. But then he recovered and threw himself back at me with double force. We scuffled, grappling, sweat and excitement rising. I wrenched him around, taking care not to let his unprotected body hit anything. He shoved me with all his might, sent me staggering back into the lockers with a clang.

Enough. I caught him in a deft arm lock, twisted him to his knees, then his stomach. And leaned.

"Pitie, pitie!" he gasped against the mat.

I felt the surge of heat and triumph, and let him go. Guy rolled onto his back, long tight body still trembling with exertion, black hair flattened with sweat. My mouth swam. Guy gazed up at me with respect. And fire.

"I forgot to say . . . the winner . . . gets fucked," he panted.

And the winner was, gladly.

It was a quiet drive back to the city. The night had slipped into a strange twilight, as if the coming day already waited in the snow that banked the highway. The plate—or as many pieces as we could find—was in a plastic bag on the back seat. Guy and I had worked together, him holding the light, me crouched between the seats, picking up shards. That physical act had settled the roller coaster of euphoria and disbelief. My knees hurt. This had to be real.

What surprised me was my regret for the plate itself. All my life Rocket Richard had loomed over me, the French Canadian hero on skates, impossibly tall and distant. Yet now that I'd hurled him away I felt a fierce blaze of kinship: we were both defiant men.

"What are your going to tell your family about the

plate?" Guy asked suddenly, reaching across the seat for my hand.

"I don't know. The next time I go home I'll have something else to tell them." I squeezed him back. "That'll be enough."

"You could get another one on eBay for about sixteen dollars. Turquoise comes up pretty often."

"But not autographed."

"Oh, no. You do that yourself. That's how I did mine."

"Yours!"

His gaze was still on the road but a grin slunk over his face, a tiger released from its cage, or the cat out of the bag. The bastard had switched my plate with another! I'd broken a forgery. I was staggered by relief, and incredulity.

"Don't tell me you knew in advance—"

"That you'd break it? No." His voice softened, the low hush he saved for secrets or promises between the sheets. "It was me. I couldn't . . . desecrate him. I may be wicked but I'm still *French,* Maurice."

I squeezed him again, amazed at my luck, the wonder of loving someone from my hometown.

A Baker's Dozen of Flashers

flasher: *n.* A complete, sizzling, sexy story in a mere one hundred words. A specialty of the Erotica Readers and Writers Association.

Black Widow

Seneca Mayfair

"Of course I killed my lover."

She tilted her head at the doctor, and smiled at him as if they were conspirators. He imagined her naked, writhing beneath him. He saw her blood-red mouth screaming in ecstasy.

"Don't you feel any remorse?" His pen was poised over his notebook, ready to absolve her.

She shifted on the overstuffed leather couch, and crossed her long legs. Her skirt rode up her thigh; he caught his breath. "Why should I feel remorse?" She leaned forward and caressed his knee with her pointed scarlet nails. "Don't you think I'm worth dying for, Doc?"

Domestic Bliss

Keziah Hill

There's someone downstairs."

"What? I can't hear anything."

"I'm sure there is. I heard a crash."

He sighs. "Do I really have to get up?"

"Yes! What if it's a burglar?"

"For God's sake!" He throws off the covers, gets up, goes down stairs, discovers the cat in the pantry, chucks it out and scurries back to bed.

"What was it?

"A homicidal maniac with an ax."

"Don't tease me."

He looks at her, all tousled and warm, and smiles, sliding his hand under her breast.

"Kiss me."

"Why?"

"I saved you from a homicidal maniac, didn't I?"

A Good Haunting

Amanda Earl

I've missed you, Veronica,"

Veronica felt a cool draft and smiled.

"I'm coming to join you, Arthur. We're going to make love again. I'll put on that French cologne you adored. We'll waltz, and you'll lower me onto the bed. I need to feel your lips on mine."

The ghost caressed his widow's body and helped her pass gently into the afterlife.

"They say the house is haunted," Jessica told her husband. "Maybe we shouldn't buy it."

They heard ecstatic sounds of moaning.

"I hear the couple who lived here was married fifty years," said Joshua. "Let's take it."

Grandmother's Inheritance

Elizabeth Daniels

It's the last thing of hers I find, an album buried in a cedar chest. The binding is time-bleached red, worn to petal fragility.

Inside, my grandmother as odalisque, preserved forever in wanton bloom. She lounges on her prized Oriental rug, wearing only a slumberous smile, a sepia-tinted siren with child-ripened curves. Beneath the image is my grandfather's florid scrawl, white ink on the stiff black page.Smiling through tears, I tuck her album beside one of my own, which is marked in my husband's hand. My grandmother's green eyes are not the only part of her I inherited.

Groupie

Lisabet Sarai

"I like your poems," she said, leaning closer across the café table, so that he could see the shadowed hollow between her breasts where the candlelight did not reach. "I like your images. I can taste them, roll them around on my tongue. They catch in my throat like unshed tears."

He sipped his chianti, adjusted his glasses, pretended to ignore her stealthy hand on his thigh. Her fingers crept over his chinos, aiming for the swelling at his root. He thought of rejection slips, the dirty laundry scattered round his flat, the bills waiting to be paid.

Useless. None of these mundane devices could prevail against her blond adoration.He stood like iron. Her triumphant hand claimed him. "I like the way you can write 'fuck,' " she said, "and make it into a poem."

"What Is Thy Name?"

Teresa Lamai

"Psychotic episodes like that can be acutely distressing," Dr. Crace murmurs, his eyes like a sad rabbit's.

I clutch the pill bottle. I shouldn't have told the doctor about Gabriel.

"Those should make the hallucinations stop, Maria."

A wave of panic blinds me. A night without Gabriel, his dark topaz skin glinting in the moonlight? His wings fill my moldy, drab room; his ancient golden tongue teases out my clitoris. My blood fills with sugar. I'm drunk on the scent of his hair.

My heart races even now.

"Thank you, doctor."

Once home, I flush the pills down the toilet.

Lost and Found

Dani Benjamin

She is lost.

His fingertips slowly trace every curve. From her toes to her knees, from belly to breasts, his fingers travel the landscape of her body. Like an explorer, he climbs every peak. With each proprietary touch, he claims her, inch by inch.

His hands slip around her throat, and his thumbs frame the hollow there. He leans forward to kiss the wildly beating pulse, singing her surrender.

She trembles uncontrollably as with each touch, each kiss he takes possession. He drinks her tears and with a whispered, "Mine," she is found.

She is home.

She is his.

Punter

Mike Kimera

Money in one hand, wedding band on the other, he stands frozen by the reality of his need.

"Anal is extra," I say taking the cash.

He shakes his head, his eyes fixed on my erection.

"Oral it is, then."

I slide the condom over him and watch him shudder.

"You can touch me if you like."

His hand twitches but doesn't grasp my cock. He can barely grasp that he's here.

Wickedly, I wank as I suck. He comes with my finger up his virgin ass. He returns to wifey relieved and ashamed. We both know he'll be back.

Maybe Next Time

Michael Michele

Ding-dong.

Eighty-five, alone; Lillian is cautious.

Who's at her door? Pranksters, robbers, Mormons?

Frank would've been amused—intrepid Lillian afraid! She misses him; he'd loved her well, with his mouth when nothing else cooperated.

Ding-dong.

Lillian contemplates the neighboring old-timer, a widower. She imagines him here, wildflowers in hand. Would he be shocked to know she's wondered how his long white hair would feel if she held it as he spread her upon the crocheted bedspread, fucking her hard, making up for the lonely years?

Finally responding, she finds an empty doorstep.

Maybe next time Lillian thinks, closing the door.

Vixen 6.9

Rachel McIntyre

Even after he rebooted his system, Viki appeared on his monitor, smirking while rubbing her cunt through her tight little shorts.

"Didn't think that'd work, did ya, Bill?"

"This can't be," he rasped.

"You programmed me to be bad."

"For the game."

"Fine," she said, disappearing into the world he'd created.

Bill watched his dark beauty blow her way past the beefy Zandorian guards, grind warriors into submission, then bind the temple priestess to her altar and fuck her with the sacred staff.

His stiff cock oozing inside his pants, Bill thought . . . *if only all system errors were this hot.*

The Rigby Legacy

Rose B. Thorny

He'd forgotten her over all the years; hadn't even remembered her name. Yet tonight, she drifted into his dream, her pale countenance reflecting the wide-eyed, youthful innocence he'd been the last to see.

She knelt between his legs, closed cool fingers around his burning shaft, lowered her mouth, engulfed him.

Time had honed her skill. He had never felt so alive as on this razor's edge of heavenly detonation.

She stopped short, gripping vise-like. Smiling coldly, she blew an icy fog and whispered, "I wasn't trash to be dumped. Enjoy eternity in hell."

He was buried along with his name.

Veronica's Knickers

Julius

The white panties had blown from Veronica's laundry line. He took them next door, knocked and asked, "Yours?"

She was an exquisite forty-something widow, he a divorcee of fifty-three.

She smiled, took the panties and offered him coffee.

The kitchen table was glass topped, her housecoat casually worn. He longed for what he saw, and she saw in him what she needed.

Never a bed-on-first-date lady, she escorted him to the door fifteen minutes later. Neither wanted the parting; neither quite knew how to prevent it.

Briefer, red panties were on his lawn next morning.

The Question

Jude Mason

What would you like, pet?" I asked, standing at his side. My hand, on his naked upturned ass, felt the heat of our last hour's session.

"More—please," he moaned, squirming, trying to rub his straining cock against something, anything.

"More?" I quipped, knowing.

"Spank me!" he growled. I watched his testicles pull in tight. A finger meandered around them, then upwards to his crinkled brown star, pressing mischievously inside. "Yes. Oh god, fuck me."

"Fuck or spank?"

Lustful indecision made him hesitate. "I'll be back in an hour for your choice." I shut the door and heard him howl.

Ten Years in Bed with the Best: The History of ERWA

Adrienne Benedicks

It's difficult to write good erotica. Authors in any fictional genre have to master the elements of the craft: plot, characterization, dialogue, and so on. Erotica authors need to go further. They need to depict sexual acts, situations, and emotions that are believable and arousing. To do this, they draw on their personal insights and images. They delve into their imaginations, lay bare their sensual fantasies, and share those visions with their readers. Authors who dare expose themselves via erotica are brave souls, indeed.

To my delight, I find myself today surrounded by these fascinating people: the writers of sexually explicit fiction. These are the people who populate the virtual world of ERWA, the world we have built together over the past ten years.

In 1996, when I first plugged into the Internet, I admit that the first thing I looked for was porn. I craved sexy stories. Much to my disappointment all I found were boring, mechanical sex scenes, and a lot of "Oh my gawd, I'm cumming" nonsense. It didn't take me long to realize that much of the adult Web was simply a digital form of male-oriented one-dimensional smut, a cyber circle-jerk. I was disappointed. As a woman I felt left out of the dirty stuff.

I thought that surely I wasn't unique in my desire for well-written, hot erotic stories—real stories, not just bits and pieces of fuck scenes. So I hit the chat rooms and asked, "Where's the quality sexy stuff?" That was like plastering a blinking "Who wants to screw me?" tag on my emails. Live and learn!

For my next attempt, I joined the Romance Readers Anonymous (RRA) email list. I thought that surely romance readers would be comfortable discussing erotic stories. In those days, though, we couldn't talk about sex in our public posts, even though many romances were highly erotic.

A few of us listers took to chatting off-list about the erotic parts of romance. I suggested that we live on the edge and start our own list. Great excitement greeted my suggestion, and on June 5, 1996, the Erotica Readers Association was born. ERA, an affectionate play on the Equal Rights Amendment, was a sister list to RRA, and the foundation of the current Erotica Readers & Writers Association.

At that time my children were in high school, and I had the opportunity to finish my degree in anthropology. As a student, I had access to various online options, and with the endorsement of my professor, the university agreed to host the ERA email list. My goal was to provide a private, secure online space where women could comfortably discuss erotic fiction and sexuality, away from the "hey baby, whatcha wearing" crowd.

Subscription was by request or invitation. Publicity worked via word of mouth. Within two months we had sixty women onboard—fabulous, fun, curious women who were eager to talk about sexy writings, and to discuss the joys, problems, or disappointments of their own sexuality.

It didn't take long before these readers decided to try their own hands at writing sexy fiction. "I bet even I can write a sex scene better that!" was a typical inspiration. We quickly learned that writing good erotica wasn't as easy as it seemed. The general assumption was that if you were capable of having sex, then surely you could about write it. Not necessarily true, but that didn't stop us from trying. We were having a lot of fun, even when our fictional efforts fell flat.

Before long, a few brave men who were friends of ERA subscribers were asking to join. They liked reading erotic stories, and they liked the idea of smart discussions about sex. So I opened the door; ERA became inclusive rather then exclusive. Most women were pleased with the change. A few stomped off the list, sure ERA would crumble into a "hey baby" chat room atmosphere.

That didn't happen. Men brought their unique sexual insight into ERA, and our horizons grew even more as people of all sexual persuasions requested subscription. ERA became a dynamic robust community of people interested in sexuality in the written word, and in their lives.

Of course, we had our fair share of narrow-minded confrontational types, rigid viewpoints, and egos too big even for the World Wide Web. Overall, though, ERA-ers were nonjudgmental, mutually respectful, and more then willing to get along.

ERA grew quickly that first year. Subscribers suggested I started a Web site to house all the material we were accumulating: book recommendations, hints about popular authors, discussions on where to buy erotica (at that time erotica wasn't sitting on bookshop shelves). A subscriber volunteered to build a site, and the domain "www.eroticareaders.com" became an online reality.

We decided to be really daring, and started putting subscribers' original stories behind a password-protected "Green

Door" on the ERA Web site. We felt so very sophisticated, and risqué, with our personal secret stash of erotica sitting right out there on the Web!

ERA continued to grow, and so did subscribers' interest in writing erotica. Writers were taking a serious interest in helping each other improve. Stories were shared on the list, and critiques and suggestions on how to improve the works were cheerfully and willingly given. ERA was evolving, moving from its readers' base to a writers' base. More and more focus was on writers helping writers.

Around this time, erotica anthologies were becoming very popular. The Herotica series (Down There Press) had made a big splash, leading the way to *The Best Women's Erotica* (Cleis Press), *Best American Erotica* (Simon & Schuster), *The Mammoth Book of Best New Erotica* (Carroll & Graf), *Best Lesbian Erotica* (Cleis Press), and *Ultimate Gay Erotica* (Alyson Press).

Web site magazines were springing up like grass (and weeds). There was a growing market for erotic short stories, and many ERA subscribers were ready to try publishing their work. They exposed themselves, so to speak, behind ERA's Green Door; the experience gave them confidence. With support and encouragement from their peers, ERA subscribers started to submit stories to various calls for submissions.

ERA already had a solid community feel. Subscribers really did care about each other. We were a virtual family. Even so, I was pleasantly surprised at how generous writers were in sharing calls for submissions. Rather than concealing the information to reduce the competition, ERA-ers said: "Hey everybody, look what I found! Let's give it a try."

At that time, the ERA Web site was still a small dot in the adult Web, but there was no doubt our growing resources and stash of sexy stories was drawing in a smart crowd. I took the plunge, and with a lot of help and suggestions from the community, gave the ERA site a new look that was sensual and classy, as well as easy to navigate.

I didn't realize the obvious: being out in the Web made my private email list, nicely hidden and hosted by the university computer center, suddenly quite visible. Subscription was still by request or invitation, but now inquiries came pouring in. People landing on the ERA Web site liked the resources they found there, and wanted to know more. Subscriptions grew, the site grew, and soon ERA was pulling in more than 13 percent of the university Web traffic. ERA had to go, they told me, and gave me two weeks to find another host.

Ah, the price of success! Fortunately, an Australian subscriber volunteered the help of her husband, who ran his own ISP service. Kevin hosted ERA for free for several years until we once again grew too big and had to move on to our present home, a major adult Web-hosting company.

By 2000 ERA had grown so large and had such a varied focus that things were getting out of hand. The sheer number of emails on the list caused confusion and havoc. Writers were frustrated in their efforts to have their stories critiqued because their works were lost in the deluge of chit-chat emails. Questions and concerns about publishing and marketing went unanswered because busy subscribers didn't have time or patience to dig through hundreds of emails, and were simply deleting it all.

Meanwhile the amount of information on the site was overwhelming. The organization was on the verge of losing itself in too much of everything. It would have been an ironic death by popularity.

At this point I understood that ERA was no longer a simple hobby. Good erotica had become a worthy pursuit. Erotica readers were hungry for the good stuff, and publishers were geared up to provide it. I wanted the ERA Web site to be *the place* where erotica readers and writers would come for the information they needed and where editors and publishers would come when looking for talented writers. I wanted ERA to be the premier Web site for quality erotica. Finally, I wanted to continue to provide an email list where erotica readers and writers could network, and where people could comfortably discuss sexuality.

The first step was to change the Erotica Readers Association name to better reflect what we had become: the Erotica Readers & Writers Association (ERWA). The second step was to create a flexible infrastructure for the site and for the email list, a foundation with enough latitude for future changes. Here's where ERWA subscribers came to the rescue, once again. Suggestions poured in, and I followed through. The evolution of ERWA was, and I suspect always will be, a community affair.

ERWA became three distinct parts that made up the whole: ERWA email discussion list, ERWA Web site, and the humorous and informative ERWA monthly newsletter, *Erotic Lure*, currently written by the editor of this anthology, Lisabet Sarai.

The ERWA Web site retained its basic design. The richness and utility of the site grew as publishers and editors recognized ERWA's potential. No longer did I spend hours searching for viable markets. Calls for submissions now came to me.

ERWA's story galleries became a source of quality erotic fiction. Editors routinely mined the galleries' content for their "Best of" erotic anthologies. Renowned erotic authors came on board as columnists, providing advice in our Authors' Resources section. The luminaries of the adult literary world offered provocative articles on hot sexual topics in the Smutter's Lounge pages.

I divided ERWA email discussion list into four opt-in sections; Admin (for news related to ERWA, calls for submissions, events, and other items of interest); Parlor (an open forum with a social ambiance); Writers (dedicated to authorship and related issues); and Storytime (an informal writers' workshop where authors share their stories for comments and critiques). The very best of Storytime works are placed in ERWA Erotica Galleries, and many of them are showcased right here in this volume.

Currently, the Erotica Readers & Writers Association hosts an email discussion list of over twelve hundred subscribers. Our newsletter goes out to more than five thousand readers, writers, editors, and publishers. The Web site is accessed over six million times each month.

ERWA has been favorably reviewed by *Playboy, Elle* magazine, AVN online magazine, *Writer's Digest*, and recommended in a host of books and articles as the premier resource for erotica readers and writers. Every month, we entertain, educate and inform millions people from all over the globe who are interested in erotica.

Although we've grown tremendously, ERWA's strength is still in community. We are diverse and far-flung, but tightly connected. The result is an ongoing effort to understand and accept all persuasions, lifestyles, and expressions of sexuality. We want to bring the very best of erotica to readers, partly by helping writers excel in a genre that is making headlines and causing the entire publishing industry to sit up and take notice.

Personally, I'm amazed at what we've built together, and extremely proud. Now I can say to those frustrated folk who are searching, like I was, for sex writing that is simultaneously intelligent and arousing: here we are. Search no further. Welcome to ERWA. You're home.